# Sarah Kane's Theatre of Psychic Life

**Methuen Drama Engage** offers original reflections about key practitioners, movements and genres in the fields of modern theatre and performance. Each volume in the series seeks to challenge mainstream critical thought through original and interdisciplinary perspectives on the body of work under examination. By questioning existing critical paradigms, it is hoped that each volume will open up fresh approaches and suggest avenues for further exploration.

**Series Editors**

*Mark Taylor-Batty*
University of Leeds, UK
*Enoch Brater*
University of Michigan, USA

**Titles**

*Contemporary Drag Practices and Performers: Drag in a Changing Scene*
*Volume 1*
Edited by Mark Edward and Stephen Farrier
ISBN 978-1-3500-8294-6

*Performing the Unstageable: Success, Imagination, Failure*
Karen Quigley
ISBN 978-1-3500-5545-2

*Drama and Digital Arts Cultures*
David Cameron, Michael Anderson and Rebecca Wotzko
ISBN 978-1-472-59219-4

*Social and Political Theatre in 21st-Century Britain: Staging Crisis*
Vicky Angelaki
ISBN 978-1-474-21316-5

*Watching War on the Twenty-First-Century Stage: Spectacles of Conflict*
Clare Finburgh
ISBN 978-1-472-59866-0

*Fiery Temporalities in Theatre and Performance: The Initiation of History*
Maurya Wickstrom
ISBN 978-1-4742-8169-0

*Ecologies of Precarity in Twenty-First Century Theatre: Politics, Affect, Responsibility*
Marissia Fragkou
ISBN 978-1-4742-6714-4

*Robert Lepage/Ex Machina: Revolutions in Theatrical Space*
James Reynolds
ISBN 978-1-4742-7609-2

*Social Housing in Performance: The English Council Estate on and off Stage*
Katie Beswick
ISBN 978-1-4742-8521-6

*Postdramatic Theatre and Form*
Edited by Michael Shane Boyle, Matt Cornish and Brandon Woolf
ISBN 978-1-3500-4316-9

*Utopian Drama: In Search of a Genre*
Siân Adiseshiah
ISBN 978-1-4742-9579-6

For a complete listing, please visit
https://www.bloomsbury.com/series/methuen-drama-engage/

# Sarah Kane's Theatre of Psychic Life

## Theatre, Thought and Mental Suffering

Leah Sidi

Series Editors:
Mark Taylor-Batty and Enoch Brater

*methuen* | drama
LONDON • NEW YORK • OXFORD • NEW DELHI • SYDNEY

METHUEN DRAMA
Bloomsbury Publishing Plc
50 Bedford Square, London, WC1B 3DP, UK
1385 Broadway, New York, NY 10018, USA
29 Earlsfort Terrace, Dublin 2, Ireland

BLOOMSBURY, METHUEN DRAMA and the Methuen Drama logo are trademarks of Bloomsbury Publishing Plc

First published in Great Britain 2023
Paperback edition published 2024

Copyright © Leah Sidi, 2023, 2025

Leah Sidi has asserted her right under the Copyright, Designs and Patents Act, 1988, to be identified as author of this work.

For legal purposes the Acknowledgements on p. xi constitute an extension of this copyright page.

Series design by Louise Dugdale
Cover image: Jessica Barden in *Blasted* at Sheffield Theatres.
(Photograph © Mark Douet)

All rights reserved. No part of this publication may be reproduced or transmitted in any form or by any means, electronic or mechanical, including photocopying, recording, or any information storage or retrieval system, without prior permission in writing from the publishers.

Bloomsbury Publishing Plc does not have any control over, or responsibility for, any third-party websites referred to or in this book. All internet addresses given in this book were correct at the time of going to press. The author and publisher regret any inconvenience caused if addresses have changed or sites have ceased to exist, but can accept no responsibility for any such changes.

A catalogue record for this book is available from the British Library.

ISBN: HB: 978-1-3502-8312-1
PB: 978-1-3502-8316-9
ePDF: 978-1-3502-8314-5
eBook: 978-1-3502-8313-8

Series: Methuen Drama Engage

Typeset by Deanta Global Publishing Services, Chennai, India

To find out more about our authors and books visit www.bloomsbury.com and sign up for our newsletters.

*For friends in dark places.*

# Contents

Acknowledgements — xi

Introduction — 1
  Why Kane? — 1
  Mental health policy in the 1990s and community care plays — 3
  *Phaedra's Love* as mental health satire — 7
  Chapter summary — 13

1 The dramaturgy of psychic life — 19
  Experientialism: Escaping from hell — 19
  Dramaturgy — 22
  Theatre and the mind — 24
    Expressionism — 25
    The historical avant-gardes — 27
    Feminist theatre — 30
  Psychic life — 31
  Exploring experientialism: *Crave* (1998) with Paine's Plough — 34
  The subject of theatre — 42

2 A dramaturgy of sexual trauma — 49
  Kane's feminist legacies — 49
  Theatre and traumatic response: PTSD and mimetic models — 56
  *Blasted*: The psychic life of sexual trauma — 59
  The mimetic model: Hiding the subject — 66
  *Blasted* in production — 71
  Shifting mimesis — 76

3 Rhythm, interruption, psychosis — 85
  A dramaturgical turning point — 85
  Closing off or opening up psychosis — 89
  Prediction and interruption in *Cleansed* — 95
  A cognitive reading: Psychosis and prediction errors — 102

| | | |
|---|---|---|
| | *Cleansed* at the National Theatre: Searching for narrative | 107 |
| | A play about love? | 111 |
| 4 | The mind-as-site | 123 |
| | (Un)Redemptive reading | 123 |
| | The ceiling of a mind | 127 |
| | Hatch opens/stark light | 138 |
| | What do you offer? | 142 |
| | It's not your fault | 150 |
| 5 | RSVP ASAP | 161 |
| | Desire and despair | 161 |
| | Kane's late style: What does theatre want? | 163 |
| | Suicidality: Returning to Kane's sources | 166 |
| | Directionless desire | 175 |
| | *4.48 Psychosis* with the Belarus Free Theatre (2014): Queer time, love and suicidality | 181 |
| | Afterword: Sarah Kane and psychic life today | 195 |
| | Bibliography | 199 |
| | Index | 213 |

# Acknowledgements

With extra special thanks to Fintan Walsh and Jacqueline Rose for their guidance, help and encouragement. Both have been truly generous with their time, wisdom and expertise – I could not have wished for better mentors. Thank you also to Louise Owen for her support as a reader and for opportunities and encouragement and to Anthony Shepherd, for his responsiveness and kindness.

This project would not have been possible without access to a range of materials relating to Sarah Kane's production history. I am grateful to Graham Saunders, who has provided guidance, and access to his Sarah Kane archive. I'd also like to thank Kim Solga for setting me on the path to writing on Sarah Kane. Thank you to Ingrid Craigie, and to Simon Kane, for giving permission for me to reproduce materials relating to the first production of *Crave*; and to Philip Venables and to the Belarus Free Theatre, for digital material relating to their respective productions of *4.48 Psychosis*.

At times, thinking with Sarah Kane has taken me to some difficult places. In these moments I have been hugely grateful to Annie Brooker, whose friendship and kindness have meant more to me than I think she realizes, and to the Fairlight community. Thank you to Laura Cushings-Harris, Kayleigh Betterton, Claire Horn, Alexis Wolf, Sasha Dovzhyk, Flore Janssen, Robbie Stearn, Anna Harpin and Francisca Stutzin for their support and encouragement at different stages of this project.

I am grateful to the Birkbeck Graduate School for supporting the PhD research which formed the basis for this book, and the Directing and Dramaturgy Working Group at TAPRA and the Feminist Scholars Working Group of IFTR, for valuable critique and feedback. I am grateful to the Wellcome Trust for two ISSF fellowships which enabled me to develop these ideas further, and to Sonu Shamdasani for creating a welcoming environment at UCL, where I could continue to develop as a researcher.

Finally, thank you to my parents and siblings who taught me how to think and continue to do so. And thank you to Iain, undauntable optimist.

# Introduction

## Why Kane?

This book starts from a simple conviction: that is it possible and necessary to communicate experiences of acute psychic pain to those who have not (yet) experienced them. Possible through a range of media, but especially through theatre. Necessary because anguish, despair, disorientation and hallucination are parts of the human condition – as much as joy, hope and rational thought. Necessary too because we live in a cultural and political moment that has created a hierarchy of human experience which sees no value in despair. It sees no value in lives that require rest, a helping hand, a network of interdependent care. It sees no value in acknowledging the pain of others and vilifies those who refuse to pull their socks up and take their meagre lot with gratitude.

This is why we need Sarah Kane's theatre today. To teach us to hold the world's cruel gaze without flinching. To understand that experiences which emphatically refuse to resolve themselves into positivity and productivity are also valuable, visionary and politically important. To find ways of existing within and alongside despair. This is not a book about hope. If anything, it is a manifesto for hopelessness.

\* \* \*

It is also, more prosaically, a book about mental distress and Sarah Kane's theatre. Sarah Kane was one of the most significant British playwrights of the late twentieth century. In her short career, Kane wrote three monologues, five plays and one short film. Her university monologues were first performed in 1992, and her last play was completed before her death by suicide in 1999 and performed posthumously at the Royal Court in 2000. Her first play *Blasted* (1994) caused a scandal when it opened at the Royal Court, provoking a media backlash because of its onstage violence and divergence from traditional theatrical forms. Her following plays – *Phaedra's Love* (1996), *Cleansed* (1998), *Crave* (1998) and *4.48 Psychosis* (2000) – each marked a significant departure in terms of theatrical form. With each new play, Kane refined and expanded her vision for a theatre which would put its audiences through unique experiences of 'real' discomfort, led by a firm belief that theatre could change people 'because experience engraves lessons on our hearts through suffering.'[1]

Central to Kane's theatrical project was the question of how to communicate something real – what she termed 'experiential' – through theatrical artifice. (Kane's understanding of experientialism is discussed at length in Chapter 1). As Graham Saunders summarized it, 'one part of her wanted to break down that demarcation between "the real" and "the performed", while her writerly instincts always wanted to impose strict formal controls over the plays.'[2] Kane took up this challenge by turning her theatre into a site in which aspects of emotional and affective reality could be shared with – even forced onto – an audience.

Kane's plays invite their audiences to look through a lens which distorts the world according to specific, historically situated forms of mental suffering. This project collapses a number of dualisms. It is not possible to fully separate out Kane's theatrical innovation and the challenging, innovative vision she consistently offers of psychic reality. Her plays are concerned with *both* psychic interiority and sociopolitical structures; her representations of violence *both* signal specific acts of political oppression and function as part of a wider dramatic structure evoking experiences of mental suffering. Finally, mental suffering in these works is *both pathological and expressive*, resistant to the resolutions promised in medical discourse even as it yearns for them.

This raises the question of where to position Kane's personal reality in relation to her theatre's claims. I propose to understand Kane as a lay expert in mental distress, and as an experimental and visionary artist who was exploring the potential for new modes of theatrical communication. Kane's works are not autobiographical or confessional, nor are they transcribed symptom. They are closely informed by life, and by an ability to look pain in the face without flinching. They are also informed by a wide engagement with theatre history, political events, religious texts, scientific and medical writing, tabloid journalism and pop culture. Kane's formal innovations are made possible by the sheer breadth of her cultural referents, and an informed boldness in her approach to theatrical traditions and norms.

Kane's biography provides part of the context, not the content, of her theatre. There is, of course, a relationship between Kane's experience as a person and her consistent preoccupations with suicide, despair and sexual violence as a playwright. This relationship has become a wide topic of critical discussion (discussed in detail in Chapter 4). Kane signalled connections with her own experience of the mental health system in her three later plays: *Cleansed*, *Crave* and *4.48 Psychosis*. *Cleansed* is dedicated to staff and patients of ES3, the psychiatric ward in the Maudsley Hospital in which she was hospitalized, and in which she carried out research for the play's representation of the schizophrenic character Robin. In *Crave*, the characters actually find themselves inside ES3 at the end of the play; and *4.48 Psychosis*, written during another period of hospitalization, clearly draws on the experience of being treated for suicidal depression and psychosis and quotes liberally from psychiatric texts and diagnostic manuals, as Antje Diedrich and Ian Marsh have demonstrated in detail.[3] This signalling demonstrates an active and thought-out engagement with the conditions of mental health service provision, and a repurposing of personal experience for theatrical ends.

It is difficult to have a conversation about theatre and mental illness today without eventually coming upon the topic of Sarah Kane – as though any thematization of mental illness on stage is in some way an 'unintended consequence' of Kane's work and death. Kane haunts her own plays. The apparently inescapable nature of her biography not only continues to colour their reception, but also creates the impression of an uncomfortable presentness, as though the works enable an immediate identification with the suffering woman herself.[4] To gain further insight into the relationship between Kane's representations of psychic suffering and the conditions of their writing, and to understand how her works continue to speak to the present, it is necessary to break this fantasy of identification. In order to do so we must ask: First, what do these works *do* as events, in relation to the discourses on mental suffering with which they coincide? And second, what do they *return* to the cultural discourses from which they emerge; how do they reveal or inflect the narratives of their moment?

## Mental health policy in the 1990s and community care plays

Experiences of mental pain and distress do not take place in a vacuum. They are shaped by the political, social and cultural environments in which they occur. These environments impact how mental distress is experienced and understood, whether someone is deemed in need of treatment, and what kinds of treatments are available. As numerous historians and sociologists of psychiatry have demonstrated, the development of biomedical approaches to mental distress in the last two centuries has taken place in a constant relationship with cultural and political forces.[5] Social, cultural and economic factors contribute to which forms of mental distress and deviances from social norms psychiatry has deemed pathological, and to how those suffering from mental distress are treated within and outside of the medical and social care systems. An often-cited example of this is the position of homosexuality in the United States, where homosexuality moved from being legally understood as a crime, to being listed in the *Diagnostic and Statistics Manual I* (DSM-I) as a mental illness, before being depathologized and removed from the *DSM-III* in 1973, and eventually broadly accepted as a legitimate sexuality.[6]

At the same time, psychiatry coexists with a number of alternative approaches to and understandings of 'madness' and mental distress which explicitly reject the medical framework. The field of Mad Studies, for example, seeks to depathologize a range of non-normative mental experiences which exist under the umbrella of 'madness', whilst still advocating for humane and respectful support for service users who choose to seek psychiatric and alternative treatments. This can lead to a complicated relationship between psychiatric survivors and medical institutions, with 'the survivor movement [. . .] often having to focus on engaging with [psychiatric services] to safeguard the rights of their peers within them. This meant that they needed to get into the system, needed its collaboration to do so and were often dependent on it and associated voluntary organisations for their funding'.[7] Beresford and Russo suggest that Mad Studies and the Mad Pride movement are an explicit rejection of both contemporary psychiatry and neoliberalism, perceiving a double threat to 'mad' people coming from the medical establishment and the economic policies of UK, US and Canadian governments. As these approaches make clear, at any one moment cultural, political and practical factors come together with dominant psychiatric approaches to form a broad and heterogeneous 'mental health context' in which mental distress is experienced and understood.

Throughout this book, I am interested in understanding Kane's engagement with mental distress through a culturally and historically specific lens. Understanding the contexts in which Kane both experienced and wrote about mental distress and psychiatry enables us to navigate the relationship between artistic works and biography without collapsing the two. Kane wrote all of her theatrical works in the 1990s, a decade of profound change and upheaval in UK mental health delivery and culture. In the rest of this introduction, I will explore how Kane engages *thematically* in this context in her second play, *Phaedra's Love*. In the rest of the book, I explore what Kane returns to this context through her theatrical *form*, which becomes a spatial and embodied critique of dominant modes of political-psychiatric thinking.

The 1990s saw a profound upheaval in the structure and delivery of UK mental healthcare. These changes impacted both the accessibility and delivery of care and the way that mental health and illness were perceived in the wider public. In 1990, the UK parliament passed the NHS and Community

Care Act, which announced the closure of long-term mental hospitals and asylums and enacted a definitive split between health and social care. The act transferred the responsibility for the long-term care of psychiatric patients, learning disabled patients, and physically disabled patients from the medical sphere (the National Health Service) into the hands of the 'community' (Local Authorities). In doing so the act formalized a process of deinstitutionalization which had been ongoing for decades, in which psychiatric care and care for the elderly and for disabled people were gradually moving from long-stay to outpatient settings.

These changes profoundly impacted the experiences of those in need of psychiatric and social services. The changes to care delivery were widely reported as abandoning service users in 'revolving door' scenarios, which established a pattern of acute care and discharge followed by a lack of 'care in the community', combined with inadequate housing and financial support. The NHS and Community Care Act was a culmination of the policy move under Margaret Thatcher and John Major's Conservative governments to transform public services into corporate, economically self-sufficient entities – for example by creating the NHS internal market and opening up procurement of care services to private providers. Whilst community care was lauded in some quarters for creating the circumstances for greater patient freedom and choice, medical practitioners and patient groups also expressed concerns that new care structures were ill thought out and failed to provide vulnerable people with adequate support.[8]

The dawn of the community care era was both the political and cultural contexts in which Kane wrote her plays, and the medical context of her experience of treatment. Kane understood the realities of mental health services in the 1990s both as a patient and as a writer. The spatial politics of her works – what I will call her *dramaturgy of psychic life* – are in part formed by a careful and deliberate engagement with the new political environment of mental healthcare developing around her. Kane's thematization of inadequate sites of psychiatric care and dramaturgical engagement with the new conditions of community care is a key mechanism by which Thatcherism is opposed in her works. It is a trope in much Kane criticism that her works somehow resist the 'Thatcherization' of English society.[9] If this claim is to be justified, Kane's works need to be examined with reference to specific pieces of legislation which constituted direct interventions of Thatcherite economics into the discursive and actual of status people living in the UK. Whilst Sierz claims that Kane was motivated by anger at 'Thatcherite subsidy cuts', the specific ways in which her works are situated in the context of Thatcherite economics are nowhere addressed.[10] The NHS and Community Care Act is a powerful instance of the impact of Thatcherite economic ideology onto the day-to-day lives of and provision for mentally ill citizens, and an example of how a single economically motivated policy transformed dominant cultural discourse.

The transition to community care made headlines in the 1990s, making madness and psychiatry into polemical cultural topics. Tabloid newspapers, television series and movies repeated the narratives of violent madmen being discharged from long-stay asylums, fuelling fear-mongering stereotypes.[11] Alongside these stereotypes, there was a flourishing of literary and theatrical works which questioned the norms of psychiatric culture and shared real-life experiences of mental illness. Elizabeth Wurtzel's 1994 memoir *Prozac Nation*, in which the American author recounts her experiences of depression in the post-asylum psychopharmacological era, is perhaps the most famous of these literary responses. (The United Kingdom and the United States followed broadly similar timelines of deinstitutionalization and might be considered as sharing in the 1990s 'mental health moment'.) In Britain, the New Writing explosion in theatre repeatedly thematized madness and mental illness. This included plays explicitly staging psychiatry and community care, as in Joe Penhall's *Some Voices* (1995) and *Blue/Orange* (2000) and Sarah Daniel's *Beside Herself* (1990); *Head-Rot Holiday* (1992); *The Madness of Esme and Shaz* (1994); interests in expanded consciousness and psychosis such as in Anthony Nielson's *The Wonderful World of Dystopia* (2001/2007) and Caryl Churchill's *The Skriker* (1994); and the parodying of mental health language and positivity culture as in Mark Ravenhill's *Shopping and Fucking* (1996).[12] These writers were shaped by, and contributed to, a cultural fabric which was reckoning with the new status of those with mental health problems in Anglo-American culture.

Kane's first two plays – *Blasted* (1994) and *Phaedra's Love* (1995) – stage failed attempts at controlling and regulating violent and excessive feeling, which mirror the profound anxieties about community care which were circulating in 1990s UK popular media. As I have shown elsewhere, the transition to community care provoked a profound and high-profile backlash from the tabloid media throughout the 1990s. Following three particularly high-profile murders by former psychiatric patients in the early 1990s, the British press consistently ran stories which stereotypically represented mentally ill people as violent and dangerous threats to society:

> Articles from the early 1990s frame community care policy as freeing dangerous individuals who 'should not have been allowed out on the street' (Hay 1993, 8). By the end of the decade, the *Sun* was carrying out a concerted campaign to end community care murders by putting mentally ill individuals 'back' into long-term institutions – demanding

that 'psychos [. . .] be taken off the streets and caged for life' (Gilfeather 1999, 14). The phrase 'community care' is invariably linked to violence in articles in the *Sun* throughout the 1990s, often appearing under scare-mongering headlines like 'Sick Killers Toll of Misery' (Reynold 1999, 15), 'Two Women Die in Stab Frenzy' (O'Reilly 1997, 1) and 'Scandal of Psycho Freed to Kill Hero Cop' (Sullivan 1998, 4). The *Community Care Act* was consistently understood as a dangerous piece of legislation in much popular press and television coverage in this period.[13]

Where tabloids did refrain from scare-mongering, they focused on the failure of psychiatric services to deliver adequate care and keep service users 'off the streets'. An article symptomatic of 'care in the community' coverage in the popular press states:

> [T]he psychiatric hospitals have never had to waste time concerning themselves with quite what community their former patients were joining. Which is why you can spot the very same people who used to have a warm, clean bed, hot meals and their drugs administered wandering round the street zombie-like by day, and living in filthy squats and cardboard boxes by night.[14]

'Care in the community' was therefore presented to the public imagination as transforming those who had a rightful location in society – the asylum where they had 'warm, clean bed[s]' – into vagrants who 'zombie-like' are neither alive nor dead, neither a part of the community nor truly separate from it.

## *Phaedra's Love* as mental health satire

Throughout her theatrical works, Kane stages the failure of medical sites and discourses to contain, regulate and cure pathologized passion and anguish. In *Phaedra's Love* and *Crave* especially, the medical or psychiatric establishment is just one of the many sites through which characters circulate in their searches for relief from mental suffering, and it is presented as particularly inadequate. In *Phaedra's Love* Kane seems to construct her dramatic universe out of the press's worst 'community care' fears. In this play failures of diagnosis lead to a complete breakdown of the social order, and Kane combines this breakdown with a dramaturgy of excess to construct a compelling parody of her contemporary moment's community care anxieties. Directing the first production in 1996, Kane also begins to incorporate spatial uncertainty into her dramaturgy, a process which would become more explicit and directly linked to the new conditions of psychic suffering in *Crave* (discussed in Chapter 1).

*Phaedra's Love* stages a dramatic universe in which the institutions charged with regulating madness are in crisis. Hippolytus's tragicomic journey from palace to grave takes him through psychiatric diagnosis and penal institutions, whilst uncontrollable violence simmers beyond the palace gates and eventually consumes him as he enters the city. *Phaedra's Love* adapts Seneca's *Phaedra* with notable changes. In Kane's version of the play, Hippolytus is transformed from a stoic into a slovenly, sex-obsessed nihilist, who spends his time masturbating to violent television reportage and playing with expensive toys. The play begins with a diagnosis:

**Doctor** He's depressed.
**Phaedra** I know.
**Doctor** He should change his diet. He can't live on hamburgers and peanut butter.
**Phaedra** I know.[15]

From the opening dialogue, psychiatric diagnosis is presented as unhelpful, and clearly not up to the task of dealing with a problem like Hippolytus. After attempting to discern the nature of Phaedra's relationship with her stepson, the doctor dismisses the whole issue and his previous diagnosis, concluding, '[h]e's just very unpleasant. And therefore incurable.'[16]

The emerging sense that it is Phaedra's desire, and not Hippolytus's nihilism, that is pathological is compounded in the following scene in which Phaedra's biological daughter Strophe advises that Phaedra return to see the doctor to discuss her own obsessive love of Hippolytus. Phaedra ignores the repeated advice of both the doctor and Strophe, and confesses her love to Hippolytus, then performs oral sex on him without his consent. Hippolytus rejects her, revealing that he has a sexually transmitted disease and that he has previously had sex with Strophe, who in turn had slept with Phaedra's husband Theseus on their wedding night. Phaedra kills, herself leaving a note accusing Hippolytus of rape. Despite Strophe's protestations, Hippolytus accepts Phaedra's accusation, interpreting it as a 'gift' that has finally broken through his apathy, and turns himself in. He goes to prison where a priest attempts to make him recant for the sake of the state's stability. Hippolytus maintains a position of haughty and ruthless honesty and has sex with the priest. Theseus returns after a prolonged absence and vows to kill Hippolytus. He joins a mob that has formed outside the prison and convinces them to murder Hippolytus. Hippolytus is grabbed by the mob as he is being transferred to court and Strophe, in disguise, tries to save him. Theseus rapes and murders Strophe, before realizing who she is. The crowd dismembers and disembowels Hippolytus. Theseus regrets the death of Strophe and cuts his own throat. Hippolytus gazes up at the vultures descending to eat his remains and wishes that 'there could have been more moments like this'.[17]

The play's heavy metaphors and excessive violence have been read as a double send-up of tragic form and the British royal family in the scandalous Diana years. Kane herself described the play as 'my comedy', and Sean Carney argues that the play is best understood 'as if the Pythons had decided to stage a parody of the Royal Family by starring them in a Roman Tragedy'.[18] Despite its usual rejection as something of a failure of Kane's oeuvre in much academic criticism, many reviewers of the first Kane-directed production found the play to be engaging, relevant and 'blackly funny'.[19] Kate Bassett suggested that Kane 'surely slips her tongue in her cheek when the expected atrocities pile in', and Kate Stratton maintained that the play had 'just the right laconic inflections and dark comic edge to her material' whilst 'blow[ing] a range of dramatic raspberries at an unmistakeably British society captured in galloping decay'.[20] Reading the play as a comedy allows for investigation into which areas of the play and genre Kane chooses to essentialize for comedic effect, and the way in which it opens these tropes up for parodic critique.

The anxieties surrounding community care form an essential context for reading *Phaedra's Love* as parody, as much of the comedy arises out of the contrasts between failed attempts at containing Phaedra's and Hippolytus's supposedly pathological behaviours and their obviously superior abilities which thwart this containment. The opening dialogue between the doctor and Phaedra is paralleled in the scene in which Hippolytus talks to the priest, as both appear insipid and unauthoritative in the face of their interlocutors. The doctor's advice for Hippolytus is a litany of platitudinous, self-help style phrases: 'He should change his diet. [. . .] And wash his clothes occasionally. [. . .] He needs a hobby'.[21] The priest's advice to Hippolytus in his prison cell is equally banal. He begins by attempting to cure Hippolytus's cynicism by telling him that '[t]rue satisfaction comes from love', and that '[l]ove never dies'.[22] Given that the only model of love so far provided in this dramatic universe is Phaedra's, which is torturous, vindictive and suicidal, the Priest's advice rings particularly hollow. It is also undermined a few moments later when he changes tack and berates Hippolytus for bringing about political instability.[23] Both dialogues (Phaedra/Doctor and Hippolytus/Priest) are stilted and highly one-sided. They try repeatedly to contain and redirect Hippolytus's depression without the linguistic capabilities to do so. In contrast, Hippolytus and Phaedra are given all of the play's poetry and witticisms. Faced with the protagonists' suicidal passions, minor two-dimensional characters such as the doctor and priest don't stand a chance.

The stilted writing of these scenes sends up the authority of institutions traditionally charged with regulating madness and unruly behaviour. The play's opening statement, 'He's depressed', is both a diagnosis and an attempt to separate the misbehaving medical subject from the popular, intelligent prince. Michel Foucault famously argued that modern psychiatry emerged out of a social need to keep forms of disorder and social deviance away from the general population – to prevent a certain kind of contagion. This contagion is not based on scientific descriptions of the actual contagiousness of madness, but a social need to separate normality from abnormality.[24] The role of psychiatry in the nineteenth century was, for Foucault, 'to protect others from the vague danger that exuded from the walls of confinement'.[25] As I have suggested, the transition to community care provoked a highly publicized crisis of confidence in the ability of the psychiatric profession to continue to uphold this separation, driven in part by the tabloid media.[26]

The impossibility of containment in the dramatic universe of *Phaedra's Love* is emphasized through Hippolytus's excessive, abject body. His presence is characterized by boundary-crossing excess. He excretes abject fluids onstage, snot and ejaculate, the latter turning out to be actually infectious when it is revealed that he has gonorrhoea. In her writing on abjection, Julia Kristeva defines ejected bodily material as causing horror and repulsion because it threatens a discursive breakdown between subject and object:

> It is thus not lack of cleanliness or health that causes abjection but what disturbs identity, system, order. What does not respect borders, positions rules. The in-between, the ambiguous, the composite.[27]

Hippolytus is an ambiguous, porous presence who threatens the sanity of those around him, as Kane satirically literalizes the tragic trope that there is something rotten in the state (of Britain). When Strophe comes to deliver the news that Phaedra has accused Hippolytus of rape and that there are riots in the streets, Hippolytus is more interested in perusing his mouldy tongue:

**Strophe** Hide
**Hippolytus** Green tongue.
**Strophe** Hide idiot.
**Hippolytus** *turns to her and shows her his tongue.*
**Hippolytus** Fucking moss. Inch of pleurococcus [*sic*] on my tongue. Looks like the top of a wall.[28]

Again, Kane takes the metaphor of contagion and boundary-dissolution to an arguably comic extreme. Hippolytus's excessive, mouldy body is finally dismembered, and his body parts thrown around a crowd and then roasted on a barbeque by the gleeful crowd. His 'sickness', far from being contained in the diagnostic category of 'depression', eventually leads to his complete disintegration and dispersal into the public sphere.

The scene of Hippolytus's dismemberment represents a final attempt to control and contain unruly subjectivity, disastrously executed by the 'community' itself. In this scene, the public rape and riotous dismembering of two people is played out as a grand day out for the family, who have

**Woman 1** Brought the kids
**Child** And a barby. [barbecue][29]

Phaedra's love – its force and its object – cannot be cured, politicized or prayed away. It is a sickness that affects both individuals and the state and turns Phaedra into a perpetrator rather than a patient. Finally, it forms the centre point for increasing absurdity, until it is destroyed by a *polis* who parodically embody the reductive, binary conservatism of tabloid rhetoric. The insults that the crowd hurl at Hippolytus cast him as a caricature of violent and perverse masculinity. Punchy and alliterative, the cry of 'Royal raping bastard!' could well be a tabloid headline.[30]

The limited and shallow nature of this speech exposes the illogical assumptions about innocence and victimhood that circulate around Hippolytus's accused act of perversity. Limited in vocabulary, the mob uses the insult 'bastard' nine times in two and a half pages of short dialogue. Both femininity and parenthood are absurdly invoked as justifications for murder and police brutality:

**Woman 1** [He] [d]on't deserve to live. I've got kids.
**Man 1** We've all got kids.
**Woman 1** You got kids.
**Theseus** Not any more.
**Woman 2** Poor bastard.
**Man 2** Knows what we're talking about then, don't he.
[. . .]
**Policeman 1** Poor bastard.
**Policeman 2** You joking?
(*He kicks* **Hippolytus** *hard.*)
I've got two daughters.[31]

Children are invoked by both the mob and the policemen as a category of inviolable innocence, even as actual children in the crowd cheer on as Hippolytus is dismembered and proceed to play with his cut off body parts.

The first production of *Phaedra's Love*, which Kane directed herself, paralleled the thematization of a failure of containment with a spatially unstable dramaturgy. As Graham Saunders describes, 'Kane's direction for the production also concentrated on attempting to break down the barriers between audience and the actors where seating was dispersed around the theatre, and no single playing space selected.'[32] Kane explained that this dispersal of the action into the audience was designed to produce shifts in the spectating process: 'It meant that for any given audience member, the play could be at one moment intimate and personal, at the next epic and public. They may see one scene from one end of the theatre and find themselves sitting in the middle of a conversation for the next.'[33]

Kane's direction undermined theatrical conventions of proximity and distance, as her audiences were neither consistently separated from the action by a boundary between audience and stage, nor were they consistently surrounded by and participating in the action as in immersive theatre. The final scene had actors 'among the squatting audience rise like a lynch mob to take matters in their own hands', which Michael Coveney interpreted as a relocating of the powers of the classical gods into the hands of the populist crowd, providing 'a powerful, genuinely effective equivalent of the monster rising from the angry sea to frighten the prince's horses'.[34] Kane's blurring of the boundary between playing space and audience through the direction of *Phaedra's Love* placed the audience literally at the centre of a dramatic universe soaked in the freewheeling violence of a populist 'community care' nightmare.

In her next three plays – *Cleansed*, *Crave* and *4.48 Psychosis* – this dramaturgical overspilling would take on a more central role in the structuring of the playtexts themselves. Here the blurring of the boundary between audience and theatrical work is executed with greater precision and subtlety, through sustained manipulations of the audiences' perspectives and identifications. *Phaedra's Love* stands out in Kane's short oeuvre as her most loosely structured work, and the only one to engage in political parody. Whilst *Phaedra's Love* immerses its audience in a deteriorating, disorientating but consistent dramatic universe, the rest of Kane's plays attempt to represent their universes through the lens of a specific form of psychic life. We might say that her three later works explore what it means to experience psychic pain from *within* a universe suffering from the dislocations which formed the basis for the world of *Phaedra's Love*.

Approaching Kane's works through this historical lens is an attempt to open up and acknowledge the gap of over twenty-five years that stands between now and the production of her first play. Initially it may seem an unusual critical approach to apply to a writer whose work is unmistakeably 'modern', and whose contemporaries are still alive and writing today. Indeed, much criticism of Kane's works emphasizes her continued and curious 'contemporaneity', suggesting, for example, that she anticipated the war on terror of the early 2000s or the challenges to gender binaries of third-wave, twenty-first-century feminism.[35] For example, Jon Venn's *Madness in Contemporary British Theatre: Resistances and Representations* includes Kane and the 'mental health plays' of the 1990s in his 2021 review of contemporary theatre practices. In doing so, he signals the relationship between contemporary mental health policies and practices and the development of community care policies in the 1990s. Nevertheless, a critical methodology which historicizes these works provides a new insight into how the plays can and do continue to speak to the present, without eliding the political and cultural changes of a quarter of a century. Especially in a post-pandemic context, situating these plays in their medico-political histories can provide a more nuanced delineation of their contemporary relevance.

## Chapter summary

In the following chapters, I turn from the external conditions in which mental distress is experienced, to Kane's experiments in staging internal life. In Chapter 1, I propose the 'dramaturgy of psychic life' as a framework for reading Kane's re-imagining of the relationship between theatre and mind. Departing from the vocabulary of 'experientialism', the dramaturgy of psychic life uses theatre to create a mode of radical sharing of aspects mental experience. Both theatre and mental distress are shaped here by a troubling of the boundary between a hidden interior and a public exterior. Drawing on psychoanalytic theories of D. W. Winnicott, I suggest that Kane departs from her mid-twentieth-century predecessors by approaching her theatre in a mode analogous to psychoanalytic playing, exemplified in her third play *Crave*. The first production of *Crave* in 1998 explicitly sought to generate the feeling of inhabiting a mental breakdown. In rehearsal Kane worked directly with the cast and director Vicky Featherstone to create a work that was simultaneously the story of four interweaving narratives and an invitation to participate in the psychic life of a single subjectivity. Drawing on previously unseen interview materials, we see how *Crave*'s experiential aims were achieved through modes of play which situated the audience somewhere on the edge of a radically open dramatic universe. The breakdown depicted in *Crave* is both highly personal and sociopolitically situated. It is shaped by and reacts to the modalities of the community care era, sharing with its audience a form of psychic life that is generated in a multifaceted encounter between self and world.

Chapter 1 introduces the term 'psyche' and 'psychic pain' to describe the states of negative subjectivity which Kane represents and embodies in her theatre. Occasionally, when discussing an experience as it has been defined by psychiatric diagnoses, this book also uses term 'mental illness'. I do not use the term 'madness'. This is not to deny the considerable work that has been done to reframe experiences which are usually explained as pathological under an expansive definition of 'madness'. As the Mad Pride movement shows us, the term 'mad' can be a liberating one and encompasses the positive and generative aspects of non-normative mental experience.[36] However this expansive definition of madness does not correlate with the kinds of interior life communicated in Kane's theatre. Hers is a theatre which is consistently concerned with experiences of violence, pain and suffering. It is these realities, rather than a broadening of concepts of the normal, which her theatrical innovations endeavour to share. 'Psychic life' encompasses a relationship between internal and social life that is both personal and political. The experiences which Kane puts her audiences through are consistently rooted in interpersonal and political dynamics of power and abuse, even as they also fall into categories of suffering and behaviour that would sometimes be pathologized.

Chapter 2 considers Kane's first attempt to integrate the shape and rhythms of internal collapse into theatrical form in *Blasted*. This chapter builds on recent feminist approaches to Kane's work from critics such as Elaine Aston, Kim Solga and Nina Kane. Beginning with an acknowledgement that Kane's dramatic universes are rife with sexual violence, I offer a historicized feminist reading of *Blasted* which locates the play within debates about the nature of traumatic experience. By incorporating and adapting the key elements of the PTSD diagnosis into her dramatic form, Kane offers a politicized revision of the psychiatric commonplaces surrounding traumatic sexual assault in the 1990s. The dramaturgy of the play as a whole spatially embodies the psychic life of a mind following sexual trauma, which is deeply transformed by the intrusion of violence. I explore the limits of this embodiment in practice by examining the 2015 production of *Blasted* at the Crucible Theatre, Sheffield.

Chapter 3 focuses on Kane's growing interest in representing psychosis on stage from *Cleansed* onwards. Building on the theatrical legacies of Strindberg and Büchner, Kane distils elements of psychotic experience into her dramaturgy in *Cleansed* without tying them to a specific character. This represents a considerable change in her approach to theatre and mind. Drawing on insights from contemporary cognitive neuroscience, I argue that Kane's play has the potential to generate predictive crises in its audiences which are analogous to those experienced in some psychotic breakdowns. Through the soliciting and thwarting of an audience's predictive capacities, *Cleansed* creates means of sharing the experience of predictive crisis with an audience. Returning to Kane's definition of 'experientialism', Kane actually puts her audience through a predictive crisis, holding them in a space of potentially 'extreme discomfort'. This approach is controversial and has led some to interpret Kane's dramaturgy is inherently 'unfinished', as demonstrated in Katie Mitchell's approach to adapting and 'finishing' *Cleansed* in her 2016 National Theatre production.

Chapters 4 and 5 take a sustained look at Kane's last two works as the most fully developed examples of her dramaturgy of psychic life. Chapter 4 argues that the playtext of *4.48 Psychosis* collapses the space between the representation of a mind in crisis and the theatrical site itself. In this play, Kane seeks to dramaturgically represent the experience of a single, fragmented consciousness. In a more extreme manner than any of her previous works, here Kane asks the audience to *reside within* a situation of sustained irresolution and demanding intimacy with an experience of mental suffering. In doing so, she provides an embodied and spatialized critique of the behaviourist turn in contemporary mental healthcare, creating a version of psychic pain which is not reducible to a neoliberal model of health and illness. Staged today, *4.48 Psychosis* goes against the grain of contemporary mental health discourses in its clear eschewing of diagnostic categorization, behaviourism and positive thinking. We see this, for example, in Philip Venables's opera of *4.48 Psychosis*, staged at the Lyric Hammersmith in 2018, which both dramaturgically and musically realized this irreducible, overspilling subject.

Chapter 5 takes us beyond the parameters of illness and distress, to address the messy question of desire in Kane's dramatic universe. In the final chapter of this book, I ask what Kane's plays might *want* from their audiences, and what it means for an artwork to want anything at all. Reading *Crave* and *4.48 Psychosis* as works that are laced through with both desire and suicidal despair, I offer a re-examination of Kane's source texts to trace the intertwining of these powerful forces in her late works. These late works offer a deeply unredemptive vision of care which resonates with queer-disabled critiques of productivity and time. I consider the queer activist performances of *4.48 Psychosis* by the Belarus Free Theatre and Deafinitely Theatre as provocations for thinking through new frameworks of hope, without productivity or progress.

## Notes

1 Heidi Stephenson and Natasha Langridge, *Rage and Reason: Women Playwrights on Playwriting* (London: Methuen, 1997), 133.
2 Graham Saunders, *About Kane: The Playwright and the Work* (London: Faber and Faber, 2009), 120.

3   Antje Diedrich, '"Last in a Long Line of Literary Kleptomaniacs": Intertextuality in Sarah Kane's 4.48 Psychosis', *Modern Drama* 56, no. 3 (2013): 374–98; Ian Marsh, *Suicide: Foucault, History and Truth* (Cambridge: Cambridge University Press, 2010).
4   Mary Luckhurst suggests that Kane's works are so bound up in her notoriety, that this has made it almost impossible to fairly assess their literary merit in 'Infamy and Dying Young: Sarah Kane 1971–1999', in *Theatre and Celebrity in Britain*, ed. Mary Luckhurst and Jane Moody (London: Palgrave Macmillan, 2005).
5   It is out of scope to summarize these approaches here. Readers wishing to approach these fields might start with Anne Rogers and David Pilgrim (eds), *A Sociology of Mental Health* (Maidenhead: Open University Press, 2005); G. E. Berrios and H. Freeman, *150 Years of British Psychiatry 1841–1991* (London: Royal College of Psychiatry, 1991); Rhodri Hayward, *Psychiatry in Modern Britain* (London: Bloomsbury Continuum, 2013).
6   Jack Drescher, 'Out of DSM: Depathologizing Homosexuality', *Behavioural Science* 5 (2015): 565–75.
7   Peter Beresford and Jasna Russo (eds), *The Routledge International Handbook of Mad Studies* (Abingdon, VA: Routledge, 2021), 4.
8   See the final section of Chapter 1 for an extended discussion of service user perspectives on the NHS and Community Care Act.
9   See Aleks Sierz, *In-Yer-Face Theatre: British Drama Today* (London: Faber and Faber, 2000), 237; Helen Iball, *Sarah Kane's Blasted* (London: Continuum, 2008), 14–16.
10  Aleks Sierz, '"We All Need Stories": The Politics of In-Yer-Face Theatre', in *Cool Brittania? British Political Theatre in the 1990s*, ed. Rebecca D'Monte and Graham Saunders (Basingstoke: Palgrave Macmillan, 2008), 25.
11  For the potency of these stereotypes, see Greg Philo (ed.), *Mediating Madness: Glasgow Media Group* (London and New York: Longman, 1996), and Leah Sidi, 'After the Madhouses: The Emotional Politics of Psychiatry and Community Care in the UK Tabloid Press 1980–1995', *Medical Humanities* (2021), Special Issue on Health Policy and Emotion.
12  Jon Venn's *Madness and Contemporary British Theatre: Resistances and Representations* (London: Palgrave Macmillan, 2021) begins his study of contemporary mental health plays with the 1990s, suggesting a continuity between this moment and the 2020s. I am more interested here in understanding the historical distance.
13  Leah Sidi, 'After the madhouses: the emotional politics of psychiatry and community care in the UK tabloid press 1980-1995', *Medical Humanities* (2021), 7.
14  Anne Robinson, 'System That's a Sick Joke', *Daily Mirror*, 14 February 1990, 13.
15  Sarah Kane, 'Phaedra's Love', in *Sarah Kane: Complete Plays* (London: Methuen Drama, 2001), 65.
16  Ibid., 68.

17 Ibid., 103.
18 Saunders, *About Kane*, 5; Sean Carney, *The Politics of Contemporary English Tragedy* (Toronto: University of Toronto Press, 2013), 273.
19 Paul Taylor, *Independent*, 23 May 1996, in *Theatre Record* 16, no. 11 (1996): 651–2, 651.
20 Kate Bassett, *The Times*, 22 May 1996, in *Theatre Record* 16, no. 11 (1996): 651; Kate Stratton, *Evening Standard*, 21 May 1996, in *Theatre Record* 16, no. 11 (1996): 653.
21 Kane, 'Phaedra's Love', 67–8.
22 Ibid., 93.
23 Ibid., 94.
24 Michel Foucault, *Madness and Civilisation: A History of Insanity in the Age of Reason*, trans. by Richard Howard (New York: Vintage Books, 1988), 205.
25 Ibid.
26 Sidi, 'After the Madhouses'.
27 Julia Kristeva, *Powers of Horror: An Essay on Abjection*, trans. Leon Roudiez (New York: Columbia University Press, 1982), 4.
28 Kane, 'Phaedra's Love', 85.
29 Ibid., 98.
30 Ibid., 100.
31 Ibid., 100, 102.
32 Graham Saunders, *Love Me or Kill Me: Sarah Kane and the Theatre of Extremes* (Manchester: Manchester University Press, 2002), 80.
33 Stephenson and Langridge, *Rage and Reason*, 134.
34 Michael Coveney, *Observer*, 26 May 1996, in *Theatre Record* 16, no. 11 (1996): 653.
35 Sierz suggests that 'Ten years before the London bombings, Kane instinctively, if unconsciously suggested the politics of Muslim disaffection, and of English reactionary racism'. Aleks Sierz, 'Looks like there's a war on': Sarah Kane's '*Blasted*, Political Theatre and the Muslim Other', in *Sarah Kane in Context*, ed. Graham Saunders and Laurens De Vos (Manchester: Manchester University Press, 2010), 45. Cristina Delgado-Garcia suggests that Kane's characters are Butlerian 'performative subversions' of heteronormative subjectivity, and Nina Kane's upcoming book locates Kane's works in relation to contemporary trans feminisms. Cristina Delgado-Garcia, 'Subversion, Refusal, and Contingency: The Transgression of Liberal-Humanist Subjectivity in Sarah Kane's *Cleansed*, *Crave*, and *4.48 Psychosis*', *Modern Drama* 55 (2012): 230–50, Nina Kane, *Sarah Kane: Queer Desires and Feminist Continuums* (Abingdon, VA: Routledge, upcoming).
36 For an excellent introduction to this area, see Beresford and Russo, *The Routledge International Handbook of Mad Studies*.

# 1

# The dramaturgy of psychic life

> *In fact the truth is I've only – I can't believe I'm going to tell a bunch of strangers this – I've only ever written in order to escape from . . . hell. And it's never worked, um, but . . . at the other end of it when you sit and watch something and think, well that's the most perfect expression of the hell that I felt, then maybe it was worth it.*
>
> Sarah Kane[1]

## Experientialism: Escaping from hell

In one of her final interviews, given at Royal Holloway in 1998, Sarah Kane placed her motivation for writing in a direct relationship with her own mental suffering. Asked by an audience member who she wrote for, Kane responded that she had 'only ever written in order to escape from hell', and that despite never achieving this escape, her works could be justified after the fact as 'the most perfect expression of the hell that I felt'.[2] This is an unusually candid moment of self-revelation for Kane whose interviews tended to be guarded and ironic, and lay down a narrative of her development as a writer which kept her personal and interior life out of the picture. I have preserved the fillers and hesitations in the full quotation in the epigraph earlier to emphasize the unusualness of this moment. In the recording of the interview, Kane sounds surprised at her own statement.

As we have seen in the Introduction, the link between Kane's own mental life, her pathology and suicide, and her work is one that holds a contested place in theatre and academic criticism. Reading Kane's works in relation to discourses on mental illness risks pathologizing the works themselves and producing unconvincing analyses in which dramatic innovation is read purely as symptom.[3] Nevertheless a too emphatic separation between Kane's works, her interest in, and her experiences of, mental distress can also lead to readings that do not do justice to the complexity of her theatrical vision. Taking Kane at her word here would mean understanding that by recreating a version of mental 'hell' for her potential audience to enter into, Kane created a theatre that explored what it is like to be 'inside' certain forms of mental suffering, at a specific historical juncture in the history of UK mental healthcare.

Kane frequently described her theatrical project as an attempt to create 'experiential theatre'. This term preoccupied much academic criticism of her works in the early 2000s. Experientialism emerges as a fluid term in this wave of Kane criticism. In his influential book, *In-Yer-Face Theatre: British Theatre Today*, Aleks Sierz grouped Kane with a series of male writers including Mark Ravenhill, Patrick Marber and Phillip Ridley, and united these writers under the banner of Kane's term. Sierz used 'experiential' to describe works that were highly visceral, full of onstage sex and violence, and meant to be 'felt' rather than carefully considered.[4] Sierz adopts the term largely to explain the use of shock as a dramatic tool, and it has come to be linked with readings of Kane's work which see her writing as driven by overflowing rage rather than formal and sociopolitical interests.[5] As Helen Iball notes, Sierz's use of the term 'became a tightrope or at worst even a trip-wire for its proponents', as it tended to lead to debate as to 'the extent to which the work achieves its experiential aesthetic' without a clear vision of what this aesthetic entails.[6]

In later criticism the notion of 'experientialism' has given way to a focus on 'feeling' as the primary mode of reception of Kane's works. Elaine Aston, for example, rejected Kane's grouping with the 'in-yer-face' playwrights on grounds that Kane's work contains a greater sociopolitical and global critique, and that rather than shock tactics her use of onstage violence has a transformational aim, encouraging her audience to 'feel differently'.[7] Clare Wallace understands Kane's experientialism as a form of theatrical intensity, creating 'a theatre that must be lived through', influenced by the theatrical strategies of the historical avant-garde; and David Ian Rabey also pursues the idea that 'experientialism' is characterized by an almost unmanageably intense theatrical experience in which the audience must choose 'to look directly or to look away'.[8] Both Wallace and Rabey link Kane's 'experientialism' specifically with the audience's exposure to intense and powerful imagery on stage, suggesting that such images provoke active responses in the audience.

If we return to Kane's own description of the 'experiential', we can trace the encounter between theatrical form and mental life throughout Kane's plays. Whilst she never gave a full definition of the term 'experiential', Kane described it most directly in an interview whilst discussing Jeremy Weller's *Mad* which she saw at the Edinburgh Festival in 1992 before writing her first full-length play, *Blasted* (1995). In her description of this 'totally experiential' play, 'experiential' theatre is directly related to imaginatively and emotionally entering into the space of mental illness:

> Instead of sitting, detached, and mildly interested, and 'considering mental illness as an intellectual conceit, [. . .] *Mad* took me to hell, [. . .] and the night I saw it I made a decision about the kind of theatre I wanted to make – experiential. [. . .] It was a bit like being given a vaccine. I was mildly ill for a few days afterwards but that jab of sickness protected me from a far more serious illness.'[9]

Kane described Weller's work as the 'only piece of theatre to have ever changed my life'.[10] In her account, it allowed her to enter the space of mental illness in a non-intellectual manner, with the pathology embodied in the drama actually enacting upon her in a kind of mental inoculation.[11] She described this theatrical encounter spatially, as an experience of moving *through* one mental space and into another, being 'taken to a place of extreme mental discomfort and distress – and popped out the other end'.[12] For Kane then, the 'experiential' ideal to which her theatre aspired was linked from the beginning with mental distress. It aimed to create a theatre in which distress is experienced *from within*, and in a genuine manner – a real, smaller dose of pain to ward off 'far more serious illness'.[13]

From the start of her playwrighting career, Kane developed combinations of contrasting theatrical styles in order to enact forms of mental breakdown through her playtexts without 'considering mental illness as an intellectual conceit.'[14] Kane's own (self-curated) account of her development as a writer suggests that seeing Weller's *Mad* represented a turning point in her artistic aims and methods.[15] *Mad* 'was a piece of devised and confessional theatre in which a group of performers, predominantly female, talked about their personal relationships, their experiences of clinical depression and the treatment they had received'.[16] In its focus on the experiences of mental illness and personal relationships of women, *Mad* resonates with the themes of Kane's first experiments with dramatic writing: a trio of monologues entitled *Sick* which she wrote whilst an undergraduate at Bristol University and which were performed at the Edinburgh Festival in the summers of 1991 and 1992.[17] These monologues written for women include *Starved*, which details the experience of a teenage girl suffering from bulimia and sectioned under the Mental Health Act; *What She Said*, which tells the speaker's story of her first experience in a same-sex relationship; and *Comic Monologue* in which an unnamed woman recounts her oral rape at the hands of her boyfriend Kevin, and concludes that the trauma of rape is one from which the victim can never recover.

Kane's move from writing monologues to writing her first play *Blasted* (via seeing Weller's play) marked a shift in the way in which the themes of mental pain or pathology, sexual assault and sexuality were to appear in her works. *Blasted*, *Phaedra's Love* (1996), *Cleansed* (1998), *Crave* (1998) and *4.48 Psychosis* (2000) all develop the themes of sexual assault, trauma, mental illness and hospitalization that were the central concerns of the *Sick* monologues, but no longer have characters narrate their interior lives. As we shall see, Kane's plays are not documentations of their characters' experiences, unlike the speakers of Weller's *Mad* or of the *Sick* monologues, but rather theatrical explorations of how such experiences shape and structure mental life.

I propose the phrase 'the dramaturgy of psychic life' in order to describe this theatre. This departs from the ideas of rawness which have been associated with experientialism since Kane's death. 'Dramaturgy' emphasizes Kane's craft and theatrical expertise as well as the inevitably collaborative nature of theatre-making. 'Psychic life' proposes a framework more political and dynamic than simply 'feeling', emphasizing how our selves are made and unmade in a messy encounter between personhood and power.

# Dramaturgy

Thinking of Kane's works in terms of dramaturgy (as opposed to simply playwrighting or text) enables a critical discussion of the demands these plays make both on their audiences and on the theatre-makers attempting to stage them. Sarah Kane's approach to staging mental life invokes a problematized boundary between interior and exterior. This boundary is both the actual boundary between audience and artwork, stage and auditorium, and the boundary between personal interior and social exterior which is thematized in the lives represented on stage. The one reflects and repeats the other. Both the terms 'dramaturgy' and 'psychic life' encompass the flexible and porous nature of this boundary, in the theatre and the mind respectively. Bringing them together thus provides fertile ground for beginning to articulate the claims Kane's theatre makes on its audience, and on the moment in which it is situated.

The term 'dramaturgy' encompasses all of the elements through which a live performance generates meaning at a given moment. This includes the literary aspects of a playtext; the visual content and effects of performance; auditory effects that might be deliberately orchestrated (the use of music and soundscapes) or unintentional (poor acoustics); spatio-temporal elements (proximity, distance, rhythm and pauses) and the interactions that take place between the performance and the audience. The dramaturgical analysis of a performance would focus on how all of these elements come together to produce a specific, situated significance. As Cathy Turner and Synne Behrndt emphasize, dramaturgy is inherently dynamic. Insofar as dramaturgical analysis addresses the many ways in which 'levels of meaning are orchestrated' in performance events, it can vary from one performance to another of the same play.[18] Kane herself noted the extent to which dramaturgies are shaped by their audiences. Reflecting on her dissatisfaction with writing for television, she said that theatre was

> Always the form I loved most because it's live. There's always going to be a relationship between the material and the audience that you don't really get with a film [. . .][W]ith *Blasted*, when people got up and walked out it was actually part of the whole experience of it. And I like that, it's a completely reciprocal relationship between the play and the audience.[19]

Dramaturgies are co-created by audience and performance-makers in this sense. This co-creation is not limited to a highly deliberate refusal of the play, as in a walkout. It may include the cultural assumptions that audience members bring with them into the auditorium, or significant events taking place in the surroundings such as noise from a protest outside, or a shocking piece of news relevant to the theme of the work. Dramaturgical analysis, as Turner and Berhndt note, 'need[s] to go beyond the idea that drama contains a simple set of signifiers for us to decode, since 'dramaturgy' also involves and implicates spectator responses'.[20]

The dramaturgy of a work takes place 'in between' its various signifying elements and the situation in which these elements are encountered together as a dramatic whole.[21] In a traditional dramatic theatre, we might imagine dramaturgy as occupying a liminal space in between the edge of the stage and the air in front of and above the audience members in the auditorium. It is neither completely contained by the 'interior' of the dramatic universe, nor is it entirely reducible to the 'exterior' of the auditorium. When examining the potential dramaturgies of a playtext, we should note how the audience–performance relationship is imagined, and what elements might provoke or destabilize this relationship. Kane engaged in dramaturgical practice in writing her playtexts, insofar as they contain direction for potential performances in which the non-literary aspects of the work are held in unresolved tension with plot and dialogue. As I shall explore at the end of this chapter, Kane uses tension and irresolution as mechanisms for disrupting the relationship between performance and audience. Her playtext

*Crave* curates the dramaturgical 'in between' space, and at the same time holds it open through an acknowledgement that 'no performance will ever be the same'.[22]

Kane's involvement in the first productions of her first four plays also points to varied additional dramaturgical practices. She directed *Phaedra's Love*, and wrote much of *Crave* through workshops with Vicky Featherstone and the cast at Paine's Plough. Her attitude to the direction of the first production of *Cleansed* was fairly detached, but she did end up playing Grace at a late point in the show's run. Kane was explicit that these productions were in no way definitive: her works could be interpreted in multiple ways.[23] Yet even the playtexts which contain no stage directions demonstrate a sustained attention to the spatial and temporal dynamics of live performance. Kane's attempts to create dramaturgies of real mental suffering – a theatre of inoculation – is deeply bound up theatre's liveness and spatiality.

## Theatre and the mind

In her extreme approach to theatrical representations of internal reality, Kane builds on a legacy of theatre-makers who have pushed at the boundaries of the relationship between the stage and the mind. The idea that a play might to some extent stage a mode of subjectivity is not new and has been central to the relationship between psychoanalysis and theatre since the former's inception. In 'Psychopathic Characters on Stage' (1905), Freud initially explored this relationship by outlining beliefs as to how identification forms between tragic hero and audience member. The audience member 'longs to feel and to act and to arrange things according to his desires – in short, to be a hero. And the playwright and actor enable him to do this by allowing him *to identify himself* with a hero'.[24] Here Freud seems to subscribe to a Hegelian notion of tragedy as the staging of an irreconcilable conflict between two equal motives which ends with a renunciation:

> Here [in psychological drama] the struggle that causes the suffering is fought out in the hero's mind itself – a struggle between different impulses, and one which must have its end in the extinction, not of the hero, but of one of his impulses; it must end, that is to say, in a renunciation.[25]

Still the subject of the play, the hero's struggle finds its correlate for Freud in the daydreams of the audience.

At the same time, in his reading of *Hamlet* at the end of 'Psychopathic Characters on Stage', Freud moves towards imagining the structure of a play as a whole as evocative of a single psychic experience. Hamlet's conflict for Freud is, of course, the Oedipus complex, a 'repressed impulse [which] is one of those which are similarly repressed in all of us, and the repression of which is part and parcel of the foundations of our personal evolution'.[26] Nevertheless, we do not explicitly identify with Hamlet's own repression. Rather, 'it is this repression which is shaken up by the situation in the play',[27] with the play actually exposing and playing out the Oedipal structures which are repressed in the audience. It is *Hamlet* the play, and not Hamlet the hero, which exposes this structure – a structure which has been derived by Freud precisely from another famous tragedy. The reception of this form of theatre thus differs from the phantasied identification which Freud describes in the first instance. Instead, what is repressed in the play 'is never given a definite name; so that in the spectator too the process is carried through with his attention averted'.[28] The relationship between theatre and the subject in Freud's writing, both on *Hamlet* and on *Oedipus Rex*, is thus premised on the possibility that a theatrical work as a whole can in some way embody and play out the psychic structures of an individual.[29]

Broadly speaking, we might think of Kane innovating on three theatrical traditions in representing the mind on stage: expressionism; the historical avant-garde; and second-wave feminist theatre. Whilst it is not in the scope of this book to give a comprehensive account of these theatrical predecessors, I will briefly note the ways in which each provides Kane with tools for her own theatre-making, in the relationship between theatre and a distinct concept of mind.

## Expressionism

Arguably the most significant shift in representing the mind on stage came at the beginning of the twentieth century from Swedish playwright August Strindberg, whose shift from Naturalist to Expressionist form was hailed as the 'beginning' of modernist theatre. Strindberg's approach to staging internal life is epitomized in *A Dream Play* (1901) which seeks to stage the dream of a single consciousness. The play follows the path of a goddess, Daughter of Indra, as she descends to earth to learn about the lives of humans, forming a pessimistic view of the human condition. Strindberg made the relationship between the associative form of *A Dream Play* and its attempt to stage internal life explicit in the Author's Note which accompanied it in the first production:

> the Author has sought to reproduce the disconnected but apparently logical form of a dream. Anything can happen; everything is probable.

> Time and Space do not exist; on a slight groundwork of reality, imagination spins and weaves new patterns made up of memories, experiences, unfettered fancies, absurdities and improvisations.[30]

The characters and the dramatic universe of *A Dream Play* are constantly changing. At the same time, they are held within a self-contained dreamscape: 'The characters are split, double, and multiply; they evaporate, crystallise, scatter and converge. But a single consciousness holds sway over them all – that of the dreamer.'[31] Strindberg's note proposes an explicit, *mimetic* relationship between the stage and a metal experience. Highlighting to his audiences that the action is the representation of the experience of a 'single consciousness . . . that of the dreamer', the action and setting of *A Dream Play* is bounded by the consciousness it represents.

This attempt to mimetically represent the dream-state marks Strindberg's transition from Naturalism to Expressionism. As a Naturalist playwright in the 1880s, Strindberg's plays had sought to display the minutiae of regular life onstage – the most well-known of these being *The Father* (1887) and *Miss Julie* (1888). Influenced by Emile Zola, Strindberg the Naturalist aimed to put the close attention which Naturalist novels paid to ordinary life on the stage. Strindberg's interest in Naturalism went hand in hand with a period of interest in empiricism and sciences, and with autobiographical writing. Both interests share a preoccupation with what is observable, verifiable and external, with Naturalism seeking to turn a scientific gaze on the realities of everyday life.[32] This dual interest in naturalism and science continued for Strindberg until 1895, when he experienced a psychological breakdown which he referred to as his 'inferno crisis'.[33]

The inferno crisis profoundly affected Strindberg's interests both in science and in dramatic writing, revealing for him a world beyond the rational and observable. In a sense, we can see the following Expressionist or post-inferno works as an extension of his interest in empiricism and Naturalism, with an expanded scope informed by his experience of psychosis and spirituality. Both approaches are essentially mimetic, with an emphasis on accuracy of representation. But whilst the Naturalist works sought to stage the material conditions of life with some attention to psychology, the post-inferno works stage a version of experience 'in which material, psychological and spiritual domains combined'.[34] Strindberg variously called his new approach 'half-reality' and *Ich-Dramatik* (I-drama) – both terms referring to the 'real' experience of a self which is expanded to include the spiritual and the imagination.

Strindberg's 'half-reality' has been hailed as the beginning of theatrical expressionism and was described by Eugene O'Neill as the precursor to Modernist theatre.[35] This desire to mimetically reproduce internal life is seen in later works of European Expressionism and American Modernism following Strindberg's influence. Hans Thies Lehmann highlights the extent to which early-twentieth-century theatrical innovations followed from a desire to represent a newly expanded internal life:

> Once *the unconscious* and the imagination are acknowledged as realities in their own right, the structure of drama – which could claim to have offered an adequate representation of what happens between human beings in the reality of *consciousness* – becomes obsolete. On the contrary, the surface logic of drama and external succession of actions prove to be an obstacle to the articulation of unconscious structures of desire.[36]

Strindberg's influence on American Modernism can be seen, for example, in Arthur Miller's use of dream and memory sequences in *Death of a Salesman* (1949) and O'Neill's interest in staging hallucinations, in *The Emperor Jones* (1920). Miller originally conceived of *Death of a Salesman* as a short play called *Inside His Head* which would directly represent 'the interior of the skull. And they would be walking around inside of him, all these people'.[37] These works retain Strindberg's idea of a mimetic approach to representing a fuller version of reality – creating works of theatre which stage the outer lives of characters and their internal states on the same stage. It is worth noting that these works do not trouble the boundary between internal and external reality. Dream or hallucinatory sequences are tied to a single character, and their boundaries are delineated. As we shall see in Chapter 4 of this book, this aspect of Strindberg's expressionism has had a profound impact on both Kane's writing and posthumous reinterpretations of her works.

## The historical avant-gardes

The concept of a theatre which mimetically represents the interior life of an individual rests to a certain extent on a Cartesian vision of selfhood – of the mind as self-contained and separate from the body. This perspective is contained, for example, in the assumption that it is possible to represent the dream without the dreamer. The theatre of the historical avant-garde, most notably of surrealist writer Antonin Artaud, takes up the same desire to represent interiority but also collapses the boundary between mind and body. Throughout his writings on theatre Artaud understands thought and mental activity as painfully physical. As Susan Sontag summarizes:

> The metaphors that Artaud uses to describe his intellectual distress treat the mind either as a property to which one never holds clear title (or

whose title one has lost) or as a physical substance that is intransigent, fugitive, unstable, obscenely mutable. [. . .] He refuses to consider consciousness except as process. Yet it is the process character of consciousness – its seizability and flux – that he experiences as hell. 'The real pain' says Artaud, 'is to feel one's thought shift within oneself'.[38]

It is the body that is the seat of the intractable self for Artaud, and as such it is also the seat of his theatre's transcendent potential. Far from proposing a mimetic relationship between the stage and a stable vision of inner life, Artaud's polemical vision was for a theatre that physically broke down the boundaries of the self. In 'Theatre and the Plague', Artaud insisted on theatre's potential to transmit paroxysms of the self into the bodies of its audience:

> Just as it is not impossible the unconsumed despair of a lunatic screaming in an asylum can cause the plague [. . .] outward events, political conflicts, natural disasters, revolutionary order and wartime chaos, when they occur on a theatre level, are released into the audience's sensitivity with the strength of an epidemic.[39]

Theatre for Artaud does not so much represent internal life as aim to explode it. Rage and 'unconsumed despair' of enormous proportions are to be forced through the body of the performer with an exacting discipline, so that they can run contagiously through the audience.

Artaud was the most prolific writer on theatre of the historical avant-garde, but wrote and produced little theatre in his lifetime. Nevertheless, his vision for theatre was taken up in different ways by highly influential theatre-makers from the 1960s onwards. Groups such as The Living Theatre, Peter Brook's Theatre of Cruelty, Richard Schechner's The Performance Group and Jerzy Grotowski's Laboratory Theatre variously incorporated aspects of Artaud's vision into their practice. These include, for example, the use of screams and glossolalia on stage, depersonalization of characters, the use of violence and gore, and an intense focus on gesture. Artaud's ideas about actors as 'automate personnel' are reflected in Robert Wilson's use of figures on stage 'moving [. . .] magically without any without any visible motivation, objectives and connections.'[40] We might think of these legacies of Artaud as expanding the breadth of tools available for theatre-making, without necessarily continuing Artaud's vision of the relationship between theatre and mental anguish. In the case of Wilson, Lehmann argues that the psychological element is removed from his theatre, staging instead postdramatic 'landscapes' devoid of action, psychological figures and context.[41] The absolute collapse of mind, body and theatre which Artaud's Theatre of Cruelty advocates might be as yet unrealized.

The influence of Artaud on Kane has been the subject of substantial attention, particularly in the light of Kane's claims that she had never read Artaud until she wrote *Cleansed* (see Chapter 3). Nonetheless there are significant connections between Artaud's and Kane's approaches to theatre which go beyond the inspiration she drew for *Cleansed*. Kane's notion of experientialism as inoculation parallels and reverses Artaud's understanding of theatre as contagion. The notions of inoculation and contagion are not merely metaphorical for both writers. Both envisioned their theatrical aims in relation to real pain. If, for Artaud, the encounter with cruelty is necessary to overcome the dangers of banality, for Kane being put through theatrical pain wards off greater infection.

Samuel Beckett's theatre was also rooted in the historical avant-garde. As De Vos notes, Beckett contributed to avant-garde journal *transition* in the 1920s, which published notable Surrealists, including Artaud. De Vos's Lacanian study traces an ahistorical line between Artaud, Kane and Beckett, arguing that each playwright attacks the 'subjectile' of language – the very material through which enunciation and selfhood are manifest.[42] Unlike Artaud, Beckett's theatre has been described as profoundly Cartesian, with its focus on 'unwording' the power of language understood as a wrestling with the *cogito*.[43] On the other hand, De Vos and Katz highlight an ambivalence in this supposedly Cartesian position, suggesting that Beckett's attack on language is influenced both by Descartes and by an avant-garde interest in materiality which would seem to pull him another way. I do not intend to outline the considerable literature and debate on Beckett's approaches to language and self here. Rather, I would draw the readers' attention to a new area of Beckett studies that more clearly addresses the question of Beckett's approach to staging the mind.

Recent research has revealed the extent to which Beckett was deeply well-read in psychoanalytic theories of mind, and in neuro-psychoanalysis and mid-century neuroscience. Beckett started writing for the stage in France in the interwar years, which was at that time a cultural hotbed for advances in the sciences of the mind.[44] These developments in psychoanalysis and neuroscience form the cultural fabric from which Beckett drew in order to create his theatrical works. Beckett was particularly interested in neurological disorders which affect speech, including Tourettes, Aphasia and Parkinson's. His mother's experience of Parkinson's is often identified as a source for the specific pattern of the breakdown of language and selfhood in *Rockaby*. As Hugh Culik notes, Beckett is careful to strip his works of expressive or even narrative detail.[45] His plays represent a relationship between mind and stage which is neither a mimetic representation nor a radical collapse of body/mind.

We might think of Beckett's approach to staging mind as one of *distillation*. Specific features of neurological diversity and distress are distilled in these works and re-enter the stage in ways that are divorced from narrative and diagnosis. They signify anew – or not at all. Beckett is, of course, a major influence on Kane's theatre.[46] In Chapter 3 we will consider how Kane might be understood as taking a similar approach of distillation to her treatment of psychosis in *Cleansed*.

## Feminist theatre

The final approach to staging the mind which I will briefly consider in this section comes from mid-century feminist theatre in the UK and Europe. This is a subject which will be expanded on in Chapter 2. I mention feminist theatre briefly here to note that the largely male groups of Expressionists, American Modernists and avant-gardists do not have a monopoly on innovation, and to re-position Kane's oeuvre in a broader lineage.

The question of how to represent interior life was a pressing one for second-wave feminist theatre-makers who wished to stage versions of selfhood that are both personal and political. French feminist playwright Hélène Cixous famously rewrote one of Freud's major case studies for the stage in her play *Portrait of Dora* (1976). Here Cixous draws on Expressionist and avant-garde models in order to stage the inner life of Freud's famous patient, re-imagining the therapeutic encounter from Dora's perspective. Cixous splits Dora's experience across the stage, incorporating voices, film and photographs into her account of Dora's encounter with Freud. The result has been described as 'a hysterical play', which incorporates the repetitions, questions and loops of hysteria itself into the dramaturgy.[47] The play draws on the Naturalist trope of the hysterical woman but structures the dramatic universe from her perspective.

Cixous's *Portrait of Dora* exposes the power dynamics embedded in both psychoanalysis and realist theatre by staging the inner life of a hysteric in a manner that emphasizes its impenetrability. As Elin Diamond notes, in the work of Cixous and several of her feminist contemporaries 'the hysteric [. . .] returns to representational space, but in text and *mises-en-scenes*, neither her character nor any other is a unitary object under scrutiny'.[48] This is a deliberately political move against a patriarchal diagnostic gaze which assumes the transparency of the female observed subject. Inner life is split across the stage space in these works in a way that is opaque, 'creat[ing] a sense of history as an assemblage of patriarchal narratives that are ripe for revision'.[49] In this sense, feminist playwrighting in the 1970s and 1980s placed interior psychological life in a constant conversation with the history and politics of observation. As we shall see in the following chapter, they trouble the boundary between interior and exterior life in a way that also becomes essential for Kane's theatrical vision.

Like Cixous's *Portrait of Dora*, Kane's works are situated at a troubled boundary between a personal/psychological interior and a political exterior. They draw on both the mimetic legacies of Expressionism and the Artaudian collapse of mind and body, whilst placing these theatres in an atmosphere in which the act of theatrical observation is understood as inherently political. Her dramaturgy thematizes the troubling of an interior/exterior boundary in the experience of mental breakdown and repeats it in her approach to the stage.

## Psychic life

Kane simultaneously innovated both on dramaturgical form *and* on models of psychic suffering, and it seems that for Kane these were to some extent one and the same. Drama is a way of representing experience which is at once social and mental; theatre is a site in which the two are inevitably enmeshed. Kane draws repeatedly on frameworks for understanding mental pathology which were particularly popular in the 1990s, most notably the PTSD paradigm in *Blasted* and *Crave*, and cognitive behavioural approaches to depression and suicide in *4.48 Psychosis*.[50] On top of this she also engages intertextually with a wide range of theatrical writing from Strindberg, Artaud, Beckett and Pinter to Shakespeare to Churchill and Weller. These discourses, from the popular to the specific, form the landscape in which and with which Kane crafts the psychic lives represented in her works.

The idea that the experience of selfhood might be at once psychological and political is encapsulated in the concept of psychic life. I propose psychic life here as a helpful prism for understanding how Kane's representations of selfhood balance the pressures of internal breakdown and external disruption. According to Lisa Baraitser, the term 'psyche' is now considered dated in contemporary theories of mental life and subjectivity, to the extent that it 'show[s] up as a kind of embarrassment' in psychological discourses:

> It goes against the grain of mainstream psychological discourse where 'psyche' gave way some time ago to 'mental' and now simply 'neuro', as the brain, albeit conceived of as plastic, emotional, responsive, porous and in some way relational, has become *the* psychological subject.[51]

Nevertheless, Baraitser argues for the importance of a return of the concept of psychic life or 'psychic reality', as a way of introducing a third term into discussions of subjecthood. As a 'third term', psychic life enables one to address subjective experience beyond binary constructions of interior/exterior, and self/other.

Psychic life is constituted through the invasive meeting of external, social-political life with a psychological interior, which both moulds and is moulded by this experience. In this framework, 'psychic reality [can] be understood to change the social norm, and not just the other way around'.[52] Judith Butler conceptualizes the psychic life of power as taking place in between social and political normative structures, and the supposedly interior reality of the individual. Butler's vision of a subject who is always-already social and relational is one that is constituted by this encounter with an object that 'is actually an already configured social world, an other who is already regulated and governed, formed by social norms'.[53]

Tracing the inherently ambivalent relationship between power and subject-formation, Butler suggests that the internalization of power through social norms also involves an 'interiorization of the psyche', in that it actually *'fabricates the distinction between interior and exterior life,* offering us a distinction between the psychic and the social that differs significantly from an account of the psychic internalisation of norms'.[54] Psychic life for Butler and Baraitser is both generated by and experienced in an *in between*, a site which is reducible neither to brain/mind, nor to social environments. Such a form of psychological in-betweenness parallels the in-between nature of Kane's dramaturgy. Psychic life allows us to articulate a 'third space' out of the encounter between work and audience (and all of the social-political conditions the audience brings) which signifies differently, socially and anew.

It is within the third space – the space of psychic life – that playing occurs. Kane's mode of engagement with her audience is distinct from those of the Expressionists and avant-gardes, as it can be understood as a mode of psychoanalytic 'play'. Psychoanalytic theory is useful in approaching Kane's work not because it explains away her theatre as symptom or (Oedipal or castration) complex, but because it provides a theoretical framework in which purportedly pathological forms of mental experience are allowed to signify in their own spaces, a framework which has been historically engaged with the relationship between psychic phenomena and site. According to D. W. Winnicott, 'play' is a mode of relating in which the distinction between interior life and external reality is blurred. Initially the way that infants mediate the difficulties of object-relating – of realizing a separation between their existence as subjects and the world of objects outside of the self – playing crucially involves the use of external, real objects within a subjectively created world.

It is through playing that we participate in the psychic lives of other people. Playing takes place in a 'transitional space', in which the boundaries between subject and object, and between psychic interior and material exterior, are blurred. It takes place in 'an intermediate area of *experiencing*, to which inner reality and external life both contribute'.[55] Playing therefore involves a kind of extension of interior reality into the external world, creating the potential for a subject's play-world to be experienced by another in a mode not strictly dictated by a separation between subject and object. For Winnicott, it is here that psychotherapeutic intervention occurs.[56] Playing is an action, to play 'one has to *do* things', and to play with another is to *do* something to that other, to have them inhabit one's play-world.[57]

Throughout her dramatic oeuvre Kane pushed the locus of her dramaturgy to occupy a site in-between the viewing subject and viewed object/artwork which is analogous to this site of play. With increasing intensity and complexity Kane's dramaturgy troubles the boundary between audience and artwork, culminating in her final works which invite her audiences to radically inhabit the inside of a spatially enacted subjectivity. This goes beyond Winnicott's suggestion that all aesthetic experience generates a nostalgia for a return to the 'transitional phenomena' of infancy.[58] Kane attempts to transform her theatre into something much closer to the type of play which Winnicott identifies in psychotherapeutic practice which creates the potential for an overlap of two subjective experiences. And whilst Winnicott understood play as always 'belong[ing] to health',[59] the modes of playing suggested in Kane's dramaturgy are closer to André Green's concept of 'negative play': a 'form of thought [. . . which includes] treacherous, cruel, and destructive plays', but remains linked to the need to mediate the 'horror' of outside reality.[60]

Kane's dramaturgy of psychic life *plays with* its audience. Returning to the idea of theatre as inoculation, it is essential that there is something real being shared in this playing. Of course, Kane's plays are representational and do not enact experiences of actual violence on their audiences. But they do invite the audiences to participate in real experiences of distress through those elements of interior life which can be shared: disorientation, waiting, refused identification, aggression and provocation, to name a few.

In the final section of this chapter, I will examine the first production of *Crave*, in order to provide a concrete example of what this dramaturgy of psychic life might look like in the theatre.

## Exploring experientialism: *Crave* (1998) with Paine's Plough

*Crave* was Sarah Kane's fourth play and was first performed by Paine's Plough in 1998, directed by Vicky Featherstone. Kane wrote the play under a pseudonym, wishing to distance it from the furore that had surrounded the first production of *Blasted* and dogged future works. The play stages the experience of four unnamed people, as their lives intersect and then descend into a psychological breakdown, ending in ES3, the psychiatric ward in which Kane herself was treated.

In *Crave*, Kane and Featherstone staged an experience of mental distress in a historical moment in which UK mental healthcare was undergoing a profound upheaval. As discussed in the Introduction, deinstitutionalization and the transition to community care can be read as key contexts for the 'mental health plays' of the 1990s. In *Crave* in particular, Kane stages the interface between personal internal breakdown and the disorientating new psycho-political context. In this play, spatial instability becomes the condition through which mental suffering is both experienced and communicated.

In *Crave* Kane returns to the theme of psychiatric treatment, which had been the focus of her unpublished university monologue *Starved*.[61] In *Starved* the speaker's experience of bulimia is charted through her journey through domestic and medical spaces. The medical site is presented as a place where the speaker is deprived of autonomy, no longer able to control her eating and purging, and is force-fed and physically restrained. Having returned to a healthy weight, however, the speaker expresses bewilderment as to where she is meant to return, unable to conceive of an outside of the medical site. By the end of *Starved* the speaker comes full circle, returning to her original refrain to describe her patterns of disturbed eating in her parents' home. One is given the impression that the whole monologue could just start all over again, and the journey from home-to-hospital-to-home will be repeated.

As Dan Rebellato has pointed out, Kane reused several passages from all three of her monologues in *Crave*, but 'it is *Starved* that she draws on the most'.[62] C's experience of trauma, disordered eating, sexual bullying and psychiatric breakdown draws on the phrases used in *Starved*, although set within a very different stylistic and dramaturgical framework. Rebellato suggests that '*Crave* [...] is a great leap forward, but in one important way is also an act of careful retrospection across the entirety of [Kane's] work'.[63] It is also a testament to the continuity of Kane's thematic as well as dramaturgical preoccupations with mental suffering and its representation. In *Starved* Kane explores different ways in which the monologue might represent the experience of bulimia, ranging from diary-like entries recording weight, date and food consumption, to narrating upsetting memories about food, to broken down, repetitive Beckettian language with which she describes the experience of hospitalization. In *Crave* this exploration takes a new form, as Kane attempts to integrate the unstable spatialities of psychiatric care into the play's dramaturgy.

*Crave* presents its audience with four narratives of pathologized mental suffering, which came together in the 1998 production to form a single expanded consciousness. The play stages four speakers: young woman C (which stands for Child), older man A (Author/Abuser), young man B (Boy) and older woman M (Mother). The characters speak in fragments of conversation, quotation and poetry, and a series of relationships emerge out of the overlapping conversations. C is traumatized by past sexual abuse, and tormented by her rejection of her mother and her seemingly abusive relationship with A, she turns to M for help; A is a self-confessed paedophile who is C's abuser and/or lover; M desperately wants a child, and has a relationship with B in order to become pregnant; she then abuses and rejects him; B is an alcoholic in love with M. The characters weave a tapestry of speech which partially reveals their narratives whilst never providing enough concrete information to fully distinguish between their 'real' and imagined relationships.

Key to this confusion is the fact that despite the speech being fairly evenly distributed across all four speakers, the play nevertheless seems to be structured by C's mental experience. Ingrid Craigie played M in the original 1998 production and noted the technical difficulty of performing such an ambiguity:

it's a paradox that you are very clearly who you are, this woman who has a fear that she is barren and desperately wants a child, but at the same time [. . .] you merge into something else [. . .] That's one level of your existence but through that more literal or concrete existence you are part of a whole, part of the experience of this disintegration, this breakdown.[64]

Craigie describes the process of rehearsing the play with Kane and Featherstone, as finding a way to negotiate the development of a single character and at the same time participating in a dramaturgy which embodies the breakdown of another.[65] This aim was outlined by Kane herself in a funding proposal for the development of the play, where she notes that 'as a whole [*Crave*] forms one voice which can be broken into four distinct and separate voices, and these in turn can be broken down into a multiplicity of voices'.[66] As 'part of the experience of this disintegration', Craigie and her fellow actors participated in the presentation of a single mental breakdown in which they were 'four individuals but really all part of one voice, one experience'.[67]

This theatrical doubling, by which Kane and Featherstone presented both the experiences of four characters and the breakdown of one mind, intended to create a theatrical version of mental anguish which was indeterminate and almost impossible to objectify. Kane emphasized the indeterminacy of the character representations and contexts as key to the play's dramatic project:

> The people in this play are representations of people rather than characters. To C, M represents her mother (even though she is not, because M is childless). A represents C's abuser (though he may 'in fact' be her lover), and also represents her lover (though he may be her abuser). All the characters represent something to each other, but these representations have little to do with actuality.[68]

Distinctions between reality and imagination are deliberately avoided. In this document Kane notes that she wishes the audience of *Crave* to be exposed to 'a multiplicity of contexts, none of which are given priority over one another'.[69] This separates Kane's approach to interiority from that of Strindberg's discussed earlier, in which authorial framing makes it clear the play-world is held within the mind of a dreamer. In *Crave* the play-world remains open, signifying more than one psychic reality at once.

The psychic life (or lives) of the speakers in *Crave* is moulded by external conditions. The play portrays a contextually indeterminate breakdown by representing mental suffering across a series of unstable and uncertain sites. The speakers narrate and refer to a number of locations throughout the play, without ever settling into a site or narrative. The first location invoked by C in the opening lines of the play is itself a non-place:

**C** You're dead to me.
[. . .]
**C** Somewhere outside the city, I told my mother, you're dead to me.[70]

The site emerges apparently as a qualifier to C's initial phrase which opens the play. The phrase appears to have a location and an interlocutor in its second iteration. However, the location is defined only by what it is not. 'Somewhere outside the city' is not the city's antithesis (the country), nor is it the city itself. The play thus begins with C's evocation of vague outskirts, on the boundary between two types of space.

Whilst the play is littered with references to urban sites, the city itself never emerges as a stable 'context' for the speakers' narratives or their suffering in *Crave*. These urban locations are intertwined with remembered or fantasized moments in rural locations, which are characterized by their impossibility. M 'remembers' seeing her grandparents embrace from a poppy field outside her grandfather's house, only to be told by her mother that 'That didn't happen to you. It happened to me. My father died before you were born'.[71] C either remembers or re-imagines her childhood sexual trauma as a terrible and ecstatic moment in the open countryside: 'A fourteen year old to steal my virginity on the moor and rape me till I come.'[72] C's assault by the fourteen-year-old at this moment in the play seems impossible, both because of its reference to orgasm and because in the earlier episodes her childhood abuse is repeatedly linked with urban locations and old men. The audience cannot know if her 'real' or 'original' traumatic encounter was with her grandfather in a car, which she is reclaiming through the fantasy of the fourteen-year-old 'his blue blue eyes full of sun'; if the 'small dark girl' in the car is someone else; or if they are both examples of the litany of abuse that C has been subjected to.[73] These flights into the rural do not provide any more context for the intense pain of the characters than the indeterminate urban locations. The mental pain which the play describes and represents overflows them both and is best characterized by its inability to be contained by any location.

*Crave*'s representation of a mental breakdown across a series of indeterminate locations can be read as a direct engagement with the new spatiality of mental suffering associated with 'care in the community', as it was experienced by patients. As discussed in the Introduction, the NHS and Community Care Act provoked a representational crisis with regard to mental illness in the UK. For centuries, those suffering from mental illness had been associated in the public imagination with asylums; places which would regulate and contain 'madness' to prevent it from touching the 'sane' population.[74] As Peter Barham notes, the Victorian asylum had a profound effect on shaping both the experience of 'madness' and the place of the mentally ill in society:

> The legacy of the Victorian asylum is, in an important sense, the abolition of the *person* who suffers from mental illness. In place of the person we have been given mental patients, their identities permanently spoiled, exiled from the space of their illness on the margins of society.[75]

Barham identifies two main consequences of care in the community for those diagnosed with mental illness. The first is a practical transformation of their experience of place, especially in relation to interactions with social and medical services. Care in the community provoked concerns about vagrancy across both popular and professional forums, caused either by stigmatization or by the very real question of where former mental patients were to go, once asylums and long-stay psychiatric wards closed.

Rather than being held for long periods in a total institution, those requiring psychiatric care were now more likely to be treated in a 'revolving door' scenario, constantly moving back and forth from acute ward to often impermanent accommodation.[76] As an article in the *British Medical Journal* noted following the Community Care Act:

> [Community care is] an unknown quantity with unknown consequences. [. . .] [A] young man with severely disabling schizophrenia might block an acute psychiatric ward bed for a year, enter a slow stream rehabilitation ward, move to a hostel in the centre of town, return to his parents' home, stay in a bed and breakfast or sleep in a cardboard box.[77]

Former psychiatric patients under 'care in the community' were, according to many in the medical establishment, at risk of homelessness and lack of treatment.[78] According to this narrative, deinstitutionalization added the stresses of vagrancy and uprootedness (moving from ward, to hostel, to street, to ward) to the experience of pathological mental suffering.[79]

We might think of the spatial and subjective transformation that patients leaving long-term psychiatric care experienced as a dramaturgical shift – one that encompasses an upheaval of physical spatial conditions (sights/sounds/smells/security/warmth, etc.) and social, interpersonal and subjective experiences. Jon Venn has described this shift as generating a 'contemporary asylum' – an assemblage of practices and interactions which shape the lives of mental health service users despite no longer providing long-term inpatient care:

> The contemporary asylum is no longer the single building. It has been replaced by scattered psychiatric wards, adjudicated by judicial hearings, enforced through community treatments orders and domesticated into the medication taken at home.[80]

Through this scattered assemblage service users are still subject to psychiatric power, and Venn emphasizes that the contemporary asylum extends and capacitates the diagnostic gaze further into home and community settings. However, Venn's term implies a stability and coordination to contemporary mental healthcare which has been starkly lacking since the introduction of community care. The experiences of many service users in the late 1990s and early 2000s have been characterized as much by waiting lists, administrative failures, punitive benefits sanctions and failed referrals as they have by psychiatric surveillance.[81]

The experience of mental distress in the community care era is thus characterized by both surveillance and uprootedness. Constant movement between services and settings also requires a shifting of identities, with service users acting variously as patients, advocates, complainants, defendants and consumers alongside their domestic and professional identities. In her introduction to *The Colour of Madness*, a collection of writing on BAME experiences of mental health, Samara Linton emphasizes the 'sheer tenacity that is demanded of us [Black service users] when we are at our most vulnerable', in order to access mental health services.[82] Accessing the right care from a range of scattered services becomes a full-time pursuit, especially for those from marginalized communities. Writing about the discharging of patients after asylum closures, Barham remarked that those suffering from mental illness were 'discharged as patients and [told] to rejoin the community as ordinary persons'.[83] This transformation from patient to 'ordinary person' is not straightforward. It involves a complex performance of different roles in a social order which demands both compliance, and autonomy and economic self-reliance, in order to navigate and receive mental health care services.

The 1990s saw a flourishing of 'community care plays' in the UK, as society struggled to respond to the new organization of psychiatric services. For example, playwrights Sarah Daniels and Anna Reynolds both developed work in this period based on real-life experiences of women leaving long-term compulsory detention. Daniels's *The Madness of Esme and Shaz* (1994) stages the story of Shaz, released from a secure wing after thirteen years into the care of her estranged aunt. The play counters popular concerns about the release of patients who have been under compulsory detainment by portraying the touching friendship that develops between aunt and niece, as both attempt to find a place in a changed world. Reynolds's *Jordan* (1992), in contrast, is a one-woman show co-written with Moira Buffini, which tells the story of Shirley Jones, who Reynolds had met when they were both detained in the secure psychiatric wing of Royal Holloway Prison. What is striking about both plays in relation to care in the community is that whilst they are both ostensibly 'deinstitutionalization narratives', they both suggest that a new subjectivity outside of psychiatric institutions is effectively impossible. Reynolds's Shirley ends her life immediately following her acquittal and release. Daniels's play ends with a utopic escape by Esme and Shaz from the police and psychiatric authorities, by joining a Mediterranean cruise and deciding to 'go mad' together.[84] Whilst both plays are preoccupied with the process of leaving institutions, neither manages to address the formation of a new subjectivity without the institution. Joe Penhall's *Blue/Orange* (2000), another self-consciously 'care in the community' play, similarly avoids addressing the life and identity *in* the community, ending as it does at the moment of patient Christopher's discharge.

In all three of these works, the identity of the patient-character remains structured by their relation to an institution and the dramatic universe itself remains tied to a number of binaries introduced by the institution: inside/outside, sanity/insanity, health/illness. In his study of total institutions, Irving Goffman states that institutionalization is constituted by the constant reinforcing of these binaries, in which the inmate is made to accept their patient status as part of a process which leverages the difference between 'inside' and 'outside':

> The full meaning for the inmate of being 'in' or 'on the inside' does not exist apart from the special meaning to him of 'getting out' or 'getting to the outside'. [...] [T]otal institutions [...] create and sustain a particular kind of tension between the home world and the institutional world and use this persistent tension as strategic leverage in the management of men.[85]

Daniels's and Reynolds's works in particular explore this boundary between the inside and outside of the institution, but nonetheless remain structured by it.

*Crave* can also be read as a 'care in the community' play, but its approach contrasts with Kane's contemporaries. Kane's play begins its account of mental suffering on the 'outside', without the explicit structure of an entrance or exit narrative to shape the speakers' experiences. The urban and medical sites through which the speakers of *Crave* experience their individual and group breakdown are characterized by indeterminacy and inadequacy. The city is returned to after C's first evocation of it in an anecdote which seems to describe her history of sexual abuse:

> In a lay-by on the motorway going out of the city, or maybe in, depending on which way you look, a small dark girl sits in the passenger seat of a parked car.[86]

'[G]oing out of the city, or maybe in', the motorway is a site of directionless movement. The incident in the lay-by is presumably an account of C's early traumatic experience. It also spatially literalizes the paradoxical sense of both stasis and movement that characterizes C's mental experience of her trauma: 'And though she cannot remember she cannot forget./ And has been hurtling away from that moment ever since.'[87] Held in a restless stasis between remembering and forgetting, and yet simultaneously 'hurtling' through time, the temporal disruptions that structure C's mental suffering seem derived from the contrasting speed of movement and spatial indeterminacy of the motorway and lay-by itself. *Crave* presents the audience with a dramatic universe in which the relationship between external and internal (mental) landscapes is porous, as the spatial structures of traumatic experience are integrated into mental suffering.

In the 1998 production of *Crave*, this contrast between movement and stasis was integrated into the dramaturgy of the performance event itself. The playtext of *Crave* is strange and poetic. The characters talk to and over one another, and out to the audience. Whilst the text contains no stage directions, it seems clear that the speakers are required to stay onstage throughout, impelled to speak their desires and mental anguish whilst not being afforded freedom of movement or action. Reminiscent of Beckett's *Play*, the dramaturgy of *Crave* is found in the contrast between the slippage, fluidity and unreliability of language, and the suggestion of an oppressively static stage space. The 1998 production compounded this sense of oppressive stasis by setting the play in a talk show. Here, the speakers were seated throughout the production, participating in a kind of obsessive sharing without being able to get up and actually dramatize the emotions they were going through.[88] Craigie notes that this was due to a sense Featherstone's part that the audience needed a concrete visual 'setting' in order to help them cope with the difficulty and fluidity of the language: 'I think that [the chat-show format was chosen] because Vicky wanted it to have a concrete existence, a way in for the audience.'[89] This sense of simultaneous restless movement and oppressive stasis thus gave dramaturgical form to the frustrating indeterminacy of the speakers' psychic lives which, in C's words, 'exist in the swing, neither one thing nor the other'.[90]

Despite the variety of experiences and suffering displayed by the characters in *Crave* they share a problematized relationship with space, which we might identify as a deinstitutionalized, or post-asylum, subjectivity. B describes this experience as one of always being located in an unstable outside:

> A circle is the only geometric shape defined by its centre. No chicken and egg about it, the centre came first, the circumference follows. The earth, by definition, has a centre. And only the fool knows it and can go wherever he pleases, knowing the centre will hold him down, stop him flying out of orbit. But when your sense of centre shifts, comes whizzing to the surface, the balance has gone.[91]

This shifting of the centre and whizzing out of orbit might be a characterization of the dramaturgy of Kane's play itself. The play never settles into a single narrative, nor does any firm understanding of the relationships between the characters ever become clear. The text itself is 'out of orbit', circulating within and around the speakers in a site which cannot bring it into order.

This production's dramaturgy thus represented painful psychic breakdown as structured by the environment of deinstitutionalization, in which those in pathological mental distress occupy practically and discursively indeterminate spaces. By incorporating the spatial and temporal qualities of this new kind of existence into its formal embodiment of a 'single breakdown', *Crave* radically suggests that this new spatiality actually structures the nature of psychic suffering in the 'care in the community' era.[92] The psychic life of the figures it portrays is created at the meeting point between internal distress and external conditions, and embodied in the dramaturgy of the work as a whole.

*Crave* thus presents its audience with a dramaturgy of psychic life for a specific historical moment, in which sufferers were perceived (by others and by themselves) as newly and inevitably out-of-place. It offers a response to the sociopolitical changes brought about by the NHS and Community Care Act by exploring its consequences for the inner lives of the people it affects. This is not to say that the play advocates for a return to institutionalization. Rather, it troubles the political narrative implicit in the act (and ongoing today) that the problems of mental health care are primarily the implicitly impersonal problems of allocation of spatial and monetary resources. The play may be understood as a politicized response insofar as it stakes a claim for the importance of considering the complex inner lives of those living with pathologized mental pain, and suggests that these inner lives are constantly being shaped by the spaces and structures they are legislated to inhabit.

## The subject of theatre

By inviting her potential audience to experience a breakdown 'from within', Kane reimagines the relationship between the stage and its representation of subjects. In *The Psychic Life of Power*, Judith Butler defines the 'subject' as a grammatical position, which is not to be seen as 'interchangeable with "the person" or "the individual"'.[93] Rather, the subject 'ought to be designated as a linguistic category, a placeholder, a structure in formation'.[94] Subjectivity is spatially imagined by Butler, as it is both a site and a mode of linguistic intelligibility: 'Individuals come to occupy the site of the subject (the subject simultaneously emerges as a "site"), and they enjoy intelligibility only to the extent that they are, as it were, first established in language.'[95] To be a subject is thus to hold a linguistic and spatial position in relation to others and oneself, to be able to experience oneself *in the first person* as opposed to in the second or third person. Spatially, we might add that it is also to experience oneself as *here*, as opposed to *there*. This distinction is important to Butler's theory of psychic life because it means that coming to know and understand oneself as a subject involves a contradiction: 'the subject can refer to its own generation only by taking a third person perspective on itself, that is, by dispossessing its own perspective in narrating its genesis.'[96]

This contradiction is relevant to any attempt to locate a subject of a play or performance, and to understanding how Kane's representations of psychic life also involve a shifting of the terms of theatrical mimesis. Colloquially (when discussing dramatic or mimetic theatre), we may talk of the 'subject of the play' as the protagonist – the character who carries out the action, and with whom the audience is invited to identify. This dynamic is at the heart of Hans Thies Lehmann's understanding of 'dramatic theatre':

> If one thinks of theatre as drama and as imitation, then action presents itself automatically as the actual object and kernel of this imitation. And before the emergence of film indeed no artistic practice other than theatre could so plausibly monopolize this dimension: the mimetic imitation of human action represented by real actors.[97]

The subject of dramatic mimesis for Lehmann is the body who imitates the actions of life beyond the theatre: 'Within the necessary fixation action seems to entail thinking the aesthetic form of theatre as a variable dependent on another reality – life, human behaviour, reality etc.'[98] The very identification of such a subject involves objectification and points to the position of the theatregoer as an observer who for the most part maintains their own subjective distance. The audience member maintains the distinction between themselves as a watching 'I' and the performing 'them', just as they know the difference between 'here' (the auditorium) and 'there' (the stage). The 'subject' of dramatic theatre both carries the audience along in an identification with their actions, and presents themselves as there to be objectified, as the other which the play is 'about'.

We can characterize Kane's dramaturgy of psychic life as an attempt to transform this relationship by positioning the play itself as a subjectivity, and thus create a theatrical experience in which the relationship between audience and art work is more difficult to pry apart. In this sense Kane neither repeats the imitation of action that Lehmann locates at the centre of 'dramatic theatre', nor does she fall easily within the terms of 'postdramatic theatre', in which the representative function of performance is abandoned.⁹⁹ The mimetic relationship at the centre of her work is the doubling of a psychic pattern rather than an external action. This doubling is created by a dramaturgy which attempts to radically close the distance between audience and artwork. In the case of *Crave*, this is achieved by putting the audience through a dramaturgy which is at once disorientating in its fluidity and claustrophobically static.

In the next two chapters, I will explore how Kane used dramaturgical tools to stage the psychic consequences of sexual violence in *Blasted*, and the disorientations of psychosis in *Cleansed*. This involved a reappropriation and transformation of the legacies of naturalist, avant-garde and feminist theatres, to new and different ends. We will return to *Crave* in Chapter 5, which will consider how the affect of desire complicates and transforms the theatrical encounter in Kane's two late works.

# Notes

1 Dan Rebellato, *Brief Encounter with Sarah Kane*, recorded interview (1998). Available online: http://www.danrebellato.co.uk/sarah-kane-interview (accessed 31 January 2017).
2 Ibid.
3 See, for example, Femi Oyebode's diagnosis of Kane's works in *Madness at the Theatre* (London: The Royal Institute of Psychiatry, 2012).
4 Sierz, *In-Yer-Face Theatre*.
5 Sean Carney understands experientialism as 'Kane seeth[ing] with antagonism at the postmodern condition'. In Carney, *The Politics of Contemporary English Tragedy*, 266. Graham Saunders tackles this assumption in his 2003 article, in which he attempts to pair the 'experiential' label with Kane's 'strict formal control'. Graham Saunders, '"Just a Word on the Page and There is Drama": Kane's Theatrical Legacy', *Contemporary Theatre Review* 13 (2003): 97–110, 100.
6 Iball, *Sarah Kane's Blasted*, 45.
7 Elaine Aston, *Feminist Views on the English Stage: Women Playwrights 1990–2000* (Cambridge: Cambridge University Press, 2003), 82.
8 Clare Wallace, 'Sarah Kane, Experiential Theatre and the Revenant Avant-Garde', in *Sarah Kane in Context*, ed. Graham Saunders and Laurens De Vos (Manchester: Manchester University Press, 2010). David Ian Rabey, *English Drama Since 1940* (London: Pearson Education Limited, 2003), 207.
9 Sierz, *In-Yer-Face Theatre*, 92.
10 Ibid.

11 Sarah Kane, 'The Only Thing I Remember Is . . .', *Guardian*, 13 August 1998, 12.
12 Sierz, *In-Yer-Face Theatre*, 92.
13 Ibid.
14 Ibid.
15 Kane, 'The Only Thing', 12.
16 Iball, *Sarah Kane's Blasted*, 28.
17 Dan Rebellato, 'Sarah Kane before *Blasted*, the Monologues', in *Sarah Kane in Context*, ed. Graham Saunders and Laurens De Vos (Manchester: Manchester University Press, 2010), 29–31.
18 Ibid., 18.
19 Saunders, *Love Me*, 13.
20 Cathy Turner and Synne Behrndt, *Dramaturgy and Performance* (Basingstoke: Palgrave Macmillan, 2008), 18.
21 Ibid., 33.
22 Saunders, *Love Me*, 17.
23 When working with James Macdonald on *Cleansed* for example, she refused to provide guidance on which directions certain lines ought to be interpreted, instead demanding that the production encompass 'all of them'. Saunders, *Love Me*, 169.
24 Sigmund Freud, 'Psychopathic Characters on the Stage (1942 [1905 or 1906])', in *The Standard Edition of the Complete Psychological Works of Sigmund Freud, Volume VII (1901–1905): A Case of Hysteria, Three Essays on Sexuality and Other Works*, ed. James Strachey, 305, emphasis in original.
25 Ibid., 308.
26 Ibid., 309.
27 Ibid.
28 Ibid.
29 André Green discusses this relationship at length in *The Tragic Effect: The Oedipus Complex in Tragedy*, trans. Alan Sheridan (Cambridge: Cambridge University Press, 1969).
30 Strindberg, 'Author's Note', in *Six Plays of Strindberg*, trans. Elizabeth Sprigge (New York: Doubleday Anchor, 1955), 192.
31 Ibid.
32 See Dan Rebellato, 'Objectivity and Observation', in *The Cambridge Companion to Theatre and Science*, ed. Kirsten Shepherd-Barr (Cambridge: Cambridge University Press, 2020).
33 Michael Robinson, 'Chronology', in *The Cambridge Companion to August Strindberg*, ed. Michael Robinson (Cambridge: Cambridge University Press, 2009), xxv.
34 Göran Stockernström, 'Crisis and Change: Strindberg the Unconscious Modernist', in *The Cambridge Companion to August Strindberg*, ed. Michael Robinson (Cambridge: Cambridge University Press, 2009), 86.
35 Ibid., 79.

36 Hans Thies Lehmann, *Postdramatic Theatre*, trans. Karen Jürs-Munby (Abingdon, VA: Routledge, 2006), 65.
37 John Lahr, 'Walking with Arthur Miller', *The New Yorker*, 1 March 2012. Available online: https://www.newyorker.com/culture/culture-desk/walking-with-arthur-miller (accessed 2 November 2021).
38 Susan Sontag, 'Introduction', in *Antonin Artaud: Selected Writings*, ed. Susan Sontag (Berkely and Los Angeles, CA: University of California Press, 1973), xii.
39 Antonin Artaud, *Antonin Artaud: Selected Writings*, ed. Susan Sontag (Berkely and Los Angeles, CA: University of California Press, 1973), 17.
40 Lehmann, *Postdramatic Theatre*, 78.
41 Ibid.
42 Laurens De Vos, *Cruelty and Desire in the Modern Theater: Antonin Artaud, Sarah Kane and Samuel Beckett* (Madison, NJ: Fairleigh Dickinson University Press, 2011).
43 Lois Oppenheim, 'A Twenty-First Century Perspective on a Play by Samuel Beckett', *Journal of Beckett Studies* 17, no. 1–2 (2009): 187–98.
44 See Elizabeth Barry, 'Introduction: Beckett, Language and the Mind', *Journal of Beckett Studies* 17, no. 1–2 (2008): 1–8.
45 Hugh Culik, 'Neurological Disorder and the Evolution of Beckett's Maternal Images', *Mosaic* 22 (1989): 1.
46 For Beckett's influence on Kane see for example: De Vos, *Cruelty and Desire*; Graham Saunders, '"Out Vile Jelly": Sarah Kane's Blasted and Shakespeare's King Lear', *New Theatre Quarterly* 20 (2004): 69–77; Sierz, *In-Yer-Face Theatre*, 96–8; Elizabeth Angel-Perez, *Voyages au Bout du Possible Les Théâtres du Traumatisme de Samuel Beckett à Sarah Kane* (Paris: Klincksieck, 2006).
47 Martha Noel Evans, 'Portrait of Dora: Freud's Case History as Reviewed by Hélène Cixous', *SubStance* 11, no. 3 (1982): 64–7, 65.
48 Elin Diamond, *Unmaking Mimesis: Essays on Feminism and Theatre* (Abingdon, VA: Routledge, 1997), 38.
49 Ibid., 39.
50 Addressed in Chapters 2 and 4 respectively. For the intertextual sources of *4.48 Psychosis* see Diedrich, 'Last in a Long Line of Literary Kleptomaniacs', 374–98, and Marsh, *Suicide*.
51 Lisa Baraitser, *Enduring Time* (London: Bloomsbury, 2017).
52 Ibid., 40.
53 Ibid., 44.
54 Judith Butler, *The Psychic Life of Power: Theories of Subjection* (Stanford, CA: Stanford University Press, 1997), 19.
55 D. W. Winnicott, *Playing and Reality* (London: Routledge, 2005), 3.
56 Ibid., 51, emphasis original.
57 Ibid., 55, emphasis original.
58 Ibid., passim.
59 Ibid., 56.

60  André Green, *Play and Reflection in Donald Winnicott's Writings* (London: Karnac, 2005), 12, 8.
61  *Starved* is one of the three monologues written by Kane at university, grouped under the title *Sick*. *Starved* is unpublished but available for public viewing at the Bristol University Theatre Collection.
62  Rebellato, 'Sarah Kane before *Blasted*, the Monologues', 28–44, 39.
63  Ibid.
64  Ingrid Craigie, private correspondence with Graham Saunders, reproduced with kind permission from Ms Craigie.
65  Kane was heavily involved in the rehearsal process, elucidating the references for every quotation with the actors and re-drafting the play substantially during the rehearsal period.
66  Sarah Kane, 'Crave by Sarah Kane', 1997, accessible via the Royal Court Theatre archive. Reproduced by kind permission of Simon Kane. As a funding proposal, it is important to note that this document was not intended as guidance to future actors or directors and Kane was insistent that the play could be staged in multiple ways, without the A, B, C and M, positions becoming rigid. At the same time, we can see that this funding proposal highlights the indeterminacy of these positions, and suggests the importance of their fluidity.
67  Craigie, correspondence.
68  'Crave by Sarah Kane'.
69  Ibid.
70  Sarah Kane, 'Crave', in *Sarah Kane: Complete Plays* (London: Methuen Drama, 2001), 155.
71  Ibid., 159.
72  Ibid., 178.
73  Ibid., 178, 157.
74  See Foucault, *Madness and Civilisation*, 207.
75  Peter Barham, *Closing the Asylum* (London: Penguin, 1992), xiii.
76  Ibid., 32.
77  T. Groves, 'After the Asylums: Can the Community Care?', *British Medical Journal* 300, no. 6733 (1990): 923–1188, 1188.
78  David King, *Moving on from Mental Hospitals to Community Care: A Case Study of Change in Exeter* (London: The Nuffield Provincial Hospitals Trust, 1991), 53.
79  Testimonies such as those collected by Barham evidence that some patients experienced 'care in the community' in this light.
80  Venn, *Madness and Contemporary British Theatre*, 21.
81  See for example Mental Health Taskforce to the NHS in England, *The Five Year Forward View for Mental Health* (London: NHS England, 2016).
82  Samara Linton, 'Introduction', in *The Colour of Madness: Explore BAME mental health in the UK*, ed. Samara Linton and Rianna Walcott (Edinburgh: Stirling Publishing, 2018) vii.

83  Barham, *Closing the Asylum*, 99.
84  Sarah Daniels, *Sarah Daniels: Plays 2* (London: Bloomsbury Methuen Drama, 1994), 507.
85  Irving Goffman, *Asylums: Essays on the Social Situation of Mental Patients and Other Inmates* (London: Penguin, 1991), 22.
86  Kane, 'Crave', 156.
87  Ibid., 158.
88  Saunders, *Love Me*, 132.
89  Craigie, correspondance.
90  Kane, 'Crave', 194.
91  Ibid., 193.
92  Craigie, correspondence.
93  Butler, *The Psychic Life of Power*, 10.
94  Ibid.
95  Ibid., 10–11.
96  Ibid., 11.
97  Lehmann, *Postdramatic Theatre*, 36
98  Ibid.
99  Ibid.

# 2

# A dramaturgy of sexual trauma

## Kane's feminist legacies

In considering the kinds of psychic life Kane represents in her theatrical works, I begin with a feminist and anti-ableist lens. This means paying attention to the particular ways in which norms associated with gender, sex, violence, capacity and sanity are deployed in Kane's theatre, and how her dramaturgy thwarts our assumptions about what constitute 'normal' minds and bodies. The initial wave of Kane criticism shied away from feminist readings, locating Kane in a tradition of notable male writers, including Samuel Beckett, Howard Barker and Edward Bond – a lineage Kane herself repeatedly endorsed. These critiques take the lead from Kane's rejection of the label of 'woman writer' in a much-quoted interview in Heidi Stephenson and Natasha Langridge's 1997 collection, *Rage and Reason: Women Playwrights on Playwrighting*.[1] Nevertheless, this rejection of the 'woman writer' label need not deter us from approaching Kane's works from a feminist perspective. Making note of the antagonistic playfulness noticeable throughout Kane's interviews, we might ask why it was in an interview specifically about women writers that Kane chose to reject the label. What kind of performance was Kane engaged with in situating herself in a lineage with Shakespeare, Beckett and Bond, rather than playwrights such as Franca Rame, Clare McIntyre, Caryl Churchill and Timberlake Wertenbaker – playwrights she is known to also have admired?[2] Kane's adamant rejection of the 'woman writer' label is perhaps best read in the context of a 1990s London theatrical scene which tended to view feminist plays as marginal, and a theatre criticism culture which had dismissed Kane's first play with accusations of petulant, immature femininity – characterizing her as 'the naughtiest girl in the classroom'.[3]

Whatever Kane's reasons for not embracing the feminist label, her works themselves call for a feminist response. Kane's dramatic worlds are imbued with sexual violence and painful, contradictory desires. Each of her plays narrates or refers to the rape of a woman by a man, and most also stage or refer to the rape of men by other men. *Phaedra's Love* and *Crave* raise the troubling question of how far women can also be considered perpetrators of sexual violence in the context of unbalanced heterosexual relationships. Given the ubiquity of sexual violence in Kane's oeuvre, it is important to begin with a perspective which takes seriously the political and ethical challenges raised by cultural representations of rape. Approaching these works from a feminist perspective means recognizing that the decision to stage a rape scene (or to relocate a rape scene offstage, as in the case of *Blasted*) is an inherently political one. Any representation of sexual violence exists within a world in which sex, as Amia Srinivasan puts it, 'is already laden with meaning'.[4] All sex acts and representations of sex acts participate in a pre-existing politically and ethically charged cultural field. As Srinivasan suggests: 'sex, which we think of as private, is in reality a public thing. The roles we play, the emotions we feel, who gives, who takes, who demands, who wants, who is wanted, who benefits, who suffers: the rules for this were set long before we entered the world.'[5] Kane's works are highly preoccupied with these rules, insofar as they pose extremely difficult questions about the relationships between desire, love and violence.

In Kane's first play *Blasted* (1994), sexual politics and the politics of sanity and capacity are intimately related. Kane stages a female protagonist who is attacked both on the grounds of her gender, and her supposed capacity and sanity. Briefly, *Blasted* stages the story of a middle-aged journalist, Ian, and a young woman, Cate, who arrive at a hotel room in Leeds. It becomes clear that Ian wishes to restart the abusive relationship which had previously existed between them. Ian bullies and intimidates Cate, and then rapes her during the scene break. In the following scene, Cate confronts Ian and then escapes through the bathroom window. The world outside the hotel room is transformed into a war zone, as a soldier appears at the door and the stage is blasted by a mortar bomb. In the wreckage, the soldier asks Ian to report his story, and upon Ian's refusal, the soldier rapes him, sucks out his eyes and then kills himself. Cate returns from the war zone carrying a baby, who dies and who she buries in the floor. She refuses to help a now-blind Ian to kill himself, and leaves in search of food. The play becomes a tableau of Ian performing abject acts on stage, before burying himself in the floor. Cate returns with food and feeds him. He thanks her. The play famously provoked a near-hysterical backlash from the press, which reported outrage that public funds should be used to support the creation of a play with such violent content and supposed formal incoherence.

From the beginning of *Blasted*, Ian draws on a constellation of stereotypes relating to mental illness, learning disabilities and sexual provocation in order to coerce and psychologically abuse Cate. In their first conversation of the play Ian classes Cate with her brother who has learning disabilities.

Calling Cate 'stupid' and a 'spaz', Ian constructs an image of Cate, to herself and to the audience, as dependent, passive and mentally deficient.[6] This characterization was emphasized in the first production, in which Cate was played as having 'the mental age of about 12'.[7] Ian's construction of Cate as deficient is inherently sexual – it is simultaneously the source of his desire and his excuse for discounting her lack of consent: '**Ian:** [You] Don't know nothing. That's why I love you, want to make love to you.'[8] When Ian forces Cate to masturbate him, the assault provokes a fit, introducing a connection between Ian's sexual coercion and her apparent mental illness. First, she stutters and then 'She starts to tremble and make inarticulate crying sounds'. When 'Ian stops, frightened of bringing another "fit" on', she 'sucks her thumb' and he goes on to manipulate her into completing the act, characterizing her as cruelly sexually provocative.[9]

Cate's supposedly pathological subjectivity, which Ian characterizes as caught between uncontrollable sexual provocativeness and the inability to be self-responsible, draws on and re-presents a popular and pernicious stereotype. As I have shown elsewhere, this misogynistic double-bind is typical of popular depictions of mentally ill women in the 1980s and 1990s. Examining the stories relating to mental illness in tabloid newspapers in these decades, I found that they overwhelmingly followed

> [a] trend in presenting female psychiatric patients [which] treads a line between presenting them as victims and in this presentation sexualising and victim-blaming them. We therefore might describe these stories as objects of arousal masquerading as objects of outrage. Read together, the articles build up a fantasy of the hypersexual, mentally ill young woman held at the mercy of a system which punishes her for her apparently unstoppable sexual behaviour.[10]

These discourses typically elide learning difficulties, intellectual disabilities and mental illnesses into a generic, stigmatized image. With the female subject bound by these stereotypes, the reader is invited to enjoy her story, even as he is allowed to preserve the position of moral righteousness and outrage.

Kane draws on this popular image of troubled, pathologized femininity in *Blasted* and simultaneously subverts it, putting it in the mouth of an abusive, sexually violent tabloid hack. The stories that Ian writes and reads out from his newspaper participate in the same sexualizing and trivializing discourse as the insults he uses against Cate. In scene one Ian dictates an article down the phone about an exotic murder of a 'bubbly nineteen-year-old from Leeds', describing her as a 'beautiful redhead with dreams of becoming a model'.[11]

Two lines later he rejects another story on the basis that the supposed victim is a provocative malingerer:

> **Ian** That one again, I went to see her. Scouse tart, spread her legs. No. Forget it. Tears and lies, not worth the space.[12]

The narratives which Ian dictates down the phone mirror the narrative he imposes onto Cate, in which sexualized passivity and disingenuousness are the hallmarks of his misogynistic view of the feminine.

This inclusion of tabloid and tabloid-style characterizations of female pathologized subjects in *Blasted* is an act of what Edward Said calls 'worldly self-situating'.[13] Without needing to include a speech about the danger of pathologizing young women, Kane's play takes on the pernicious assumptions surrounding women's experiences of mental illness dominant in 1990s media and popular culture. Her play acknowledges this discourse, and as such is historically situated within it. Nevertheless, the discourse sits uncomfortably within the rest of the play. It is re-presented in heightened form and associated with a violent protagonist. By re-staging psychiatric narratives of the tabloid press in this light, Kane 'introduces circumstance and distinction where there had only been conformity and belonging [and creates] distance, or what we might also call' – feminist – 'criticism.'[14]

In taking on the particular conflagration of ableism and misogyny of the tabloids, Kane also unwittingly anticipated the tone of much of her play's reception. The tirade of negative criticism which met *Blasted* when it opened at the Royal Court in 1995 consistently cast Kane herself in the model of psychiatrically sick femininity. Jack Tinker of the *Daily Mail* famously suggested that 'the money [from the Jerwood Foundation grant which funded the play] might have been better spent on a course of remedial therapy', whilst Roger Foss described the play as 'the prurient psycho-fantasies of a profoundly disturbed mind' and Kate Kellaway's *Observer* review hoped that '[Kane] wakes up from the nightmare of her own imagination'.[15] Such reviews toe the same line between passivity and provocativeness in their characterization of Kane, as popular presentations of female mental illness on which Kane draws. Not only is Kane a victim of the 'prurient psycho-fantasies' of her own imagination in these reviews, she is simultaneously cast as 'the naughtiest girl in the class, trying to find out just how far she can go before being sent to stand in the corridor'.[16] 'Adolescent', described repeatedly as a 'girl' rather than playwright, and haunted by incoherent monstrosities, the mode through which many of the reviewers of *Blasted* went about dismissing its author seems to draw on the very tropes which the play seeks to expose. This response thus embedded questions surrounding Kane's sanity and femininity into the ongoing, publicly adversarial relationship between Kane and newspaper criticism. Kane becomes part of a developing conversation about how to talk about both atrocity and mental illness which extends beyond her works, but also defines the place her works hold in popular discourse of the 1990s.

By bringing together physical violence and an offensively ableist and stereotyping vocabulary, Kane's characterization of Ian contributes to a growing concern in feminist theatre in the 1980s and early 1990s about the abuse of mentally unwell women. Plays developed by feminist theatre and campaigning groups represented psychiatric wards as destinations in which abused women face further abuse. Sarah Daniels's *Head-Rot Holiday* was developed with Clean Break and performed in 1992. Set at Christmas at Penwell Special Hospital (a psychiatric prison for women), it stages the absurd situation in which a group of female prisoners, most of whom have been abused, are made to attend a festive disco and dance with male prisoners to prove the success of their psychiatric recovery – secure in the knowledge that their dance partners are convicted rapists. The inmate Ruth in particular presents her situation as being caught in a cycle of sexual abuse and humiliation at the hands of family members, fellow inmates and facility staff:

> It's happened all my life, in much worse ways in the past, much worse than any of the category A blokes have done to me in here. There are people out there who have really fucked me over. [. . .] [I]f a man wants to do something to me, anything, I let him. I hold my breath until it's over. [. . .] I've been forcibly stripped by six men in here and left naked without even a tampon. I've been watched in the bath by men. They get paid to do it.[17]

Punished for causing a fuss after being groped by one of the 'category A blokes' at the disco, Ruth's sexual provocativeness is deplored by the psychiatric nurses, and the play presents sexual double-standards as central to the functioning of the institution.

Daniels's play is typical of feminist approaches to sexuality and madness in this period, insofar as it demonstrates the absurdities and double standards of the psychiatric system. As fellow patient Dee muses following Ruth's seclusion: 'if I was on the outside, and I made a relationship with a serial killer, or rapist or both you'd consider me mad, but that's what you'd have to do here to prove you're sane.'[18] Daniels's psychiatric subjects take it upon themselves to ridicule their own situations, and her plays about mental illness humanize their subjects through comedy – as Daniels notes, 'ridicule can often be a more devastating weapon than argument.'[19]

Kane shares an interest in the relationship between psychiatric and sexual abuse with her feminist peers. Having begun her writing career in the 1980s, Sarah Daniels can be read as an interesting interlocutor for Kane's theatre. Daniels's radical feminist play *Masterpieces* premiered at the Royal Court a decade before *Blasted* provoking a similarly vicious public and critical outcry, with its suggestion that there is a direct line connecting misogynist humour, pornography and actual rape.[20] As Elaine Aston has pointed out, *Blasted* is reminiscent of *Masterpieces* not only for the critical response it provoked, but also for the feminist sensibility with which it links sexual violence and explicit *representations* of sexual violence.[21] Where Daniels attempts to establish a link between misogynistic humour, consumption of pornography and sexual violence in *Masterpieces*, Kane has misogynistic storytelling coming from a journalist who is an actual rapist. In each case, sexual violence and patriarchal culture (today we would call this 'rape culture') are represented as two sides of the same, very thin coin. Like Daniels, Kane's first polemical play was partly inspired by the violence of hard-core pornography. Both plays are concerned with how to live in a world in which sexual violence is both hidden and hyper-visible. The female protagonist of *Masterpieces* rages at the sexual-double standards of a world in which snuff movies are shown in cinemas and accusations of rape are disbelieved. The play ends with a monologue condemning rapists, pornographers and 'men who tell misogynistic jokes'.[22] In *Blasted* the representational politics are more complex. Kane's play stages an encounter between a young woman and a violent sexual abuser but locates the major act of violence against Cate's body offstage. In a dramatic world which is saturated with misogyny, it is Ian's body which is repeatedly exposed and violated in front of the audience. We might consider this an act of resistance – even of care – for the play's female protagonist, as the play attempts to stage a story of sexual abuse without exposing the female body.[23]

Kane thus departs formally from her feminist contemporaries in *Blasted* by relocating her critique of sexual violence into the dramaturgy of her first work. Throughout *Blasted*, Cate thwarts the characterization Ian imposes upon her through the persistence of her refusal, her reticence and the psychosomatic fits that Ian classes as signs of her mental deficiency. Rather than placing Ian in conflict with an eloquent interlocutor who might debate his ableist and misogynistic narrative, Kane places him opposite two characters, Cate and the soldier, both of whom remain outside his narrative control: the soldier because he presents stories so horrific that Ian cannot narrate them, and Cate because she preserves a form of mental life that is non-linguistic, and beyond Ian's reach and understanding.

The reticence and absence of *Blasted*'s female protagonist highlight the complex relationship between supposedly pathological behaviour and sexual abuse. Throughout scenes one and two Ian does everything in his power to insist on Cate's narrative of sexual availability coupled with helpless stupidity; repeatedly sexually assaulting her, raping her, infantilizing her and locking her in the room. Nevertheless, Cate repeatedly undermines this narrative by retreating into a mental space in which she cannot be reached and suggesting a subjectivity that is beyond Ian's gaze:

> **Cate** The world don't exist, not like this.
> Looks the same but -
> Time slows down.
> A dream I get stuck in, can't do nothing about.
> One time[24]

Cate reveals nothing about the experience of the fits themselves here, other than the absolute difference between the experience of a fit and the experience of reality.

Kim Solga suggests that by revealing the origins of Cate's pathology from the outset, Kane undermines the forms of narrative suspense that would make such a 'discovery' a source of pleasure for the audience. The fits have ominously begun 'since Dad came back', and the play also strongly suggests that Ian's own relationship with Cate began when she was underage:

> **Cate** We used to always go to yours.
> **Ian** That was years ago. You've grown up.[25]

(In early drafts of *Blasted*, it is explicit that this abusive relationship began whilst Cate was at school.) Comparing Kane's narrative structure to Ibsen's, Solga notes that *Blasted* eschews the moment of revelation of sexual history usually bestowed upon Ibsenite heroines. Rather than having a personal narrative that unfolds as the play progresses, Cate arrives onstage already-damaged:

> the trajectory of events in scenes one and two makes so obvious the link between Cate's abused body and her mental illness that any analysis of these scenes as a version of the realist medical melodrama needs to state the obvious: the pleasurable 'discovery' of the source of Cate's illness is a startling let-down.[26]

For Solga, the play deprives Cate's story of sensationalism. The fits themselves thwart both Ian and the audience in search of a narrative.

Throughout *Blasted* Kane thus draws on the tropes of passivity and victimhood associated with female mental illness in the 1990s and invites the audience to identify these tropes in Ian's speech. At the same time, the play represents these patriarchal discourses as dislodged from reality, as they cannot adequately expose Cate's identity or render it legible to the audience. If as feminist readers and spectators we are to search for the play's understanding of what it means for a young woman to experience a sexually violent world, we will find our answer not in the words of its female protagonist, but in the structure of the play itself.

## Theatre and traumatic response: PTSD and mimetic models

*Blasted* dramaturgically enacts the psychic consequences of sexual abuse on its potential audience. This dramaturgy is situated in a network of culturally influential debates surrounding trauma. Read alongside one of the major debates in current trauma studies, Kane's first play can be seen to bring together two apparently conflicting theories of trauma: 'unrepresentable model' trauma and the 'mimetic model' of trauma. I will briefly outline both models and their consequences here, in order to better discuss Kane's relationship with them in the rest of the chapter.

The 'unrepresentable' model of trauma understands trauma as a problem of reception. According to this understanding, psychological trauma occurs when the victim of a violent event cannot receive and integrate the memory of this event into their consciousness. This understanding of trauma is broadly derived from Freud's *Beyond the Pleasure Principle*, and formed the basis of the modern PTSD diagnosis, as well as the works of several important literary and clinical trauma theorists such as Shoshanna Felman, Dori Laub, Cathy Caruth and Bessel van der Kolk.[27] In *Beyond the Pleasure Principle*, Freud famously sets out to theorize the phenomena of 'traumatic neurosis', which is characterized by the persistent repetition, for example, in dreams, of unpleasant past events. In such cases, Freud notes:

> The patient cannot remember the whole of what is repressed in him, and what he cannot remember may be precisely the essential part of it. [. . .] He is obliged to *repeat* the repressed material as a contemporary experience rather than, as the physician would prefer to see, *remembering* it as something in the past.[28]

Central to Freud's understanding of repression was the inability of the patient to integrate the unpleasant experience into their own timeline. This inability is not caused by the nature of the traumatic event itself, but by its reception and relationship to the fundamental structures of the human psyche:

> These reproductions, which emerge in their unwished-for exactitude always have, as their subject, some portion of infantile sexual life – of the Oedipus complex, that is, and its derivatives.[29]

This belief that traumatic repetition is caused not by the specific nature of the unpleasant experience itself but by its relationship to the repression of the Oedipus complex marked a shift in Freud's thinking on trauma. Here Freud moves away from his previous theory of trauma known as 'seduction theory', in which he posited that hysterical patients' symptoms were caused by the repressed memories of actual sexual abuse in childhood.[30] In *Beyond the Pleasure Principle* in contrast, traumatic phenomena are understood to be a temporal disruption in the patients caused by the universally traumatic experience of the Oedipus complex. Events become traumatically repeated only insofar as they excite the repressed Oedipal memory.

This relationship between traumatic repetition and a form of universal unrepresentability is central to the trauma theory of Cathy Caruth, arguably one of the most influential writers in the field of 'trauma studies.' Key to this version of trauma is the idea that a rupture takes place in the reception of a traumatic event, which leads it to be stored in a manner which bypasses consciousness (and therefore representability). Never consciously experienced, the traumatic moment returns in repetitive and persistent forms in flashbacks or dreams. Caruth summarizes:

> The pathology cannot be defined either by the event itself – which may or may not be catastrophic, and may or may not traumatise everyone equally – nor can it be defined in terms of a *distortion* of the event, achieving its haunting power as a result of distorting personal significance attached to it. The pathology consists, rather, solely in the *structure of its experience* or reception: the event is not assimilated or experienced fully at one time, but only belatedly, in its repeated *possession* of the one who experiences it.[31]

For theorists such as Caruth and Felman, traumatic phenomena point to something inherent in the human psyche, a structural enigma that leads to some forms of reception being disrupted. For Caruth, the phenomenon of traumatic repetition becomes a foundation for a theory of enigmatic psychic life, as she argues that 'the notion of trauma has confronted us not only with a simple pathology but also with a fundamental enigma concerning the psyche's relation to reality'.[32]

The influence of this 'unrepresentable' model of trauma on the PTSD diagnosis can be found in its insistence on the preservation of the traumatic memory somewhere in the mind and the necessity of its reintegration for the purposes of cure. The traumatic event is somehow integrated into the psyche without being touched by consciousness· As such, the event remains enigmatic, but literally preserved until it emerges symptomatically and can be integrated into a patient's timeline through therapy. Allan Young emphasizes this in his study of 'prolonged exposure therapy' as the 'gold standard' of treatments for PTSD in veterans in the United States. In these cases, the patient is asked to recount a traumatic event in extreme detail, or watch footage of such events repeatedly, until it is re-assimilated in the patient's memory.[33] In such an understanding of PTSD, trauma is a temporal disruption in the receiving of an overwhelming event, and its cure involves a reordering into the 'correct' temporality – that is, leaving the past in the past.

Didier Fassin and Richard Rechtman have argued that psychoanalytic 'trauma theory' has had an important impact in turning the specific diagnosis of 'combat stress disorder' into the more widely applicable PTSD diagnosis in two ways. First, by repositioning the traumatic experience 'to become a testament to the unspeakable', it enlarged the psychiatric questions surrounding trauma into wider questions about the limits of knowledge. And, second, perhaps more importantly, it turned PTSD into a social issue, a question of how the psyche is capable of living through atrocity:

> In contrast to the image offered by the combat shock patient of soldiers psychologically damaged by battle, the trauma of survivors testified to the transgression of a fundamental boundary, beyond which social life had been destroyed.[34]

The model of 'unspeakable trauma' thus understands trauma as a structural psychic response to atrocity, in which the repetitive return of the traumatic event is not so much a symptom of the damage a specific event has wrought on the psyche, but evidence of the psyche's inability to represent such an event that is by its very nature unrepresentable.

In response to this increasingly wide definition of trauma, alternative understandings of the psychic consequences of violence have emerged. The 'mimetic model' of trauma focuses less on reception and memory, and more on the ways in which traumatic events transform subjectivity. The 'mimetic model' is partly based on the work of Sándor Ferenczi, who was a Hungarian psychoanalyst and student of Freud's. In his final paper, Ferenczi returned to the question of childhood trauma, rejecting Freud's turn away from seduction theory. Ferenczi focuses specifically on the impact of sexual abuse on childhood psychic development. According to Ferenczi's mimetic model, the survivor's ability to perceive is shattered by the traumatic sexual assault to the extent that they are no longer able to experience themselves as an autonomous subject. It alters the way the survivor actually sees the outside world, enacting 'a pervasive change in someone's perceptual world'.[35] Ruth Leys argues that in this framework, the survivor 'mimetically incorporate[s] the thoughts and feelings of the aggressor', and their own subjectivity becomes occupied by the traumatizing 'other'.[36] The survivor is 'shocked out of consciousness into a condition of trance-like incorporation or imitation of the violent other'.[37]

This model of trauma thus emphasizes the disruptive power of the act of aggression, and the encounter between victim and perpetrator. It understands the event as entering consciousness and causing potentially irreparable damage by forcing the subject to recreate themselves in the model of their aggressor in a bid for survival. In this way it has a closer relationship to the diagnostic category of 'complex PTSD', which feminist psychiatrist Judith Herman proposes to describe the complicated, ongoing impact of long-term domestic abuse and child abuse.[38] The traumatic mimesis which it describes is more extreme than the form of imitation, or re-presentation denoted when we talk about theatrical mimesis. Mimetically experienced trauma involves the subject actually *remaking herself* in a new image, as she unwillingly incorporates her aggressor into her psychic life. It becomes a model for understanding the way in which psychic life can be reshaped, even entirely remade by a violent encounter.

## *Blasted*: The psychic life of sexual trauma

Throughout her works, Kane presents a version psychic life following sexual violence which speaks to both of these models. *Blasted*'s dramaturgy is structured according to a logic of distortion and repetition, which is found in the processes of mental breakdown associated with a PTSD diagnosis. The definition of PTSD which was included in the *Diagnostic Statistics Manual III* in 1980 (a hugely influential diagnostic guidebook published and revised at least once a decade by the American Psychiatric Association) contained four main symptoms by which the disorder was to be identified. These were:

1) the experiencing of 'an event that is outside the range of usual human experience and that would be markedly distressing to almost anyone';
2) the persistent 're-experience[ing]' of the event in some form';

3) 'avoidance of stimuli associated with the trauma or numbing of general responsiveness'; and
4) 'persistent symptoms of increased arousal' including physiological responses to situations reminiscent of the traumatic event.[39]

According to the PTSD diagnosis the actual 'original' traumatic event is not remembered, or if it is, it is remembered with a sense of detachment or 'numbing' which prevents it from being affectively integrated in the individual's history. Instead, it is intrusively repeated in the form of dreams, flashbacks or hypersensitivity to events that resemble the traumatic moment. The patient's timeline is effectively disrupted, and they are unable to understand the event as past because it keeps re-erupting into their present.

*Blasted* performs this loss and recurrence of a traumatic moment by temporally eliding the rape of Cate in a scene break and using it as the hidden catalyst for the overwhelming scenes of violence that follow. Kane introduces disruptions and repetitions into the form of the playtext in order to manipulate the experience of a potential spectator, and create an 'experiential' style which places the reader or spectator *within* the experience of post-traumatic repetition. Much has been said of the stylistic changes *Blasted* undergoes, but it is necessary to recap them here for the sake of argument. The play begins in the mode of Ibsenite realism: two people enter a hotel room, previous connections between them are revealed through dialogue and conflict between them occurs. The opening scene more or less follows the formal rules of this mode, as everything that does occur can be explained by the internal logic of the plot – either suggested (Cate's fits are caused by abuse) or explicit (Cate is here because Ian asked her to be). At the beginning of scene one, for example, there is a bunch of flowers in the hotel room. Their presence is consistent with the classiness of the room, the champagne provided and the romantic intentions of Ian. It is therefore easy for the audience to assume that Ian has requested for them to be there before arriving.

In the beginning of scene two the flowers have begun to function in terms of a new signifying logic, for which the audience has been unprepared: 'The bouquet of flowers is now ripped apart and scattered around the room.'[40] Whilst it is possible that either Ian or Cate themselves ripped apart and distributed the flowers, the event is neither discussed, nor does it fit with the events of the night as they emerge from Ian and Cate as the scene progresses. A botany-destroying stand-off does not feature in the narrative the audience pieces together regarding the events of the night in which Cate and Ian go to bed together and hold hands, following which Ian rapes Cate and performs violent oral sex on her causing her to still be bleeding the following day.

The bouquet, in other words, no longer responds to the '*structure*[s] [. . .] *of experience* or reception' of Ibsenite realism that were established in scene one.[41] Instead they belong to a new form of reference and signification, in which their destruction obliquely points to the unseen violence that occurred in the scene break, and is now emerging outside of realism's representative channels. The blasting of a hole into the back wall of the stage at the end of scene two is an escalation of the blasting of the bouquet, as the violence of and towards the set escalates alongside the violence perpetrated by and towards the characters.

The disruption of the play's narrative logic is also detectable on the level of the acts of the characters onstage. As some of *Blasted*'s initial reviewers noted, even before the entrance of the soldier Cate and Ian's characters emerge with inconsistencies. Ian was a journalist in scene one, but scene two reveals him as a Pinteresque character: a slightly unbelievable secret agent – or a journalist with paranoid fantasies in which he is a secret agent. Cate, on the other hand, goes from being so shy and averse to sexual contact that she has a psychosomatic fit in response to being kissed with tongue, to a woman willing to perform oral sex and bite her aggressor's penis as an act of revenge. Whilst neither of these is totally unbelievable, it nevertheless destabilizes the kind of narrative logic that scene one has established for its audience. Whereas in scene one aggression and violence were contained within the logic of a domestic narrative, in scene two they emerged unexpectedly and unbelievably from sources outside of the premised plot: the changes to the room, the unexpected character twists and the newly violent world outside the door. The viewing experience for a potential spectator might become disorientating and split, having to observe the unfolding of the plot and experiencing emotional response to it on the one hand, and simultaneously attempting to assimilate the illogical additions to it on the other. As Michael Billington asked in his review of the first production: 'who exactly is meant to be fighting whom on the streets?'[42] Whilst one could argue that questions such as this demonstrate a failure to understand either the Bosnian reference or the formal innovativeness of the work,[43] it is nevertheless a valid question that may well occur to the viewer whilst watching the play. The emergence of a soldier from an unmentioned location bringing the horrors of an unnamed war in tow is an escalation of the increasing disorientation that has been playing itself out since the unstaged rape of Cate.

Kane structures *Blasted*'s dramaturgy so as to perform the repetition of Cate's rape in increasingly amplified and distorted forms. According to the PTSD framework, this repetition disrupts the survivor's internal chronology, holding them in a traumatic present rather than allowing memory to be consigned to the past. Ruth Leys summarizes the supposed effects of this disrupted temporality: 'As a result, the victim is unable to recollect and integrate the hurtful experience into normal consciousness: instead she is *haunted or possessed by intrusive traumatic memories*. The experience of trauma, fixed or frozen in time refuses to be represented *as* past, but is *perpetually re-experienced as painful, dissociated, traumatic, present*.'[44] Kane describes this experience in *Crave*: 'And though she cannot remember she cannot forget/ And has been hurtling away from that moment ever since.'[45]

The violence enacted upon Ian by the soldier in scene three, and his subsequent breakdown in the expressionist tableaux of scene five, contain thematic and formal escalations of his aggression towards Cate in the first two scenes of the play. The representation of Ian's rape especially parallels the simulation of his rape of Cate in scene two:

**Cate** *trembles and starts gasping for air.*
*She faints.*
**Ian** *goes to her, takes the gun and puts it back in the holster. Then he lies her on the bed on her back.*
*He puts the gun to her head, lies between her legs, and simulates sex.*
*As he comes* **Cate** *sits bolt upright with a shout.*
*Ian moves away, unsure what to do, pointing the gun at her from behind.*
*She laughs hysterically, as before, but she doesn't stop.*
*She laughs and laughs and laughs until she isn't laughing anymore, she's crying her heart out.*[46]

-

*The* **Soldier** *turns Ian over with one hand.*
*He holds the revolver to* **Ian**'s *head with the other.*
*He pulls down* **Ian**'s *trousers, undoes his own and rapes him – eyes closed, and smelling* Ian's *hair.*
*The* **Soldier** *is crying his heart out.*[47]

The connection between the simulated rape of Cate and the actual rape of Ian is one that Kane herself was emphatic about, deploring her reviewers for 'ignoring [. . .] the fact that [the soldier] does it with a gun to his head which Ian has done to Cate earlier – and he's crying his eyes out as he does it'.[48] But the violence of scene three is not simply a reiteration of the simulation of scene two. They are both repetitions, references to an assault that is not staged but eclipsed by the chronological structuring of the play which elides the rape of Cate in the scene break.

Following the rape of Ian the violence gets worse; his eyes are removed and eaten by the soldier who subsequently kills himself. Each act of violence builds on the last in a reiterative rather than narrative logic that does nothing to explain what has come before. The play's penultimate scene is a series of tableaux separated by blackouts, in which Ian cries, laughs, masturbates, defecates, attempts to eat the baby and buries himself in the floor. By the time we get to this the narrative logic of the play has broken down completely. Ian's abject acts escalate the thematic concerns of act one. Masturbation is a repetition of the first (forced) sex act performed onstage, cannibalism an escalation of Cate's disgust at Ian's meat-eating, defecating reminiscent of the constant trips to the bathroom, burying himself in the floor an escalation of the hole in the back wall – the first violation of the stage itself. Rather than a simple litany of degradation the play follows a careful pattern of distortion, repetition and escalation, giving its audience visual and thematic connections between the scenes without a traditionally unfolding narrative that provides a logic of 'before' and 'after'.

Scene five marks the biggest shift in the play's temporality as Kane abandons narrative chronology altogether. Yet again, the breakdown is a form of repetition. Eight tableaux are separated with eight blackouts, reminiscent of the play's first blackout in which the unstaged violation occurs. The blackouts are also reminiscent of Cate's fits, which themselves point to a traumatic symptomatic structure. Rather than returning at the expected interval after the length of a scene, the blackouts are now piling up, within the scene, with under a minute between them. The acts that they frame are singular, unrelated to one another and without specific narrative precedent. In this moment in the play the audience is held in a present, totally cut off from any narrative experience and yet constantly being referred back to that which has not been seen.

I have been explicit in the ways in which these 'formal' developments refer back to the unseen rape in order to emphasize the connection between the violence and stylistic changes of the play and the character and body of Cate. This is not to say that the soldier's rape of Ian is a vengeful repetition of his assault on Cate. Such an interpretation would actually maintain Ian as the play's primary referent, figuring him as an anti-hero receiving his comeuppance. There are two ways in which the act simultaneously signifies. On the level of plot the soldier rapes Ian in the context of war, and the atrocities he has committed and submitted to unwitnessed. On the level of overall dramaturgy violence begins to break in, destroying the play's narrative logic and filling the field of vision, and referring us back to an invisible source. These levels of signification do not cancel each other out. Throughout Kane's work the psychic and the actual, which is imbued with the global-political, are tightly bound together. The boundary between gendered violence, political violence and psychic breakdown is rendered untenable in this work, as psychic life is in itself worldly and the boundaries between interior and exterior, and personal and global, are deeply troubled.

This is what separates my argument from those of Patrick Duggan and Peter Buse, who both read *Blasted* as a 'traumatic' text but fail to note the elision of the rape of Cate. Duggan's reading does attempt to locate an 'originary' moment for the dramaturgical breakdown that takes place afterwards, but does so in a scene he reads as Ian's metaphorical castration. Duggan's reading of *Blasted* figures Cate as the primary perpetrator, who threatens Ian's masculinity, thus inciting him to traumatic violence (i.e. violence routed in Ian's trauma):

> Cate's laugh and the fracturing it causes in Ian's understanding of himself is a psychologically violent attack which marks the beginning of a traumatic cycle that rumbles throughout the play.[49]

Having identified Cate laughing at Ian as the key traumatic moment, and ignoring both her history of psychosomatic fits and the implied previous abuse, Duggan goes so far as to suggest that Cate brings her rape upon herself:

> Perpetrators have the traumas they have committed turned upon themselves: Cate rebuffs and laughs at Ian, but, as T. G. A. Nelson warns, laughter can be treacherous because 'people laugh when they feel superior, but the tables may turn so that the laughter become the butt' (1990:6) and so Ian rapes Cate, returning the traumatic experience to her.[50]

A critical perspective which does not look into the 'blind spot' of the play here (i.e. to look directly at the circumstance and elision of the rape of Cate) can lead dangerously close to adopting the rape apologism of Ian himself, figuring Cate as a castrating mother-figure, participating in the (anti-)hero Ian's degradation.[51] By following Ian's anti-heroic narrative arc as the only structuring principle of the play, such criticisms miss the specific pattern of repetition and distortion that takes place in the play's dramaturgy. For both Duggan and Buse, Ian is the traumatic victim and the bomb and generalized 'chaotic violence' that follow are the consequences.[52]

On the other hand, embarking on a feminist reading encourages us to pay attention to the marginalized body of the female protagonist. When we interpret the rape of Cate as the originary perpetration, the violence and breakdown reveals itself not to be chaotic at all, but to be a careful and structured series of repetitions and distortions. Kane explained this in an interview with Nils Talbert:

> [T]he soldier is the way he is because of the situation, *but the situation exists because of what Ian has created in that room, of what he has done to Cate*

[. . .] So, basically, it's a completely self-perpetuating circle of emotional and physical violence. If you skip the connection between all this, if you skip the emotional reason, the play does appear to be completely broken backed, just split into two halves which means it fails totally.[53]

Placing Cate at the centre of the play's dramaturgical structure not only gives scope to a feminist reading of the play but also enables us to articulate a specific thesis as to the kind of mental life Kane awards the traumatized subject.

This connection situates *Blasted* in a critical relationship with feminist trauma studies. The concept of rape-trauma as PTSD had a significant influence on the literary and artistic culture within the women's movement in the UK. Lisa Appignanesi notes how the focus on trauma and rape in the 1980s shaped the women's movement, moving the focus from empowerment to overcoming victimhood. 'A dynamic abuse narrative had been moulded,' Appignanesi says, 'it took for granted that the entirety of a life was misshaped by the experience of early sexuality.'[54] Pressure emerged from within the women's movement for this narrative to be voiced repeatedly: 'Speaking the horror in front of sympathetic witnesses, perhaps in a women's group or in therapy or most controversially in the courts, took on, particularly in the USA, the force of a moral injunction.'[55] The cultural importance of this kind of 'speaking up' about women's traumatic experiences found its way into feminist theatre in Britain, where the 'practice of performances that [drew] on personal, lived experiences, [became] coterminous with the history of "Second Wave" Western feminism'.[56] Whilst it is unclear how far Kane was aware of specific ideas and theories of trauma, both *Blasted* and her university works speak to this cultural concern. Kane's early experimentation with the rape monologue in *Comic Monologue*, and her decision to direct Franca Rame's seminal feminist monologue *The Rape* whilst an undergraduate, demonstrate her interest in feminist strategies for voicing of traumatic sexual experiences.[57]

Kane's presentation of violence in *Blasted* is open to the same criticisms of universalism that have been levelled against the PTSD diagnosis and its appropriation by feminist discourse. As a framework for understanding the psychic consequences of violence, PTSD emerged as a bridging term, connecting the consequences of the violence of war, political oppression, state violence and the violence of patriarchy. As a diagnosis, PTSD gained popularity in the 1980s and 1990s in part due to two widespread and vocal campaigns which pushed the diagnosis into the medical establishment and the public imagination: the Vietnam veterans' campaign in the United States and the North American and European women's movements.

After the introduction of PTSD as a veteran's disease, feminist psychiatrists in the United States led by Judith Herman battled for the *DSM-III* definition to be enlarged to include the trauma of rape and child abuse. Herman and her contemporaries had political and practical motivations for including abuse in the PTSD diagnosis, as Appignanesi notes:

> [S]ince diagnoses do make their way into court in the form of expert witnesses, since they do affect divorce, custody or the rarer murder trials and also serve to release insurance expenditure for treatment, the battle to find a diagnosis for the abused of the private sphere had a sense of justice about it. The diagnosis which Herman and her colleagues battled to attach to abused women was PTSD.[58]

The effect of these vocal campaigns was to create a symptomatic structure through which to understand and interpret psychic pain following a variety of experiences of abuse, one which it was necessary to subscribe to if treatment or legal consequences and compensation were to be forthcoming. PTSD therefore provided a framework which was capable of navigating the personal and the political, domestic rape and atrocities of warfare.

Kane follows this lead by integrating the violence of war and domestic gendered violence into a single dramatic universe. Readings of *Blasted* as a play about domestic rape-trauma do not preclude readings of *Blasted* as a political response to the British public's apathy to the Balkan conflict.[59] Rather, it adds to this already widely addressed perspective by suggesting that the acts of warfare take place within a dramatic space shaped by a single act of domestic rape. In her important book on the history of rape, Joanna Bourke warns of essentializing or universalizing sexual violence. For Bourke, such an attitude risks eliminating the specific social and political circumstances in which rapists commit violence.[60] Kane's representation of sexual violence in *Blasted* seems to take place somewhere between these two poles, as the play presents violence as thematically universal but dramaturgically specific.[61]

## The mimetic model: Hiding the subject

The specificity of the rape of Cate in *Blasted* is the fact of its invisibility. *Blasted* is not a wholesale regurgitation of the effects of violence according to the definition of PTSD. Rather, it presents a modified version of these effects, as Kane's dramaturgy enacts and represents a mental scene in which violence engenders a new form of traumatized subjectivity. Kane uses Cate's literal absence from the stage to suggest that the consequences of domestic rape and child abuse include the obliteration of the victimized subject from her own psychic experience. In this way *Blasted* resonates with Ferenczi's 'mimetic model' of trauma, which Herman has built on to describe the 'complex PTSD' or chronic trauma suffered by victims of long-term abuse. This model understands the sexual traumatic event as so decimating that it voids the victim of her own subjectivity, and forces her to build another in response to a violent environment.

In *Blasted* Kane represents and simulates a version of traumatic vision in which the traumatized subject *cannot continue to exist as she is* following sexual abuse. The play's female protagonist is not only damaged by traumatic sexual violence, she is also occupied by it. This occupation is militaristic in its nature, metonymically linked to the soldier's occupation of the hotel room.[62] Cate, her narrative, her body and the glimpses we catch of her interiority are displaced from the play itself by the overwhelming scenes of violence that follow. The reader or potential spectator is taken out of a pseudo-naturalist situation in which it was possible to empathize with the female protagonist, 'to a place of extreme mental discomfort and distress',[63] in which the images of male violence are so explicit they seem to render the first half of the play irrelevant.

Following the rape of Cate in *Blasted*, the world of the play and Cate's interior world become overrun by Ian's worldview. Cate's tentatively established interiority in contrast begins to disappear. Throughout scene one Ian views the outside world as violent and threatening, and expresses this through paranoia and rampant racism. Entering the room he takes out a gun, 'checks it is loaded and puts it under his pillow'.[64] His constant use of racist slurs is linked to a sense of threat, to himself and to the city beyond the window. Afraid that the 'Wogs and Pakis' are taking over the city outside the window and that the woman he is attempting to possess is a 'nigger-lover', Ian already perceives himself as under attack from a myriad of others.[65] In scene one Cate resists both his racism and his sense that the outside world is a threat. Whilst Ian needs to answer the door with a loaded gun, Cate knows the name of the waiter bringing up the room service. The world that Ian reads as teeming with violence is one that Cate is happy to interact with:

**Ian** And when was the last time you went to a football match?
**Cate** Saturday. United beat Liverpool 2-0.
**Ian** Didn't you get stabbed?[66]

After the scene break between scenes one and two, in which the rape of Cate occurs, the violent and threatening fantasy through which Ian sees the world begins to seep into the rest of the play, through the dramaturgical fracturing discussed earlier, and through the change in Cate's own perspective. Throughout scene two Cate begins to introject Ian's fear of the outside world. She colludes with his earlier assessment of the view from the window commenting that it 'looks like there's a war on.'[67] And whilst she was incredulous at Ian's fear of opening the door in scene one, in scene two she responds to knocks at the door with terror:

*There is a knock at the door. They both jump.*
**Cate** DON'T ANSWER IT DON'T ANSWER IT DON'T ANSWER IT
*She dives on the bed and puts her head under the pillow.*[68]

Following Cate's coming around to the perspective that the world is filled with violence and threat, the world of the play actually changes. It becomes full of more violence than even Ian could have imagined. Following her rape Cate repeatedly calls Ian a 'nightmare' just as his worst nightmare is realized in the following scenes. He is attacked, emasculated, symbolically castrated through blinding, all by a generically 'foreign' other who emerged through the door he has been terrified of since scene one. Ian's worldview and his subsequent suffering take over the play, leaving Cate physically absent, and absent from the narrative.

The psychic consequences of sexual trauma here are therefore staged as interminable. In the final scene of *Blasted*, when Ian's body, the stage set and the play's form have been mutilated almost beyond recognition, Cate returns. Dan Rebellato has interpreted this return as an overcoming on the part of Cate, and a significant departure for Kane from her rape monologue, *Comic Monologue*. *Comic Monologue* ends with a condemnation of rape, as the speaker states that the consequences of such an attack cannot be overcome. Rebellato argues that this is 'editorial commentary' which is removed in *Blasted*.[69] For Rebellato, Cate's return to the stage at the end of *Blasted* marks a change of heart for Kane, and a chance for recovery following trauma. Nina Kane has taken this claim further, writing that 'Cate reclaims her sexuality and agency in the face of violence throughout the play, emerging as a survivor, not a victim, her humanity intact'.[70] Whilst it is tempting to try to find a hopeful final message in *Blasted* through Cate's return, when examined in the context of the rest of the play the final scene provides no such relief. Cate returns to a world in which the violence perpetrated upon her 're-circulates in the images of war that follow'.[71]

What's more, asking at what cost survival is found is certainly not to undermine the play's feminist potential, or to underestimate Cate 'as a character'. Cate is forced by the violence of war to abandon the few signs of personal identity and interiority which she showed in scene one. Having begun the play as a vegetarian, disgusted by Ian's alcoholism, and committed to monogamy, she returns at the end without any of these attributes:

**Cate** *enters carrying some bread, a large sausage and a bottle of gin.*
*There is blood seeping from between her legs.*
*[. . .] She eats her fill of the sausage and bread, then washes it down with gin.*[72]

Cate returns from the war-torn world outside with the very food and drink (gin and pork) that she refused to eat at the beginning of the play, food she has only been able to acquire through a violent sexual encounter. This is reminiscent of Herman's observations in her work with survivors of long-term abuse, where she notes that the 'final step in the psychological control of the victim is not completed until she has been forced to violate her own moral principles and to betray her basic human attachments'.[73] Cate's return marks a new set of behaviours and a new subjectivity which has been constituted through violence. To suggest that this return is an act of overcoming or empowerment is to undermine how Cate is present as a subject. Her return marks a total submission to the logic of a new, violent world in the name of survival – a submission that has led to the repetition rape on her body and an inability to continue to live life according to the values that previously defined her. Whilst there is no explicit statement that the trauma of rape is unrecoverable in the dialogue of the play, the dramaturgy itself provides this 'editorial commentary' by enacting a form of subjectivity structured by Cate's psychic life.[74]

The rape of Cate acts as a catalyst for the domination of the theatrical site by male violence, leaving the audience with only Ian and the soldier with which to identify. Following this unstaged act of violence, all subsequent violence is presented with startling explicitness and the dramatic universe of the play becomes a site of extreme aggression. For Ferenczi, traumatic confusion takes place in an abused child because there is no language or framework for the child to understand what has happened to them. The attacker's own shame and guilt creates a silence around the attack, which is imposed on the child. This introjection for Ferenczi 'arises mainly because the attack and the response to it are denied by the guilt-ridden adults, indeed, are treated as deserving punishment'.[75] This traumatized subject literally leaves themselves in order to avoid feeling the pain of abuse, and takes up the subjectivity of their own aggressor instead: 'I do not feel the pain inflicted upon me at all, because I do not exist. On the other hand, I do feel the pleasure gratification of the attacker, which I am able to perceive.'[76] Jay Frankel emphasizes the extent to which this identification is a survival mechanism: 'Knowing the aggressor "from the inside" in such a closely observed way allows the child to gauge at each moment precisely how to appease, seduce, flatter, placate, or otherwise disarm the aggressor'.[77] This is not done consciously. Rather, '[i]dentifying with the aggressor involves feeling what one is expected to feel, whether this means feeling what the aggressor wants his particular victim to feel or feeling what the aggressor himself feels'.[78] The attack itself causes a voiding of subjectivity, but it is the guilt and ambivalence of the attacker that fills the void, as Kane herself suggested: 'when people are intensely violent they manage to make the victim feel guilty'.[79]

In *Blasted*, however, Kane alters this introjection. Ian's violent misogyny and entitlement are so strong that he feels no guilt with regard to his abuse of Cate, and therefore no guilt is introjected by Cate, or into the form of the play. Instead, the world of the play becomes soaked in the violence of Ian and the soldier which is presented so as to seem to block out and overwhelm everything else. Ian as the victim and perpetrator of this violence (against himself and the baby) becomes the play's epicentre, and it is difficult to look past his dominance onstage to see Cate at all. If the play's dominant features and aesthetic identity are its onstage violence, as newspaper reviews and academic criticism seem to suggest, then what needs to be acknowledged is that this violence is engendered by the rape of Cate. In other words, the representational challenges of her rape shape the dramatic universe itself, forming a novel dramaturgy out of the obliteration of the first act of violence.

By both drawing on the patterns of repetition of PTSD on the one hand, and enacting a version of trauma in which the perpetrator invites identification and interminably occupies psychic space on the other, *Blasted* therefore sits uncomfortably between two major, ostensibly conflicting theories of trauma.[80] Ferenczi's 'mimetic model' differs most from both the PTSD diagnosis and Caruth's trauma theory in one key aspect: the 'mimetic model' understands trauma as disruption of *identity*, rather than of memory and reception. In Caruth's work and the PTSD framework, the memory of the traumatic moment is inscribed *in some way* into the mental life of the subject, and is to that extent recoverable. In psychiatric and therapeutic contexts, the recovery of the 'lost' memory of a traumatic moment has become a key to many treatments.[81] In contrast Ferenczi 'would attribute the patient's lack of memory of the trauma [. . .] to the vacancy of the traumatised subject or ego in a hypnotic openness to impressions or identifications occurring prior to all self-representation'.[82] This perspective leads us to a point of contention between Ferenczi and other theorists. If at the moment of trauma the victim is affectively absent, then a 'true', accurately remembered version of the event simply cannot exist. We, as potential audience members within the traumatic structure, must experience the distress of this event without being provided with a historical 'cause' which would frame the rest of the play into a clear narrative. The rape of Cate is both obvious and cannot be 'proved', and the consequent damage it inflicts to the world of the play is clearly manifest despite taking place in her absence.

*Blasted* thus provokes a different mode of relating with the potential audience, outside of straightforward identification. This dramaturgy relates to its audience through the mode of psychoanalytic play which 'is in fact neither a matter of inner psychic reality nor a matter of external reality'.[83] Rather, it is located in a 'potential space' that is in between the inner lives and external realities of the participants. Through her manipulations of theatrical form, Kane invites her audience into a potential space in which they might experience distortions, repetitions akin to those of the trauma following sexual abuse. By voiding Cate from the stage space altogether, the play invites a troubling identification with its primary perpetrator which repeats the internalizing of his world view into Cate's psychic life. The challenge issued by *Blasted*, for theatre-makers and potential audience members, becomes whether and in what way to integrate the absence of Cate into the play's reception.

## *Blasted* in production

The extent to which *Blasted*'s disappearance of Cate has been successful in production is demonstrated in the newspaper reviews of the three major London productions that have taken place since its opening. The now-infamous reviews of the play's 1995 premiere largely follow the same pattern: a short summary of scenes one and two followed by an extensive list of the abject and violent acts committed onstage, and some gleeful condemnation of them and of the Royal Court's decision to stage the play. Reviewers of the Royal Court's 2001 revival of the production were largely preoccupied with retracting some of the negative sentiment of their previous reviews following Kane's death by suicide. Nevertheless, one feature familiar to reviews of both the original production of *Blasted* and its 2001 revival is the focus on onstage violence and the degradation of Ian's body.[84] The 2001 reviews largely attempt to justify the onstage violence in the face of Kane's death, either with the argument that scenes just as violent can be seen on news channels,[85] in Beckett plays or in Jacobean drama,[86] or with speculation that Kane was making 'a point' about Bosnian violence,[87] or about the personal horrors of depression.[88]

Reviews of Sean Holmes's 2010 production at the Lyric Hammersmith are more nuanced, the event being at a greater distance from Kane's death. Nevertheless, the reviews emphasize the image of Ian's body as the most impactful of the play, and Danny Webb's portrayal of Ian as its standout performance. Several reviewers viewed Ian as a modern-day Lear,[89] and others made a comparison between Ian's body at the end of the play and the religious paintings of Francis Bacon.[90] The directing, design and performances of the 2010 production established Ian as the anti-hero of the play, who 'rapes his epileptic former girlfriend and thereby unleashes a surreal storm of retributive horrors that blast the play into a different shape'.[91] These productions, none of which diverged too far from Kane's text, presented their reviewers with a dramatic world which revolved around Ian, in which Cate's narrative was seen as a stepping stone and coda to the savagery suffered and perpetrated by the male characters.

These reviews point to the inevitable problem of attempting to enact a process of forgetting or disappearing on an audience. Solga argues that the unique status of the rape of Cate in Kane's oeuvre as a dramatically and temporally hidden act might make it stand out from an intellectual perspective, but onstage its being a non-event does not make it noticeable. If it does, it does so only after the fact, when the subsequent sexual assaults refer us back to an original victim, and then only if directing, design and performance decisions choose to point an audience in this direction. The rape of Cate is not something we are made to notice so much as something we have to make an effort to see, a 'blind spot' in the visual field of the play.[92] Nevertheless, as we have seen, the violence of the second half of the play appears 'broken backed' and 'chaotic' without the pattern which links it back to the invisible source.[93] Sean Carney has noted Ian's position as the site of representational ambivalence in *Blasted* – both impossible to like and an extreme sufferer.[94] Carney concludes that this ambivalence makes for a play that is very self-conscious, revealing the contradictions inherent in tragedy itself as containing both thought and feeling.

Richard Wilson's 2015 production of *Blasted* at the Crucible Theatre in Sheffield approached this challenge unusually, by situating the character of Cate firmly at the centre of his production. This production thwarted the invisibility of the rape of Cate and her narrative by pushing Cate into the foreground of the play's dramaturgy. In doing so, Wilson diverged from the tradition of London productions mentioned earlier, which have tended to place a greater emphasis on the visual impact of Ian's body in the later scenes of the play. By considerably downplaying the visual impact of Ian's violation and bodily breakdown Wilson's production opened *Blasted* up to a feminist re-reading which spoke to specifically twenty-first-century concerns surrounding victimhood and sexual abuse. Rather than maintaining the representational ambivalence surrounding Ian in the playtext, Wilson resolved it by making Cate more central to the *theme* of the play, turning it more clearly into an abuse-narrative.

This was partially achieved by reducing the explicitness with which the onstage violence was staged. Toning down the violence of the second half (no screaming or spurts of fake blood), the production disappointed some critics, who suggested 'a certain amount of sanitised coyness about the showing of sexual depravity, male rape, eyeball gauging, eating a dead baby and so on'.[95] One reviewer complained that 'in some places the violence and sex were so sanitized that it actually became unclear what was meant to be occurring – which somewhat detracted from the visceral power of the play because it was clear that some of these things weren't "really" happening' – a reflection that says as much about the voyeuristic fascination with which Kane's plays are anticipated as it does about the production itself.[96]

By avoiding a gore-fest interpretation (the litany of horrors implied in 'and so on') in favour of a slow-paced, stylized production Wilson allowed space for greater articulation of Cate's character. The majority of reviews of this production dedicated more time to Cate's narrative than is usually seen in reviews of the play and highlighted the visual impact of Cate's body on the production. Whereas the reviews of the 2010 production at the Lyric Hammersmith frequently return to the vision of 'Ian pinned in a shaft of white light in Bacon-like poses of miserable suffering', reviews of the Sheffield Theatres production dwell on the haunting image of 'Jessica Bardem's cracked, porcelain doll-like Cate' as the production's lasting image.[97]

By placing a greater emphasis on the character of Cate, Wilson made her mental pathology a central thematic concern of the play and connected it explicitly to her history of abuse. In doing so Wilson risked the trap of 'considering mental illness an intellectual conceit' which Kane was so keen to avoid.[98] Jessica Bardem's performance as Cate in the 2015 production clearly characterized her as an abuse victim. Bardem was slow-speaking, fragile and highly dissociated – seeming numb and detached from the world around her, withdrawn from her own narrative. She spoke in a flat tone, slightly too loud, and stared out of the hotel room window with a disturbingly blank expression. This blankness was contrasted with moments of child-like excitement in which she bounced on the bed, and of child-like vulnerability, at one point curling her entire body into a small armchair and sucking her thumb.

Previous performances of Cate in the 1995 and 2010 London productions performed Cate with various pathologies. Lydia Wilson's performance in the Lyric Hammersmith's 2010 production was noted for its range of emotion. Critics noted, for example, that 'Lynda Wilson's enigmatic, epileptic Cate switches between helplessness, affection, furious disgust and disinterest',[99] and praised her ability to 'change from sweet pathos to shrieking anger'.[100] Reviewers of the 2010 production understood Cate's fits as epileptic rather than psychosomatic.[101]

According to *Financial Times* critic Ian Shuttleworth, Lydia Wilson's Cate was 'less obviously "damaged"' than previous characterizations, and had the agency and strength to resist Ian's abuses.[102] Interestingly, Shuttleworth notes that such an interpretation of Cate served to emphasize the dominance of Ian's character in the production's reception: 'Conversely this interpretation scores in that it thereby emphasises Ian's utter inability to even conceive of being anything other than the bastard he is, as his sexual and linguistic violence continue regardless.'[103] In the Lyric Hammersmith production therefore, Cate was portrayed as an independent woman with a health problem who reacted emotionally to her abuses but ultimately took a backseat compared to Ian's downfall. The portrayal of Cate in the original 1995 production was at the other extreme, as actress Kate Ashfield played Cate as extremely vulnerable and developmentally disabled, 'with a mental age of about 12'.[104]

Whilst they are contrasting, both of these performances of Cate defined her pathology outside of her personal history, and therefore provided no clear connection for the audience between the breakdown of Cate's mind and that of the dramatic universe – a connection which Kane emphasized in her claim that 'the play collapses into one of Cate's fits'.[105] Bardem's performance in 2015, on the other hand, did just that. Her laughter during Cate's fits was loud and hollow, and the fits themselves were most disturbing for their similarity with the waking Cate. Bardem portrayed a woman who was already-vacant, who had already retreated from a violent world into 'another place', which '(b)locks out everything else'.[106] As such Bardem's performance thematized the kind of affective withdrawal which is found in classic trauma theory and the PTSD diagnosis. Through this powerful characterization of Cate, the production obviously thematized sexual trauma and the 'blind spot' of the play was brought into the audience's field of vision.

The continuity between the waking Cate and her fit behaviour was reflected in the Crucible Theatre's production in the continuity between the two halves of the play. Whilst the onstage violence was shocking, and the blasting of the hotel room effectively achieved, both were staged in the same slow, drawn-out rhythm of the first half, so that there was more a sense of seeping violence than sudden escalation. When the soldier laboriously chewed Ian's eyeball in scene three, the sound and pace of the act recalled each previous incident of eating in the play and reminded the audience of the physicality and time-consuming nature of bodily processes. Ian's rape took place on the same spot on the bed as Cate's simulated rape. And Cate took up the same position looking out onto the war-torn city whilst cradling the baby in scene four as she had when she commented that it 'look[ed] like there's a war on' in scene two. As Velda Harris noted, 'Wilson's slow-paced direction allow[ed] plenty of time to consider the implications of verbal exchanges, and to adjust to the metaphorical significance of the later action.'[107] James Cotterill's set was key in achieving this connection. The raised box set was surrounded at the top and bottom by windows. As the explosion took place, underfloor lighting flashed, and the audience were able to see themselves through these windows. By introducing the opportunity for the audience to see themselves fairly late in the production, Wilson provoked a moment of dissociation for the audience drawing a parallel with the interpretation of Cate's character as seemingly already outside of herself. The dramaturgy of psychic life which the play shared with the audience was less an encounter with breakdown and ricocheting images of violence, and more a sense of being held in a painfully slow, dissociated present in which the onstage violence was both nauseating and strangely without emotional affect.

The decision to place such a focus on Cate in this production can be seen as a reflection of specifically twenty-first-century concerns with child abuse, trauma and victimhood. Coming at a time when the UK newspapers are rife with stories about aging male celebrities being taken to court on historical abuse and rape charges, it may be that 2015 audiences and theatre-makers were hypersensitive to narratives of child abuse and that the production was part of a larger national process of re-focusing the gaze onto historical victims, attempting to give them a voice they were unable to find in the 1970s and 1980s. As one reviewer put it: '(Set i)n Leeds too: impossible not to think of Jimmy Saville.'[108] Wilson felt that 'one of the most fascinating aspects of the play is the relationship between Ian and Cate, and exactly what is happening there'.[109] Highlighting a traumatized pathology in Cate's character, and downplaying the subsequent stage violence, the play's child-like first victim haunted the remainder of the play, perhaps rehearsing a vision of voiceless victimhood that is so prevalent in public consciousness and tabloid newspapers today. The production reflected a shift in public perceptions of the consequences of sexual abuse, especially the sexual abuse of children, that has taken place since the play's writing.

Looking back at this production today, it also serves as a chilling reminder of the recent historical allegations regarding the conduct of Max Stafford Clark at the Royal Court, whose artistic directorship ended the year before Kane's debut. Such circumstances suggest that *Blasted* was first directed and produced at a moment in which the Royal Court had itself only just been a site of silencing culture around sexual abuse. The invisibility of Ian's rape of Cate, from this perspective, also reflects the obscuring and making-invisible of sexual misconduct and violence by theatres themselves. By foregrounding this aspect of the play's narrative, Wilson created a framework for the interpretation of *Blasted* by his audience and reviewers that resonated strongly with the public concerns of 2015.

At the same time, Wilson's decision to turn Cate's invisible rape into a central thematic concern of the production in some sense simplifies and resolves some of the serious tensions to be found in the playtext. It has been my argument in this chapter that *Blasted* carries an inherent critique of the effects of rape on mental life in its form; and that this critique had to be held *only* in the play's form in order for Kane to simulate the decimating effects of this violation of personhood for the audience. That Wilson's production articulated this critique so strongly may be an indication that the challenge the *Blasted* issues, that we see into its 'blind spot', cannot be achieved onstage without some adaptation. Personally, I found Wilson's production to be a compelling work, and successful in achieving the 'experiential' aims of Kane's theatre: for me the production simulated the experience of being simultaneously held at a distance from a violent event and yet viscerally affected by it, and I left the theatre feeling both numb and nauseous.

## Shifting mimesis

Reading *Blasted* through the lens of the psychic life of its female protagonist, therefore, leads us to reconsider the nature of Kane's dramaturgy itself. This is a dramaturgy which actively *plays* with its potential spectators, inviting them to repeat aspects of traumatic psychic life. In so doing Kane creates a work which performs a kind of psychic mimesis, placing the experience of a subjectivity, rather than action, at its centre. As I suggest earlier, this experience is historically situated in a period in which trauma and, especially, PTSD were central to popular and feminist understandings of the consequences of sexual violence. As such, the mimesis of psychic life which *Blasted* performs also reflects the time in which it was written, and constitutes an attempt to find new ways of focusing on the consequences of sexual violence beyond the traditions of second-wave feminist theatre.

*Blasted* differs from Kane's following plays insofar as the psychic life that the dramaturgy enacts is linked back to the interior life of a single character. *Blasted* thinks Cate's trauma, and both the literary shape of the play and its spatio-temporal existence, are constituted in relation to her invisible traumatic moment. The play *makes itself* out of its inability to recover from Ian's rape of Cate.

In the next chapter, I suggest that Kane abandons this link from *Cleansed* onwards. The dramaturgy of *Cleansed* prevents any sustained identification or immersion into a distinct dramatic universe. This aesthetic development takes place in conjunction with a move from concerns in *Blasted* and *Sick* with the traumatic, to a sustained concern from *Cleansed* to *4.48 Psychosis* with the psychotic. These later works mark a progression from considering the way in which an external, empirically experienced event might mould and destroy interior life, to a radical questioning of the boundaries between interior and exterior life altogether. Whereas *Blasted* thinks through the trauma of an individual which overspills and shapes the dramatic universe, *Cleansed* attempts to put the potential audience through the experience in which the signposts distinguishing reality, imagination and hallucination are fully removed.

The traumatic dramaturgy examined in this chapter and the psychotic dramaturgy in the next come together to make one crucial claim: for the validity of the experiences which they embody. Dramaturgy exceeds narration. It creates the potential for affirming the epistemological validity of experiences which are repressed, unrepresentable or unreal.

## Notes

1. Stephenson and Langridge, *Rage and Reason*.
2. Kane-directed plays by Rame, McIntyre and Churchill, as well as Shakespeare, Barker and Bond whilst an undergraduate. The influence of Rame's *The Rape* on her *Sick* monologues in unmistakeable.
3. Charles Spenser, *Daily Telegraph*, 20 January 1995, in *Theatre Record* 15, no. 1–2 (1995): 39–40.
4. Amia Srinivasan, *The Right to Sex* (London: Bloomsbury, 2021), xi.
5. Ibid., xii.
6. Ibid., 8.
7. Dominic Cavendish, 'Debut: Interview with Kate Ashfield', *Independent*, 9 September 1998.
8. Sarah Kane, 'Blasted', in *Sarah Kane: Complete Plays* (London: Methuen Drama, 2001), 23.
9. Ibid., 15.
10. Sidi, 'After the Madhouses', 6, Special Issue on Health Policy and Emotion.
11. Kane, 'Blasted', 12–13.
12. Ibid., 13.
13. Edward Said, *The World, the Text, the Critic* (Cambridge, MA: Harvard University Press, 1983), 15.
14. Ibid.
15. Jack Tinker, *Daily Mail*, 19 January 1995, in *Theatre Record* 15, no. 1–2 (1995): 42; Roger Foss, *What's On*, 25 January 1995, in *Theatre Record* no. 1–2 (1995): 38; Kate Kellaway, *Observer*, 22 January 1995, in *Theatre Record* no. 1–2 (1995): 40–1. Such characterizations continue in later productions, with Charles Spencer's review of *Phaedra's Love* for example ending 'It's not a theatre critic that's required here, it's a psychiatrist.' Charles Spenser, *Daily Telegraph*, 21 May 1996, *Theatre Record* 16, no. 11 (1996): 652.

16 Charles Spenser, *Daily Telegraph*, 20 January 1995, in *Theatre Record* no. 1–2 (1995): 39–40.
17 Sarah Daniels, 'Headrot Holiday', in *Plays 2* (London: Bloomsbury Methuen Drama, 1994), 233.
18 Ibid., 238.
19 Stephenson and Langridge, *Rage and Reason*, 7.
20 *Masterpieces* did not have a second professional staging until it opened to mixed reviews at the Finborough Theatre in April 2018, where it was lauded as 'relevant' to the sexual harassment scandals in the theatre industry revealed by the #MeToo movement. However, its return might also be put into a wider context of the increased attention paid to victims of sexual assault in the public sphere and the growth of popularity of third-wave feminism.
21 Elaine Aston, 'Reviewing the Fabric of Blasted', in *Sarah Kane in Context*, ed. Graham Saunders and Laurens De Vos (Manchester: Manchester University Press, 2010), 23.
22 Sarah Daniels, 'Masterpieces', in *Sarah Daniels: Plays 1* (London: Methuen Drama 1991), 203.
23 Thank you to Rachel Clements for this observation.
24 Kane, 'Blasted', 22.
25 Ibid., 10, 13.
26 Kim Solga, '*Blasted's* Hysteria: Rape, Realism, and the Thresholds of the Visible', *Modern Drama* 50, no. 3 (2007): 361.
27 The unrepresentable nature of trauma is the focus of: Shoshanna Felman and Dori Laub, *Testimony: Crises of Witnessing in Literature, Psychoanalysis and History* (London: Routledge, 1992), and Cathy Caruth, *Unclaimed Experience: Trauma, Narrative and History* (Baltimore, MD: John Hopkins University Press, 1996).
28 Sigmund Freud, 'Beyond the Pleasure Principle', trans. James Strachey in *The Standard Edition of the Complete Psychological Works of Sigmund Freud, Volume XVIII (1920–1922): Beyond the Pleasure Principle, Group Psychology and Other Works*, ed. James Strachey (London: The Hogarth Press and the Institute of Psycho-Analysis, 1955), 18.
29 Ibid.
30 See Freud's *Studies in Hysteria* for an account of seduction theory. The move away from seduction theory has been subject to extensive debate. Some commentators, most notably Jeffrey Moussaieff Masson, have argued that Freud abandoned seduction theory out of a desire not to address the reality of child abuse – either unconsciously or in order not to offend the psychiatric establishment (see *Assault on Truth: Freud's Suppression of Seduction Theory* (New York: Farrar, Straus and Giroux, 1984)). On the other hand, commentators as varied as Juliet Mitchell and Roger Luckhurst argue that seduction theory was ever really abandoned, just reintegrated into a version of the psyche in which memory and fantasy are inextricably

intertwined. Juliet Mitchell, *Psychoanalysis and Feminism: A Radical Reassessment of Freudian Psychoanalysis* (New York: Basic, 2000, first published 1974) and Roger Luckhurst, *The Trauma Question* (Abingdon, VA: Routledge, 2008).
31 Cathy Caruth, 'Introduction', in *Trauma: Explorations in Memory*, ed. Cathy Caruth (Baltimore, MD: John Hopkins University Press, 1995), 4.
32 Caruth, *Unclaimed Experience*, 91.
33 Allan Young, *The Harmony of Illusions: Inventing Post-Traumatic Stress Disorder* (Princeton, NJ: Princeton University Press, 1997), and Allan Young, 'Trauma and Harm', podcast recording, The Birkbeck Trauma Project, 14 April 2016. Available online: www.bbk.ac.uk/trauma/events/trauma-and-harm (accessed 2 February 2017).
34 Didier Fassin and Richard Rechtman, *The Empire of Trauma* (Princeton, NJ: Princeton University Press, 2009), 73. Luckhurst makes a similar argument, suggesting that the widening of the category of trauma leads to a loss of political and historical specificity in discussions on violence.
35 Jay Frankel, 'Exploring Ferenczi's Concept of Identification with the Aggressor: Its Role in Trauma, Everyday Life and the Therapeutic Relationship', *Psychoanalytic Dialogues* 12, no. 1 (2002): 101–39, 102.
36 Ruth Leys, *Trauma: A Genealogy* (Chicago, IL: University of Chicago Press, 2000), 173.
37 Ibid., 175.
38 Judith Lewis Herman, *Trauma and Recovery: The Aftermath of Violence – from Domestic Abuse to Political Terror* (New York: Basic Books, 1997), 127.
39 *Diagnostic and Statistical Manual of Mental Disorders*, 3rd edn. (Washington, DC: American Psychiatric Association, 1980), 236.
40 Ibid., 24.
41 Caruth, 'Introduction', 4.
42 Michael Billington, *Guardian*, 20 January 1995, in *Theatre Record* 15, no. 1–2 (1995): 39.
43 As Graham Saunders implies in his influential reading of Kane's woks in *Love Me or Kill Me: Sarah Kane and the Theatre of Extremes* (Manchester: Manchester University Press, 2002), 40–1.
44 Leys, *Trauma*, 3, my emphasis.
45 Sarah Kane, 'Crave', in *Sarah Kane: Complete Plays* (London: Methuen Drama, 2001), 158.
46 Kane, 'Blasted', 27.
47 Ibid, 39.
48 Saunders, *Love Me*, 46.
49 Patrick Duggan, *Trauma-Tragedy: Symptoms of Contemporary Performance* (Manchester: Manchester University Press, 2012), 120.
50 Ibid., 123.
51 Solga, '*Blasted's* Hysteria', 346.

52 Duggan, *Trauma-Tragedy*, 126.
53 Saunders, *Love Me*, 45–6, my emphasis.
54 Lisa Appignanesi, *Mad, Bad and Sad: A History of Women and the Mind Doctors from 1800 to the Present* (London: Hachette UK, 2008), 469.
55 Ibid.
56 Dee Heddon, 'The Politics of the Personal: Autobiography in Performance', in *Feminist Futures? Theatre, Performance, Theory*, ed. Elaine Aston and Geraldine Harris (Basingstoke: Palgrave Macmillan, 2006), 130.
57 For Kane's directing of Franca Rame's monologue, see Nina Kane, 'Breath and Light: Blasted, Sheffield Theatres and New Directions in the Staging of Sarah Kane', *Litro*, 19 April 2015. Available online: http://www.litro.co.uk/2015/04/breath-and-light-blasted-sheffield-theatres-and-new-directions-in-the-staging-of-sarah-kane (accessed 31 January 2017).
58 Appignanesi, *Mad, Bad and Sad*, 482.
59 See for example Duška Radosavljević, 'Sarah Kane's Illyria as the Land of Violent Love: A Balkan Reading of Blasted', *Contemporary Theatre Review* 22, no. 4 (2012): 499–511.
60 Joanna Bourke, *Rape: A History from 1860 to the Present* (London: Virago, 2007).
61 Whilst Kane's staging of violence in *Blasted*, *Phaedra's Love* and *Cleansed* would seem to represent a certain universalism, in interviews Kane moves from making sweeping connections with different forms of violence to discussing the cultural specificity of rape in certain fields of war. See Saunders *Love Me*, 48.
62 Christopher Wixson has drawn parallels between the set of *Blasted* and Cate, seeing the room itself as an extension of Cate's body. The allying of bodily and spatial violence opens up the potential for greater political critique in the play for Wixson, linking Kane with Churchill and Wertenbaker as playwrights concerned with responsibility and the global community. For both Churchill and Wertenbaker (according to Wixson), spatial boundaries and privacy (space-as-property) are to be destroyed in the aim of communality. Christopher Wixson, '"In Better Places": Space, Identity, and Alienation in Sarah Kane's Blasted', *Comparative Drama* 39, no. 1 (2005): 75–91.
63 Sierz, *In-Yer-Face Theatre*, 92.
64 Kane, 'Blasted', 3.
65 Ibid., 4 and 5.
66 Ibid., 19.
67 Ibid., 33.
68 Ibid., 34.
69 Rebellato, 'Sarah Kane before *Blasted*, the Monologues', 44.
70 Kane, 'Breath and Light'.
71 Aston, *Feminist Views*, 85.
72 Kane, 'Blasted', 61.

73 Herman, *Trauma and Recovery*, 83.
74 Rebellato, 'Sarah Kane before *Blasted*, the Monologues', 41.
75 Sándor Ferenczi, *The Clinical Diary of Sándor Ferenczi*, ed. Judith Dupont, trans. Michael Balint and Nicola Zarday Jackson (Harvard, MA: Harvard University Press, 1988), 178.
76 Ibid., 104.
77 Frankel, 'Exploring', 104. See also the argument of chapter 5 of Herman, *Trauma and Recovery*.
78 Ibid.
79 Saunders, *Love Me*, 46.
80 Shoshanna Felman's ferocious extended footnote in *The Juridical Unconscious: Trials and Traumas in the Twentieth Century* (Cambridge, MA: Harvard University Press, 2002) is evidence of the heatedness of this debate, 175.
81 See Allan Young on 'Prolonged Exposure Therapy', in *The Harmony of Illusions*.
82 Leys, *Trauma*, 32.
83 Winnicott, *Playing and Reality*, 129.
84 Elaine Aston argues that the original reviews of *Blasted* 'affect stripped' the play, by focusing only on the body of Ian, in 'Reviewing the Fabric of Blasted'.
85 Nicholas De Jongh, *Evening Standard*, 4 April 2001, in *Theatre Record* 21, no. 7 (2001): 418.
86 Kate Bassett, *Independent on Sunday*, 8 April 2001, in *Theatre Record* 21, no. 7 (2001): 420; Benedict Nightingale, *The Times*, 5 April 2001, in *Theatre Record* 21, no. 7 (2001): 421; Brian Logan, *Time Out*, 11 April 2001, in *Theatre Record* 21, no. 7 (2001): 422; Charles Spencer, *Daily Telegraph*, 5 April 2001, in *Theatre Record* 21, no. 7 (2001): 419.
87 Michael Billington, *Guardian*, 4 April 2001, in *Theatre Record* 21, no. 7 (2001): 421; Nightingale, 2001; Georgina Brown, *Mail on Sunday*, 8 April 2001, in *Theatre Record* 21, no. 7 (2001): 422; Spencer, *Daily Telegraph*, 2001; De Jongh, *Evening Standard*, 2001.
88 John Gross, *Sunday Telegraph*, 8 April 2001, in *Theatre Record* 21, no. 7 (2001): 420; Andrew Smith, *Observer*, 8 April 2001, in *Theatre Record* 21, no. 7 (2001): 421; Billington, *Guardian*, 2001; Brian Logan, *Time Out*, 2001.
89 Susanna Clapp, *Observer*, 31 October 2010, in *Theatre Record* 30, no. 22 (2010): 1240; Charles Spenser, *Daily Telegraph*, 1 November 2010, in *Theatre Record* 30, no. 22 (2010): 1240; Siobhan Murphy, *Metro (London)*, 3 November 2010, in *Theatre Record* 30, no. 22 (2010): 1241.
90 Murphy, *Metro (London)*, 2010, 1241; Paul Taylor, *Independent*, 2 November 2010, in *Theatre Record*, 30, no. 22 (2010): 1241; Henry Hitchins, *Evening Standard*, 29 October 2010, in *Theatre Record* 30, no. 22 (2010): 1240; Michael Billington, *Guardian*, 29 October 2010, in *Theatre Record* 30, no. 22 (2010): 1240.

91 Paul Taylor, *Independent*, 2010, 1241.
92 Solga, 'Blasted's Hysteria', 346.
93 Saunders, *Love Me*, 46, and Duggan, *Trauma-Tragedy*, 123.
94 Sean Carney, 'The Tragedy of History in Sarah Kane's Blasted', *Theatre Survey* 46 (2005): 275–96.
95 Roger Foss, 'Blasted Review', *The Stage*, 10 February 2015. Available online: https://www.thestage.co.uk/reviews/2015/blasted-2/ (accessed 15 September 2016).
96 Ruth Deller, *Broadway World Reviews*, 14 February 2015. Available online: www.broadwayworld.com/uk-regional/article/BWW-Reviews-BLASTED-Crucible-Studio-Sheffield-February-10-2015-20150214 (accessed 15 August 2016).
97 Murphy, *Metro (London)*, 2010, 1241; Lyn Gardner, 'Blasted Review – Unflinching Revival of Sarah Kane's Prescient Horror Show', *Guardian*, 11 February 2015. Available online: https://www.theguardian.com/stage/2015/feb/11/blasted-sheffield-crucible-sarah-kane-richard-wilson-review (accessed 15 February 2019).
   The following reviews of the 2015 production also emphasize the impact of Bardem's physical performance and her portrayal of an already-traumatized Cate: Velda Harris, 'Blasted Review', *British Theatre Guide*, 3 February 2015. Available online: http://www.britishtheatreguide.info/reviews/blasted-crucible-studio-11191 (accessed 15 February 2019); Foss, 2015; Verity Healy, 'Blasted - Crucible Theatre Sheffield', *Theatre Bubble*, 16 February 2015. Available online: http://www.theatrebubble.com/2015/02/blasted-crucible-theatre-sheffield/ (accessed 15 February 2019); Matt Trueman, 'Blasted (Sheffield Crucible) - Anniversary Revival Does Sarah Kane's Play Full Justice', *What's On Stage*, 11 February 2015. Available online: http://www.whatsonstage.com/sheffield-theatre/reviews/blasted-sheffield-crucible-sarah-kane_37128.html (accessed 15 February 2019).
98 Sierz, *In-Yer-Face Theatre*, 92.
99 Murphy, *Metro (London)*, 2010.
100 Paul Callan, *Daily Express*, 5 November 2010, in *Theatre Record* 30, no. 22 (2010): 1242.
101 The following reviews describe Cate as 'epileptic': Murphy, *Metro (London)*, 2010; Hitchins, *Evening Standard*, 2010; Billington, *Guardian*, 2010; Ian Shuttleworth, *Financial Times*, 1 November 2010, in *Theatre Record* 30, no. 22 (2010): 1240; Spenser, *Daily Telegraph*, 2010; Paul Taylor, *Independent*, 2010; Maxie Szalwinska, *Sunday Times*, 7 November 2010, in *Theatre Record*, 30, no. 22 (2010): 1242.
102 Shuttleworth, *Financial Times*, 2010, 1240.
103 Ibid.
104 Cavendish, 'Debut'.
105 Stephenson and Langridge, *Rage and Reason*, 130.
106 Kane, 'Blasted', 22.

107 Harris, 'Blasted Review'.
108 Trueman, 'Blasted (Sheffield Crucible)'.
109 In Nick Ahad, 'The Lasting Legacy of Sarah Kane's Genius', *Yorkshire Post*, 13 February 2015. Available online: http://www.yorkshirepost.co.uk/what-s-on/theatre/the-lasting-legacy-of-sarah-kane-s-genius-1-7105126 (accessed 15 February 2019).

# 3

# Rhythm, interruption, psychosis

## A dramaturgical turning point

In Kane's quest to create a dramaturgy that experientially shared 'real' psychic pain, she constructed an original and insightful vision of the psychic phenomena of trauma and psychosis. Clearly eschewing diagnostic labels, Kane's dramatic works represent a constant entanglement between psychotic, depressive and traumatic phenomena which diverges from the containment with which they were treated in her student monologues: *Starved* confines itself to an account of bulimia, and *Comic Monologue* to trauma following sexual assault. As I demonstrated in the previous chapter, the representations of trauma (especially of sexual trauma) in Kane's dramatic works build on and are in dialogue with discourses on trauma and PTSD which were popular in the 1990s in clinical settings, as well as in feminist theory and theatre. Unlike this largely historically situated engagement with trauma, Kane's representations of psychosis diverge significantly from those to be found in either popular discourses or contemporary theatre concerned with mental health. With regard to her portrayal of psychosis, Kane strikes out on her own to create a theatre of psychotic psychic life which posits psychosis as a radically open experience of subjectivity, one that is both deeply painful and disorienting and at the same time constantly attempts to reach out of itself and into social life.

Kane's third play *Cleansed* (1998) represents a turning point in her dramatic project. Whilst the dramaturgies of *Blasted* (1995) and *Phaedra's Love* (1996) played on the expected tragic arcs of their male protagonists, in *Cleansed* Kane moves her theatrical apparatus further from narrative forms of theatre. Here and in *Crave* and *4.48 Psychosis* Kane draws on the techniques of expressionist theatre and the historical avant-garde, particularly the works of Georg Büchner, Antonin Artaud and August Strindberg in order to create a dramaturgy which interacts with, but is nonetheless separate from, the plot-like goings on of the figures on stage.[1] This development in her dramaturgy coincides with a closer engagement with mental illness in her works, in particular an engagement with her own biography. As Kane put it in an interview with Nils Talbert, *Cleansed* holds a complex, indirect relationship with Kane's own mental distress. *Cleansed*, Kane reflects, had 'certainly been written as a reflection of my life. Without being autobiographical'.[2] In this interview Kane describes the 'extreme state' which she experienced writing *Cleansed*, which enters in some way into her dramatic universe.[3]

In her final three works, Kane also signposts a relationship to her own psychic life and experience of the mental health system. *Cleansed* is dedicated to ES3, the psychiatric ward at the Maudsley Hospital in which Kane was hospitalized in between her writing of *Phaedra's Love* and *Cleansed*, and to which she arranged research trips during the rehearsal for the first production. The relationship between the authoritarian institution in the play and the hospital is itself ambivalent. The dedication expresses gratitude towards the 'patients and staff of ES3' on the one hand, whilst on the other, there is a suggested connection between psychiatric hospitalization and the torturous environment of the play. In *Crave* ES3 finds its way into the playtext itself, as the speakers end up in the ward at the end of the play. As Ingrid Craigie notes, this is just one of numerous personal references that Kane included in the work, in order to transform them into 'something different' in the context of the dramaturgy.[4] (Craigie notes, for example, that A's love monologue in *Crave* was lifted from an actual love letter written by Kane, which is 'utterly transformed' when put into the mouth of an abuser.[5]) These inclusions and transformations of biographical material, as well as the much speculated-upon relationship between *4.48 Psychosis* and Kane's experience of suicidal depression, point to a development in Kane's theatre both in terms of the extent of her engagement with pathologized mental pain and the methods through which it is addressed.

This development in approaches to mental pain coincides with a period of experimentation with directing and with film in Kane's career. Between *Blasted* and *Cleansed*, Kane created three works which widened her perspectives on what it is possible to achieve through theatre: writing and directing *Phaedra's Love* (1996), directing Büchner's *Woyzeck* (in 1997) and writing a short television film *Skin* (1997). Kane's shift from the anti-heroic arcs of Ian and Hippolytus to the accumulative dramaturgy of *Cleansed* is partly drawn from *Woyzeck*. *Woyzeck* is a play by Georg Büchner, which was left uncompleted when he died in 1837. An important text for both Naturalist and Expressionist theatre of the late nineteenth century, *Woyzeck* staged the ill-fated experiences of a lowly soldier, who is betrayed by his friend and the woman he loves, persecuted by his superiors, experiences hallucinations and paranoia, and murders his fiancée. The manuscript is made up of twenty-four scenes which have no definitive order and have been staged in a variety of sequences. For Kane, the eponymous hero is not attempting to master his own fate but is 'batted around by everyone'. In Kane's estimation Woyzeck 'is the first hero who has absolutely nothing going for him [. . .] Woyzeck's only way of expressing himself is through violence'.[6] In directing *Woyzeck*, Kane experienced creating a theatrical work which was not structured by the journey of a single character but by the relentless persecution of the dramatic universe in which he resides. Kane identified a split between form and narrative in the dramaturgy of the work which was important for her own production: 'The thing I found really extraordinary about this piece, that I wanted to capture myself, was that for me the scenes were like balloons that in a way float above ground but at the same time are tied to the earth, rooted but floating'.[7] Whilst Kane found these scenes to contain a 'clear meaning', they were not structured around the story of the play. As we shall see, this formal split became an important structuring principle for *Cleansed*.

In writing her short film *Skin*, Kane continued to experiment with form, but was frustrated with the limits of working with film as a media. *Skin* is a ten-minute film which portrays the obsessive love of a skin head Billy for a Black woman, Marcia, against the background of the racist violence of the National Front. Borowski argues that *Skin* is the 'missing link' that is often ignored by critics in tracking the development of Kane's form, because it is Kane's first clear engagement with the Expressionism.[8] Thematically, *Skin* shares a lot with *Cleansed* – androgyny, unfulfilled obsessive love, political violence and cruelty at the hands of the love-object. It draws directly from Expressionist cinema through techniques such as doubling, the unfocused gaze and blurred boundaries between awake and dream states. As its name suggests, *Skin* is highly preoccupied with surface identity. Borowski suggests that the film seems to 'demonstrat[e] that a sense of integrity [of identity . . . is built] merely on a set of external traces, bodily features and behaviours'.[9] In this sense, the film is quite separate from the intense focus on interiority that characterizes Kane's theatrical work, as well as through its focus on a specific political problem. Frustrated with the limits of writing for film, Kane set out in her following works to make theatre that 'could never be shot for television [. . .] that could only be staged'.[10] What Kane clearly does take from the experience of creating a short Expressionist film, at the same time as directing *Woyzeck*, is an understanding of the potential of interruption as a dramatic tool. In both Büchner's play and in Expressionist film, the audience is never allowed to settle into a scene and have their perspectives constantly disturbed. As we shall see, *Cleansed* takes this interruption further, using it to simulate the possibility of a predictive crisis.

A final observation on this period of directing and film in Kane's oeuvre can be made on the subject of site-lines. In *Cleansed*, *Crave* and especially *4.48 Psychosis* Kane's dramaturgy becomes more focused directing and troubling the audiences' gaze. Reflecting on her experiences directing, Kane emphasized that her understanding of the director's role was the creation of 'exactly the images I had written' on stage.[11] In directing *Phaedra's Love* at the Bush Theatre in 1996, Kane experimented with surrounding the playing space with the audience, and having actors appear from within the audience in the final scene. Here, the movement and redirection of the audiences' gaze becomes key: 'it meant that for any given audience member the play could be at one moment intimate and personal, at the next epic and public. They may see one scene from one end of the theatre and then find themselves in the middle of a conversation the next.'[12] This emphatic direction of the gaze of the audience is, of course, much more controlled in film-making, in which the camera confines and directs the gaze of the viewer. As I will outline herein, compared with *Blasted* and *Phaedra's Love* the playtext of *Cleansed* contains a much greater attention to the direction of the gaze of the audience and thinks through how a theatrical space might solicit or refuse the gaze of a spectator.

*Cleansed* thus represents a turning point in both the formal tools Kane uses to create her theatrical work and the vision of psychic life which she represents on stage, as she moves towards creating a dramaturgy which approximates psychotic experience. This chapter argues that Kane's use of dramaturgical irresolution and unpredictability invites the audience to participate in the creation and thwarting of theatrical expectations. This process evokes the temporalities and disorientations of psychotic breakdown. In doing so it suggests that aspects of psychotic experience are sharable when they are understood as spatially enacted. This shareable, 'open' understanding of psychotic experience finds its resonances in a thread of psychoanalytic thinking leading from Melanie Klein to Christopher Bollas. These thinkers can be brought into productive dialogue with Kane's work as they understand psychosis as routed in relatable, *social* experience. They therefore help us to read both what is being shared in Kane's representations of psychotic psychic life, and what Kane's mode of sharing might reflect back to contemporary understandings of psychic life in psychosis.

Such ideas about the shareability of psychosis are not unique to psychoanalysis, but find their correlates in new research by both experience-led researchers and in cognitive neuroscience. This chapter goes on to draw a parallel between narrative disruptions in Kane's play and a cognitive neuroscience understanding of psychosis as caused by prediction error. I suggest that this parallel might help us to understand what is 'done to' the audience via Kane's dramaturgy, and to approach the openness of Kane's final works within the logic of experimentation upon the audience itself. This experimental attitude is highlighted in contrast to the way psychosis is staged by Kane's contemporaries, which follow a more conservative 'closing off' of psychotic phenomena.

In the final section of this chapter, I consider the durability of Kane's open dramaturgy in relation to Katie Mitchell's 2017 production of *Cleansed* at the National Theatre in London. Staged in a new mental health landscape, Mitchell's production produced a play which ran counter to the interpretation of Kane's works which I present here. Such a production highlights the difficulty of maintaining openness on stage, as well as perhaps revealing anxieties about the staging of fragmented works in a historical moment that is so preoccupied with aetiology. This preoccupation ultimately 'closes off' the play's sharing of psychosis in favour of a simpler vision.

To understand Kane's unique intervention into the representation of psychotic experience, it is necessary first to lay out a brief outline of some perspectives on psychosis. The purpose of the following section is not to be comprehensive, but to situate Kane's works in ongoing psychoanalytic debates as to the nature of psychosis. I suggest in this and the following chapter that Kane uses the theatrical site to create a radically 'open' interpretation of psychotic experience, which is shareable via its spatial enactment. As I shall demonstrate in the following section, this version of psychosis finds a resonance in a particular strand of psychoanalytic thinking, which can in turn be used to better articulate Kane's intervention into this field.

## Closing off or opening up psychosis

It is out of scope of this work to provide a comprehensive account of writing on psychosis in psychiatry, psychoanalysis or wider cultural work. Instead, I propose to examine briefly how psychoanalytic and biomedical accounts have imagined the relationship between persons experiencing psychotic symptoms and those who are observing or accompanying them, be this as clinicians, carers or friends. This will allow us to situate Kane's work in relation to some of the overriding assumptions about psychosis prevalent in our society, and to see how her theatre refocuses our gaze onto the encounter between the subject who experiences psychosis, and those they interact with. With this focus in mind, I consider understandings of psychosis as either 'closed' or 'open'.

Psychosis, especially in the context of a diagnosis of schizophrenia, has overwhelmingly been understood as a 'closed', inaccessible experience. In her study of clinical and cultural representations of schizophrenia, Angela Woods identifies the extent to which schizophrenia remains an enigmatic, seemingly inaccessible experience in modern psychiatry. Tracing clinical discourses on schizophrenia from Emil Kraepelin's 'discovery' of the disorder in the early twentieth century to twenty-first-century medical journals, Woods suggests that schizophrenia continues to be constructed as psychiatry's 'sublime object': at once an exciting puzzle to be solved and a fundamentally '*un*understandable' phenomenon. The *DSM*'s description of schizophrenic delusions as 'bizarre', for example, introduces a decidedly non-scientific vocabulary into the diagnostic criteria.[13] It locates schizophrenic phenomena as firmly outside the realm of the rational and suggests an even greater distance between clinician and patient than is usually described. Woods observes two fundamental constants in clinical writing on schizophrenia in the last century. First, an insistence on a clear collection of symptoms that identify schizophrenia as a verifiable diagnostic entity, and second, the unsolved question of its cause or aetiology. By bringing these features together, psychiatry has 'ensured that schizophrenia is perceived as a definite disease entity but one that attracts ongoing analysis in order to prove this is so'.[14]

The inherently enigmatic nature of schizophrenia as it is described in psychiatric discourse, Woods argues, has had a profound effect on the discipline of psychiatry itself. Explaining the aetiology (the clinical cause) of schizophrenia and finding an effective cure are repeatedly framed in clinical literature as psychiatry's ultimate challenge. When medical texts present schizophrenia 'as an opaque and bizarre disorder of unknown or unknowable aetiology, it exceeds and thus marks disciplinary limits as a form of unreason which can be neither adequately represented nor analytically mastered'.[15] It is precisely this discourse of mastery which is most disturbing in Woods' overview of the clinical literature. Schizophrenia becomes a 'sublime object' in her analysis not simply because it is awe-inspiring and mysterious, but because it reshapes the relationship between the clinician/researcher and person experiencing psychosis.

Following Kant's definition of the sublime, Woods argues that the sublime 'affirm[s] the rational subject's ascendancy over nature and hence it actively re-centr[es] the subject'.[16] The sublime status which schizophrenia is afforded by psychiatry allows clinicians preserve their status as rational observers when faced with the distress of psychosis, precisely *because* it frames experience of psychosis as inherently unknowable and renders schizophrenia as an intellectual puzzle. What's more, the 'normal' clinician's inability to empathize actually becomes a diagnostic indicator, a measure of the bizarreness of the schizophrenic experience. As Woods notes in relation to the work of Karl Jaspers, 'the immediately perceptible collapse of the psychiatrist's empathetic structures of understanding is pathognomonic of a disorder unequivocally construed as sublime'.[17]

By understanding schizophrenia as inherently enigmatic, clinical psychiatry positions persons experiencing psychosis as fundamentally separate from those treating them. Departing from clinical language, I use the broader term 'psychosis' (rather than 'schizophrenia') in this chapter to emphasize Kane's own avoidance of diagnostic labels in her works. The psychotic experiences which are approximated and represented in her work could be situated in a range of diagnostic categories, including depression. Until recently, psychiatric texts broadly defined psychosis as 'gross impairment in reality testing' or 'loss of ego boundaries', and psychosis still carries these significations in psychoanalytic and therapeutic contexts. The current *DSM-5* limits the definition of psychosis to a list of the symptoms of schizophrenia – further closing the diagnostic loop that separates schizophrenia so definitively from other psychiatric experiences. Given that 'psychosis' is the term used by Kane herself, it is the term I will use from here on in, unless referring to a psychiatric text.

Like psychiatry, psychoanalysis initially understood psychosis as an inherently 'closed', inaccessible experience. Freud himself maintained that psychotic individuals were unreachable through the psychoanalytic method because they were unreachable through transference.[18] Freud initially distinguished between neurosis and psychosis on the basis that psychosis involves a complete rejection of reality and retreat into a created world. Freud suggested that psychotic experiences share an initial retreat from reality provoked by a traumatic scene with the first stage of neurosis.[19] However whilst in neurosis the psychic disturbance is caused by a repressed moment of trauma, in psychosis disturbance gives way to the complete replacement of one reality with another, more pleasurable one: 'the creation of a new reality which no longer raises the same objections as the old one that has been given up.'[20] The picture Freud paints of psychosis here has almost no relationship with reality. It involves an 'initial flight' from reality, which is succeeded by an 'active phase of remodelling' which builds reality anew.[21] As such, the psychotic patient appears unreachable, as they no longer occupy a similar or relatable psychic space to that of the analyst, or 'normal' (non-psychotic) subject.

However, the psychotic loss of reality presented here is also a dynamic one. The Freudian neurotic subject is frozen between a desire to flee a libidinal reaction to reality, and this reaction's manifestation or return through the symptom. The psychotic subject, on the other hand, by participating in an 'active phase of remodelling', continues to assert itself as an ego with some agency; only the agency is misdirected from the outside world to the inner. Freud thus suggests that the remodelling the psychotic subject engages in is analogous to that of a 'normal' subject changing his circumstances to better suit his needs or desires. As such, Freud's version of the psychotic ego is closed, but not disintegrated or split. It participates in a wholesale retreat from the world, after which it continues to try to pursue its aims in an alternative world of its own creating.

This picture of the psychotic ego as isolated but nonetheless 'whole' is linked to Freud's developmental theory. In *On Narcissism*, he suggests that the withdrawal or 'flight' of the ego in psychosis is a form of regression to a state before the development of object-cathexis (i.e. the ability to relate to objects outside of oneself, and distinguish between self and other).[22] This is a state of 'primary narcissism' in which the ego can only relate to itself, via a drive Freud calls the ego-libido. The psychotic ego regresses to a paranoid and megalomaniacal state in which it experiences only the ego-libido which gets 'dammed up' and is trapped, as it were, in a relationship with itself.[23] Freud suggests that the aspects of psychosis which are usually understood as symptoms (i.e. hallucination and delusion) are secondary to this regression and represent not psychosis itself but the ego's attempt to resolve the unpleasant tension caused by this damming-up of the ego-libido. Psychosis here is imagined as regression to a state of primary narcissism, which the ego attempts to escape by re-creating the object-world from which it has withdrawn.

Freud therefore frames psychosis as the experience of complete withdrawal, and regression to a stage of development in which the infant's ego is whole and relates only to itself. In this state, the ego is unreachable by anyone including the psychoanalyst. Woods suggests that for Freud and later Lacan psychosis remains an object of *interest*, even as the person experiencing it is understood as uncurable. In this sense Freud and Lacan follow the trend identified in Woods' critique of psychiatry of distancing the doctor from the schizophrenic *patient* in order to better focus on the schizophrenic *puzzle*:

> Lacan [. . .] follows Freud in distancing the psychotic patient from psychoanalytic technique (insisting that people diagnosed with schizophrenia are beyond cure or even therapy, Lacan transforms the patient into a purely interpretive problem) while simultaneously suggesting that psychoanalysis provides the master theory of schizophrenia's aetiology, structure, and symptomatology.[24]

Whilst it is tempting to say that Freud's theory of psychosis is premised on his developmental model, in fact the opposite is true: Freud arrives at the theory of primary narcissism through his limited observations of psychotic patients.[25] This relationship between ego-formation and psychosis points to the fact that a belief in a fully withdrawn psychotic subject rests on and contributes to a belief in a fully isolated primary subject. Such a narrative of subject-formation would be challenged in the late twentieth century by psychoanalytic thinkers who conceived as the subject as always already-social. As we shall see, this perspective makes room for a more 'open' view of psychotic experience.

This open view of psychosis is one that Kane's works reflect. In an interview about *4.48 Psychosis*, Kane emphasized the experience of disintegration as key to psychotic phenomena. She describes 'psychotic breakdown' as 'what happens in a person's mind when the barriers which distinguish between reality and different forms of imagination completely disappear [. . .] you no longer know where you stop and the world starts'.[26] This idea that the experience of psychosis involves not so much a withdrawal from the exterior world but a *disintegration into it* finds a particular resonance in psychoanalytic understandings of psychosis from the object-relations school, which depart strikingly from both Freud and Lacan.

Following the influence of Melanie Klein, object-relations psychoanalysts in Britain did develop psychoanalytic treatments for psychosis. These psychoanalysts understand subjectivity as social from its inception and constituted by relations to the outside world (as we have seen in the discussion of Winnicott in Chapter 1).[27] For Klein, psychosis is a not a regression to a form of narcissism, but to a moment of profound, painful sociality. In this model, psychosis involves being trapped within the experience of projective identification, in which the ego is painfully split and redistributed in the surrounding objects. Klein links the failure to 'work through' projective identification with schizophrenia, which she defines as a process of 'falling to pieces', 'under the pressure of this threat [the anxiety about being destroyed from within by the ego's own destructive impulse]'.[28] In its explicit focus on disintegration rather than retreat, and its implicit positioning of the subject as (in) a liminal space *between* objects, Klein's writings on schizophrenia therefore differ considerably from Freud's.

The understanding of psychosis as an experience of dangerous immersion into the world is echoed by Kane's vision of psychosis in her theatre. For example, Kleinian analyst Hebert Rosenfeld describes how his patients experienced psychosis as dissolving the boundary between themselves and the world. One patient describes his experience of being 'all broadened out' as he felt threateningly incorporated into the world:

> His behaviour, gestures and the few sentences and words he uttered showed that he felt he had destroyed the whole world outside, and he also felt he destroyed the world inside himself. [. . .] He felt he had taken the destroyed world into himself, and then felt he had to restore it.[29]

This experience is more complex than the Freudian 'retreat' into narcissism.[30] Here the patient both takes the world into himself and simultaneously disintegrates into it, and is 'broadened out' *into* the world to the point that he cannot separate himself from it. This experience of psychosis is figured as radically open, in part because of Rosenfeld's decision to focus on the feeling of the relationship between his patient and the world, rather than the textual content of his hallucinations.

This open view of psychosis is taken a step further by the object-relations psychoanalyst Christopher Bollas. Firmly abandoning the concept of primary narcissism, Bollas suggests that subjective experience emerges through an initial encounter with alterity. For Bollas subjectivity is constituted through encounters with the others, as early as in the late stages of gestation. In such encounters, '[t]he object can cast its shadow' on the child, influencing and shaping their identity 'without a child being able to process this relation through mental representations or language'.[31] These encounters take place prior to the development of thoughts, and act as 'unthought knowns'.[32] 'Unthought knowns' can refer to a range of experiences. Whilst the parent might force their desire or envy onto the infant, positive experiences of nurture, play and rhythm also make their way into the infant's psychic life as unthought knowns.

Bollas thus radically suggests that subjectivity is formed through an experience of alterity prior to object relation (or representation) which has a lasting effect on the structure of psychic life; and which, when it goes awry, impacts the development of psychosis. He thus understands psychotic experience as essentially caused by the encounter with and continuing presence of an other which remains outside of representation. Throughout his psychoanalytic career, Bollas has developed adaptations to standard psychoanalytic techniques in order to treat early-stage schizophrenia and psychotic breakdowns.[33] Key to Bollas's interventions is the belief that it is possible to reverse the early effects of schizophrenic breakdown through intensive psychoanalysis, if the unthought knowns precipitating the breakdown can be rendered into thought (i.e. can be represented). By bringing the disorganizing associations and objects into representation 'so that [they] are no longer part of the unthought known', patients can '*subject* [them] to thought'.[34] Far from being inherently enigmatic, Bollas's unthought knowns can be brought into thought and communicated to others, bringing the subject out of psychotic experience and back into social, representable life.

Bollas thus understands psychosis as radically open, adding that it is an experience which is *accessible* and translatable into non-psychotic, representational thought. Perhaps because of this conviction, Bollas's most recent work on schizophrenia, *When the Sun Bursts*, is also a remarkable account of the phenomenology of the psychosis, tracking aspects of the *experiences* of breakdown of his many patients, as well as theorizing on them. His writing provides a rich account of the varied ways in which psychosis develops during schizophrenic breakdown, and the radical transformation of a subject's 'aesthetic of being' during this process.[35] Beginning as it does with the conviction that psychosis is a shareable experience, it is a powerful text to read alongside Kane's works. With this in mind, we can now turn back to the structure of *Cleansed* in order to consider what kind of psychic life it shares with its audience.

## Prediction and interruption in *Cleansed*

In *Cleansed*, Kane creates an experience of sustained irresolution for her potential audiences which is designed to disorientate the spectator. The play's twenty short scenes are structured episodically and clearly eschew the narrative arch of psychological realism. The play tracks the experiences of five inmates – Grace, Graham, Rod, Carl and Robin – who are being held in an institution built on the site of a university. The institution is run by Tinker, variously a doctor, torturer, drug dealer and prison warden. The play begins with Tinker killing Graham with an overdose of heroin. Graham's sister Grace arrives at the institution looking for him and is committed to the institution as an inmate herself. She sees and physically interacts with Graham even though he is dead. Grace faces a series of tortures at the hands of Tinker, culminating in a forced mastectomy and phalloplasty without anaesthetic, so that she might 'become' Graham. At the same time, in another room of the university, Tinker tests Rod and Carl's homosexual relationship by torturing Carl after each of his expressions of love, until Rod finally agrees to die for Carl. The fifth character, Robin, is a young illiterate inmate who has been committed because he hears voices. Grace teaches him to read and count, and upon finding out the length of his sentence, he kills himself. Additionally, there is an unnamed woman working as a striptease performer in a shower cubicle, who is visited by both Tinker and Robin. Her name turns out to be Grace. The strands of the play interact with one another without ever coalescing into a single narrative, and its increasing violence is combined with images of flowers springing from the ground and rats swarming the stage, reminiscent of the surrealist theatre of Apollinaire, and Artaud's Theatre of Cruelty.

The scenes function as a series of pairings, with each pairing haunted by a bystander – usually Tinker or Graham. Whilst the actions of these pairings seem to unfold in chronological time, the pairings (Grace/Graham, Carl/Rod, Tinker/Woman, Grace/Robin) operate in parallel with one another, showing a cross-section of individuals under similar tortures, rather than tracing the disintegration of heroes or situations as in Kane's first two plays. The link between the scenes is the site they take place in: the university, the responsiveness and violence of the environment, and the regime of violence perpetrated upon them by Tinker in this place. The use of pairings and locations to provide a loose structure to the play draws on Strindberg's *The Ghost Sonata*, in which pairs of characters are bound to specific rooms in Hummel's ghostly house. In Strindberg's play, the colours of the rooms and their pairings with characters give a sense of stability and signification which is not found in the plot itself. The protagonist in this play is convinced that Hummel's house will yield a great secret, only to find it a place of torture. Yet, as Saunders argues, the torturous journey of *The Ghost Sonata* does become a transformational experience for the student as 'the use of rooms as places of discovery or revelation for characters constitutes a form of ongoing journey or pilgrimage'.[36] In *Cleansed* Kane retains the idea of a spatial structure from *The Ghost Sonata*, but abandons the sense of a coherent journey. We might think of *Cleansed* as using the spaces of Strindberg's theatre and inserting Büchner's non-cohering structure into this space.[37]

Rather than being structured via an unfolding journey, *Cleansed* takes the form of a cruel call and response in which the inmates attempt to communicate, to give accounts of themselves and their loves, only to be punished by Tinker for their linguistic failure. The episodic nature of the scene structure in *Cleansed* represents an extension of the tableaux of Ian that end *Blasted*, as well as an anticipation of the parallel, yet overlapping, testimonies and desires that make up *Crave*. In *Crave* the play's structure seems to emerge out of the unanswered and unanswerable call of the desires of the speakers. *Cleansed*, on the other hand, embodies a painful call and response predicated on an all-hearing, Orwellian authority.

This is most explicitly demonstrated in the relationship between Rod and Carl. In their first encounter onstage, Carl professes his love for Rod through exaggerated linguistic tropes which he nonetheless appears to believe. Convincing sceptical Rod to exchange rings in an unofficial marriage Carl professes his undying love for Rod:

**Rod** You'd die for me?
**Carl** Yes.
**Rod** (*Holds out his hand.*) I don't like this.
**Carl** *closes his eyes and puts the ring on* **Rod**'*s finger.*

**Rod** What are you thinking?
**Carl** That I'll always love you.[38]

Tinker, audience to this conversation, responds in scene five by threatening Carl with death by anal penetration until he denies his commitment to Rod, breaking his own love narrative that he had established in the marriage scene:

**Carl** Please don't fucking kill me God
**Tinker** I love you Rod I'd die for you
**Carl** Not me please not me don't kill me Rod not me don't kill me ROD NOT ME ROD NOT ME
[...]
**Tinker** Show me your tongue
**Carl** *sticks out his tongue.*
**Tinker** *produces a large pair of scissors and cuts off* **Carl**'s *tongue.*[39]

This scene is an obvious borrowing from Orwell's *1984*, but unlike Orwell's version, which marks the end of secrecy and the possibility of a private self, Kane's play oscillates back to Carl and Rod's relationship which continues despite the betrayal.[40] Carl is systematically deprived of all his means of communication and sources of joy throughout the play, losing his hands after writing, his feet after dancing and, finally, his genitals after making love.

The experience for the audience, depending on the individual and the directing, is either harrowing or pornographic. It is also likely to be deeply disorientating. The mutilations are repetitive and sequential, and do not end when Rod finally agrees to give up his life for Carl. Kane stages both rejection and death in the relationship between Rod and Carl, but allows neither to terminate their love, nor to provide the dramatic high point or termination of the narrative. As Susanna Clapp commented with regard to James Macdonald's first production, 'It does not so much unfold or develop as accumulate.'[41] Whilst Carl fails to live up to his own romantic narrative, he persists on stage. The conflict within the call and response structure here remains unresolved at the end of the play, with Tinker offstage and yet alive, and Carl mutilated and reduced but still living. The cumulative nature of the scene structure in *Cleansed* is thus generative of a tension for the audience from which Kane withholds a coherent resolution.

If the linking strand between the scenes in *Cleansed* is the site or environment in which they occur, then this too falls short of being a coherent structuring principle. The scenes take place in a series of rooms on the site of a university, each room with a colour and each relating to a different pairing: The College Green (Rod and Carl), The White Room (Graham and Grace),

The Red Room (Tinker's torture chamber), The Black Room (Tinker and Woman), The Round Room (Grace and Robin). The symbolism relating to the overlaying of university and a site of torture is clear, and presents a continuity with the suggestion implicit in *Blasted* that violence is present under the surface of any apparently civilized setting. But the set is more than a flat symbol as Kane creates an active environment which is responsive to the emotions of the characters, both allowing them a voiceless means of expression and perpetrating Tinker's tortures. As Hilary Chute suggests, the fictional site of the play and the physical stage itself acts in a relationship with Grace.[42] In the moments of high romance in her relationship with Graham, after they have made love and after he has protected her from an array of bullets, flowers emerge from the floor. However, the stage is not only in a relationship with Grace. It also perpetrates violence through invisible attackers on Grace's body, confinement through the conversion of a shower cubicle into the Woman's peep show, and becomes the means of both Robin's education and his suicide. Like the bodies of the characters, the stage itself is a conflicted environment which moves from acting in a poetic metonymy through the growth of Grace's flowers to becoming the means by which her attempts at love and subjectification are violently repressed.

In the first production at the Royal Court in 1998, the destabilizing treatment of space in the play was compounded by Jeremy Hubert's set design, which created the impression that the various rooms in which the play is set were being viewed from different perspectives. At certain moments in the production, the actors and props were lifted and pinned to a wall to create the impression for the audience that they were being viewed from above and with the actors 'sprawl[ed] on steeply raked platforms as if stuck to a fly trap'.[43] The changeability of the relationship between set and onstage characters was therefore reiterated in the relationship between audience members and the stage space. Terry Brawn identified this lack of continuous spatial logic as the most disorientating aspect of the production:

> And my most disorientating response was one of confusion as to where this story was taking place. And no, I don't mean literally – we were obviously in the realm of fable or allegory. I was trying to map the world of the play. I must admit I never succeeded.[44]

The setting and visual effects of this production was both hostile to the characters onstage and profoundly destabilizing for the audience. The set presents a site that is at once a coherent 'whole' (a university complex) and a variable space which changes its functions from scene to scene. The site of *Cleansed* is at once an agent of poetic expression and torture, and is variously compliant with the desires of the inmates, static, or actively used against them.

Through the dramaturgy of *Cleansed* Kane creates a theatrical experience which provokes the desire to create narrative or temporal/historical coherence in the reader or potential audience member and then thwarts it. It is important to elaborate here what form the 'non-coherence' of the features I have been mentioning so far takes. To say that the scenes of the play and the visual eruptions therein do not cohere in the form of a narrative is not the same as saying that they are nonsense. Taken as particularities, the scenes and events do each have an internal logic. However this is a logic which constantly requires revision, as it changes from episode to episode. When flowers burst through the floor, for example, the event can be explained by a form of aesthetic internal logic; that Grace is in a metonymic relationship with her environment which responds to her happiness. When the environment attacks Grace through the form of invisible voices a new logic is proposed; that the environment is a manifestation of the violent cultural norms also embodied by Tinker. And whilst both of these instances seem to fit within the realms of surrealist theatre, the storyline relating to Robin is painfully realistic. Detained in a medical facility for being a difficult child Robin is illiterate and innumerate, and therefore has no understanding of the length of his detainment. He learns to read and count from fellow inmate Grace, and kills himself upon realizing his detainment will last thirty years.

The cruelties perpetrated against Robin take the form of humiliation which is both shocking and believable in the context of countless media reports of institutional abuse of this kind, such as the public enquiry into Ashworth hospital which was taking place during the production's first run.[45] This, of course, brings us back to the relationship between Kane's work and popular discourses on mental illness, including scandals and enquiries relating to psychiatric hospitals, which was addressed in the Introduction to this book. Were Robin's story line to stand alone one could draw out a plausible socio-realist play bent on exposing abuse in institutions such as young offenders institutions or care homes. This reference was picked up by one of the play's initial reviewers who suggested; 'It might be of more consequence to read or listen to the ongoing public inquiry into Ashworth Hospital for the criminally insane.'[46] It is telling that reviewers of several different productions have identified the scene in which Robin is made to eat an entire box of chocolates as 'one of the most disquieting scenes' of the play as it provides a moment of painfully realistic tragedy in the otherwise surreal environment.[47] Through the scenes relating to Robin, Kane therefore creates an interruption of the surreal logics of earlier scenes, returning the play to a form of realism which it then repeatedly discards. Rather than being incoherent in the sense of failing to signify anything, the non-coherence Kane manifests in *Cleansed* requires constant re-evaluation. It signifies through various apparently contradictory frameworks in sequence without giving one dominance over the rest.

In this way, *Cleansed* is an attempt to immerse a potential spectator into a situation of sustained irresolution, in which the need to establish a narrative history is encountered as both violent and necessary, and impossible. Critics of the 1998 production used language relating to insideness to describe the experience of viewing Kane's play. David Benedict wrote that '[director James] MacDonald and [designer Jeremy] Herbert take you by the hand, allowing you to become a prisoner of Kane's fierce but fiercely controlled imagination', and Jon Peter commented that the action took place 'like a nightmare it unreels somewhere between the back of your eyes and the centre of your brain with unpredictable but remorseless logic'.[48] These spectators encountered *Cleansed* as a phenomenon of being trapped *inside a mind*, without the agency or control to halt the nightmarish accumulation of scenes, or the identification with a single hero or narrative which would provide the reassurance that the action is taking place outside of oneself.

The 'unpredictable but remorseless logic' of the play was achieved in the first production by depriving the audience of the ability to use an established past narrative to predict the events ahead.[49] This tension between the necessity to create a narrative and its impossibility is evocative of Christopher Bollas's accounts of the experience of psychotic breakdown. Bollas provides some of the most creative and provocative accounts of psychoanalytic treatments for psychosis in young people, suggesting that the long-term effects of psychosis can be diverted with the correct early treatment.[50] Bollas highlights the importance of narrative and predictability in coping with everyday life:

> In normality we live with the illusion that we foresee the future, or at least a range of future possibilities. We prepare ourselves for being let down or socially derided. We carry the assumption that a well-prepared self is a safe haven, and the illusion of safety in the present has implications of how we look back on the past.[51]

The dramaturgy and structure of *Cleansed* is an attempt to undermine this 'illusion of safety', and to put the spectator through the experience of trying to make sense of compelling, even destructive, imagery without preparation.

*Cleansed* deliberately disorientates, thwarting attempts to establish a history of the dramatic universe on the one hand or anticipate a future narrative on the other. In doing so it pushes the locus of the dramaturgy from the dramatic universe represented on stage to an in-between space which is the site of the audience–artwork encounter. Bollas's description of the kind of disorientation that takes place in schizophrenic breakdowns makes for an interesting comparison with this process, and points to the kind of mental experience that the dramaturgy of *Cleansed* might be simulating. A shocking event takes place in the narrative of the young individual, perhaps a disappointment or a rejection, and the ability to contextualize this event, place it in the past and continue in reality is lost. 'Most people rebound,' says Bollas, 'But not all. Some are hijacked by a shock that becomes an eternal present. The self is suspended, remaining on constant watch, and this means they can no longer inhabit everyday reality. Past-present-future ceases to have any meaning. The temporal structures are lost.'[52] It is within a simulated voiding of temporal structures that Kane stages Tinker's violent attempts to force the characters and world of *Cleansed* back into a narrative history and predictability. Of course, this voiding is not complete, as works staged in traditional theatres are always bounded by temporal and physical frameworks. However, whilst theatre's temporal boundaries are usually used as the framework for narrative-making, in *Cleansed* the relationship between temporal progression and history is suspended.

Kane described this technique of historical suspension in a distinction she named the difference between 'plot' and 'story'. Speaking with students at Royal Holloway, Kane identified 'story' as the historical narratives in a play, 'chronologically what happens over time.'[53] 'Plot', on the other hand, she identifies as what the audience actually encounter. She describes the process of writing *Cleansed* as one of initially writing out the stories of each character pairing individually: 'I wrote out all the story-lines if you like, the Rod and Carl story, the Grace/Graham story, the Tinker/ stripper story.'[54] These 'stories' were then rearranged into individual scenes in which only the moments of 'high drama' were preserved. Kane used a diagram in order to explain this process of voiding her 'stories' of history in order to transform them into compelling theatre, which showed a straight horizontal line, with a wavy line running through it:

> If the wiggly line [...] which goes up and down is the story, the bits which go up are the moments of high drama, which tend to be violent [...]and the bits under [the line] are the build-up. So that's the story. Everything [above] the line is the plot. So all the stuff underneath it you just shed. [...] Anything remotely extraneous or explanatory is completely cut, all you get are the moments of extremely high drama.[55]

This process of dehistroicizing the plot becomes essential to create the intensity of affect which the work attempts to generate:

> In a lot of plays there are things like, 'then a messenger comes on [and explains what is happening]', all of which is much easier to take and gives you time to calm down. But I didn't want to give anyone time to calm down.[56]

*Cleansed* thus aims to enact a situation of sustained temporal irresolution and extreme emotional agitation onto its potential audience, which undermines the audience's predictive capacities in a psychosis-like process.

## A cognitive reading: Psychosis and prediction errors

That an inability to predict the future is a feature of psychotic breakdown is not unique to Bollas's psychoanalytic observations; it is also an increasingly popular position in neuroscientific thinking, and correlates with accounts from those living with psychosis. The prediction error minimization (PEM) framework for understanding cognition places prediction and its failures at the heart of all cognitive processes. As Jakob Hohwy summarizes it, PEM is a theory that suggests 'that the brain is a sophisticated hypothesis-testing mechanism, which is constantly involved in minimizing the error of its predictions of the sensory input it receives from the world'.[57] This theory understands all cognitive processing as a balancing act between 'bottom-up' intake of perceptual information and 'top-down' prediction of what is expected to be perceived based on former perception. As Hohwy notes, this is a particularly broad way of conceptualizing the activity of the brain/mind, as 'the mechanism is meant to explain perception and action and everything mental in between' and therefore suggests that 'prediction error minimization is all the brain ever does'.[58]

From within this broad framework the hypothesis has emerged that the experience of positive psychotic symptoms (delusion and hallucination) is brought about through specific disruptions of the mind's predictive capacities. This hypothesis rests on a model of the brain which is hierarchical. It suggests that there is a low-level system which predicts and confirms prediction through perception. When perception errors occur, the error is referred up to a higher-level (more complex) system which figures out whether the abnormal perception should be discarded (i.e. that it is noise), or whether the body of knowledge on which the predictive capacity depends needs updating. Neuroscientists Paul Fletcher and Chris Frith suggest that delusions and hallucinations can be accounted for by the dysfunction of this system – specifically by disruption in the processing of prediction errors:

> Persistence of the disruption up the hierarchy can mean that the attempts at the lower levels to explain the world will fail. Achieving a world model that is not continually being signalled as wrong will require more complex changes. [. . .] Ultimately, someone with schizophrenia will need to develop a set of beliefs that must account for a great deal of strange and sometimes contradictory data.[59]

The suggestion here is that due to faults in the processing of prediction errors, changes need to be made at a higher, more conscious level of cognition which leads to the phenomena of delusion and hallucination.

Whilst this model for understanding psychosis may seem sterile when paired with Kane's plays, with its language of data inputs and hypothesis-testing, it has the advantage of bringing together cognitive mechanics with a phenomenology of hallucination. The study cited in the paragraph earlier attempts to posit PEM as a mechanism of transition, from one world view to another: 'If one imagines trying to make sense of a world that had become strange and inconsistent, pregnant with sinister meaning and messages, the sensible conclusion may well be that one is being deliberately deceived.'[60] This picture of the experience of psychosis, as one of constantly trying to map out and account for an incoherent world, certainly resonates with descriptions from writers with lived experience of psychosis. In *The Collected Schizophrenias*, Esmé Weijun Wang describes the experience of confusion which immediately precedes the onset of her delusions:

> The more I consider the world, the more I realize that it's supposed to have a cohesion that no longer exists, or that it is swiftly losing – either because it is pulling itself apart, because it has never been cohesive, because my mind is no longer able to hold the pieces together or, most likely, some jumbled combination of the above.[61]

Wang describes this experience of confusion as one of extreme distress that passes into a phase of delusion.

> Something's wrong; then it's *completely wrong*. After the prodomal phase, I settle into a way of being that is almost intolerable. The moment of shifting from one phase to the other is usually sharp and clear; I turn my head and in a single moment realize that my coworkers have been replaced by robots.[62]

As Wang notes, much discourse on psychosis and schizophrenia has a limited ability to describe 'how it feels to be under the skin and believe things that aren't real'. Whilst we can 'rattle off the symptoms of a panic attack [...] there is no corresponding checklist from the sensations of psychosis'.[63] Despite its cognitive vocabulary, the PEM framework provides a useful structure for discussing the spatial and temporal scuppering experienced during the psychotic breakdowns of some people.

In *Cleansed*, Kane transforms the theatre into a site of erroneous prediction. This is achieved, as I have been arguing, not simply by creating a surreal theatrical landscape, but by repeatedly *soliciting* the potential audiences' predictive capacities and then thwarting them. This creates a dramaturgy which is actively unpredictable, in which the voiding of predictive capacities (at a conscious level) is not represented but *done to* the audience. As such, a shift in the locus of the dramaturgy itself is performed. The theatre becomes a site of play or experiment, with audience and artwork meeting in an active encounter with each other. The artwork is no longer the passive object of the audience's gaze, nor is it creating an entirely active, immersive world in which the audience is rendered passive. Instead, the audience and artwork might meet in the processes of soliciting and thwarting prediction, and the experience of psychosis-like psychic life is evoked at this meeting point.

One might, of course, express reservations about pairing understandings of psychosis which are neuroscientific with those derived from psychoanalysis, given that the cognitive neuroscience model would appear to leave little room for interior life, and for the unconscious in particular. This theoretical problem is addressed at length in the work of philosopher Catherine Malabou, who suggests that the impasse can be resolved through the concept of 'cerebrality', which would incorporate both the activity of the brain and the events of psychic life.[64] Malabou suggests that the brain's capacity to regulate its own affects, 'auto-affectation', can be understood as the unconscious of the cerebral: '*cerebral auto-affectation is the unconscious of subjectivity*'.[65] It is this ability of the brain to regulate its own affects, which according to Malabou allows a person to feel themselves as a subject, or as an other. A reorganization of this process, due to accident, trauma, brain disease or schizophrenia, leads to an irrecoverable transformation of psychic life.[66] The disruption of 'auto-affectation' for Malabou is a '*point of no return*'.[67]

Malabou can be usefully brought to bear on the PEM framework, although not without some problems. The concept of auto-affectation can find its correlate in the hypothetical prediction-testing mechanisms, which regulate pre-conscious perception in order not to overwhelm the conscious brain, whilst managing and evaluating the brain's relationship with its own contents. On the other hand, Malabou's understanding of psychotic experiences, both in terms of schizophrenia, and in brain diseases such as Alzheimer's, presumes a complete discontinuity with a previously existing subject, and as such a radical break between the subject of mental 'health' and the subject of illness.[68] Such a break is particularly problematic when applied, as Malabou suggests, to hallucinatory phenomena experienced by those with schizophrenia diagnoses, given the growing evidence for the role of psychic histories of trauma on the contents of hallucinations.[69] This difference is clearly relevant to the applicability of either framework to Kane's works, given their entanglement of sexual violence, trauma and psychotic breakdown. The framework of the predictive mind, on the other hand, suggests a greater continuity between a person's psychic history and the generation of hallucinatory experience. Rather than being irreparably broken, this framework suggests that the mechanisms of cognition are *disrupted*; as a consequence the mind mines its own history (figured here as a bank of data) in order to create a new understanding of the world which fits with unpredicted perceptual information. Understood in this light, PEM might actually run parallel to the concept of psychic life, as it understands one's experience of oneself (as a subject) as constantly in the process of being constituted through an encounter between interiority and exterior life – which may indeed be disordered, violent or traumatic.

Rather than proposing either cerebrality or PEM as ontological certainties, I wish to identify the latter as useful in defining and tracing mechanisms for understanding both how the mind relates to itself and to its environment. The mechanisms of prediction which are proposed as existing inside the brain also exist and can be simulated in artificially created environments – such as the theatre.[70] By triangulating Kane's radically unpredictable dramaturgy, psychoanalytic understandings of psychosis as a disintegration of boundaries and narrative capacities, and the PEM model of psychosis as prediction error, we open up the possibility for a spatialized sharing of psychotic phenomena in a concrete way. Rather than explicitly representing psychosis, Kane distils elements of how it *feels* to undergo psychotic breakdown and puts them to work in her dramaturgy. Kane might be therefore be read as conducting an experiment into the extremity of theatre's ability to put people through curated alternative psychic states – states which are traditionally understood as 'closed off' or irrecoverable.

The uniqueness of Kane's vision, especially at the time of her writing, is exemplified in her prioritizing of epistemological uncertainty for her audience. Whilst the structure of *Cleansed* surrounds the audience in a series of scenes that thwart efforts to impose a historical structure on the work, the content of the scenes represents a collapse of interior, imaginary life and actuality. At the same time Kane's dramatic universe in *Cleansed* contains enough traces of the characters' individual narratives and histories to imply a reality outside of their interior lives. Grace and Graham may exist in an ahistorical moment onstage, in which Graham is both alive and dead, but Graham's desire does have a history:

**[Graham]** *hesitates.*
*He kisses [Grace], slowly and gently at first, then harder and deeper.*
Graham I used to . . . think about you and . . .
I used to . . . wish it was you when I . . .
Used to . . .[71]

Graham's desire is both physically manifest here and contains its own history of prohibition and the realization of past fantasy. Likewise, Robin very much exists within a narrative of his own, in which he has a mother who he is not allowed to see due to a past misdemeanour, and who he longs to return to. The tragedy of Robin's character is that by learning to count he becomes aware of his own external reality, in which he is condemned to remain in the institution for thirty years, and consequently ends his own life. As mentioned earlier, this almost socio-realist storyline is played out in parallel and overlapping with the stories of Rod and Carl, who have no external references at all, and Grace and Graham who seem to operate in a metonymic relationship with the stage in the style of surrealist theatre.

By not providing a moment of revelation explaining Graham's return from the dead as psychosis, dream or imagination, Kane differs from her contemporaries dealing with a similar real/unreal boundary. Anthony Nielson's *The Wonderful World of Dissocia* (2004) and Joseph Penhall's *Blue/Orange* (2000) are a few examples of Kane's contemporaries attempting, like Kane, to represent a mind for which the distinction between internal and external has broken down. In Nielson's and Penhall's plays, the resolution is found within the medical establishment, which finally provides a boundary between real and unreal, allowing one side of the patient's staged experience to be delegated to psychosis. These take place in different ways in each of the plays. *The Wonderful World of Dissocia* takes place within the psychotic world of 'Dissocia' in which Lisa has a surrealist adventure which is at once thrilling, confusing and terrifying. Slowly sounds of the 'outside' world, such as traffic, break into the dissociated world represented onstage. The nature of 'dissocia' as unreal is clearly confirmed in act two in which the protagonist wakes up in a hospital bed on a psychiatric ward, having been sectioned during a psychotic episode.

In Penhall's *Blue/Orange* a similar moment of revelation takes place, although this time between the doctors who are debating the status of a patient who thinks oranges are blue, and believes that Ugandan dictator Idi Amin is his father. In an effort to clear bed space, psychiatric consultant Robert convinces himself and attempts to convince his colleague Bruce that there is reasonable doubt that the patient Christopher may in fact be the son of Idi Amin, and that designating this belief a psychosis is racism. The turning point comes when the junior psychiatrist Bruce reveals that previously Christopher has believed himself to be the son of other internationally renowned figures, such as Muhammad Ali:

**Robert** Don't you think you're being a bit arbitrary?
**Bruce** What?
**Robert** Why should he put [a newspaper cutting about Idi Amin's wives and children] away?
**Bruce** Why?
[. . .]
Because he cut it out of *The Guardian* on Saturday. I watched him. Where do you think he got a pair of scissors from?
*Pause.*
**Robert** *snatches the article from* **Christopher** *and examines it.*
**Robert** So . . .?
**Bruce** Three weeks ago it was Muhammad Ali. He'd seen Muhammad Ali on the television winning 'Sports Personality of the Century' and put two and two together.[72]

Having explored and represented a certain ambiguity as to the reality of the patient's beliefs through the conflict between Robert and Bruce, Penhall nevertheless confirms the psychotic, 'unreal' nature of Christopher's fantasy parentage to his audience. In differing ways both Penhall's and Nielson's plays reinstate the boundaries between what constitutes fact and psychotic fiction in their dramatic universes. In so doing they end up subordinating the confusing experience of psychosis to a medical discourse that closes off internal 'fiction' from external 'fact'.

## *Cleansed* at the National Theatre: Searching for narrative

In her production of *Cleansed* for the National Theatre in spring 2016 director Katie Mitchell introduced a staging and narrative structure for Kane's play which attempted to resolve the play's disorientating aesthetic. This production was the first major production of *Cleansed* in London since it debuted in 1998, and the first play of Kane's to be performed at the National Theatre. Mitchell's production represents an interpretation of *Cleansed*'s dramaturgy which runs counter to the argument presented so far in this chapter, as Mitchell set out to resolve the play's non-coherence and provide a meta-narrative for her production. Examining Mitchell's production in the context of this chapter, I invite us to think about the resistances a dramaturgy of disorientation might raise in audiences and theatre-makers alike.

In the playtext of *Cleansed* Kane blurs the boundary between the real – the external and empirically verifiable – and the imaginary – that which takes place only within the mind, be it psychotic figment, dream or imagination. This blurring can be seen, for example, through the character of Graham, who, like Ian in *Blasted*, returns from the dead with enough physicality as to trouble the interpretation that he is ghost or imagination. Whilst Graham seems only to be seen by Grace and Tinker, he nevertheless physically interacts with the stage, characters and soundscape, and causes no surprise through his appearance. In *Blasted* Ian wakes from death only to find everything is the same except that it is now raining, a final irony which extends the ruthlessly ironic treatment he receives at the hands of the play. Graham's return is related to the arrival of his sister Grace but also carries the implication that he has never left the institution in which he was killed. For Grace, Graham is alive enough to love, make love and protect her from bullets. In other words, Graham is *as real* as the tortures which are inflicted upon Grace in the university and the environment which makes up the rest of the play. In her production for the National Theatre Mitchell set out to separate the real and 'unreal' elements of Kane's play through her directorial choices, thus modifying the play's disorientating affect.

Mitchell attempted to resolve this central ambiguity by shutting off the open dramaturgy suggested in Kane's playtext. Speaking in conversation with Matt Trueman at the National Theatre, Mitchell identified a major adaptation that she had made to Kane's dramaturgy by having the character of Grace remain onstage throughout the play. This adaptation was made, according to Mitchell, in order to render the play more 'coherent' to the audience.[73] With the aim of coherence, Mitchell decided that the action 'was the dream of one of the characters and that was Grace'.[74] For Mitchell this decision allowed a unity of genre in which to situate the play which better allowed her to direct it. She used 'the genre of surrealism as opposed to naturalism' in which 'characters can be happily inside this dreamscape'.[75] Within this decision regarding genre, Mitchell further imposed a criteria for the action itself to be as naturalistic as possible. With regard to the sexual and violent events taking place onstage, these were to be done with cinematic accuracy: 'it's just how I understand the material when I read it, like a piece of literature, I see it like a film.'[76] Overall Mitchell remarked that the framework she had given her actors to work with was that of an exceptionally realistic and vivid nightmare, with Grace at its centre.

By placing Grace at the centre of her production of *Cleansed* and insisting on the dreamscape as its cohering element, Mitchell set out to eliminate the disorientating changeability of the playtext. For Mitchell as a director, consistency to an ongoing genre is essential: 'genre is very important to me. Once I decide it is surrealism every single thing has to follow the rules of surrealism.'[77] Mitchell's own understanding of what surrealism means in terms of directing is set out in her book *The Director's Craft*:

> It is like being in a dream. Strange things happen but people might not comment on them as they would in real life.
> You pursue the things you want with intensity.
> You are often misunderstood by the people you are talking to.
> Objects may take on a significance out of proportion with their import.
> The physical laws of the universe may be subject to alteration.[78]

Mitchell insists several times throughout *The Director's Craft*, as she did in conversation with Mat Truman, that the surrealist logic is essentially the logic of the dream. Whilst the surrealist logic does allow for a certain amount of confusion to take place onstage, 'where the banal and the fantastical can co-exist in the same space unchallenged', Mitchell's approach to style nevertheless alters the audience's perspective, requiring them to adopt a single stylistic view point: 'style and genre define the world that the audience see and the way in which the characters interact in that world.'[79] For Mitchell, then, a play which she has chosen to direct in the style of surrealism will portray a dreamscape.

By interpreting the play as a dream and introducing new elements to emphasize this interpretation to her audience, Mitchell introduced a reality-testing function which is absent in the playtext of *Cleansed*. When Graham comes back from the dead in Mitchell's version of *Cleansed*, unlike in the playtext, he is accompanied by a funeral procession which slowly walks back and forth across the stage carrying umbrellas, implying the intrusion of Grace's memory of her brother's funeral onto the dream. At the end of scene eleven in the playtext Graham shields Grace's body from a very physical attack of gunfire.

*The wall is being shot to pieces and is splattered with blood.*
*After several minutes the gunfire stops.*
**Graham** *uncovers* **Grace**'s *face and looks at her. She open's her eyes and looks at him.*

**Graham** No one. Nothing. Never.
*Out of the ground grow daffodils.*
*They burst upwards their yellow covering the entire stage.*[80]

Whilst this took place in Mitchell's production, she added a funeral procession which crossed the stage and left behind an urn. Graham opened the urn with Grace, and poured his own ashes through her fingers. The symbolism of the urn in this moment was obvious: Graham is truly dead; he is affirming his status as dead to Grace through her imagination by showing her the content of his own urn.

It also introduces a strong implicit connection between Grace's loss of Graham and the gunfire. The production contained an impressive, continuous soundscape, combining the sirens and music with sounds of a war taking place on the outside of the building, created by sound designer Melanie Wilson. The penetration of the sound of gunfire into the set with the slow motion opening and pouring out of Graham's ashes onto Grace created a link between the two, implying that the destruction taking place beyond the building and throughout the dream-world emanated out from Grace's primary loss. At moments of particular distress or confusion for Grace in this production, the characters moved in slow motion, or the funeral procession walked backwards. The procession was carried out by suited individuals in balaclavas – the same individuals who seem to be running the facility. The occasional metonymic relationship between Grace and the stage which takes place in some of the scenes in the playtext, such as when flowers grow in response to her happiness, was used by Mitchell to become the overall structuring principle, in order to 'define the world which the audience see'.[81] The entire play was staged as Grace's nightmare journey through imaginary tortures, occasioned by her grief at the loss of Graham. Grace in this version is a lot more like the dreamer in Strindberg's *A Dream Play* who travels through a self-contained dreamscape observing the horrors of humanity.

In an interview at the National Theatre, Mitchell explained her approach to *Cleansed* was to work with the play as though she were staging an unfinished text, using her skills as a director to mould the scenes in an 'actual play'. Reflecting on her general preference to stage adaptations of novels or non-theatrical forms, she compared directing *Cleansed* to an adaptation, pulling together and re-working non-dramatic fragments into a coherent whole: 'It's not really a play [. . .] I'm] not sure I can do plays anymore [. . .] It's just fragments that have to be ordered and resist cohering'.[82] This approach, which has been much commented upon in regard to Mitchell's theatre practice as a whole, subordinates the text of the play to the vision of the director leaving it to Mitchell to create out of supposedly incomplete source material.[83] In this way it differs radically from the directing philosophy of James Macdonald, who directed the first production of *Cleansed* and with whom Kane had previously worked on *Blasted*. For Macdonald, the director's role is to be invisible: 'I don't have anything I need to express about myself. My job is to enable other people to express themselves.'[84] It also shuts off the openness of the play's dramaturgy, so that the nightmarish content no longer takes place somewhere between the audience and the stage, but is held in an objectifiable stage space, mediated by a single character. The play becomes about telling a story, rather than sharing a state of heightened, disorienting drama.

The National Theatre production of *Cleansed* was in a sense born of two opposing projects. On the one hand Kane's playtext contains a uniquely un-cohering vision, in which the audience is challenged to remain in a liminal space in which knowledge of the boundaries between the interior and the actual is suspended. On the other Mitchell's directorial project was to erect a coherent 'whole' out of the work, and move from accumulation towards narrative. A simple example of this intervention may be that at the end of Mitchell's version of the production, Tinker kills the woman he loves and shoots himself. The playtext leaves our final image of Tinker alive, suggesting that the play's call and response are not complete and that further cruelties and transformations in the institution could be perpetrated. Killing Tinker off itself raises interesting questions. Does he feel guilty? Is he as affected by the despair of the institution as his victims? Has he performed these acts under duress? Is the 'love' he feels for the woman simply too much to cope with? These questions arise at the end of Mitchell's production, but they are only able to arise because Tinker is dead. The story is closed, and by being closed it has realized itself *as a narrative*. In this way Mitchell partially removed the disorientation that I have been arguing is key to Kane's work. The result was a production that was at times painful to watch, and at times numbing, and which several viewers and reviewers ultimately found boring.[85] The accumulation of acts was deprived of its ability to disorient, and therefore felt like a repetitive and uninteresting narrative.

## A play about love?

The suggestion that *Cleansed*, *Crave* and *4.48 Psychosis* all form part of a project to dramaturgically open up psychotic subjectivity both specifies and complicates a trope of Kane criticism: that her works are ultimately about love. The trope, for example, largely characterized the press reception to Mitchell's production following Mitchell's comment on Radio Four's *Front Row* that the play 'is not about violence, it's about love'.[86] This claim comes from Kane herself who decided it would be the defining line on the play during an interview with James Christopher in *The Observer* in 1997:

> 'It's a completely different play [to *Blasted*] in every way. The trilogy will eventually amount to three responses to war.' [Says Kane.]
> She is suddenly struck by a thought from which the interview never quite recovers. 'I've changed my mind what the trilogy is about just in that second. They are not about war at all but about faith, hope and love in the context of war' says Kane wonderingly. '*Blasted* is about hope. *Cleansed* is about love. Scrap that bit before the war. It's suddenly become clear to me. After three years. How amazing.'[87]

The trope that the play is 'about love' has been repeated throughout critical and journalistic material since this interview, with little attention to the kind of self-fashioning Kane may well have been engaged in when suddenly changing her mind mid-interview. Perhaps due to the circumstances of her death and the limited availability of interview material available, Kane sound bites tend to be treated as gospel by academics and reviewers alike. *In what way Cleansed* might be 'about love', and *what kind of love* it may be about are not addressed.

To interpret the play as thematizing a generic, Hollywood-style version of love as salvation, in which every 'I love you' is regarded as both 'true' and a sign of ethical redemption is patently unconvincing. Susanna Clapp noted that Mitchell's production made this binary more pronounced and dully unconvincing due to the realistic interpretation of stage directions:

> Its morals stuck out a mile. Its targets were too obvious: torture bad, love good. [. . .] In 1998 it had the particular interest of presenting itself in a new form: installation theatre. [. . .] [T]he lexicon which Mitchell draws on is so familiar. So much of it seems to have come out of a toolkit of theatrical despair.[88]

These reviews suggest that the production did not leave room to examine what love actually consists of for Kane, and what risks it involves. Clapp's review also refers to the altered spatial logic of the play in Mitchell's production. Whereas the 1998 production had the budget to create a dynamic hydraulic set that represented the various rooms of the university with striking artistry and allowed the audience the impression of looking through various perspectives, Mitchell's budget at the Dorfman theatre did not allow for this.[89] Mitchell and her team resolved this by choosing to stage the entire play in a single site, which looked like a concrete bunker. In this oppressive space, Grace's love seemed doomed to fail, and the (arguably impossible) malleability and variability of the space in the playtext was not expressed. The 2016 production of *Cleansed* was understood by newspaper critics as the presentation of a militarized site containing a straightforward choice between love exemplified by Grace and violence exemplified by Tinker, an interpretation which seriously limits the scope of the play.

The extreme kind of love that Kane presents in the play may be a reference, deliberate or unwitting, to the obsessions of psychosis. As I mentioned earlier, the play is clearly rooted in a relation to the real psychiatric establishments in the outside world, through its dedication to the patients of ES3 and the pseudo-medical actions of Tinker. During the rehearsals for the first production Kane took Daniel Evans, who played Robin, on a research trip to the ward in the Maudesley hospital where she herself had stayed.[90] In rehearsal for this production, Kane also identified Robin as 'a schizophrenic', revealing a direct thematic link between a character in the play and its possibly psychotic form.[91] The medical link in *Cleansed* therefore sits across both thematic and intellectual concerns with a diagnosis, and Kane's lived experience of being a patient. Reflecting on this visit and a further one made after Kane's death, during the rehearsals for *4.48 Psychosis*, Evans reflected 'going to the Maudesley for me showed and justified absolutely the anger that flows through *4.48 Psychosis*, against the way the medical profession treats people who fall ill'.[92] The theme of incarceration in the play, which is most poignantly expressed through Robin's narrative and suicide, is therefore tied up with the kind of rebellion against medical authority that is so pronounced in *4.48 Psychosis*. Likewise, the potentially lethal pain of unrequited love in *Cleansed* is inseparable from the thread of concerns with pathological psychic suffering which runs throughout her oeuvre.

Understanding the 'love' thematized in *Cleansed* as linked to psychotic suffering nuances the claims Kane herself made about the play's relationship to obsession. Kane claimed that inspiration for the play came from reading Roland Barthes's *The Lovers Discourse*, in which he compares 'the situation of the love-sick subject to that of an inmate of Dachau'.[93] On reading it, Kane commented:

> When I first read that I was appalled he could make that connection, but I couldn't stop thinking about it. And I gradually realized that Barthes is right: it is all about loss of self. When you love obsessively, you lose your sense of self. And if you lose the object of your love, you have no resources to fall back on. It can completely destroy you.[94]

As with the interview earlier, this statement has largely been taken as an unproblematic given by critics of Kane's work, as if to compare love with the experience of being a Holocaust victim is not highly polemical. Indeed, David Nathan's 1998 review of *Cleansed* in the *Jewish Chronicle* seems to be the only critical voice to have found issue with this connection.[95] That falling in love involves a loss of selfhood so radical, humiliating and violent that it can be equated with the experience of a concentration camp is clearly not the case for all love stories, or even all love stories staged by Kane. Ian's love for Cate in *Blasted* is based on dominance and a reaffirmation of his own masculine power over her. Ian's identity is bolstered in scene one of *Blasted* by Cate's passivity and his fantasy that her forced acquiescence is a sign that this love is requited.

However there is one kind of love that involves a radical and life-threatening loss of self, and that is the love experienced in the form of psychotic empathy. Bollas describes the radical empathy that can be felt in the experience of psychosis as deeply threatening to the boundaries of the psychotic person's sense of self:

> Because of [a psychotic person's] skill in projecting himself into objects, of hiding his mind, he is at risk when it comes to relationships with other people. If the other for whom they feel affection comes to harm, either through a breakdown or by suffering some physical injury, the schizophrenic can have become so identified with the person that this becomes his own suffering [...] the inability to cure the other of the state they are in, and the fact that he is fated by identification to *be* the other, ties him to an indeterminate vector that mirrors his own history of being fated by external factors.[96]

The experience of psychotic empathy is, according to Bollas, based on a loss of affective boundaries between interior and exterior life – a total breakdown in the ability distinguish between self and beloved other. The ability to recognize pain in others is replaced by an actual experience of that pain, making any form of empathetic or affectionate relationship for the psychotic individual a risk of losing the sense of self.

This obsessive love which is experienced as radical and dangerous identification finds its way into the dramaturgy of *Cleansed*, through the blurring of boundaries in the incestuous relationship between Grace and Graham. Their relationship involves a merging of bodies, from making love and dancing identically on the one hand, to Grace's transformation into 'Graham' on the other. In scene eleven Graham's body absorbs Grace's wounds:

> **Graham** *presses his hands onto* **Grace** *and her clothes turn red where he touches, blood seeping through.*
> *Simultaneously, his own body begins to bleed in the same places.*[97]

In the following scene Grace's identification with Graham's body is so complete that it is interpreted as threatening and pathological by Tinker and the voices, who attempt to '(b)urn it out' using a crude form of electroconvulsive therapy:

**Grace** My balls hurt.
**Tinker** You're a woman.
**Voices** Lunatic Grace.
[. . .]
**Tinker** Can make you better.
[. . .]
**Voices** Frazzle it out.[98]

Grace and Graham's relationship does indeed stage a love so extreme that it involves a 'loss of self' and at the same time a loss of boundaries between the bodies on stage. This is compounded by Graham's dead-and-alive status discussed earlier, as the audience may or may not understand him to exist 'inside' Grace's psychic life. A thematic collapse of the couple's identities is enacted via this confusion, and the constant images of doubling which appear on stage. Understanding *Cleansed* as an exploration of love-as-psychic-disintegration points us forward to the extreme form of collapse which Kane would attempt to stage in *Crave* and *4.48 Psychosis*.

I have argued in this chapter that the dramaturgy that Kane calls for in the playtext of *Cleansed*, and which she and Macdonald achieved in the first production, is one that pushes the play out into the shared psychic site of the theatre itself. The refusal to resolve apparently contradictory modes of narratives, formal logics and theatrical styles in *Cleansed* makes for an experience which Turner and Behrndt identify as one of 'complete undecideability, while the possibility of interplay and exchange is as much a source of terror as it is a source of energy or solace'.[99] Turner and Behrndt have argued in relation to *4.48 Psychosis* and *Crave* that 'the openness of Kane's dramaturgy means that these plays – more than most – are only completed by the decisions made in the performance-making process'.[100] Given the literal impossibility of many of Kane's stage directions in her first three plays, it is evident that in order to transition from playtext to production a number of production decisions must be made which alter the theatrical work itself.

Nevertheless to understand this process as 'complet[ing]', and resolving the 'openness' of the works – as Turner and Behrndt do and as Mitchell stated she did earlier – imposes a notion of final signification and reduction which Kane herself was highly resistant to.[101] Evans describes how Kane insisted that each line, action and image in the playtext was open to several meanings, and that this multiplicity of meanings was to be (impossibly) preserved:

> I remember distinctly the day we were discussing something, and it was to do with Stuart McQuarrie who was playing Tinker. There's one word – just 'no'. We went around and discovered five different possible meanings for it, so we turned to the playwright and said, 'which one?' And she said, 'all of them, play them all'. Which of course is impossible, but you just leave it open.[102]

In linking this irresolution to mental pathology through a comparison with the processes of psychotic thinking, I do not intend to introduce a theoretical structure with which to 'close' this openness. Rather, I wish to suggest that in *Cleansed* irresolution is a valid mental experience itself, and not a sign of unfinished business. The challenge to maintain this painful irresolution is issued not least to anyone attempting to stage the play, as theatre-makers must grapple with the physical impossibilities of the playtext as well as the narrative, storytelling challenges that the dramaturgy poses.

This very irresolution in *Cleansed*, which is sustained throughout Kane's later works, might also be read as issuing a wider challenge to the reductive conceptions of mental life encountered both in the medical discourses discussed by Woods and in today's neoliberal society more largely. That an experience may be heavily imbued with 'unreal' content, highly painful, unresolved and yet still 'true' is in itself a radical claim. Whilst Kane's dramaturgy may be variously 'completed' by different theatrical productions, the irresolution of the playtext nevertheless leaves it open to constant reinterpretation, and its visions of supposedly pathological mental states still have the potential to disturb assumptions about contemporary subjectivity over two decades after her death.

## Notes

1  Kane identifies Strindberg's *The Ghost Sonata* as one of main influences for *Cleansed*, notes the importance of Artaud in her late works in Nils Talbert, 'Interview with Sarah Kane', in *Playspotting: Die Londoner Theatreszene der 90er*, ed. Nils Talbert (Reinbeck, IA: Rowohlt Taschenbuch Verla, 1998), English transcript kindly made available by in Graham Saunders. For the influence of Strindberg on *Cleansed*, see Mateuz Borowski, 'Under the Surface of Things: Sarah Kane's *Skin* and the Medium of the Theatre', in *Sarah Kane in Context*, ed. Graham Saunders and Laurens De Vos

(Manchester: Manchester University Press, 2010) and Louise Lepage, 'Rethinking Sarah Kane's Characters: A Human(ist) Form and Politics', *Modern Drama* 57 (2014): 252–72.
2   Talbert, 'Interview with Sarah Kane', 5.
3   Ibid.
4   Craigie, correspondence.
5   Ibid.
6   James Christopher, 'Her First Play was About Defecation, Cannibalism and Fellatio. The New One's About Love.' *The Observer*, 2 November 1997.
7   Saunders, *About Kane*, 42.
8   Borowski, 'Under the Surface'.
9   Ibid., 188–9.
10  Rebellato, *Brief Encounter with Sarah Kane*.
11  Talbert, 'Interview with Sarah Kane', 6.
12  Heidi Stephenson and Natasha Langridge, *Rage and Reason: Women Playwrights on Playwriting* (London: Methuen, 1997), 134.
13  Angela Woods, *The Sublime Object of Psychiatry: Schizophrenia in Clinical and Cultural Theory* (Oxford: Oxford University Press, 2011), 55.
14  Ibid., 54.
15  Ibid., 63.
16  Ibid., 28.
17  Ibid., 51.
18  Sigmund Freud, 'On Narcissism', in *The Standard Edition of the Complete Psychological Works of Sigmund Freud, Volume XIV (1914–1916): On the History of the Psycho-analytic Movement, Papers on Metapsychology and other works*, trans. James Strachey (London: Hogarth Press, 1957–66), 74.
19  Sigmund Freud, 'The Loss of Reality in Neurosis and Psychosis', in *The Standard Edition of the Complete Psychological Works of Sigmund Freud, Volume XIX (1923–1925): The Ego and the Id and Other Works*, trans. James Strachey (London: Hogarth Press, 1961), 184.
20  Ibid.
21  Ibid., 185.
22  Freud, 'On Narcissism', 75.
23  Freud links this regression to primary narcissism to paranoia initially in the Schreber case. Here a repressed libidinal impulse, somewhere between narcissism and homosexuality, is projected outwards into a hallucinated, all-powerful persecutory figure. See 'Psychoanalytic Notes on an Autobiographical Account of a Case of Paranoia (Dementia Paranoides) (Schreber)', in *The Standard Edition of the Complete Psychological Works of Sigmund Freud, Volume XII (1911–1913): The Case of Schreber, Papers on Technique and Other Works*, trans. James Strachey (London: The Hogarth Press and the Institute of Psycho-Analysis, 1958), 3–84. Freud's contemporary Victor Tausk built on this idea considerably, arguing that the often-mechanized persecutory figure in paranoia is a projection of

'the patient's body onto the outside world.' Tausk, 'On the Origin of the Influencing Machine in Schizophrenia', *Journal of Psychotherapy Research and Practice*, trans. Dorian Feigenbaum 1, no. 2 (1992): 192.

24 Woods, *The Sublime Object of Psychiatry*, 57.
25 In his reflections on the Schreber case, Freud highlights the difficulty of observing cases of psychosis for psychoanalysts like himself who are not attached to an asylum. Most of Freud observations on psychosis were therefore derived from written accounts such as Schreber's, or as in *On Narcissism* from neurotic patients with some psychotic symptoms. Freud, 'Schreber', 138.
26 Saunders, *Love Me*, 112.
27 Gregorio Kohon, *The British School of Psychoanalysis: The Independent Tradition* (London: Free Association Books, 1986), 21. Kohon emphasizes that whilst the British Psychoanalytic Society did split, and the Independent Group (of which Winnicott was eventually part) diverged from Klein's work, both Kleinian and Independent psychoanalysts agree on the basic idea that the infant always relates to objects. This idea, which the Independent Group would call the theory of object relations, suggests that 'it is not only to the [infant's] real relationship with others that determines the subject's individual life, but the specific way in which the subject apprehends his relationships with his objects (both internal and external). It always implies an unconscious relationship to these objects'. Kohon, *The British School of Psychoanalysis*, 20. What Klein, Winnicott and the thinkers discussed in the rest of this section share is an apprehension of internal life as containing multiplicity – constituted by a network of both internal and external objects which mediate the individual's relationship with alterity.
28 Melanie Klein, 'Notes on Some Schizoid Mechanisms', in *The Selected Melanie Klein*, ed. Juliet Mitchell (London: Penguin, 1990), 180, emphasis added.
29 Ibid., 79.
30 Although it does bear some resemblance to Schreber's own description of his psychotic experience, as reported by Freud. Nevertheless, Freud understands Schreber's projections of himself into the world and consequent apocalypticism as a consequence of his libidinal withdrawal and regression to a state of primary narcissism: 'his subjective worlds has come to an end once the withdrawal of his love from it.' Freud, 'Schreber', 208. Whilst Freud sees this immersion as a consequence of libidinal withdrawal Rosenfeld seems to understand it as the primary affect of psychosis, and positions withdrawal as a secondary consequence.
31 Christopher Bollas, *The Shadow of the Object: Psychoanalysis of the Unthought Known* (London: Free Association Books, 1987), 3.
32 Ibid., 9.
33 For Bollas's interventions into early-stage schizophrenias and adaptations of the psychoanalytic method, see Christopher Bollas, *Catch Them Before They Fall: The Psychoanalysis of Breakdown* (London: Routledge, 2013).

34 Christopher Bollas, *When the Sun Bursts: The Enigma of Schizophrenia* (New Haven, CT; London: Yale University Press, 2016), 183, emphasis original.
35 Bollas, *The Shadow of the Object*, 13.
36 Saunders, *Love Me*, 94.
37 For a closer examination of Büchner and Strindberg's influences on Kane, see Borowski, 'Under the Surface'; Lepage, 'Rethinking Sarah Kane's Characters', 252–72, and Wallace, 'Sarah Kane, Experiential Theatre and the Revenant Avant-Garde'.
38 Sarah Kane, 'Cleansed', in *Sarah Kane: Complete Plays* (London: Methuen Drama, 2001), 110.
39 Ibid., 118.
40 See chapter five of George Orwell, *1984* (London: Penguin, 1949).
41 Susanna Clapp, 'Kane's New Play is a Howl of Horror with the Sensibility of a Damien Hirst', *Observer*, 10 May 1998, in *Theatre Record* 18, no. 9 (1998): 566.
42 Hilary Chute, '"Victim, Perpetrator, Bystander": Critical Distance in Sarah Kane's Theatre of Cruelty', in *Sarah Kane in Context*, ed. Graham Saunders and Laurens De Vos (Manchester: Manchester University Press, 2010), 164.
43 Ibid.
44 Terry Braun, 'Another Angle on Smack City', *Sunday Business: Life Section*, 10 May 1998.
45 Illtyd Harrington, 'Cleansed – Royal Court', *Camden New Journal*, 14 May 1998.
46 Ibid.
47 Clare Allfree, 'Sarah Kane's Pageant of Torture Tests the Furthest Boundaries of Love', *The Telegraph*, 24 February 2016. Available online: http://www.telegraph.co.uk/theatre/what-to-see/sarah-kanes-cleansed-tests-the-furthest-boundaries-of-love/ (accessed 17 February 2017), see also Matt Trueman, '*Cleansed* is more than just shock theatre', *What's On Stage*, 29 February 2016. Available online: http://www.whatsonstage.com/london-theatre/news/matt-trueman-cleansed-sarah-kane-national_39853.html (accessed 1 January 2017).
48 David Benedict, 'Real Live Horror Show', *Independent*, 9 May 1998; Jon Peter, 'Short Stark Shock', *Sunday Times*, 10 May 1998.
49 Peter, 'Short Stark Shock', 1998.
50 Bollas, *Catch Them Before They Fall*.
51 Bollas, *When the Sun Bursts*, 178.
52 Ibid., 178–9.
53 Rebellato, *Brief Encounter with Sarah Kane*.
54 Ibid.
55 Ibid. Image of the diagram is available online: http://www.danrebellato.co.uk/sarah-kane-interview/ (accessed 24 January 2020).
56 Ibid.

57 Jakob Hohwy, *The Predictive Mind* (Oxford: Oxford University Press, 2013), 1.
58 Ibid., 1, 7.
59 Paul Fletcher and Chris D. Frith, 'Perceiving is Believing: A Bayesian Approach to Explaining the Positive Symptoms of Schizophrenia', *Nature Reviews Neuroscience* 10, no. 1 (2009): 48–58, 56.
60 Ibid.
61 Esmé Weijun Wang, *The Collected Schizophrenias* (London: Penguin 2019), 127.
62 Ibid.
63 Ibid., 126.
64 Catherine Malabou, *The New Wounded: From Neurosis to Brain Damage* (New York: Fordham University Press, 2012).
65 Ibid., 42, original emphasis.
66 Ibid., 10 for Malabou's inclusion of schizophrenia in the category of the 'new wounded'.
67 Ibid., 59.
68 Ibid., 80.
69 Lisa Blackman's work with the Hearing Voices Network has highlighted the roles of abuse and trauma in shaping the content of auditory hallucinations. See Lisa Blackman, 'The Challenges of New Biopsychosocialities: Hearing Voices, Trauma, Epigenetics and Mediated Perception', *The Sociological Review Monograph* 64, no. 1 (2016): 256–73.
70 Hohwy uses the example of binocular rivalry to demonstrate how the confusion of predictive capacities can be simulated in an artificial, experimental setting. Hohwy, *The Predictive Mind*, 20.
71 Kane, 'Cleansed', 120.
72 Joe Penhall, *Blue/Orange* (London: Metheun Drama, 2000), 97.
73 Katie Mitchell, 'Katie Mitchell Platform', public interview with Katie Mitchell, National Theatre, London, 2 March 2016.
74 Ibid.
75 Ibid.
76 Ibid.
77 Ibid.
78 Katie Mitchell, *The Director's Craft* (London: Taylor and Francis, 2008), 51.
79 Ibid., 50.
80 Kane, 'Cleansed', 133.
81 Mitchell, *Director's Craft*, 50.
82 Mitchell, 'Platform'.
83 For Katie Mitchell's *auteur* status see for example Dan Rebellato's essay 'Katie Mitchell, Learning from Europe', in *Contemporary European Theatre Directors*, ed. Maria M. Delgado and Dan Rebellato (Abingdon, VA: Routledge, 2010).

84 James Macdonald interview with Matt Trueman, 'I'm Drawn to Plays I Don't Know How to Do', *Independent*, 19 January 2016.
85 See, for example, Susanna Clapp, '*Cleansed* Review – The First Cut was the Deepest', *Observer*, 28 February 2016; Sarah Hemming, *Financial Times*, 13 February 2016; Jess Denham, *Independent*, 24 February 2016; Michael Billington, *Guardian*, 14 February 2016; Holly Williams, *I*, 25 February 2016.
86 *Front Row*, BBC Radio 4, 2 February 2016, 7:15pm. Available online: http://www.bbc.co.uk/programmes/b071fyq9 (accessed 20 April 2016).
87 Christopher, 'Her First Play Was About Defecation, Cannibalism, and Fellatio'.
88 Clapp, '*Cleansed* Review'.
89 Records in the Royal Court Theatre Archive show that the set of the 1998 production exceeded the budget for any London West End theatre production that preceded it. See Katie Mitchell, 'Platform' for the set restrictions resulting from the 2016 production budget.
90 Saunders, *Love Me*, 172.
91 Ibid., 169.
92 Ibid., 172.
93 Roland Barthes, *A Lover's Discourse: Fragments*, trans. Richard Howard (London: Vintage, 2002), 49.
94 Sierz, *In-Yer-Face Theatre*, 116.
95 David Nathan, *Jewish Chronicle*, 15 May 1998, in *Theatre Record* 18, no. 9 (1998): 568.
96 Bollas, *When the Sun Bursts*, 139.
97 Kane, 'Cleansed', 132.
98 Ibid., 134–5.
99 Turner and Behrndt, *Dramaturgy and Performance*, 29.
100 Ibid., 30.
101 Ibid.
102 Saunders, *Love Me*, 169.

# 4

# The mind-as-site

## (Un)Redemptive reading

The relationship between the openness of the form of *4.48 Psychosis*; the play's claim to 'experientially' represent psychotic, suicidal depression; and Kane's own suicide make it a particularly difficult play to write about in relation to mental pathology. The idea that the play has something to say about the experience of psychotic depression itself, with its obvious corollary that this knowledge comes *in some way* from the author's experience, leans close to the claim that *4.48 Psychosis* is an account of Kane's own mental suffering and is thus 'nothing but' a '75-minute suicide note'.[1] The dilemma of where to place Kane's death in relation to her work haunts approaches to this play, as the play both very clearly is and is not a representation of her suicidal state. As her agent Mel Keyon suggested at the time of the first production, the play provokes a profound ambivalence in relation to Kane's suicide: 'I pretend that [*4:48 Psychosis*] isn't a suicide note but it is. It is both a suicide note and something much greater than that.'[2] Both Kenyon and director James Macdonald, who directed the play's posthumous debut, note the intertwining of Kane's personal experience and theatrical innovation in a way that has been treated with wariness by critics. James Macdonald reflects simply, 'I think she set out to described her 'illness' experientially – to find a theatrical form which would mirror this experience.'[3] This comment reflects the argument I have been making throughout this book, that Kane's works all, to some extent, invite their audiences into a version of interior life. Reactions to this dilemma regarding *4.48 Psychosis* from journalists, theatre-makers and critics have tended to produce readings of the play which fall along one of two axes: either the play is emphatically *not* about Kane's experience (and is instead about the breakdown of form/ the demise of humanism/ the death of God, etc.), or the play *is* about Kane's final days and as such is a 'positively heroic' communication from the other side (or, in the case of a few commentators, simply transcribed symptom).[4]

Responses to the work on both sides of the biographical dispute participate in what Leo Bersani identifies as 'the culture of redemption'. This is a

> critical assumption [. . .] that a certain type of repetition of experience in art *repairs inherently damaged or valueless experience*. Experience may be overwhelming, practically impossible to absorb, but it is assumed [. . .] that the work of art has the authority to master the presumed raw material of experience in a manner that uniquely gives value to, perhaps even redeems, that material.[5]

This approach is clearly visible in commentaries such as those by fellow playwrights Edward Bond and David Greig which raise Kane to a prophet-like status. Greig comments that:

> *4.48 Psychosis* is a report from a region of the mind that most of us hope never to visit but from which many people cannot escape. Those trapped there are normally rendered voiceless by their condition. That the play was written whilst suffering from depression, was an act of generosity from the author. That the play is artistically successful is positively heroic.[6]

In his elegiac afterward to Graham Saunders's book, Bond takes these claims a step further. Here he frames Kane's suicide and her theatre as a prophetic indictment of the ills of the twentieth century:

> The confrontation with the implacable created [Sarah Kane's] plays. Did she – the dramatist in her – know she might not be able to go on confronting it in her plays? Our economy and theatre are against it. [. . .] If she thought perhaps the confrontation could not take place in our theatre, because it is losing the understanding and the means – she could not risk waiting. Instead she staged it elsewhere. Her means to confront the implacable are death, a lavatory, and shoelaces.[7]

Highly reminiscent of Artaud's 1947 essay 'Van Gogh, the Man Suicided by Society', Bond's elision of Kane's death and her art is at once grandiose, crude and extreme. However it also reveals, by virtue of its extremity, a tendency which runs through much Kane criticism. For both Greig and Bond, the suffering in the work is redeemed by virtue of its communication, an act that transforms it into form of generous sharing. This response is perhaps the most straightforward when it comes to addressing the fundamental question which confronts us when reading or viewing *4.48 Psychosis*: What to do with

Kane's suffering, and what to do with the suffering the play presents us with? Bond and Greig respond to this suffering directly by redeeming it, which at least allows it to remain central to the play's concerns.

However, this redemption can also function as a critical blindness to the staging of certain forms of pain. In a play so imbued with expressions of pain, and so unwilling to provide its audience formal guidance as to how this suffering ought to be interpreted, it is perhaps unsurprising that many critical approaches have sought to eliminate it completely from their critical framework. Analyses by Antje Deidrich and Ian Marsh have focused eloquently on the intertextual use of medical texts in the play, arguing that *4.48 Psychosis* functions as a discursive critique of diagnostic psychiatry. I have already drawn briefly on these analyses in Chapter 1 and will return to them herein. Both analyses valuably situate Kane's work in the context of a changing mental health landscape in the UK, and suggest the authorial position as one of detached, informed critique. In doing so they follow Graham Saunders's argument that the play finds its structure and meaning 'through the division of the play into a series of *discourses*'.[8] However, the idea that one might be able to both be an informed observer and a sufferer seems to be absent from their argument. Here, as elsewhere, is the sense that in order to confer value onto the artwork, one must distance it from the pain it represented.

Other works have sought to address the suffering expressed in *4.48 Psychosis* as responding to ontological crises. Sean Carney, Erhen Fordyce and Juliet Waddington highlight that the disintegration of this mind responds to a wider crisis as to the nature of the subject. Carney identifies this crisis as the universalizing of a search for metaphysical love, in a Godless dramatic universe; Waddington as a conflict between humanist and Cartesian experiences of subjectivity; and Fordyce as a conflict between the imperative to re-present the violence of the world and violence identified in the authorial position itself.[9] Whilst Waddington does state that the disintegration of the subject of *4.48 Psychosis* 'resembles psychosis', these criticisms nonetheless all shy away from addressing the psychotic nature of the subject(s) at the centre of the play. Like discourse, ontology becomes a means of separating the work, and specifically its author, from the muddy waters of personal suffering. The work is placed seemingly outside of (we might say 'above') biographical concerns, and gains validity through its relationship to philosophy.

Redemptive readings therefore promote a critical hierarchy, in which the representation of mental suffering, if acknowledged at all, is subordinate to the play's 'intellectual' interventions, into medical discourses, philosophy or aesthetics. Throughout her career, Kane's works become increasingly characterized by dramaturgical indeterminacy. Several critics have written about this indeterminacy in relation to the aesthetics of *4.48 Psychosis*. David Barnett, Ken Urban, Eckhart Voigts-Virchow and Mathew Roberts all view the play as eschewing the representative function of dramatic theatre in favour of either non-representative textual collage (Urban) or postdramatic, non-mimetic 'presentation' (Barnett and Roberts).[10] Focusing on the play's textual indeterminacy from a different perspective, Christina Delgado-Garcia has argued that in *Crave* and *4.48 Psychosis* Kane moves from having staged a critique of liberal-humanist subjects to eschewing the staging of subjects altogether.[11] However, as approaches which read the play *purely* in terms of aesthetic innovation they also clearly participate in this kind of supposed elevation. These approaches share a conviction, first, that the play's success lies in its non-representational textual indeterminacy, and second, that this indeterminacy (and therefore the play's innovativeness and power) is undermined in the conditions of performance, in which it must necessarily become embodied (Delgado-Garcia) and risks being transformed into 'drama' (Barnett). For this strain of criticism, *4.48 Psychosis* is a work which *uses* the challenge of representing pain for aesthetic/philosophical ends, (barely) thematizing suffering on the pathway to artistic innovation. Despite their variety, these criticisms all participate in the kind of redemptive practice which Bersani identifies, whereby the artwork is seen as *repairing* valueless (painful, psychotic) experience through its repetition in a higher register. Such criticism 'erases, repeats and redeems' the 'damaged' experience at the centre of *4.48 Psychosis* precisely by declining to address the nature of this experience itself – that is to say its painful content and its materiality.[12]

Restoring the question of representing mental pain to the centre of a reading of Kane's works allows for the articulation of the demands Kane's dramaturgy makes on its audience, and addresses the consequences of her radical conflation of theatrical and psychic space. The suggestion that Kane's play might 'just' be a representation of psychotic and suicidal suffering, valid, informed, somehow linked to 'life', and artistically proficient should not be critically intolerable. *4.48 Psychosis* presents a form of suffering that does not seek to be redeemed from the outside, but rather invites its audience to participate in its material presence. This is not to say that the subject(s) of *4.48 Psychosis* do not want to be cured or released from suffering, or that the play is an anti-psychiatric glorification of psychosis. Rather, it suggests that *4.48 Psychosis* aims at creating new formal potentials for understanding the experience of psychosis, in a manner that is not uniquely oriented towards cure. In the final two chapters of this book, I propose that Kane's theatre offers her audience an unredemptive mode of sharing, oriented towards coexistence rather than cure, with a history and with a consistently fraught relationship with 'life'. These relationships remain deliberately open: to paraphrase Bersani we never know if the play voices Kane's suffering, the speaker(s) suffering or abstracted suffering derived from ideals by the speaker(s). The following analysis of Kane's dramaturgy does not aim to close any of these down, but to explore what kind of alternative mode of engagement with mental pain we might find in Kane's work, through the articulation of a form of knowing rooted in the materiality of theatre.

This chapter suggests that Kane's final two works push the relationship between theatrical site and psychic life to its limits, a relationship that she had been troubling since she turned from writing monologues to creating the 'experiential form' of *Blasted*. As I discussed in Chapter 1, Western philosophy and theatre criticism have long maintained some level of equivalence between theatre, or specifically drama, and the representation of some form of mental experience. Freud most famously used *Oedipus Rex* as the prototypical structure for his mapping of the human psyche, using not just the representation of a hero, but of a dramatically generated structure of relations and site (a dramaturgy, perhaps). Freud's Oedipal subject is not simply analogous to King Oedipus but is constituted by the set of theatrical relations described in Sophocles's tragedy. Kane literalizes this relationship in *Crave* and *4.48 Psychosis* attempting not only to convey a sense of certain affects generated by mental pain but to actually represent the experience of mental suffering for the audience through the space of the stage itself.

## The ceiling of a mind

The playtext of *4.48 Psychosis* calls for a spatial encounter with mental suffering. The playtext begins and ends with an evocation of the mind experienced as a cavernous site. *4.48 Psychosis* opens with a frustrated attempt by a medicalized voice to have its interlocutor provide a transactional account of themselves, asking repeatedly, 'What do you offer your friends to make them so supportive?' only to encounter a series of '*long silence*(s)' in response.[13] Following this initial, failed attempt to engage the interlocutor on its own transactional/behaviourist terms, the medicalized voice disappears and is replaced by a highly poetic register, which provides an account of its experience of mind that is at once plural, unstable and spatial:

> A consolidated consciousness resides in a darkened banqueting hall near the ceiling of a mind whose floor shifts as ten thousand cockroaches

when a shaft of light enters as all thoughts unite in an instant of accord body no longer expellant as the cockroaches comprise a truth which no one ever utters.[14]

This dense opening image and its contrast with the preceding failed dialogue largely encapsulate the thematic and formal concerns that will unfold throughout the rest of Kane's short final play.

Throughout the playtext of *4.48 Psychosis* and especially throughout many productions, a constant tension is generated between the subject(s) experience of themselves as plural and spatial, and an imperative to have the subject(s) enter into a behaviourist, transactional form of discursive exchange in which this experience is actively denied. The description of the 'consolidated consciousness' which opens the play immediately establishes the mental experience which it evokes in a paradox – this consciousness is at once singular and plural, both '*a* [. . .] consciousness' and something consolidated, assembled out of a variety of pieces that are held together. The extent to which such a consolidation can be considered successful is thrown into question in the multitude of images which follow in quick succession – the banqueting hall, the ceiling of the mind, the cockroaches, the shaft of light, the body, the impossibility of speech – images which will return repeatedly throughout the play. This complex opening series of images also contains a suggestion of a mode of engaging with this apparent cacophony. Consciousness 'resides in a darkened banqueting hall near the ceiling of a mind whose floor shifts', generating an unstable site reminiscent of the skull cavity in which multitudes, 'ten thousand cockroaches', are allowed to circulate. A few lines later the consciousness experiences itself once again in a contained site in which the presence of plurality is both a pleasure and a torment: 'the broken hermaphrodite who trusted hermself alone finds the room in reality teeming and begs never to wake from the nightmare'.[15]

Through these images, the opening of *4.48 Psychosis* offers two alternative ways of encountering mental suffering and isolation: the first, encapsulated in the repeated question, 'What do you offer?' asks the subject(s) to re-present a (palatable) version of themselves to the outside world, as the basis for understanding and intimacy. The second, evoked in the images of the banqueting hall, the mind's ceiling and the teeming room, emerges out of the notion of *residing*. The first act of self-expression by the suffering consciousness in the play thus evokes the experience of *entering-into* and *living-in* an unstable site. The dramaturgy of the play takes this loose assemblage of mental experience as its starting point, suggesting a dramatic site in which language, sound, image and bodies circulate and coexist without ever resolving themselves into a truly consolidated singular consciousness.

The audience is invited to reside within this dramaturgy for seventy-five minutes and is faced with a choice between painful coexistence with or imposed resolution of the mental suffering held therein.

*4.48 Psychosis* represents psychotic suffering as a painful disintegration of spatial boundaries. Kane identified the evocation and disintegration of a bounded space as key to her representation of psychotic breakdown, as we have already seen in Chapter 3:

> I'm writing a play called *4:48 Psychosis* [. . .] It's about a psychotic breakdown and what happens in a person's mind when the barriers which distinguish between reality and different forms of imagination completely disappear [. . .] you no longer know where you stop and the world starts.[16]

The image of the mind as cavernous site returns throughout the play, through references to the mind's 'ceiling', the floor of cockroaches and the repeated phrase 'hatch opens/stark light'. In each instance it troubles the demands for self-representation in a dyadic relationship voiced in the opening questions.

After having undergone a litany of chemical treatments which form the central scene of the play, the image of the mind-as-site returns with greater complexity, reviving the images of the first description. Here however, the mind-as-site has obtained a dangerously porous quality. The scene begins, 'Hatch opens/stark light', and this suggested spatial opening is followed by an influx of anxiety relating both to the plurality experienced within the mind, and its lack of boundaries.[17] Having previously deplored the constant medical gaze to which it has been exposed ('A room full of expressionless faces staring blankly at my pain, so devoid of meaning there must be evil intent'),[18] the image of tormenting spectators returns as both within and outside of the mind:

the television talks
full of eyes
the spirits of sight
       and now I am so afraid
I'm seeing things
I'm hearing things
I don't know who I am.[19]

Both spectator and spectated, speaker and listener, are assimilated in the site suggested in this scene. The 'I' states that it is seeing things, and both the 'I' and that which it views are 'full of eyes'. Unable to create a clear division between viewed object and viewing subject, the 'I' is thrown into a spatio-temporal crisis:

Where do I start?
Where do I stop?
How do I start?
(As I mean to go on)
How do I stop?
How do I stop?
How do I stop?
How do I stop?
How do I stop?
How do I stop?
How do I stop?
How do I stop?[20]

The repeated question, 'How do I stop?' contains both a temporal question, ironically denied in its own repetition, and a spatial one. The 'I' literally asks how it might 'stop', how it may be bounded in space. For Kane this spatial fluidity is at the heart of psychotic suffering, and one which she attempts to embody dramaturgically, 'making form and content one'.[21]

The experience presented here of losing a bounded sense of self into a porous environment is an important feature of psychoanalytic accounts of psychotic suffering. In this scene, and throughout *4.48 Psychosis*, representation of disintegrated spatial boundaries is achieved through attention to the disturbance of the speaker's gaze in attempts at self-representation. The disruptions in the speaker's gaze throw the unity of the 'I' into question. When spectator and spectated are assimilated, the question, 'Where do I stop?' becomes imperative. Christopher Bollas identifies the breakdown of the 'I' and its spreading into the environment as the major process in psychotic breakdowns:

> In schizophrenic breakdown the integrity of the I is fragmented and projected into the environment for safekeeping. The pronominal present may remain in a superficial way, but much else is lost.[22]

For Bollas it is the consistency of the 'I' in self-representation which allows non-psychotic people to retain a sense of separateness from the world around them: 'The I is crucial. The act of speaking for oneself sustains the essential illusion of a continuous perspectival authority.'[23] In *4.48 Psychosis* Kane deliberately stages the breakdown of such a 'continuous perspectival authority', staging (or voicing) the breakdown of the speaker's ability to perceive from a single viewpoint.

Simultaneously, the play represents an experience of selfhood which has been expanded into the surrounding environment. Near the end of this short scene the speaker(s) returns to the image of mind-as-site. These painful expressions of self-disintegration are summarized as 'a dismal whistle that is the cry of heartbreak around the hellish bowl at the ceiling of my mind'.[24] Evocative of the image of the wind whistling through a drafty interior, the image of the cavernous mind no longer provides the containment that it did in its initial incarnation. Instead, the 'dismal whistle' describes the experience of unpleasant sounds circulating through a porous space, drawing attention to the relationship between sound and site that has been played out in the repetitiveness and visual invocations throughout this scene. The audience are invited to notice and reside within a spatiality that is increasingly unstable, whose bounded-ness cannot be relied upon.

The dramaturgy suggested by the playtext of *4.48 Psychosis* establishes an unstable spatial encounter for its potential audience, which is analogous to the one described in the scene addressed earlier. Kane achieves this spatiality by placing the audience's gaze at a point which allows them to participate in the specular splitting and collapse enacted by the psychotic subject(s) on stage. Throughout the play, the potential audience encounter contradictory imperatives with regard to their own spectatorship. At the same time, they must attempt to follow the trajectory of an 'I' for whom self-representation is almost impossible, and self-spectatorship is considered a torment. As in the incorporation of the 'television[. . .]/ full of eyes' into the subject's own specular identity, the speaker(s)'s attempts at self-spectatorship are invariably described in terms of failure or of the collapse of the spectator/spectated positions.

These collapses are preceded, followed by or concurrent with challenges to the audiences' positions as spectators which might lead the audience into a contemplation of their own spectating practice, or provoke a crisis in the audience member who does not know *where to look*. Throughout the more 'medical' sections of the play, the speaker(s) continually solicits and refuses the gaze of both doctor/therapist and audience member. The medical situation is first described in a line that could just as easily be an address to the audience: 'A room of expressionless faces so devoid of meaning there must be evil intent.'[25] The spectator's gaze is once again vilified a few lines later, this time specifically referring to the gaze of 'Dr This and Dr That and Dr Whatsit':

Watching me, judging me, smelling the crippling failure oozing from my skin, my desperation clawing and all-consuming panic drenching me as I gape in horror at the world and wonder why everyone is smiling and looking at me with secret knowledge of my aching shame.[26]

Having perhaps somewhat comically (depending on the delivery) interpolated the audience into the position of watching doctor in the first instance, the play now implicates the audience in the gaze that is actively causing the onstage subject pain.

This has the potential to push the spectator into a position of visual and ethical uncertainty. This uncertainty is again compounded when moments later the speaker yearns for a remembered positive visual encounter, with 'the only doctor who ever touched me voluntarily, who looked me in the eye, [. . .] who lied and said it was nice to see me.'[27] Certain forms of looking are mocked, rejected and solicited within the space of a few moments, as if inviting the audience to cast their eyes around for a place where it is permissible for them to rest.

The playtext of *4.48 Psychosis* therefore implicates its potential audience into the speaker(s)'s ethical-specular crisis. As the play continues, the pressure on the audience's gaze is increased, as acts of looking towards and looking away are directly implicated in the suffering of the onstage subject(s). The speaker(s) on stage both desires and refuses the gaze of their audience with increasing urgency. The act of symbolization required to represent oneself as a bounded subject, to oneself and to an audience, becomes impossible for the speaker(s) in the second half of the play. As the speaker(s) laments: 'Every act is a symbol/ the weight of which crushes me.'[28]

In response to the crushing nature of the imperative to hold oneself together and represent oneself to the outside, the speaker(s) changes tack in the following scene, multiplying and spreading the boundaries of the 'I' to take responsibility for a litany of global atrocities and personal wrongs:

> I gassed the Jews, I killed the Kurds, I bombed the Arabs, I fucked small children when they begged for mercy, everyone left the party because of me, I'll suck your fucking eyes out and send them to your mother in a box and when I die I'm going to be reincarnated as your child only fifty times worse and mad as fuck and make your life a living fucking hell I REFUSE I REFUSE LOOK AWAY FROM ME.[29]

As several commentators have pointed out, the outburst seems to represent an example of psychotic responsibility, an experience common to schizophrenia whereby the psychotic subject takes on responsibility for often global wrongs they cannot possibly have committed.[30] However, *4.48 Psychosis* builds on the idea of psychotic responsibility here in order to implicate its audience.

This scene presents a consistent 'I' to the audience, one with which they may choose to identify with as a character. This 'I' is in crisis, expanding to occupy roles of perpetrators of terrible crimes. At the same time, the emotional intensity and unpalatability of this expansion pushes the audience away. By the time the speaker(s) asks the audience to 'LOOK AWAY FROM ME', the elision between the 'I' and atrocity has already made the identification, and the gaze, almost impossible to sustain. By expanding of the notion of 'I' into universal perpetrator, Kane provokes the refusal of the audience's gaze even before it is demanded. Faced with the pressure of being looked at, the only form of self-symbolization the 'I' can achieve is one that is radically open, which causes it to merge with perpetrators of atrocity.

This short scene invites its audience to participate in the specular crisis of the 'I', meta-theatrically collapsing the positions of spectator and spectated. The openness of the outburst can be read both as a psychotic symptom and an ethical claim. Indeed, Bollas has suggested that encountering persons with psychotic responsibility can be profoundly disturbing to a non-psychotic person's sense of responsibility and normality. Bollas describes working with schizophrenic children in the late 1960s, during which time 'many of [the] students thought they had killed King and Kennedy'.[31] Bollas and his colleagues noticed the extent to which the claims of their students nonetheless reflected their own anxieties as to the social responsibility they had for the political situation: 'Had we, indeed, murdered our leaders? How could we have stopped these murders from happening?'[32] For Bollas working with schizophrenic patients, especially those who experience a form of psychotic responsibility, is difficult because they undermine the 'capacity for denial' which non-psychotic people exercise in order to continue living in a violent world:

> They [the students] would interrogate the clinicians about the illusions that comforted us and allowed us to live in a bearable world, and as we engaged in our in-depth conversation with them we would have to bear the erosion of the illusory in their own lives. To work with a psychotic person over a long period is distressing, not so much because of their psychosis, but because of how they deconstruct the defences crucial to our own peace of mind.[33]

Finally representing 'hermself' to the audience as a repeated and sustained 'I', the speaker(s) in *4.48 Psychosis* does so in a context which invites the audience into an identification which would take on a wide-ranging ethical responsibility for atrocity. In doing so it invites distressing questions of individual and group responsibility for acts and war crimes perpetrated by the audiences' own governments.

Such an identification, as Bollas suggests, is very difficult to sustain. By the time the speaker in *4.48 Psychosis* refuses the audience's gaze, and the position of responsibility which comes with it, the audience has already been put into an almost impossible situation. This scene therefore acts on its potential spectators in two seemingly contradictory ways. On the one hand it suggests that the pressure of self-representation – the pressure of the spectator's gaze – is provoking suffering in the speaker by pushing it into an unsustainable position of universal responsibility and leads the speaker to emphatically reject the position of being looked at. On the other, it solicits the spectator to join in a difficult, perhaps unsustainable, identification with a radically open subjectivity. In this perspective, the voice arrives at the demand for refusal at the same time as the spectator, and both turn away from a form of ethical responsibility which they cannot bear. The scene's potential audience is thus both asked to interrogate their own viewing practice *and* invited to *reside within* an unsustainable identification.

This short scene can be read as a highly succinct condensation of the technique of both eliciting and refusing identification which Kane had already developed in the dramaturgy of *Blasted*, and which I have outlined in Chapter 2.[34] Whereas in Kane's first play this technique was developed through the contrast between anti-hero and dramaturgy, here it is collapsed into an intense dramaturgical interrogation of the spectator's position in relation to the staged subject. The phrase 'look away from me' is repeated another four times from this point. Ariel Watson argues that this rejection of the audience's gaze, and of the gaze of the doctor-figure, represents a rebellion against the spectatorship implicit in psychiatric treatment: 'The weight of the spectatorial gaze (the gaze of medical analysis, of the refracted self-examination of depression, and of the theatrical audience), [. . .] is too much at times, yielding some of the fiercest rejections of the theatricality of treatment.'[35] Whilst Watson's argument is enlightening in terms of her examination of the theatricality of medical and psychiatric encounters, it does not make room for the apparently contradictory imperatives imposed on the audience with regard to looking.

After having refused the spectator's gaze in the middle of the play, *4:48 Psychosis* also repeatedly addresses its spectator to demand a witness to its disintegration. The play ends with a plea to be looked at, and the implication that the subject's salvation is only possible through audience's gaze:

I have no desire for death
no suicide ever had
watch me vanish
watch me
        vanish

watch me
watch me
watch.³⁶

The question of whether to look at or look away is implicated in the suffering of the staged subject(s). The audience is held in an ethical double-bind in which the gaze is both rejected as a form of aggression and solicited as the only possibility of redemption.

Such a technique suggests how far *4.48 Psychosis* subverts usual modes of theatrical presentation. André Green suggests that in the context of theatre criticism:

> the aim of psychoanalytic reading is the search for the emotional springs that make the spectacle an affecting matrix in which the spectator sees himself involved and feels himself not only solicited but welcomed, as if the spectacle was intended for him.³⁷

Kane subverts this 'affecting matrix' most completely in her final work so as to make the spectator undergo a kind of dislocation whereby they are at once welcomed *and rejected* by the artwork. The pressures on the audience's gaze share in the perspectival crisis of the subject(s) of the play. Both solicited and refused, the spectator, like the speaker(s), may well feel that they 'don't know where to look anymore'.³⁸

Through these challenges the spectator/spectated dynamic is reversed, and both audience and performer share in a site of troubled looking. The audience are both looking and *looked at* – implicitly by the onstage speaker who critiques and refuses their gaze, and meta-theatrically by themselves. By forcing the audience to note their own spectating practice, the play transfers the burden of self-observation and self-representation onto its audience. This was literalized in the design of the first production, directed by James Macdonald and designed by Jeremy Herbert (the same team who worked with Kane on *Cleansed*):

> While the stage props of table and chairs were functional to the point of being anonymous, the intriguing feature that dominated the set was a mirror slanted at a 45-degree angle, cutting off the back of the set so that it resembled a small attic room. The mirror's presence meant the audience could simultaneously see the drama on two planes, so that they could both witness the actors playing in front of them and above their heads. Audience members seated further back could also observe a vertical view of the first two rows of theatre-goers.³⁹

Jeremy Herbert's set design here gave the audience a number of options as to where to direct their gaze: at the bodies on stage, at their reflection or at other audience members. Whilst several commentators have emphasized the meta-theatricality of this technique, it is also notable that the creation of the attic-like space literalizes the images of being close to the 'ceiling of the mind', which are repeated throughout the play.[40] For those audience members seated at the back, the mirror not only created new options for spectating the play: by highlighting the presence of other audience members, it also highlighted their own positions as occupying a shared space of looking, in continuity with the stage. This space – attic-like, disorientating and 'full of eyes' – is highly evocative of the unstable spatial images used to describe the mind throughout *4.48 Psychosis*. A continuity is established between the literal space of the theatre (including stage and auditorium) and the metaphorical space of the mind. The dramaturgy of this production might be said to have extended beyond the stage, in order to create a situation in which the audience might experience a sense of *residing within* the site lodged at the 'ceiling of the mind'.

The nature of this theatrical space and its desired effect on the potential audience member are best described in relation to Bollas's psychoanalytic concept of 'transformational space'. In this way it totalizes the mode of 'playing' which I have been tracing throughout Kane's works. Derived from D. W. Winnicott's 'transitional space', 'transformational space' (more frequently described as a 'transformational object' in which the object exists as object-as-process) describes an environment created for the infant by the 'good enough' mother, or in the therapeutic site by analyst and analysand. This is an environment in which and through which the subject undergoes a 'process of alteration of self experience'.[41]

Bollas understands the transformational space as a process which is organized in spatial terms: through gaze, gesture, touch, proximity/distance and so on.[42] When a mother acts as a transformational object by generating this space/environment for the infant, her modifications of the environment organize it and give it its own character (or 'idiolect'), generating an 'aesthetic of being' that is transferred to the infant who inhabits it.[43] Crucially, Bollas proposes that this process creates an alternative way of knowing that is rooted in the experience of an environment and is not reducible to language.[44] The form of understanding generated in this environment exists, as Bollas suggests in his book title, as the *shadow* of the object, insofar as it is experienced 'without [...] being able to process this relation through mental representations or language [...] While we do know something of the character which affects us, we may have no thought yet'.[45] In other words, the experience of the transformational object involves 'a kind of existential, as opposed to representational knowing', which Bollas calls the 'unthought known'.[46]

The notion of an object which acts as an 'enviro-somatic transformer of the subject' finds its echo in Kane's experiential aims for her theatre, especially in relation to her experience of Weller's *Mad*, discussed in Chapter 1. In several interviews Kane identified *Mad* as an experience of transformation, calling it 'the only play ever to have changed my life'.[47] This transformation was achieved through spatial immersion, being 'taken to a place of extreme mental discomfort and distress – and popped out the other end'.[48] Bollas associates this form of spatialized knowing specifically with the experience of psychosis, in which subjects go through a process of designification through which they might lose themselves in the surrounding objects or environments. Key to Bollas's psychoanalytic therapy for schizophrenia is the naming of objects and associations, 'so that [they] are no longer part of the unthought known' and can be '*subjected* to thought'.[49] For this process to be successful, the therapist must to some extent enter into an understanding of the unthought known of the patient, sharing the transformational environment.

Whilst Bollas understands aesthetic experience as the nostalgic *memory* of the transformational object/environment, I suggest that Kane's theatre creates such a site of 'enviro-somatic transformation' for her audiences and does so most completely in *4.48 Psychosis*. Through manipulations of the audience's spatio-temporal and narrative experience, and oscillation between inviting and rejecting the audience's identification, Kane's final work acts at the boundary between spectator and spectated. Kane thus generates a site of play – the 'basic form of living' which makes up Winnicott's transitional and Bollas's transformational space.[50] Play is a precarious mode of thought, as it is 'always on the theoretical line between the subjective and that which is being objectively perceived'.[51] Whilst play can and does fail, when it succeeds it is through the balancing and intermingling of the internal and the external experiences through spatio-temporal *action*:

> [P]laying has a place and a time. It is not *inside* by any use of the word [. . .] Nor is it *outside*, that is to say, it is a not part of the repudiated world, the not-me, that which the individual has decided to recognise (with whatever difficulty and even pain) as truly external, which is outside magical control. To control what is outside one has to *do* things, not simply to think or to wish, and doing *things takes time*. Playing is doing.[52]

The playtext of *4.48 Psychosis* demands a staging which participates in a kind of overspilling between the work's interior (representational/fictional site) and its exterior reality in the auditorium. The audience of *4.48 Psychosis* are placed *both* within and outside of the spectacle, which itself both *represents* the experience of mental suffering and attempts to immerse the audience *inside* it.

Through the work's oscillation between immersion and representation *4.48 Psychosis* asks its potential audience to determine their own measure of participation in the theatrical space. As I shall explore herein, the audience of *4.48 Psychosis* (and indeed its directors and performers) are given a measure of choice as to how far to enter into the play's own perceptual crisis. For the play's *playing* to succeed, both audience and production must participate in it and generate the possibility for an '*overlap of the two play areas*'.[53] Kane's play (in both senses of the word) creates the possibility for a mode of knowing to be realized, should the theatre-makers choose to create and the audience-member choose to actively reside in the enviro-somatic experience which the playtext suggests. This qualifies the claims I have been making about Kane's dramaturgy so far as 'simulating' specific non-normative mental experiences for its audience. Kane's works cannot truthfully simulate an 'actual' experience of the trauma or psychosis of another, as clearly no work can. Instead, Kane's dramaturgy in *4.48 Psychosis* attempts to place us in what Bollas might refer to as the 'shadow of the [psychotic experience]'. The work invites its audience to participate in a disordered and pathologized representation of psychotic suffering without the tools to objectify it. Instead, they are 'compelled [...] to experience' a site of enviro-somatic knowledge, in which they are faced with an 'I' that has distributed itself into a transformational environment.[54]

## Hatch opens/stark light

The specular dynamics in the playtext of *4.48 Psychosis* (i.e. the splitting and collapsing of the speakers' and spectator's gazes) and its use of spatial metaphors for mental experience set a precedent for a dramaturgical evocation of mind-as-site, which has repeatedly provided the basis for directing and set design in production. Since the first production directors and set designers have used a variety of concepts to generate spatial equivalents to the cavernous mind-as-site, indicating the role of these spatial metaphors in shaping *4.48 Psychosis*'s ever-evolving dramaturgy. Anna Harpin has highlighted the use of rays of light and areas of onstage darkness in three productions, which literalize the repeated phrase 'Hatch opens/stark light', as a starting point for set design: the TR Warsaw production at Kings Theatre, Edinburgh International Festival in 2008; the Arcola Theatre production in 2006 and a production at St Ann's Warehouse, New York, in October 2004.[55] Like the set design of the first production, these examples point to the site of the play being imagined as a kind of ceiling, this time with light piercing through its surface, mirroring the porous quality of the mind-as-site/mind-as-cavern evoked in the second half of the play. Jon Venn similarly focuses on the use of light in the original production, highlighting the connection between the use of stark light and the exposing nature of the medical gaze in the play.[56]

In the productions Harpin describes, 'directors [. . .] commonly realise these textually-implied ambiguous spaces (pits, ponds, chambers and so forth) through shards of brilliant light, white boxes and the multiplying surface reflections on glass'.[57] Harpin links the piercing of light into these sets with a call for spatial proximity with madness. Building on Juliet Foster's sociological research into cartographical metaphors for mental illness, she emphasizes the extent to which madness is often figured through metaphors of distance:

> To be mad is, according to common idiom, to be out-of-place. [. . .] A person descends into madness or is driven there. Two things are apparent here. First there is a sense of journeying that attends to madness. Secondly, the dominant notion of place renders 'mad' experience an inherently geographical encounter.[58]

Foster and Harpin both note that the 'mad' individual is typically figured as somehow outside of or away from themselves, and spatial metaphors are used to emphasize the gulf between the pre-illness, 'true' self and the mentally ill subject. This is reinforced in schizophrenia narratives 'in which the pre-illness person goes missing, seemingly abandoned by the disorder'.[59] Harpin suggests that these productions of *4.48 Psychosis* propose a new spatial logic by allowing the literalized 'stark light' to break into the isolated, distant site of madness and create a new site 'oppressive in its expansive luminosity'.[60] The bright, porous stage spaces in these productions 'disturb notions and associations of space, place and perception' in order to create 'a kind of phenomenological empathy through [Kane's] arresting evocations of iridescent solitude'.[61]

In these productions, as in the first production by McDonald and Herbert, the visual qualities of the experiences described onstage are transferred into the set itself, thus generating a form of expanded consciousness in which the theatrical site both represents and embodies the mental experience it stages. The frequency with which such decisions are made suggests a widespread decision on the sides of set designers and directors to use the playtext itself as a call for the creation of a particular type of space. *4.48 Psychosis*'s radical manipulation of its potential audiences' perspectives, along with an expanded auditory quality, thus suggests a kernel of dramaturgical specificity which seems to be repeated throughout many productions.

Theatre-makers are offered a choice as to how far to construct the theatrical site as an embodiment of the kind of spatial experience embedded in the playtext. *4.48 Psychosis* as a *site* into which the 'I' is fragmented and projects itself forms the basis for perhaps one of its most innovative recent dramaturgical re-imaginings. The 2016 production co-produced by the Lyric Hammersmith (London) and the Royal Opera House re-staged *4.48 Psychosis* as an opera, composed by Philip Venables and directed by Ted Huffman. In this production it was not the visual but the auditory features of the playtext which were used as the basis of the production's dramaturgical decisions. Venables used the playtext of *4.48 Psychosis* as a starting point for developing new ways of integrating non-sung modes of text delivery into opera. Taking the play's polyphonic nature as a starting point, Venables and Huffman created a theatrical experience in which the multi-directional nature of sound and wide-ranging assignment of spoken and sung text created an auditory equivalent of the disorientating 'mind-as-cavernous-site'.

In their words, Huffman and Venables sought to create a 'hive mind' in which musical and textual expressions of mental suffering were spread across the bodies, set and instruments on stage:

> No single cast member would take on a truly fixed role, with the exception, perhaps, of one person carrying some of the solo arias on behalf of the main character (the patient). The whole ensemble would at times represent the main character, at other times they would step out to play the roles of doctors, lovers, carers. The polyphonic inner voices could be mapped into real vocal polyphony, solo arias or speeches could be distributed between the cast, some parts could be left open in the score and allocated in the rehearsal room, leaving the director more flexibility with staging.[62]

The composition made use of both spoken and sung recordings as well as live speech and singing, and projected text accompanied only by percussion. Venables innovated on 'five varying approaches to dealing with non-sung text' as part of the opera, which were included alongside 'singing in many forms'. These were:

1) the 'opera thought-bubble', 'a synchronisation of solo sung gesture and voiceover, to indicate the inner thoughts of the performer who is singing'
2) the voiceover, 'pre-recorded voice over music, with or without projected text'

3) mid-phrase switching 'singers switch from sung to spoken text mid-phrase'
4) tape-cutting, 'implementing cut-and-splice and stuttering/scratching techniques to make stream-of-consciousness spoken text'
5) 'percussion dialogues', 'dialogue scenes where projected text is synchronised with two percussion soloists'.[63]

All of these techniques involved further splitting of the already-polyphonic voices of the play texts, so that the voices ranged across speech and song, and also across differing positions within the stage space.

In the 'opera thought bubble' sections for example, soprano Gweneth Ann Rand stood alone onstage singing wordlessly, whilst the sung text was broadcast as a pre-recorded voiceover from speakers above her head. The sound clearly came from above, as was occasionally emphasized by Rand looking upward, directing the audience to search to a source for the disembodied speech. The impact of this auditory splitting was both polyphonous and spatial. Whilst it was clear that both the spoken text and the wordless singing were meant to be expressive of Rand's suffering, the means of this expression were extended to incorporate the theatrical site itself.

The spatial dynamics of this experience were emphasized by Hannah Clarke's set design, which located the orchestra above the back wall of the set, which was dressed to look like an anonymous waiting room. The orchestra was partially lit, so that one could see the teeming movement of musicians in a dark space above the sparse, brightly lit stage. In the *'very long silence'* which opens the play in the original text, elevator *muzak* was played from a speaker above the back wall. This music maddeningly returned in all of the many 'silences' that followed, contrasting with the rich orchestral music and intense percussion which travelled down from the orchestra in the more poetically expressive sections of the play. The combination of musical polyphony and innovative set design formed an auditory and spatial parallel to the textual evocations of mind-as-site. The use of *muzak* especially evoked the 'dismal whistle [. . .] around the hellish bowl at the ceiling of [a] mind'.[64] By placing the orchestra and speakers significantly higher than the singers, Clarke, Huffman and Venables created a phonic equivalent to the unstable, cavernous site, reminiscent of the set of the first production. In both cases this was achieved through the introduction of an unusual measure of choice as to where the audience might direct their gaze or ear, and a set design which undermined a dyadic relationship between stage and audience member by drawing the audience's perception to areas above and around the stage.

The penultimate line of *4.48 Psychosis* returns to the conflict between the possibility of residing within a disordered dramaturgy, and demand for self-representation: 'It is myself I have never met, whose face is pasted to the underside of my mind.'[65] Here the metaphorical link between the richly imagined mind-as-site and the skull cavity are collapsed, into a single image in which it is the body's physicality itself which prohibits the encounter with a fully formed, representable 'self'. The line evokes a highly visual image of a material face, 'pasted' like a photograph in a location that is at once interior and utterly inaccessible. The cavernous mind-as-site which has provided dubious containment for mental suffering throughout the play is now implicated in the apparent impossibility of the subject's self-representation. If this cavity also represents and to some extent reflects the boundaries of the theatrical site itself, as I have been suggesting, then the very idea of traditional forms of knowing through theatrical identification is also being challenged. The play never yields a traditional, knowable subject to its audience, the sort that could perhaps be summarized on a promotional poster with the image of an actor's face. Instead, it created an environment into which the audience member is invited to reside, and in which they might participate in the inability of the 'I' to place itself.

## What do you offer?

The 'transformational site' evoked by *4.48 Psychosis* is populated by fragments of medical and behaviourist discourse. As noted earlier, *4.48 Psychosis* opens with an incomplete dialogue, in which a possibly medical voice repeatedly asks an other to give an account of themselves:

(*A very long silence.*)

– But you have friends.

(*A long silence.*)
You have a lot of friends.
What do you offer your friends to make them so supportive?
(*A long silence.*)
What do you offer your friends to make them so supportive?
What do you offer?
(*Silence.*)[66]

The account required by the speaker in this opening scene is a transactional one, seeking a set of representable attributes which can be exchanged for interpersonal support. The scene is usually interpreted as the first of seven doctor–patient dialogues in the play, in which the 'patient-voice' repeatedly resists, complicates and thwarts their medical interlocutor, whilst simultaneously seeking for a meaningful connection with a 'doctor' who resists getting emotionally involved. As Ariel Watson and Alicia Tycer, among others, have noted, the use of the long silences in response to the repeated question immediately establishes a relation of resistance between the patient and doctor voices (assuming they are voiced by different individuals in production) and silence becomes a key 'tool' for resisting the medical gaze throughout the play: 'Silence is a tool or a weapon here, resisting the scriptedness of the therapeutic encounter, its inability to deviate from the expectations of depression and illness or from the prescriptions of cure.'[67] Depending on the rest of the dramaturgy and the length of the silence in production, the opening '*very long silence*' can also work meta-theatrically, drawing the audience's attention to their growing discomfort at the lack of speech or action on stage. The onstage silence can variously be read or staged as active resistance by the interlocutor to the medical-voice's demand, or alternatively as a sign of the impossibility for the interlocutor of finding an answer – perhaps even the absence of such a representable subject to begin with. In the latter case the failure of the dialogue may be read as undermining a specific conceptualization of subjecthood and relationality based on transactionality.

The failure of this initial (presumed) dialogue and the nature of its demands also sets a precedent for the kinds of intervention the 'medical' voice will make throughout the play. Throughout the patient/doctor dialogues which follow, the voice returns to repeatedly frame the 'patient' in terms and techniques derived from behavioural psychology, notably using techniques espoused by cognitive behavioural therapy (CBT). The opening failed dialogue appears to begin the play with a fragment of a session in which the therapist is attempting to use the CBT technique of 'guided discovery', in which a patient is repeatedly questioned in order to lead them to challenge 'maladaptive core beliefs'. Through this technique:

> Therapists use questions to probe a patient's assumptions, question the reasons and evidence for their beliefs, highlight other perspectives and probe implications. [...] Guided discovery is central to the interventions aimed at each level of cognition.[68]

Later in the play, Kane quotes from the Beck Depression Inventory, a key diagnostic tool created by the founder of CBT, Aaron Beck, in which patients assess their own depression by rating the relevance of twenty-one statements. Key to the behaviourist approach is the notion that successful therapy is required to address patterns of thought rather than actual experiences by the patient: '[CBT] hypothesises that people's emotions and behaviours are influenced by their perceptions of events. It is not a situation in and of itself that determines what people feel but rather the way in which they *construe* a situation.'[69] Challenging the veracity of the patient's perception of and emotional reaction to an event is thus key to the techniques of CBT, either directly or through indirect means such as 'guided discovery', behavioural experiments or written exercises.

The representation of cognitive behaviourism in *4.48 Psychosis* is critical of such an approach, as both the failure of the first dialogue and the antagonism of the following ones demonstrate.[70] Nevertheless, Kane does more than stage the inadequacies of a therapeutic technique at the hands of an incompetent therapist. Rather, the doctor–patient dialogues draw out two key aspects of behaviourist ideology and practice: first, the denial of the emotional veracity of the patient's experience; and second, its insistence on patient-responsibility and the link between this conceptualization of the patient and neoliberal constructions of subjectivity.

*4.48 Psychosis*'s representation of the medical voice both exposes and ridicules the claims to epistemological certainty and sovereignty found in the cognitive behavioural model. This is clearly demonstrated in the second doctor–patient dialogue, in which the patient-voice is silenced for using poetic, rather than behavioural, language in order to characterize their emotional state:

- I feel like I am eighty years old. I'm tired of life and my mind wants to die.
- That's a metaphor, not reality.
- It's a simile.
- That's not reality.
- It's not a metaphor, it's a simile, but even if it were, the defining feature of a metaphor is that it's real.
(*A long silence.*)[71]

Placed in the context of a theatrical work which is masterful in its use of rich metaphors, the obstinacy and linguistic narrow-mindedness of the doctor-voice in this dialogue appears foolish (almost) to the point of being parodic and is reminiscent of the extreme banality of the doctor in *Phaedra's Love*. At the same time, the exchange exposes the foundational beliefs of the behaviourist approach in which the patient is to be drawn away from maladaptive 'false' beliefs and emotions, thus implying a rigid emotional-epistemological hierarchy which denies the depressive's reality in favour of the reality of the positive or the 'well'. Under this approach, the patient is encouraged to constantly monitor their interior life, identifying when to approach their own thoughts with suspicion, and deny their suffering. As William Davies argues, CBT and behavioural sciences more widely encourage individuals to 'come to interpret and narrate their own lives according to this body of expertise. [. . .] [W]e train ourselves to be more suspicious of our thoughts, or more tolerant of our feelings'.[72]

Using *4.48 Psychosis* as an example, psychoanalyst Darian Leader identifies this process as one of the most damaging aspects of modern psychiatry. Leader introduces the experience of one of his patients, who 'described how she was forced into a set of concepts and categories that were alien to her, like the protagonist of Sarah Kane's *4.48 Psychosis*, whose fury grows as her doctor refuses to go beyond the question of whether her act of self-harm provided relief or not'.[73] Leader suggests that the denial of the patient's inner life parallels the violence with which patients were treated under Victorian regimes of 'mental hygiene':

> The clinician who attempts to graft his own value system and view of normality onto the patient becomes like the colonizer who seeks to educate the natives, no doubt for their own good. Whether the system is secular and educative or religious, it still bulldozes away the culture and the history of the person it purports to help.[74]

For Leader, a clinical approach which insists on a rigid epistemological framework and tells the patient 'how her behaviour is incorrect, and how she need[s] to learn to think differently and see herself [differently]' doesn't attempt to transform the patient's relationship to themselves so much as truncate it. Eschewing the patient's desire to reveal their interior life in their own idiom, the 'violence' of this approach 'is present each time we try to crush a patient's belief system by imposing a new system of values and policies on them'.[75]

In *4.48 Psychosis* the 'medical voice' largely follows the techniques of CBT in order to quietly and persistently erase those parts of the patient's interior life which do not conform to that of a behaviourist subject. Having been semantically thwarted by the patient-voice, the doctor-voice returns to the 'guided discovery' technique in order to lead the interlocutor into a position of suspicion as to their own metaphorical-thinking:

– You are not eighty years old.

(*Silence.*)
Are you?

(*A silence.*)
Are you?
(*A silence.*)
Or are you?
(*A long silence.*)[76]

Alternating between a denial of the patient's mode of self-expression and an irritatingly repetitive insistence on its own regime of truth, the presentation of the behaviourist doctor-voice in *4.48 Psychosis* reveals the behavioural-medical position as one predicated on the denial, even the elimination of, the patient's interior life.

The persistent thwarting of the emotional-epistemological hierarchy proposed by the doctor-voice, which takes place throughout *4.48 Psychosis*, frames such systems of knowledge as antithetical to understanding mental pain. Throughout these dialogues the patient-voice is increasingly trapped in paradoxical claims made with regard to their ability to 'take responsibility' for their emotions. Any affirmations of the patient's suffering (always through the vocabulary of 'illness') from the doctor-voice are swiftly accompanied by a call to responsibility:

- And you don't think you're ill?
- No.
- I do. It's not your fault. But you have to take responsibility for your own actions.[77]

As well as denying the patient-voice an opportunity to represent 'hermself' in terms that contain paradox or ambiguity, the medical interlocutor uses the notion of responsibility as a double-bind through which to objectify the patient's illness whilst constructing an implicit culture of blame around them.

- I don't feel contempt.
- No?
- No. It's not your fault.
- It's not your fault, that's all I ever hear, it's not your fault, it's an illness, it's not your fault, I know it's not my fault. You've told me that so often I'm beginning to think it *is* my fault.
- It's *not* your fault.
- I KNOW.
- But you allow it.
  (*Silence.*)
  Don't you?

- There's not a drug in on earth that can make life meaningful.
- You allow this state of desperate absurdity.[78]

The notion of responsibility here is used to erase the question of 'fault', and thus the possibility that the patient might consider their suffering as a (possibly political) consequence either of their own actions or of the conditions to which they are exposed.

By denying any discursive space for the notion that there might be *causes* for the patient-voice's suffering, 'responsibility' also becomes a means for discounting the truth-content in the patient's observations, and their history. In a dramatic world which is coursed through with violence, fraught relationships and power-play, this framework is striking in its reductiveness. The patient's own claims are framed as irresponsible, whilst their suffering is given no weight, as it is implicitly permissible – 'allowed by' the patient. Nevertheless, as with the previous exchange, the doctor-voice is unequal to the patient's expressive power and to the work's dramaturgical representation of suffering. Kane fragments the cognitive behavioural framework, so that it is a persistent and aggressive presence in the theatrical space, but never becomes a dominant meta-discourse. By presenting both its persistence and its cracks, *4.48 Psychosis* creates space for an epistemological and ethical critique of the power dynamics hidden in CBT's supposed scientific neutrality.

Kane uses the fragmented medical voice in *4.48 Psychosis* to articulate a specific critique of reductive models of mental suffering which is rooted in late 1990s psychiatric culture. In these short exchanges Kane reveals one of the key paradoxes and strategies central to the neoliberalization of healthcare: the marrying of epistemology, responsibility and a (dubious) ethical system. In the introduction to this book, I suggested that Kane wrote during a period of crucial transition in UK mental health care. This was a period of flux, during which mental health care moved from an asylum system to one in which care was delivered by multiple-service providers in the community. Having written about and experienced the mental health care system in the UK in the decade following the NHS and Community Care Act 1990, Kane would have witnessed a period of fundamental transition in the way in which mental illness was conceptualized and treated in the UK. As the first act of parliament to introduce private sector providers into the health and social care systems and to establish an internal market within the NHS, the act began a process of neoliberalization of health and social care which has perhaps reached its apotheosis today.[79] The new legislation enabled further implementation of a conception of the NHS based on the idea of patients-as-consumers and NHS Trusts as competitive corporate-style service-providers.

Using the framework of neoliberalism to describe the subsequent changes in UK mental health care is useful, as it enables one to address the way in which structural and ideological changes combine to create new discursive and practical conditions for subjectivization.

Key to analyses of neoliberalism from Foucault onwards is the idea that as a 'governmental rationality' it acts as a series of economic and governing practices which impact the lives of individuals, *and* simultaneously creates a new epistemic order in which all forms of knowledge are subsumed into an economic logic. For Foucault, neoliberalism is a system of governance in which the logic of the market is expanded beyond the economic:

> Analysis in terms of the market economy, or, in other words, of supply and demand, can function as a scheme which is applicable to non-economic domains.[80]

Not only is market logic applied to non-economic realms under such a system, but the market is posited as the ultimate arbiter of governmental decision-making, acting as an epistemological and ethical meta-discourse:

> *Laissez-faire* is thus turned around, and the market is no longer a principle of government's self-limitation; it is a principle turned against it. It is a sort of permanent economic tribunal confronting government.[81]

A system can be described as neoliberal therefore, insofar as it holds the market as the standard against which all other forms of value are to be judged.

Foucault emphasizes the way in which neoliberal economic theory lays claim to the entire concepts of the real and the rational. Neoliberalism's chief proponents and theorists promote an epistemic order in which 'rationality', 'health' and 'sanity' are subsumed under the banner of economic productivity. Proponents of economic neoliberalism from the Chicago school both drew on and contributed to the field of behavioural psychology. The behavioural economics model espoused by the Chicago school applies 'price theory' 'beyond the limits of market consumption, to apply to *all* forms of human behaviour'.[82] Crucially, it posits single a form of rationality to which all 'sane' individuals conform.

> *Homo economicus* is someone who accepts reality. Rational conduct is any conduct which is sensitive to modifications in the variables of the environment and which responds to this in a non-random way, in a systematic way, and economics can therefore be defined as

the science of the systematic nature of responses to environmental variables.[83]

In classic neoliberal theory therefore, the individual is redefined as an autonomous agent who reacts 'rationally' (i.e. according to the logic of a cost-benefit analysis) to changing environments in order to survive changes to the market-environment, whose continuance is the only end-in-itself. Reactions that do not follow such a principle are defined as aberrant or irrational, to be altered if the subject is to survive. One can easily see the link with the cognitive behavioural framework here: targeting 'maladaptive thoughts', CBT does not seek to identify an aetiology of suffering but focuses instead on guiding patients to have 'reasonable' or proportional reactions to their environment. As such, the behavioural approach sees the subject as an autonomous, though maladapted, agent, to be brought in line with the dominant epistemological-emotional regime.

In identifying the neoliberal, behaviourist trend in mental health care and having it largely characterize the medical voice in her final play, Kane presented a highly prescient vision of the direction of UK mental health care. In the UK, the redefinition of the psychiatric subject along neoliberal and behaviourist lines has had profound practical consequences since the 1990s, as patients with mental health problems are increasingly figured as faulty economic agents. As William Davies points out, the recent adoption of CBT as the dominant mode of therapy in the NHS was largely a neoliberal economic decision.[84] In the proposal for the creation of the largely CBT-based Increasing Access to Psychological Therapies (IAPT) scheme in 2006, Richard Layard argued specifically that 'the money which the government spends will pay for itself. For someone on Incapacity Benefit costs us £750 a month in extra benefits and lost taxes. If the person works just a month more as a result of the treatment, the treatment pays for itself'.[85] Since its inception IAPT has had links with the UK Department for Work and Pensions, with employment advisers integrated into the service, and return to employment a key marker for measuring recovery. In 2014, the Conservative Party sought to make Employment and Support Allowance for those diagnosed with depression dependent on individuals receiving CBT, with sanctions for non-attendance.[86] What's more, 2017 proposals sought to further embed the link between employment and recovery, by mandating that economic self-sufficiency be both the *aim* and the *focus* of IAPT therapies. Under the heading 'Changes to clinical practice for IAPT therapist', a joint DWP and DoH presentation states:

> During therapy keep informed of the progress of employment support and in collaboration with the client *take the necessary action to ensure*

*that employment support is successful by focussing on psychological blocks,*
*for example, fear or anxiety around interviews.*[87]

The change marks a notable escalation in the application of neoliberal thinking and the relationship between work and therapy. Whilst the ability to work has long been a marker in the mapping of illness and health, the new proposal takes this a step further. The 2006 Layard report had already collapsed the distinction between health and work, proposing employment as a sign of recovery. In the 2017 guideline to clinicians this logic is reversed, and unemployment itself identified as the major pathology: the role of the clinician becomes to 'ensure that employment support is successful', and mental pathology is only understood in terms of 'psychological blocks' to the return to work. The shift is at once practical, epistemological and coercive: with their livelihoods and benefits often dependent on receiving such therapies, subjects are entered into a therapeutic process which asks them to *redefine themselves* as behaviourist-economic subjects, and the therapeutic site ceases to be one in which a variety of subjectivizations can be explored.

## It's not your fault

In this context, contemporary stagings of both *Crave* and *4.48 Psychosis* go somewhat against the grain of current mental health discourses, in both professional and theatrical contexts. There is an element of cultural dissonance when these works are compared to contemporary playwrighting on mental illness, especially with those works staged in London's West End theatres. This dissonance is generated both by the staging of the inadequacy of the CBT therapeutic encounter in *4.48 Psychosis*, and by its spatialization of the mind. Recent successful new writing around the subject of mental suffering includes Alice Birch's *Anatomy of a Suicide* and Duncan Macmillan's *People, Places, Things*, staged at the Royal Court, and National Theatre/Wyndhams respectively. Both productions opened to highly positive reviews, with *People, Places, Things* securing a West End transfer. Whilst they vary dramatically in style and dramaturgy, these new plays share two notable similarities: first, they represent dramaturgically innovative attempts to represent mental suffering, and second, they are all structured around a journey out of mental illness which takes the form of a precarious return to 'normal' or productive life.

This return is most clearly noticeable in *People, Places, Things* which tells the story of an actress, possibly called Emma, who enters a rehabilitation centre for drug and alcohol abuse. The play stages her two cycles of rehabilitation, in which she struggles to accept the program, eventually accepting her helplessness but not the role of Christianity in Alcoholics Anonymous process. Instead of repeating the serenity prayer, she attempts to remember a corporate monologue which she had performed for her first acting job, and which she subsequently rehearsed with her late brother and uses for auditions. The play contains interesting dramaturgical evocations of Emma's mental anguish during the withdrawal process, with her dissociation and pain represented through the emergence of multiple 'Emmas' on the stage, writhing and shaking under flashing lights, generating a confusion in the audience as to whether we are witnessing hallucinations, or a self no longer experienced in coherent spatial and chronological terms. This confusion is compounded by the fact that Emma's substance abuse is combined with an 'addiction' to acting, as she presents successive 'roles' to the audience and her therapy group, repeatedly undermining her own past narratives and casting doubt on her real name and identity.

Nevertheless, the play ends with the suggestion of possible return both to 'health' and to economic productivity. Having left rehab, Emma returns to her toxic family environment, ignoring the injunction to avoid the 'people, places and things' that cause the addict to want to use. Instead, Emma returns to the site that makes her want to use the most, stating that if she can stay sober whilst living with her mother, she can be sober anywhere. In the final scene, the bedroom in her parents' house moves away, and Emma is left standing on a bare stage, finally correctly reciting the corporate monologue as though in an audition. The final monologue functions in a number of ways in this scene: it is at once a sign of Emma's recovery, her defiance of her toxic family environment and her return to economic subjecthood. The end of the play combines the language of defiance and combat with illness, increasingly applied in the mental health context, with that of economic identity and corporate banality to generate an uncertain sense of cure and restoration to 'life'.

Alice Birch's *Anatomy of a Suicide* ends with a similar transformation of the stage space in order to indicate the lifting of illness and the cure-filled future. Birch's play, directed by Katie Mitchell at the Royal Court in 2017, owes a clear debt to Kane's *Crave* in its presentation of three generations of suicidal women, all of whom occupy the stage at the same time. Like *Crave*, the narratives of *Anatomy of a Suicide* unfold in unclear chronologies, with scenes from each generation taking place simultaneously, and speech overlapping. However, Birch introduces narrative certainty and transformation which are very different from Kane's dramatic universes. The play's exploration of genetically inherited suicidality ends when the woman from the youngest generation decides to sell her grandmother's house, the site of her mother's and grandmother's suicides, and to have her ovaries tied. Refusing to continue an apparent biological compulsion towards suicide and distancing herself from the traumatic history held in her maternal home, Jo causes a transformation of the stage space. For most of the play, the set was a concrete-like cell, with three doors along the back wall, with a date projected above each door to indicate the time of each narrative. Action from each time-period took place in front of the assigned door, so that one had a sense of separate narratives being played out in parallel. Jo's escape from her suicidal heritage is represented as a literal lifting of this depressive landscape, as the back wall rises in the final scene, to reveal the 'actual' house flooded with light behind it.

Both plays are thoughtfully critical of the promise of cure. Jo is restored to the health only through an elimination of the possibility of reproduction, as if the mental illness which she has inherited is not so much suicidal depression as motherhood. Emma's return to her life as an actress is rendered dubious both because of the extent to which acting has been represented as part of her addiction to begin with, and because she literally returns to where she had started – on stage, where, at the start of the play she had been drunkenly performing the end of Chekhov's *The Seagull*. Nevertheless, these doubts are made possible within dramaturgical representations of mental illness which track the journey from psychiatric intervention to home, and back to work, and follow chronologies in which cure is an end point.[88] Rather than being direct or indirect engagements with the conditions and power relations in which mental suffering takes place, both Birch and Macmillan ultimately stage narratives of personal strength leading to autonomy, and dubious self-fulfilment or cure. In contrast, Kane's unrelenting portrayals of seemingly irresolvable mental suffering make significantly different demands on contemporary audiences.

When restaged in the current neoliberal mental health context Kane's plays provide audiences with the opportunity to think otherwise, by presenting them with versions of metal suffering which are incoherent within the neoliberal framework. As I discussed in the reading of *Crave* in Chapter 1, one of the lasting consequences of the NHS and Community Care Act has been the conversion of the psychiatric patient into a 'service user', who is positioned as a consumer in the centre of a number of service providers. Returning to this shift now, we can see how deeply Kane's final play provides a charged response to its political moment. This repositioning assumes a level of capability, autonomy and expert knowledge by the service user which is not necessarily present, as well as transferring the liability for any failure of the services on to poor navigation by the user. As Barbara Taylor observes in her account of community care, those living with pathological mental suffering are now 'looked after (or not) [. . .] through a network of services provided by the voluntary sector, private companies and local NHS mental health trusts', with 'the guiding principle behind this vision [. . .] that the best way of life – for everyone, sick or well – [is] one of personal independence'.[89]

This shift towards autonomy as the founding principle of service provision has been described by economic and sociological critiques of neoliberalism as the process of 'responsibilization'. Under a 'regime' of responsibilization patients are understood in a system which 'provides the illusion of control, autonomy and sovereignty' and in which 'capability (and the failure to exert it successfully) is perceived as fully under the control for consumers'.[90] As such, the space for criticism of structural causes of distress or patient-capabilities is effectively eliminated:

> When individuals are asked to make choices and conform to the ideals of responsibilisation, but are unable to do so because of structural tensions within the service system, the self-blame effect magnifies and induces a vicious-cycle. [. . .] Not succeeding in integrating resources from their personal domain with those from providers and the service system becomes a reflection of consumer deviance, incompetence, and inadequacy under the neoliberal logic of responsibilisation.[91]

The logic of responsibilization thus aims to transform the individual into a successful and autonomous economic unit and condition their responses to the failure to realize oneself as such a unit into a personal inadequacy. Such a logic is noticeable in both Birch's and Macmillan's narratives of recovery, with Emma finally 'taking responsibility' for the harm she caused due to her addiction and returning to independence, and Jo's radical choice to become infertile in order to avoid passing suicidality on to a future generation, taking responsibility for future suffering and dependency by eliminating its possibility.

In *4.48 Psychosis*, the doctor's attempts to guide the interlocutor into a transactional account of themselves are eventually revealed to be based on a fearful rejection of interdependency. The patient's silences force the medical voice into an unprofessional moment of self-disclosure, which reveals its previous calls for self-responsibility and for transactional self-representation as above all attempts to distance the patient, and isolate their pain from others:

> (*Silence.*)
> – Most of my clients want to kill me. When I walk out of here at the end of the day I need to go home to my lover and relax. I need my friends to be really together.

(*Silence.*)
I fucking hate this job and I need my friends to be sane.
(*Silence.*)
I'm sorry.
– It's not my fault.[92]

Fearfully refusing the patient's desire for friendship and constantly denying their request to be believed, the therapist's confession here exposes the limits of the neoliberal/responsibilized therapeutic encounter. The kind of sustained engagement with the patient's suffering which speaker(s) seeks, and which is perhaps described by Bollas when he comments on the psychotic's ability to challenge the foundations of their therapist's beliefs, is impossible under a behavioural/neoliberal framework which works on the assumption of subject-autonomy.

Kane renders this form of autonomy incoherent by inviting the audience to reside *within* a spatially realized version of a painful psyche. From this position of insideness, we are invited to perceive the demands of the doctor-voice as both intrusive and impossible. The ideal responsibilized subject is autonomous and above all bounded – contained in a single, capable body. By creating a dramaturgy of mental breakdown which spreads the representation of a single consciousness across a number of bodies, temporalities, sounds and sites, Kane communicates a version of mental suffering which experiences the demand for autonomy as an unwanted and unanswerable intrusion.

In Venables's opera production, the essential contradiction between the demands of the medical voice and the audio-spatially realized 'hive mind' of the play was ingeniously and comically underlined through the staging of the dialogues. Venables developed these scenes into 'percussion dialogues', in which text was projected onto the back wall of the set accompanied by percussion, to the rhythm of natural speech. Both text and percussionists were spatialized:

> One percussionist stage right played the Doctor and one percussionist stage left played the Patient. The text for each role was projected onto the upstage white wall of the set stage right and left respectively, close to the location of the performers, who were in the corresponding left and right positions on the raised gantry. The left-right spatialisation helped make the dialogue aspect clearer, and highlighted the adversarial nature of the characters' relationship in these scenes.[93]

During these dialogues the stage was occupied either just by soprano Gweneth-Ann Rand, the 'leader' of the hive mind/ensemble who carried most of the solo arias, or by Rand and Lucy Schaufer who was frequently choreographed as a doctor/therapist figure. The representation of the patient/doctor scenes was thus spread across a variety of visual and auditory modes of expression. The 'patient-voice' was at once text and percussion, and expressed through the visible body of the percussionist, the blankness of the back wall of the set and Rand's onstage presence.

Each 'voice' was given its own quality through use of specific instruments. The patient's voice was expressed with a bass drum and the doctor's variously using a military drum, a metal scaffolding pole and a wood saw. Question marks in the text were marked with the pinging of a counter bell. This variation of instruments allowed for the articulation of different levels of intrusiveness on the part of the medical voice:

> The doctor interferes, annoys, niggles, often with trite or ridiculous questions. Instruments were chosen to reflect this, for example with the penetrating, invasive sound of metal scaffolding with metal-headed hammers (Scene 6), or the comic effect of sawing a piece of wood with heavy amplification applied (Scene 12). Only in Scene 23, when the Doctor finally shows her own humanity, flaws, emotions and vulnerabilities, does the Doctor also play the orchestral bass drum.[94]

Venables thus used the percussion dialogues to create a sense of impossible demands entering an expanded mind-as-site through auditory effects which varied from banal to aggressive and, in the case of the wood saw, almost unbearable. The splitting of the dialogue across singers, sounds, percussionists and texts made it impossible to assign the 'voices' to a specific body, whilst nonetheless maintaining the doctor–patient split through the assigning of bodies and sounds to the left- or right-hand sides of the stage. The result was a staging of the dialogues which was significantly funnier than that of other productions (at least those I have witnessed). Placed in the theatrical context of an *environment* of mental suffering, the doctor's repetitive questioning and calls for the patient to 'take responsibility for your actions'[95] became absurdly comical, with the incongruity of such demands emphasized by the return of banal, waiting-room-style muzak on either side of the dialogues.

Reflecting on the distance between therapeutic voice and patient, the psychoanalyst Marguerite Sechehaye wrote that

> When we try to build a bridge between the schizophrenic and ourselves, it is often with the idea of leading him back to reality – our own – and to our own norm. He feels it and naturally turns away from this intrusion.[96]

This bridge for Sechehaye is the psychotherapeutic situation which, she suggests, is usually constructed for the purpose of leading the other 'back to reality – our own – and to our own norm'. Such an invitation is felt as intrusive and can lead to a loss of the very connection it seeks to maintain: 'he feels it and naturally turns away from this intrusion.'[97]

Kane's final works have the potential to build a similar bridge, in a theatrical, rather than therapeutic, situation. The purpose of this bridge is emphatically not to coax the suffering psyche 'back' to normality. Rather, it contains the opposite invitation. It asks that those of us in the audience who bring the norms of the outside world into the theatre with us take a few steps out onto this bridge. In doing so it asks us to put aside those norms for a fixed period of time and reside in a psychic and physical space that might be quite different from those we have experienced before. This space is filled with contradiction. It contains the intrusions of the behaviourist therapy and is moulded by psychiatric medication. It is angry, desiring, poetic, desperate for a cure even as it shuns the possibility of recovery.

It is in this invitation, which might be experienced as a demand, that I believe Kane's works find their most urgent and radical politics. It speaks both to the conditions of the regulation of psychic life in which Kane was writing, and to a number of contemporary circumstances. In the following chapter, I consider how far Kane's demands on her audiences create the possibility for a host of varied political significations – from the UK neoliberal mental health context to the Belarus Free Theatre's resistance to the oppressive legislation of everyday life in totalitarian regimes. Kane's dramaturgy asks us to think psychic life otherwise, to understand it as somehow inherently spatial, and therefore inhabitable and shareable in the psychic in-between of theatrical space.

## Notes

1 Michael Billington, 'How Do You Judge a 75-Minute Suicide Note?', *Guardian*, 30 June 2000, 5.
2 Quoted Ken Urban, 'An Ethics of Catastrophe: The Theatre of Sarah Kane', *PAJ* 23, no. 3 (2001): 36–46, 44.
3 Saunders, *Love Me*, 124.
4 David Greig, 'Introduction', in *Sarah Kane: Complete Plays* (London: Methuen Drama, 2001), xvii. For a reading of Kane's works as symptom see Femi Oyebode, *Madness at the Theatre* (London: The Royal Institute of Psychiatry, 2012).
5 Leo Bersani, *The Culture of Redemption* (Cambridge, MA: Harvard University Press, 1990), 1, emphasis added.

6   Greig, 'Introduction', xvii.
7   Saunders, *Love Me*, 191.
8   Ibid., 112.
9   Carney, *The Politics of Contemporary English Tragedy*; Juliet Waddington, 'Post-Humanist Identities in Sarah Kane', in *Sarah Kane in Context*, ed. Graham Saunders and Laurens De Vos (Manchester: Manchester University Press, 2010), 139–48; Ehren Fordyce, 'The Voice of Kane', in *Sarah Kane in Context*, ed. Graham Saunders and Laurens De Vos (Manchester: Manchester University Press, 2010), 103–14.
10  David Barnett, 'When Is a Play Not Drama? Two Examples of Post-Dramatic Theatre', *New Theatre Quarterly* 24 (2008): 14–23; Echart Voigts-Virchow, '"We are anathema" – Sarah Kane's Plays as Postdramatic Theatre Versus the 'Dreary and Repugnant Tale of Sense', in *Sarah Kane in Context*, ed. Graham Saunders and Laurens De Vos (Manchester: Manchester University Press, 2010), 195–208; Mathew Roberts, 'Vanishing Acts: Sarah Kane's Texts for Performance and Post-Dramatic Theatre', *Modern Drama* 58 (2015): 94–110, and Urban, 'Ethics'.
11  Delgado-Garcia, 'Subversion, Refusal, and Contingency', 230–50.
12  Bersani, *Culture of Redemption*, 11.
13  Sarah Kane, '4.48 Psychosis', in *Sarah Kane: Complete Plays* (London: Methuen Drama, 2001), 205.
14  Ibid.
15  Ibid.
16  Saunders, *Love Me*, 112.
17  Kane, '4.48 Psychosis', 224.
18  Ibid., 209.
19  Ibid., 224.
20  Ibid., 226.
21  Kane in Saunders, *Love Me*, 112.
22  Bollas, *When the Sun Bursts*, 169.
23  Ibid.
24  Kane, '4.48 Psychosis', 227.
25  Ibid., 209.
26  Ibid.
27  Ibid.
28  Ibid., 226.
29  Ibid., 227.
30  See Oyebode, *Madness*.
31  Bollas, *When the Sun Bursts*, 28.
32  Ibid.
33  Ibid., 35, 36.
34  See the argument of chapter 2.
35  Ariel Watson, 'Cries of Fire: Psychotherapy in Contemporary British and Irish Drama', *Modern Drama* 51, no. 2 (2008): 188–210, 193.

36 Kane, '4.48 Psychosis', 244.
37 Green, *The Tragic Effect*, 18.
38 Kane, '4.48 Psychosis', 240.
39 Saunders, *Love Me*, 115.
40 See Watson, 'Cries of Fire'; Saunders, *Love Me*.
41 Christopher Bollas, 'The Transformational Object', *International Journal of Psycho-Analysis* 60 (1979): 97–107, 97.
42 Bollas, *The Shadow of the Object*, 13.
43 Ibid.
44 Bollas suggests that this form of knowing 'remains symbiotic [. . .] and coexists alongside other forms of knowing.' Ibid., 16.
45 Ibid., 3.
46 Bollas, 'The Transformational Object', 97. See Chapter 3 for Bollas's connection between the 'unthought known' and the development of psychosis.
47 Kane, 'The Only Thing', A12.
48 Kane, quoted Sierz, *In-Yer-Face Theatre*, 92.
49 Bollas, *When the Sun Bursts*, 182.
50 Winnicott, *Playing and Reality*, 67.
51 Ibid., 68.
52 Ibid., 65.
53 Ibid., 72.
54 Bollas, *Shadow of the Object*, 5.
55 Kane, '4.48 Psychosis', 225, 230, 239 and 240.
56 Venn, *Madness and Contemporary British Theatre*.
57 Anna Harpin, 'Dislocated: Metaphors of Madness in British Theatre', in *Performance, Madness and Psychiatry: Isolated Acts*, ed. Julia Foster and Anna Harpin (London: Palgrave Macmillan, 2014), 190.
58 Ibid., 187.
59 Ibid.
60 Ibid., 192.
61 Ibid., 194.
62 Philip Venables, '4.48 Psychosis: Opera as Music and Text. A Mini-site for the Doctoral Submission About the Opera 4.48 Psychosis', 2016. Shared by kind permission of Philip Venables.
63 Ibid.
64 Kane, '4.48 Psychosis', 227.
65 Ibid., 245.
66 Ibid., 205.
67 Watson, 'Cries of Fire', 194.
68 Kristina Fenn and Majella Byrne, 'The Key Principles of Cognitive Behavioural Therapy', *InnovAiT* 6, no. 9 (2013): 579–85, 581. See also J. S. Beck, *Cognitive Therapy: Basics and Beyond* (New York: Guildford Press, 1964), 10 and 23–5.

69 Beck, *Cognitive Therapy*, 30, original emphasis.
70 See for example Watson, 'Cries of Fire'; Alicia Tycer, '"Victim. Perpetrator. Bystander": Melancholic Witnessing of Sarah Kane's 4.48 Psychosis', *Theatre Journal* 60, no. 1 (2008): 23–36.
71 Kane, '4.48 Psychosis', 211.
72 William Davies, *The Happiness Industry: How the Government and Big Business Sold Us Well-Being* (London: Verso, 2016), 258.
73 Darian Leader, *What is Madness?* (London: Penguin, 2011), 6–7.
74 Ibid., 6.
75 Ibid., 7.
76 Kane, '4.48 Psychosis', 211–2.
77 Ibid., 217–18.
78 Ibid., 220.
79 This is also the argument of the epilogue to Barbara Taylor's *The Last Asylum: A Memoir of Madness in Our Times* (London: Penguin, 2015).
80 Michel Foucault, *The Birth of Biopolitics: Lectures at the Collège de France, 1978–79*, trans. Graham Burchill (Basingstoke: Palgrave Macmillan, 2008), 243.
81 Ibid., 247.
82 Davies, *The Happiness Industry*, 151.
83 Foucault, *The Birth of Biopolitics*, 269.
84 Davies, *The Happiness Industry*, 111.
85 Richard Layard, 'The Depression Report. A New Deal for Depression and Anxiety Disorders', in *Centre for Economic Performance Special Papers* (London: London School of Economics, 2006), 2.
86 Tim Ross, 'Tories Discuss Stripping Benefits Claimants Who Refuse Treatment for Depression', *Telegraph*, 12 July 2014. Available online: https://www.telegraph.co.uk/news/politics/conservative/10964125/Tories-discuss-stripping-benefits-claimants-who-refuse-treatment-for-depression.html (accessed 18 February 2019).
87 Kevin Jarman, 'Employment Advisers in IAPT – Providing Integrated IAPT and Employment Support', New Savoy Partnership Conference, 2017. Available online: https://www.newsavoypartnership.org/2017presentations/kevin-jarman.pdf (accessed 18 February 2019) (Slide 12), my emphasis.
88 I consider the politics of Birch and Macmillan's plays in relation to the history of psychiatry in 'Naturalist Hauntings: Staging Psychiatry in Anatomy of a Suicide, People Places Things and Blue/Orange', in *Routledge Companion to Performance and Medicine*, ed. Gianna Bouchard and Alex Mermikides (upcoming).
89 Taylor, *The Last Asylum*, 249.
90 Wendy Brown, *Undoing the Demos: Neoliberalism's Stealth Revolution* (New York: Zone Books, 2015), 113; L. Anderson et al., 'Responsibility and Well-Being: Resource Integration under Responsibilization in Expert Services',

*Journal of Public Policy and Marketing* 35, no. 2 (2016): 262–79, Available online: https://pure.qub.ac.uk/ws/files/120912347/Responsibility_and_Well _Being.pdf (accessed 18 February 2019).
91  Ibid.
92  Kane, '4.48 Psychosis', 237.
93  Venables, '4.48 Psychosis'.
94  Ibid.
95  Kane, '4.48 Psychosis', 219.
96  Sechehaye, *A New Psychotherapy in Schizophrenia* (New York: Grune & Stratton, 1956), 38.
97  Ibid.

# 5

# RSVP ASAP

*This takes us back to the earlier question: not just the phenomenological question 'what is it like to live in courageous time', but the ethical question, 'what does it mean to decide to know about those who live in impossible time?' If we think about this question with Freud, we might say that to know something that is impossible to know requires a form of 'working through.' Working through involves an approach towards the truth, a veering away, and an approach again, in an ongoing attempt to keep proximal what is difficult and painful to know about ourselves and others. Working through is the name for the 'again and again' of interpretation of unconscious motives and desires that we refuse to know about.*

Lisa Baraitser, *Enduring Time*.[1]

## Desire and despair

Very little has been written about the representation and role of desire in Sarah Kane's theatre.[2] Nevertheless, it would not be inaccurate to suggest that desire is the major, even overwhelming, cause of mental and physical suffering in her plays. As we have seen in Chapter 2, Kane's work is threaded through with themes of sexual violence and domination. In Kane's words, her early works are concerned with why we hurt those we desire and love, and why we desire those who hurt us: 'it was about violence, about rape, and it was about these things happening between people who know each other and ostensibly love each other.'[3] The entanglement of desire and abuse is one of the most challenging aspects of watching Kane's earlier works, from *Blasted* to *Cleansed*. As I suggested in Chapter 2, it takes a sustained and deliberate centring of the female experience in these plays to see beyond the stark images of abuse, to the traumatic and feminist vision that the dramaturgy suggests. As the subjectivities represented in Kane's work are increasingly internalized into her late plays' dramaturgies, the theme of desire does not disappear. Rather, in *Crave* and *4.48 Psychosis* desire remains thematically important, whilst bleeding into the demands made on the act of spectatorship in both works. *Crave* and *4.48 Psychosis*, especially in their first productions, invite us to consider what it might mean for a play to palpably *want something* from its audience. Through a meta-theatrical awareness of their own frames, these dramaturgies solicit, impose, demand and depend on the gazes of their audiences. They require serious affective work of the watching other, not unlike that of navigating unwelcome desire.

My contention in this chapter is that something can be productively brought out of these texts by thinking through their presentations of suicidality and desire *together*. It is through the intertwining of these that Kane's two late plays generate and sustain an intense demand upon their potential audiences – the demand to recognize as legitimate the pain of the suicidal subject which is on the continuum of experience of acceptable social and political life. Completely eschewing a cause-and-effect approach to suicidal pain, Kane nonetheless places this pain in a complex personal, sexual and social history in both works. In *Crave* this history is made up of fraught kinship relations, the legacies of violence, sexual awakenings and frustrations. In *4.48 Psychosis* it is structured through the repeated return to moments of failed recognition, from lovers, doctors and strangers. More so than her earlier works, *Crave* and *4.48 Psychosis* explore desire in a queer landscape, in which sexual and gender identities are fluid and fraught. The queering of desire in these works is manifested through the fugitive nature of desired objects, as the plays loop back repeatedly to the search for an unnamed, desired other.

This endless looping evokes the queering of time which has been an important part of queer theory since the 1990s. In the work of queer theorists such as Lee Edelman, Judith (Jack) Halberstam and Alison Kafer (to name a few) queer lives have been evoked in order to explore a different experience of temporality, which is not structured around social reproduction. That is to say, Edelman, Halberstam and Kafer ask in different ways what it means to live and create outside of the bounds of heterosexual reproduction and without the idea of creating for the next generation. In recent years, writers working in critical disability studies have returned to the notion of a temporality that is not oriented towards heteronormative reproduction. Robert McCruer's work on 'crip time' examines forms of protest which take place in a rebellious present, whilst Jasbir Puar brings together queer and crip temporalities to explore the experience of living in 'prognosis time'.[4] Lisa Baraitser likewise builds on crip and queer theories of time in order to explore a number of experiences which could be described as chronic.[5]

Kane's late works, I argue, exist in the chronic. They are not end-oriented, but rather are holding patterns which give time to forms of non-(re) productivity which are denied in normative time. Later in this chapter, I examine how this alternative approach to time and orientation opens up *4.48 Psychosis* for activist productions by the Belarus Free Theatre and Deafinitely Theatre. These productions exploit the queer temporality of the play in order to imagine futures which are outside of the norms of productivity and reproduction. They are self-consciously queer, present forms of living in which there is no clear divide between psychological, political and social suffering.

## Kane's late style: What does theatre want?

*Crave* and *4.48 Psychosis* might best be described together as Kane's 'late works', and her stylistic shift in these two plays reflective of a 'late style'. The phrase 'late works' emphasizes that both plays represent a shift in dramaturgical handling of her major themes, as well as being the last plays she wrote. *Crave* and *4.48 Psychosis* present clear formal differences from Kane's earlier works, first, in their abandoning of *dramatis personae*, setting and stage directions, and second, in the increased density of their explorations of psychic life. These plays thus demonstrate a progression of Kane's dramaturgical vision, as well as a reflexive reconsideration of her earlier work. Dan Rebellato has demonstrated the extent to which *Crave* constitutes a return to the language and themes of Kane's first monologues, performing what he terms a 'wholesale cannibalisation' of *Starved*.[6] In both *Crave* and *4.48 Psychosis* psychic life forms a knot at the centre of the dramaturgy, increasingly difficult to parse into a coherent dramatic universe.

I wish to use the language of 'lateness' to highlight the sense of temporal dislocation which is present in these works. To be late is to be dislocated from expected temporal frameworks. It is to thwart expectations, to refuse productivity – to be both in time and disrupting time. In his posthumously published work on *Late Style*, Edward Said rejects the idea that artists creating late in life 'confer a spirit of reconciliation and serenity on late works'.[7] Turning to examine works written at the end of artist's lives which are void of serenity, Said asks: 'What if age and ill health don't produce serenity at all' but are instead, 'an occasion to stir up more anxiety, tamper irrevocably with the possibility of closure, leave the audience more perplexed and unsettled than before?'[8] Late style rejects chrononormativity, and troubles our assumptions about the relationship between a body of work, expectations of completeness and the author's position in the life course.

Kane's late plays share the combination of an attention to mortality and a 'deliberately unproductive productiveness' with which Said characterized late style.[9] Like the works of Ibsen, Genet and Beethoven that Said examines,

Kane's late works are emphatically inconclusive. They also share a deep and untimely preoccupation with death and mortality. In *4.48 Psychosis* the speaker feels aged and oppressed by their life, 'like I'm eighty years old. I'm tired of my life and I'm ready to die.'[10] This oppressiveness is distinctly untimely – a closeness to age creeping into a voice whose chronological location should be closer to youth (and is usually performed as such). In *Crave* too, an awareness of death disrupts the supposed conformity between selfhood and location in the life course. At the same time, these considerations of mortality in Kane's works operate outside of typical tragic frameworks, 'tampering irrevocably with the possibility of closure' and 'leaving the audience more unsettled and perplexed than before.'[11] There is no finality to these works, and the playtexts issue ongoing challenges to theatre-makers to stage them in a multiplicity of different ways. A tendency in theatre criticism to heavily biographize these works (especially *4.48 Psychosis*) might even be read as uncomfortable attempts to introduce finality into their unsettling inconclusiveness.

In thinking of *Crave* and *4.48 Psychosis* as examples of 'late style' I wish to avoid the crude implication that Kane's premature death was either inevitable or somehow 'foreseen'. Such an inference is pointless and reductively biographical. Considering Kane's last two plays in terms of their 'lateness' has a further advantage. As well as signalling their subversive relationship with time, it avoids a language of finality which would structure the sequence of Kane's works from their (and her) end. Had Kane lived a longer life, it is highly likely that she would have written more works of different styles, and the language of finality (describing *Crave* and *4.48 Psychosis* as the 'penultimate' and 'final' works) leans close to the suggestion that these works and her subsequent death somehow 'completed' her theatrical project.[12] The language of lateness, on the other hand, simply points to the fact that these are the latest of Kane's works that exist, and that they contain a stylistic consistency which separates them from earlier works.

Kane's late works turn to the audience in a new, and newly unsettling, mode. The shock of onstage violence had been a key dramaturgical tool in *Blasted*, *Phaedra's Love* and *Cleansed*, repeatedly unsettling the relationship between audience and artwork. In *Blasted* and *Phaedra's Love* this creates an unstable identificatory field for the audience, and in *Cleansed* it holds the audience in a state of visual stress whilst provoking and thwarting their predictive capacities (as I have argued in Chapters 2 and 3). This use of violence has been described in some productions as a veritable assault on the audience. More recently, debates around the use of trigger warnings surrounding the performance and teaching of Kane's works indicate the extent to which we continue to understand their explicit content as their major impact.[13] In the past chapters I have argued that by looking beyond the shock factor of the onstage violence in Kane's earlier plays, we can identify the role of violence in transforming the theatrical site into a space of negative (Winnicottian) play. Explicit content becomes a factor in the complex negotiation between artwork and potential audience member, as the artwork invites the audience to occupy a fraught psychic middle ground between stage and auditorium.

Essential to Kane's late style is a transformation of this dynamic. In *Crave* and *4.48 Psychosis* it is no longer violence that thwarts identification but a direct meta-theatrical mode of address. These plays face their audiences head on and actively demand specific modes of spectatorship from them. As I described in Chapter 4, *4.48 Psychosis* renders the spectator's position almost untenably fraught. The spectator is implicated directly into the suffering of the onstage subject(s). Herein I take a closer look at the mechanics of this implication, suggesting that through a radical revisioning of her source texts Kane generates a vision of psychic life which is at once despairing and desiring. In both late plays, the dynamics of desire transcend the dramatic worlds and extend out into the audience. The psychic space generated by productions of these works can feel filled with the sense that the work itself *wants something*. As Anna Harpin puts it in her study of madness and contemporary art practices, 'I am less concerned with what madness [in the theatre] *is* than what it *wants* and *needs*.'[14] Desire enters the space of negative play as an affect in these works and circulates uncomfortably between staged subject(s) and potential audience.

Suggesting that desire functions as an affect in the late works, alongside anger, fear, irritation and confusion, moves us beyond the psychoanalytic framework. Thinking of desire as an affect rather than a psychoanalytic drive means thinking of it as something which circulates between bodies and things, including between an artwork and an audience. It can be passed backwards and forward, offered, refused or accepted. Feminist theatre criticism has explored the ways in which desire might be generated within the situation of performance, between performers and audience members. In her classic book of feminist criticism *Unmarked*, Peggy Phelan widened this investigation of the role of desire in the act of looking, noting that '[w]hile the notion of the potential reciprocal gaze has been considered part of the "unique" province of live performance, the desire to be seen is also activated by looking at inanimate art'.[15] Desire as an affect can circulate in a less direct way in the play-space between audience and artwork. In the same way that an audience member can feel aggressed by a performance, it is possible to feel *wanted* by a performance. To feel solicited, in Green's terms, to be something for the performance which goes beyond the role of spectator.[16] This solicitation can be mingled with aggression and pain, creating a difficult encounter in the auditorium.

## Suicidality: Returning to Kane's sources

The role that desire plays in the representation of suicidal pain in Kane's late works is revealed through close attention to her transformation of intertextual source material. In *Crave* and *4.48 Psychosis* Kane makes use of texts which are explicitly concerned with pathology, relocating them in a dramatic world which capaciously intertwines the experiences of longing, desire and despair. In the case of *4.48 Psychosis* these include the Beck Depression Inventory (see Chapter 4) and Edwin Shneidman's book *The Suicidal Mind*. In *Crave* Kane draws on a huge number of personal and intertextual sources. Her most consistent source text, as Rebellato has demonstrated, is her own university monologue *Starved*, which explicitly described an experience of bulimia. This integration of intertextual source material enables a re-mapping of the relationship between desire and despair in the late works.

Kane moves from representing suicides onstage in *Blasted*, *Phaedra's Love* and *Cleansed* to giving voice to suicidal suffering in *Crave* and *4.48 Psychosis*. This move is both a thematic and a structural one. Thematically, the late works focus not on the act of suicide but on *suicidality*. 'Suicidality' is a term drawn from the study of suicide and refers to the experience of suicidal thoughts, feelings and pain, often but not necessarily leading to suicide attempts. It is also used to describe 'the risk of suicide, usually indicated by suicidal ideation or intent, especially as evident in the presence of a well-elaborated suicidal plan'.[17] It is in the former sense that I use it here, to refer to the experience of living whilst in some way wanting to die or wanting not to be alive. Suicidality is distinct from the experiences of those seeking to end their lives due to progressive or terminal illness, or in the name of a cause or military endeavour. Furthermore, it is one of a number of medicalized experiences which may lead to an act of suicide, others including the suicides of people in the midst of psychotic experiences. *Crave* and *4.48 Psychosis* offer presentations of a specific type of suicidal experience, which is not universal.

The decision to explore suicidality rather than to stage suicides constitutes an important formal shift in Kane's exploration of mental pain. The representation of 'completed' suicides on or off stage has been a staple of Western theatre since the days of Greek tragedy, and has a complex history too vast to review in this chapter. It is worth noting, however, that in many cases, plays which represent completed suicides are not about the experience of wanting to die. Instead, they understand death by suicide from the outside, as an act taken due to interlocking social and political challenges and frustrated choices which has tragic consequences for the individual and the community in which it occurs. Approaches to suicide narratives which seek outside (social or political) explanation find their correlate in sociological approaches to suicide, most notably in the work of Émile Durkheim. As Jon Venn notes, Durkheim shifted from 'the amoral de-political biomedical model into one that positions society as the cause, and therefore responsible. It pushes the possibility (and moral necessity) of a political response'.[18] Plays which represent suicide as a sociopolitical phenomenon invite speculation as to the reasons the onstage subjects take their lives, and to a certain extent the subject becomes eclipsed by this speculation. Phaedra's suicide, for example, can be understood variously as an act of vengeance following Hippolytus's rejection, of shame in the face of her confession to Hippolytus, or an attempt to escape her fated passion. Each of these interpretations has different resonances for the themes of honour, gender politics and the stability of body politic in the play. Yet from the perspective of the community in which completed suicide took place, the reasons and the person behind the act itself are always ultimately opaque.

Any staging of plays that are about completed suicide raise serious representational challenges. In his work on theatrical representations of suicide, Venn draws on the work of philosopher Jean Améry to suggest that a completed suicide is always an *aporia* – an act that both eliminates the possibility of expression and is itself an expression. The representation of suicide on stage generates an inherent contradiction:

> These difficulties, in theatrical engagement, arise intrinsically from the nature of the suicide. The completed suicide ushers in the question of self-erasure. Suicide obscures active articulation; suicide eliminates communication even as it is uttered. Yet, suicide is simultaneously an act, a performance; if it is the elimination of the self, this elimination is necessarily written upon and through the body. As a result, suicide figures as *aporia*, an act that precludes its own utterance.[19]

As Venn notes, interpretations of suicide as either inherently silent or politically explainable are both lacking. Sociological reasons for committing suicide obscure the personal, and the personal seems to transcend sociopolitical explanations:

> From the sociological perspective, the suicide is often understood through examination of what has led to suicide, identifying causes in the surrounding sociopolitical environment. Yet, the suicide is also a self-imposed suicide, a deliberate withdrawal. The suicide silences themselves, a self-created silence. So, our understandings of suicide can shift between the imposed and the wilful.[20]

The death of Robbie in *Cleansed* might be a key example here. In Chapter 3, I repeated the usual summary of Robbie's character trajectory: That Robbie is an illiterate schizophrenic teenager who commits suicide after learning to read and count, and thus realizing the length of his sentenced imprisonment. Robbie's character is to a certain extent completed, wrapped up by the representational mode of his death. At the same time, because of his death, we never really know him. His death eclipses his character. *Crave* and *4.48 Psychosis* are not plays about suicide in this sense. In fact, nobody dies by suicide during these plays (despite the frequently cited erroneous trope that there is a suicide in each of Kane's work). What they represent is not completed suicide but the ongoing experience of suicidal pain.

Kane's approach to representing suicidality is informed by Edwin Shneidman's book *The Suicidal Mind*, which she quotes liberally from in *4.48 Psychosis*. In this foundational work on the study of suicide, Shneidman provides in-depth case studies of three of his patients: Ariel Wilson, Beatrice Bessen and Castro Reyes. He argues that suicides in most cases are 'caused by pain, a certain kind of pain – *psychological* pain' which he calls '*psychache*'.[21] This pain 'stems from thwarted or distorted psychological needs'.[22] Shneidman traces different sets of these 'vital needs' in the testimonies in each of his case studies. Of all of Kane's diverse sources, Antje Diedrich identified Shneidman's work as providing the basis for the type of endlessly desiring subject staged in *4.48 Psychosis*:

> *4.48 Psychosis* clearly reflects Shneidman's notion of suicide as 'a drama in the mind' with the self focusing in on a thwarted vital need and moving to psychological constriction and suicide. Within this drama in the mind, the world of psychiatry is represented in negative terms, not responding to but worsening the I's *psychache* and suicidal intentions.[23]

Kane draws on the notion of 'vital needs' in both *Crave* and *4.48 Psychosis*, in which the speaker yearns for the fulfilment of 'this need I have for which I would die'. Vital needs are experienced as extreme yearning and desire in Shneidman's text. Like the speakers in Kane's late works, the subjects of his case studies experience intense craving and despair side by side.

Nevertheless, *4.48 Psychosis*'s presentation of the relationship between desire and suicidal psychic life is strikingly different from Shneidman's. Shneidman's suicidal dramas are perhaps best characterized novel-like, as he presents his case studies as compelling narratives in which the patient (hero) struggles against the nemesis of their unfulfilled need. Patients are presented as intriguing characters, with suicide attempts forming the central point in their narrative arc. The subject of the first study is introduced in this mode:

> Ariel's appearance was somewhat unusual, certainly memorable. She had a lovely face, touched with brooding – she reminded me of a young Dolores Del Rio, the movie actress of my youth – pale skin and ebony hair. She wore a floor-length dress, blue, with tiny white polka-dots; the sleeves were to her wrist; at her throat, a choker collar, decorated with the same white lace.[24]

Having established the attractiveness and movie-star-like charisma of this subject, the stage is set for a dramatic revelation: 'she undid her collar and her sleeves and from what I saw I could estimate that, except for her lovely hands and face, every part of her was covered in angry keloid scars'.[25] The subsequent case studies are introduced in similar style. The subject of the second study, Beatrice Bessen is

> an attractive, slender, handsomely dressed woman. [. . .] Not hostile, but deeply rebellious; not iconoclastic, but thoroughly unimpressed by authority; not surly, but beyond being captivated by anyone.[26]

and the third, Castro Reyes is 'handsome, and robust, with a penchant for cutting corners and defying the establishment'.[27]

Following these introductions, Shneidman documents his conversations and reproduces edited extracts of correspondence with each subject in which they describe their experiences up to and including a failed suicide attempt. The accounts are followed by an identification of the vital needs of each patient, and how their inability to meet these needs led to the suicide attempt. Ariel and Castro's accounts are each accompanied by a short section headed 'A Sad Postscript', which recounts the circumstances of their death. Character-driven and structured by their endings, Shneidman's case studies follow a tragic structure. Indeed, Shneidman actually describes suicide as 'the tragic drama of the mind' in the introduction to his book. In these case studies, like in tragedies, characters emerge to as objects of narrative. In *4.48 Psychosis* Kane borrows words and phrases from these case studies, but absolutely refuses the kind of characterizations in which Shneidman indulges.

Instead, Kane draws specifically on moments in which the subjects of the case studies seem to reach a crisis of communication or are out of touch with the completeness of the characterizations provided by Shneidman. Beatrice Bessen's feelings of separation between 'me and my body' recur

*4.48 Psychosis*'s 'here I am/ and there is my body/ dancing on the glass.'[28] Of the three case studies, Kane quotes the most from Castro Reyes's lengthy correspondence with Shneidman. The reproduction of parts of Shneidman's 'vital needs form' near the end of the play quotes most extensively from Castro's 'need for affiliation'.[29]

Kane distils moments from each case study in *4.48 Psychosis* which focus specifically on the potential space between self and other. In one of the letters Shneidman cites, Castro writes: 'Please reply soon. I must regain control and find the solution. R.S.V.P . . . I now reach out to you for help.'[30] In Kane's reworking, this phrase becomes the basis for a single scene made up of two acronyms:

RSVP ASAP.[31]

The scene is bracketed by two more scenes which draw on Castro's complaints: his sense of existing in a 'Living Death' ('I have been dead for a long time') and the torment of being in love with 'a person who does not exist'.[32] In both instances, Kane draws on the parts of Castro's testimony in which he attempts to reach out beyond himself, navigating the space between suicidal pain and desire – for an interlocutor, a lover and a sense of being alive.

Castro finds his way into *4.48 Psychosis* without being named or described. Kane's condensation of his lengthy plea for help into the simple and urgent:

RSVP ASAP

exemplifies her reappropriation of Shneidman's correspondence. Where Shneidman converts his case studies into characters, Kane uses their words to form a dramatic sense of openness which searches for an absent interlocutor. In doing so she allows the audience to apprehend the speaker in the midst of their suicidal experience, without the retroactive narrative frame which is generated after a completed suicide occurs. Kane removes the framework through which to understand Castro's plea and it becomes, like his and the speaker(s)' desire, painfully objectless. The *desire for a reply* becomes the unique content of this scene, and thus the play opens up a potential space, in which the audience is invited to consider what a response might consist of, and what kind of intimacy is being demanded.

Kane's reworking of her own early monologue in *Crave* similarly re-orients her textual sources towards a confrontation with the audience. In her university monologue *Starved*, Kane had told the story of a teenager suffering from bulimia. The monologue loops through the young woman's binges and purges, her family drama and periods of hospitalization. The monologue is a powerful piece of writing which portrays the experience of being trapped in a cycle of disordered eating, and finding enjoyment as well as pain in the experience. In *Crave*, Kane reuses sections of *Starved* in a new context. Here the pressures expressed in sections of *Starved* are presented outside of clear diagnostic or kinship structures, in a radically unstable dramatic setting. For example, the following lines recur in both *Starved* and *Crave*:

He buys me a make-up kit, blushers and lipstick and eyeshadow. And I paint my face with bruises and blood and cuts and swelling and one the mirror in deep red, UGLY
[. . .]
Be a woman, be a woman, FUCK YOU.[33]

In *Starved* the lines refer to a gift the speaker receives from her father whilst in hospital. In this context it references the pressures the speaker feels from her family and doctors to control her body, her difficult identification with her mother's body and rejection of her father's attempts a reconciliation. In other words, it is deeply embedded in a diagnostic and family drama.

In the mouth of C in *Crave*, however, the same line achieves very different resonances. The preceding lines introduce the dissonance between C's experience of herself and the appearance of her body:

**C** I want to feel physically like I feel emotionally.
Starved
**M** Beaten.
**A** Broken.[34]

C then takes on both her own bodily dissonance and those of M and A as she describes the episode of painting her face. Her desire to externalize her own internal bruising and that of others complicates the dramaturgy of this moment, as the bodies and experiences of the characters merge and collapse. What's more, the burden of performing normative gender (the demand C feels to 'be a woman') is generalized when the scene is removed from its original context. Speaking out into the audience, C identifies the source of the burden in the gaze of the spectator, the stage itself being a location in which women's bodies are scrutinized and made to manifest the trappings of femininity.[35] Later in *Crave*, C repeatedly yearns for obscurity, turning away from the gaze of an other with the request: 'Let me hide myself.'[36] Borrowing a further line from *Starved*, C laments being held in a location (the stage or psychiatric ward) in which 'even dreams aren't private'.[37] In *Crave* then, Kane transforms the torment of the speaker of *Starved* to focus specifically on experiences of exposure and self-representation – experiences which are particularly pertinent to the encounter between performer and audience.

In this way, Kane changes the *orientation* of these expressions of despair. The explorations of suicidality in her late works are not end-oriented, which is to say they are not oriented towards cure or by death. In her work on *Queer Phenomenology*, Sara Ahmed describes orientation as it relates to physical objects:

> We are turned toward things. Such things make an impression upon us. We perceive them as things insofar as they are near to us, insofar as we share residence with them. Perception hence involves orientation; what is perceived depends on where we are located which gives us a certain take on things.[38]

For Ahmed, we can also be turned towards things which are not physical objects. People, ideas and affects also orient us, giving us a 'take' on a particular situation or (self-) experience. (The idea of 'home', for example, is important to Ahmed's phenomenology.) Building on Ahmed's insights, I would suggest that narrative and discursive objects also orient our 'take' on experiences of suffering or mental illness. Take, for example, the doctor–patient dialogues of *4.48 Psychosis*. In these exchanges, the doctor repeatedly offers the patient the same narrative object through which to understand their experience: the image of a mentally well, self-responsible version of the self who has 'something to offer'. This narrative object is frequently introduced into the dialogues, turning the patient-voice towards it. It regulates the discourses of selfhood available to the patient-voice. As Ahmed notes, the way we are oriented impacts our sense of what is possible or reachable:

> What is reachable is determined precisely by orientations we have already taken. Some objects do not even become objects of perception, as the body does not move toward them.[39]

As we saw in Chapter 4, when the patient-voice attempts to understand themselves in a different register in these dialogues, these alternative versions of selfhood is placed firmly out of reach. A specific version of cure through responsibility and self-management is presented as an object *towards* which the patient is expected to orient themselves here. We might understand the speaker's objections in these scenes as a *turning away from* this object of cure.

Today, much mental health discourse is heavily oriented towards this image of cure. Cure or self-management might be said to be the objects of psychiatry and mental health interventions, both in the sense of being their focus and end goal. The orientation towards cure has a temporal and disciplinary dimension, as Alison Kafer notes in *Feminist, Queer, Crip*:

> Futurity has often been framed in curative terms. A time frame that casts disabled people (as) out of time, or obstacles to the arc of progress. [...] Within this frame of curative time, the only appropriate disabled body/mind is one cured or moving toward cure. Cure in this context most obviously signals the elimination of impairment but can also mean normalising treatments that seek to assimilate the disabled body as much as possible.[40]

Today's mediatized mental health landscape is largely turned towards the object(ification) of the self-managing and self-responsible service user. As Anna Harpin has noted, this orientation also finds its pervasive manifestation in anti-stigma campaigns which typically offer up the image of a self-responsible recovered individual, who maintains their mental health through a regime of wellness, medication and self-management. For Harpin 'consciousness-raising anti-stigma campaigns [...] reinscribe this as *the* narrative of "positive" madness – of positive overcoming through self-management'.[41] *Crave* and *4.48 Psychosis* change the orientation of their representations of mental distress. Rather than turning towards an idealized version of cure the speakers in both plays turn instead towards the present, orientating themselves through an encounter with a real or imagined interlocutor.

This alternative orientation came strikingly to the fore in Deafinitely Theatre's production of *4.48 Psychosis* at the New Diorama Theatre in London in 2018. Deafinitely Theatre is a D/deaf-led theatre company that makes bilingual work in British Sign Language (BSL) and spoken English. In this production, director Paula Garfield split the text over four actors: two deaf BSL-speaking actors who played 'patients' (Adam Bassett and Brian Duffy), and two hearing BSL-speaking actors who play doctors (Jim Fish and Matt Kyle). The play took place behind a Perspex screen, on a plain, clinical-style set with lime green doors on either side. Difficulties in communication defined the psychiatric experience in this production. The doctors' obtuse and patronizing attitudes are compounded by their stilted signing, lacked the expressive quality from that of the patients. Standing on the opposite side of the stage from the patients, white coat on and clipboard in hand, one had the sense of an unbreachable gulf between hearing medical establishment and the eloquent BSL-speaking patients.

Performing *4.48 Psychosis* in BSL revealed and highlighted orientations of the different voices in the play. As writers in the field of Deaf Studies have long argued, sign language cultures have their own unique understandings of interpersonal dynamics which can widen and contradict the understandings of hearing, non-signing people. Of particular interest here is the way in which sign language makes explicit the role of deliberate orientation in listening. Baumann and Murray suggest that the 'Deaf walk' might be considered an area of deaf gain, as it generates forms of collectivity among signers:

> Significantly, when deaf people walk, however, they engage in constant eye contact, and more significantly, they must take care of the other person, extending their peripheral vision to ensure that the other person does not walk into any objects. Although this may seem a minor point, there is a larger lesson about the nature of Deaf collectivist relations. Signers take care of each other, whether strangers or intimate friends, when engaged in a peripatetic conversation.[42]

Deafinitely Theatre's production of *4.48 Psychosis* made use of this necessary emphasis on orientation to expose the extent to which the orientation towards cure could constitute a form of hostility.

This took place at the point in the playtext of *4.48 Psychosis* in which the medical voice breaks their professional distance. Drawn out by the obstinate silence of the patient, the doctor breaks down momentarily and admits their own difficulties with their work:

Most of my clients want to kill me. When I walk out of here at the end of the day I need to go home to my lover and relax. I need my friends to be really together.
(*Silence.*)
I fucking hate this job and I need my friends to be sane.
(*Silence.*)
I'm sorry.[43]

In most productions this moment marks the possibility of connection between doctor and patient, a glimpse at a relationship which can be honest, even if it is antagonistic. Garfield's production presented a bleaker vision. The 'I'm sorry' was spoken with disdain as the doctor turned his back on the patient, literally blocking him out of the field of signed conversation. At this point, Duffy was left to sign his compassionate response to the doctor's back. The antagonistic doctor–patient relationship in this production highlighted the extent to which the clinical encounter truncated the expression of the patient. The patient-voice was only allowed to speak as an object of cure – the doctor figures would only orientate themselves towards Duffy and Bassett in these moments. In the absence of recognition from the medical establishment, the play became a moving exploration of solidarity, as the patient voices turned away from the clinical encounter and towards each other.

## Directionless desire

Refusing to be oriented by an expected end, Kane's late plays hold open a painful and intense presentness. Kane invites us to consider suicidality as the endurance of suicidal pain, without the structuring finality of a 'completed' suicide. In *Crave* and *4.48 Psychosis* the suicidal subject is also a desiring subject – a *living* subject who navigates complex interpersonal webs of desire and despair. The desires for love, sex, recognition and salvation are folded into one another in both plays so that they become deliberately difficult to disentangle. They are expressed through the turning towards an interlocutor, out in the auditorium.

This orientation to the present moment of performance is generated and maintained by a dynamic in which lovers, spectators and potential saviours are always fugitive. Both *Crave* and *4.48 Psychosis* draw on and manipulate the conventions of monologue and soliloquy to make visible the trajectory of the speakers' demands from the staged consciousness into the audience. As I argued in the last chapter, this is achieved in *4.48 Psychosis* through an invitation to the spectator to identify with the speakers' acts of looking. In the first production of *Crave,* director Vicky Featherstone collaborated with Kane to stage the play around the idea of a talk show. Featherstone explained that this idea was developed through discussions about emotional burdens: 'we felt that we lived in a society that invites us to unburden our emotional baggage – and yet what happens when we do that? Do we take responsibility for that? And we felt that in most cases we didn't, but culture in the West was desperate to encourage people to do this unburdening without taking responsibility.'[44] The notion of unburdening highlights the trajectory between speaker and listener. A burden is passed from one body to another – it cannot disappear. To use Ahmed's phrase, an unburdening in conversation 'presses' onto the interlocutor orienting them towards the burden. By having the speakers turned facing the audience the Featherstone production made clear in which direction the highly emotional content of the play was headed. The directness of the demands of the speakers highlights and troubles the fourth wall in this work, circulating in the negative play-space. In *Crave* in particular, the burdens and secrets which the speakers unload onto the audience are laden with desire and sexual content, and desire as well as despair becomes one of the affects the audience is asked to navigate.

By guiding the audience to notice the trajectory of demands from stage to audience, Kane's late works make their potential audiences conspicuously aware of their own frames. These playtexts *play* with the conditions of their own potential performance, blurring or highlighting their objects of address. This introduces a rhetorical complexity to the dramaturgy of both works. As psychoanalytic critic Barbara Johnson reminds us, the self-conscious highlighting of a text's frame can actually serve rhetorically to undermine the very boundaries it seems to point out: 'The "frame" thus becomes not the borderline between the inside and the outside, but precisely what subverts the applicability of the inside/outside act of interpretation.'[45] *Crave* and *4.48 Psychosis* disturb the act of interpretation, turning to their audiences via modes of address that both are and are not meta-theatrical exclamations. In both plays speech begins within a dramatic world which is troubled rather than eliminated by the throwing out of demands onto the audience. As such, the audience is involved to the point that it renders the boundaries of theatrical space psychically porous.

In both plays, desire is characterized by a yearning for something that is impossible to find and is sought for in unlikely urban and medical sites. The speakers yearn for loved others who they present as fugitive, always slipping away from the speaker and the speaker's attempt to describe them. This is perhaps best characterized in the relationship between C and M in *Crave,* in which M occupies an uncertain position as possibly C's mother, doctor or loved other. Usually cast as an older woman, M's initial refers to 'mother', corresponding to C's which stands for 'child'.[46] Nevertheless, Kane's reduction of the titles to initials was a deliberate attempt to open up possibilities for different relations to emerge in future productions of the play: 'I didn't want to write those things down because then I thought they'd get fixed in those things forever and nothing would ever change.'[47] M describes and acts out her own narrative, in which she seduces and abuses B in an attempt to have a child. Yet she also occupies a position as the implicit female love-object and/or mother-figure for C. M moves through different positions in relation to C, taking up roles that respond to C's craving for something or someone who will end her suffering.

*Crave* opens with C's apostrophe: 'You're dead to me.'[48] Identifying the object of the apostrophe in her next line, 'Somewhere outside the city, I told my mother, you're dead to me', C seems to denote M as her addressee, at least in productions which follow the original casting. Later M and C perform a mother–daughter pair, discussing the infidelity of a husband and father:

**M** When he's generous, kind, thoughtful and happy, I know he's having an affair.
**C** He thinks we're stupid, he thinks we don't know.
**M** A third person in my bed whose face eludes me.[49]

Ingrid Craigie noted that when playing M in the original production, 'there were sections where I definitely felt, [. . .] I was her mother and that A was the father, and that there was a father, mother, daughter [relationship] here.'[50]

This implicit kinship between C and M is destabilized in the middle of the play, in which M emerges as the clinical voice, first introducing the clinical site ('Sunny landscapes. Pastel Walls. Gentle air conditioning'[51]), and then taking C's medical history. In this version of their relationship, M rejects the maternal relation with C outright:

**C** You could be my mother.
**M** I'm not your mother.[52]

Instead, another relation emerges in which M, in her role of doctor/therapist, becomes the object of C's desire, even as C acknowledges that she had 'fallen in love with someone who does not exist':[53]

**C** My entire life is waiting to see the person with whom I am currently obsessed, starving the weeks away until our next fifteen minute appointment.[54]

We might note an Oedipal reference here, in the elision of mother, doctor and lover. At the same time, the representational slippage with which M is presented to the audience repeats the frustrating nature of C's experience of desire in which the potential loved object never quite comes into focus, or into language. C's unclear desire for M, or some version of M, takes place in the shadow of the much clearer abusive relationship which C has with A. Unlike the heterosexual pairings in the play (again, dependent on casting: A/C, B/M), the nature of the C/M relationship never becomes clear in the playtext, inviting a potential audience to repeat C's search for an impossible object as spectators.

The indeterminacy of the loved object-position in which C casts M in *Crave* becomes total in *4.48 Psychosis*. In *4.48 Psychosis* Kane pushes this representation of desperate and impossible desire in the shadow of sexual violence to an extreme. There are moments of romantic and sexual attachments threaded throughout the playtext of *4.48 Psychosis*, none of which are possible to pick out as objective relationships. The speaker(s) identifies a male lover in the moment they plan their suicide: 'I am jealous of my sleeping lover and covet his induced unconsciousness.'[55] Alongside this lover who is present only in his sleep, references and addresses to another (or several other) absent love-objects emerge. The third scene introduces two references to absent love-objects, at least one in the medical sphere:

> It wasn't for long, I wasn't there long. But drinking bitter black coffee I catch that medicinal smell in a cloud of ancient tobacco and something touches me in that still sobbing place and a wound from two years ago opens like a cadaver and long buried shame roars its foul decaying grief.[56]

> I want to scream for you, the only doctor who ever touched me voluntarily [. . .] I trusted you, I loved you, and it's not losing you that hurts me, but you're bare-faced fucking falsehoods that masquerade as medical notes.[57]

Characterized only by the subject's sense of betrayal and lingering pain, these lovers barely achieve referential status as they come from a past or life outside of the play which remains obscure.

For the rest of the play, these lovers are increasingly addressed through the rhetorical figure of apostrophe: 'the direct address of an absent, dead, or inanimate being by a first-person speaker'.[58] The speaker(s) positions themself(ves) as repeatedly reaching out to a source of satisfaction (and increasingly salvation) that is at the same time revealed to be vacant:

> No one touches me, no one gets near me. But now you've touched me and somewhere so fucking deep I can't believe and I can't be that for you. Because I can't find you.[59]

Absent because they are dead, lost or non-existent, the object(s) of the apostrophes seems to give the lie to the form of address itself which is unequal to the strength of feeling which it attempts to carry. This becomes clear when the apostrophe simultaneously becomes a rejection:

> Fuck you. Fuck you. Fuck you for rejecting me by never being there, fuck you for making me feel shit about myself, fuck you for bleeding the fucking love and life out of me, fuck my father for fucking up my life for good and fuck my mother for not leaving him, but most of all, fuck you God for making me love a person who does not exist, FUCK YOU FUCK YOU FUCK YOU.[60]

Moving from an apostrophic insult, into an address to God and back into a general curse, this outburst destroys the object it set out to find. As Johnson notes, the act of apostrophe is always to some extent fictive:

Apostrophe is thus both direct and indirect: based etymologically on the notion of turning aside, of digressing from straight speech, it manipulates the I/Thou structure of direct address in an indirect, fictionalized way. The absent, dead, or inanimate entity addressed is thereby made present, animate, and anthropo-morphic. Apostrophe is a form of ventriloquism through which the speaker throws voice, life, and human form into the addressee, turning its silence into mute responsiveness.[61]

For Johnson, apostrophe seems like an orientation towards an absent other, whilst actually being an orientation towards oneself. The speaker's apostrophe in *4.48 Psychosis* undoes its own ventriloquism. Rather than constructing a version of the other for the audience, or indeed for the speaker, this form of address in *4.48 Psychosis* underlines its own emptiness. An unstable 'I' reaches out to address a 'you' which is not only absent but non-existent, and thus unable to fill the object-position the speaker seeks to form for them. Behind this non-existent 'you' is the actually present audience, who receive the apostrophe in the object's absence. To a certain extent, this is true of all apostrophic modes of address. Kane exploits this vacancy at the centre of apostrophe to have the demands of her late plays fall heavily at the feet of the audience.

Through this hollow addressing of absent objects, *4.48 Psychosis* extends its demands onto its audience. Kane's play disturbs its own thematics of desire by converting address into apostrophe, and then apostrophe into an objectless expression of desire. As Johnson reminds us, the absence of objectification does not mean that a text (or indeed a performance) does not make demands on its audience – 'for in spite of the absence of mastery, there [may be] no lack of *effects of power*'.[62] Through a deliberate dramaturgical confusion of spectator, lover and doctor, *4.48 Psychosis* implicates its audience into its own demands. In the short scene,

RSVP ASAP

the speaker(s) at once addresses a medical interlocutor, lover and audience-members.[63] Imposing this condensed demand for reply onto an audience in a site which by its very nature prevents such a response places its audience in an ethical bind. The question, 'what do you offer?' is turned outwards towards the audience who remain seated, hyper-aware of the theatricality of a situation in which they can offer nothing, and yet are simultaneously and repeatedly asked to respond.

As the speaker(s) advances further into their breakdown in *4.48 Psychosis* this demand becomes increasingly urgent, apparently bound up with the speaker(s) own survival. The play's final moments combine a demand for a spectator's response, be it lover, doctor or audience member, with a heartbreaking plea:

I have no desire for death
no suicide ever had

watch me vanish
watch me

    vanish
watch me
watch me

    watch.[64]

The thematics of desire and dependency overspill their frame here, until the words of a staged subject seeking salvation from suicidal pain becomes both a demand on the supposed interlocutor and a distillation of the only response possible from the audience.

That this response is inadequate and unredemptive for the speaker is obvious when compared to the demands it made moments earlier, again with meta-theatrical undertones:

No one speaks
Validate me
Witness me
See me
Love me.[65]

Like the absent object of desire, the silent audience cannot produce a form of validation, love or witnessing that is in any way meaningful to the staged subject(s), precisely because of the theatricality of the situation of which they are constantly reminded. All the audience can do is watch and participate in the specular collapses the speaker(s) undergoes. Such watching does not provide the speaker(s) with the kind of witnessing which would enable the transition into narrative and alleviation of pain.[66] Instead it asks the audience to remain involved with the pain that is communicated to them, to sit through it without retreating into the busy separateness of the orientation towards cure.

Through a combination of the construction of a theatrical, psychotic mind-as-site which the audience is invited to inhabit and the invitation to the audience that they occupy the position of the impossible desired other, *4.48 Psychosis* forces its audience into a position of endurance. Christopher Bollas suggests that in the therapeutic encounter, the analyst is '*compell[ed]* [. . .] to experience the patient's inner object world'.[67] Acting under this powerful demand, the analyst enters the world of the analysand's 'unthought known', experiencing and eventually naming the object with the patient, allowing them to 'reliv[e] through language that which is known but not yet thought'.[68]

Throughout Kane's dramaturgy, there exists an element of this compulsion. The meeting between audience and spectator is never neutral in these works. The forces of disorientation, representations of physical and verbal violence are put to use in an attempt to actively mould the audiences into specific, spatialized experiences of great intensity. Reflecting on her relationship with her audiences, Kane noted that she did not aim to 'create a reaction', but instead was very clear about 'what I want *to do to them*'.[69] However, this is not to ask that the audience acts as the object-naming analyst. Instead, the dramaturgy holds the audience in a looping present, in which the consciousness at the centre of *4.48 Psychosis* demands over and over again to been seen, watched, validated and saved. At the same time, the speakers of both works ask emphatically *not* to be named or described. The play overreaches itself, making deeply uncomfortable demands on its audience to sit with the unburdening of the onstage subject's despair and tolerate but not resolve the subject(s)' impossible demands for salvation.

## *4.48 Psychosis* with the Belarus Free Theatre (2014): Queer time, love and suicidality

So far, this chapter has argued that Kane's late works issue demands that their audiences sit with the extreme expressions of suicidal suffering and objectless desire. According to my argument, demands enter the theatrical space in Kane's late plays, introducing desire as an affect which circulates in the play-space between audience and artwork, among the other possible experiences of identification, refusal, anger and hopelessness which the plays may provoke. As several critics have noted, the demanding nature of these works interrogate the audience's specular practices, drawing attention to the ethics of looking. According to this interpretation, *Crave* and *4.48 Psychosis* hold the audience in a meta-theatrical double-bind, making them consider their own spectating practices. For both Venn and Alicia Tycer, witnessing remains in the field of the visual, looking across the separation between auditorium and stage and receiving the testimony of the speaker.[70] I have suggested that the demand to witness is inevitably bound to fail, and it is through the inevitable failure of witnessing and validation that *4.48 Psychosis* invites its audience to participate in the 'intermediate area of experiencing' between subject and object, which takes place in the overlap between the audience and the psychic life represented on stage.[71]

In this section, I would like to look beyond this interpretation to examine productions in which additional ethical and political issues are introduced into *4.48 Psychosis*. What is it about the dramaturgy of this play that makes it both a powerful challenge to the question of how we regard the mental pain of others, *and* a vessel for the political demands of contrasting activist theatre groups?

Despite having been initially heavily interpreted through a biographical lens in the UK, *4.48 Psychosis* has repeatedly been used by political and activist theatre companies in order to raise awareness on a number of political issues. Deafinitely Theatre's production, for example, widened the focus on mental illness in the play, to make it a powerful work on the exclusion of D/deaf people from health and support services in the UK. One of the most striking of these adaptations is the curious and unexpected afterlife of the play in the repertoire of the Belarus Free Theatre company. In many ways, this trajectory seems quite separate from the role Kane's work has played in the history of British theatre. In 2005 Vladimir Shcherban, then the director of the National Theatre of Belarus, came across Kane's play after reading plays by Mark Ravenhill. Shcherban was struck by the resonances that he found in the work with the experience of living under dictatorship in Belarus and attempted to stage it at the National Theatre. The production was banned, and Shcherban and his creative collaborators performed it anyway, secretly rehearsing in the back of the National Theatre and then touring it in clandestine locations. As a consequence of this production, Shcherban and a number of performers soon joined forces with theatre-makers Natalia Kaliada and Nicolai Khalezin to form the underground theatre company Belarus Free Theatre (BFT). In 2011, 'the company's three artistic leaders, Natalia Kaliada, Nicolai Khalezin and Vladimir Shcherban were forced into exile. Becoming political refugees in the UK, BFT was given a home in the Young Vic, London and became an associate company of Falmouth University'.[72]

In 2015 the BFT revived *4.48 Psychosis* as part of their *Staging a Revolution* festival in collaboration with the Young Vic. The production was similar to the original staging – a staging which the company still puts on in secret in Belarus and directs over Skype. As the introduction to the production reminded audiences, both homosexuality and suicide are illegal in Belarus, with dictator Lukashenko having declared that suicide and depression 'do not exist' in the country. It is in the face of this violent denial of both homosexuality and despair that Shcherban declares:

> that Sarah Kane is a British playwright but we think she is a Belarussian national treasure. She was speaking the language that we were thinking.[73]

The BFT is campaigning on a specific geopolitical issue – freedom and democracy in Belarus – as well as producing works that have wider political resonances for Western audiences. The *Staging a Revolution* festival in 2015 united both these aims in a series of performances which challenged the separation between theatre and audience in which the *means* of transmitting politically charged material – both traditional theatre and digitization – itself became a performance.

The revival of the BFT's *4.48 Psychosis* as part *Staging a Revolution* festival introduced a complex layering of time and space into and prior to the performance itself. The production was one of several to take place in a secret site-specific location. On the day of the performance audience members were texted a meeting place to arrive at for about 7pm, and told to bring ID documents. I arrived and loitered on a street corner as other audience members turned up. Unidentified members of the theatre company began approaching groups of people within the crowd and led them to the secret location, which was House of Detention, Farringdon. ID was checked on the way in (I didn't have mine and they let me in anyway). The performance space was set up with benches and cushions on the floor, and blankets were provided. In the room at the back of the performance space free homemade soup and bread were being served for the audience. There was also a paying bar for drinks and a stall for programs and T-shirts. At the start of the performance one of the BFT's artistic directors Natalia Kaliada introduced the performance, and explained that the special conditions were a reference to the way in which the company conducts performances in Belarus. Belarusian audience members are asked to bring their passports as, if the make-shift theatre is raided and they get arrested, the period of detainment will be shorter if they have ID. The BFT often perform in disused or abandoned spaces and so provide blankets for warmth. After the performances the BFT feed their audience and hold discussions about the plays. In Belarus, Kaliada said, these discussions keep going until everyone gets arrested or falls asleep, but, she added, here in London we have something called 'health and safety' so we need to be out of here by 11pm.

After this mimicking of the attendance practices of a Belarusian audience, Kaliada picked up a laptop and told us that there was also an audience in Belarus currently joining us for the performance over Skype, and that if those audience-members were found to be watching they could be arrested. She showed us the stream of the Belarusian audience and we waved at them. The performance then began with the two actors Maria Sazonava and Yana Rusakevich emerging from behind an archway with candles. On the back wall of the performance space was projected a grainy recoding of the BFT's first banned performance of *4.48 Psychosis* from 2005 in Belarus, in Russian with English subtitles also projected onto the back wall. Their own performance was more or less a reproduction of the original performance (marketed as a revival) and used props such as matches, candles, a thermos and fruit, which had been chosen originally because they were lying around in the rooms of the Belarus National Theatre where they had secretly rehearsed the play in 2005.

The introduction of the original production and the present ongoing political situation in Belarus into the London production was enabled by the openness of the playtext's dramaturgy. It also revealed and exploited the unusual approach to time found in *4.48 Psychosis*. The playtext's potential to hold open an unresolved sense of the present became key to the production's success. This present was actually stretched across many locations and times: the 2005 recorded production in Belarus, the live 2015 production in London which revived the actions and speech of the original, and the clandestine live-streamed viewing in Belarus. Each of these situations was mapped onto another in a theatrical encounter in which a number of different audiences were implicated into the act of looking. This mirrored the repeated attention to a present moment of encounter in the playtext of *4.48 Psychosis*, which itself suggests an alternative temporality, in which both spectator and spectated loop back to moments of potential recognition which remain unfulfilled. This looping is not rigid, as in a traditional understanding of traumatic time. It might be better understood as counterproductive, an approach to time which runs against the chrono-normative orientation towards productivity. The rhetorical orientations towards the audience in *Crave* and especially in *4.48 Psychosis* are structured by this counterproductivity, so that they neither culminate nor disappear. Close attention to the temporality of the demands in *4.48 Psychosis*, both in the play and in the BFT's performance, reveals more about the transferability of the playtext's politics to new contexts.

The revealing of alternative temporal experiences can itself be considered a political move. As Lisa Baraitser argues in *Enduring Time*, there is political potential in paying attention to the forms of time that are typically erased from late capitalist ideas of production. Drawing on the work of Sarah Sharma she writes:

> Accelerated technologically driven capitalist societies that are ultimately organized around the urgency of seeking new markets and profits require

new mechanisms for managing the outcomes of speeding time. But, as Sarah Sharma has shown (2014) these new mechanisms play out differently across bodies and spaces. The politics of time and space ushered in by global capitalism is not simply about speed, but involves power relations as they emerge in time, and have to do with interrelated, relational and entangled ways that one person's time is used in the service of another's.[74]

Typically, capitalist time is the time of production – a time which is defined by its end goal. But, as Baraitser and Sharma note, these high-speed and profit-making experiences of time (think of a broker on a trading floor) are not the only forms of temporality that exist in a late capitalist society. What's more, they are not even the only forms of temporality on which capitalism depends. Other forms of temporality outside of producing are inherent in our experience of time, and are 'folded into' end-oriented, productivist chronologies. Baraitser highlights the political and social shifts required to pay attention to temporal practices such as: *staying, maintaining, repeating, delaying, enduring, recalling, remaining* and *ending*.[75]

This attention to alternative forms of time reveals modes of living which are not given value in dominant social and political discourses – be these in late capitalist or nationalist authoritarian regimes. It builds on the classic feminist observation that male (capitalist) productivity is underpinned by female (unpaid) labour. Baraitser and Sharma suggest that this labour, and many other forms of unpaid and unvalued activity, contain their own chronologies in the context of global capitalism.

> Everything does not simply get faster even though everybody appears to run out of time. What proliferates is a multiplicity of contradictory temporalities, although few of them escape the relentless push towards the accumulation of profit.[76]

Baraitser notes that this relentless push forces certain groups into repetitive temporalities which are not valued but at the same time exist in an ongoing relationship with capitalist time. These include, for example, 'the busy 'work' the unemployed do for their benefits in post-industrial societies'.[77] We might include the work of mental health service users in this category, especially those dependent on the benefits system, and whose 'recovery' is increasingly understood in relation to a return to productivity.[78] In this context the time of recovery or of therapy is end-oriented, and conceived of as a process of restitution of the individual into the productive workforce. As we saw in Chapter 4, it is this kind of temporal mode that the doctor-voice attempts (and fails) to introduce into *4.48 Psychosis*. On the other hand, times in which one suffers debilitating pain, experiences mental anguish or radical dissociation from the 'real' world are understood as valueless almost to the point of not being acknowledged socially at all. These are 'hidden forms of time', folded into the lives of many people without being recognized in our social-political structures.[79]

In *4.48 Psychosis* Kane returns these unproductive forms of living to the stage, allowing them to take up much of the time of the play. These 'hidden forms of time', Baraitser suggests, 'have a relation to the trapped time of disavowed durational activities that sustain people, situations, phenomena, institutions and art objects, and thereby underpin the maintenance of everyday life'.[80] In Baraitser's work these hidden temporalities range from active forms of maintenance (from childcare to public sanitation) to simply paying attention to and 'dwell[ing] in and with' ways of living outside of the realm of the productive. I would extend Baraitser's argument to suggest that in some contexts, these acts of 'dwell[ing] with' can themselves be understood as maintenance. To live with suicidality and psychosis is at times to experience life as a form of psychic endurance – a position expressed by the speaker(s) in *4.48 Psychosis* who is 'tired of life and [] want[s] to die'. Staying alive, getting out of bed, not getting out of bed, not eating, retreating from the world into psychosis – all of these are practices which can make up the maintenance of a life in the face of extreme mental pain. In her playtext, Kane suggests a dramaturgy in which these modes of *continuing to live* in the face of extreme mental suffering are allowed to expand and take up the time of the play.

The Belarus Free Theatre production of *4.48 Psychosis* could well be interpreted as an exploration of how one continues to live in the face of personal and political despair. One of the most impressive aspects of the performance was the emotional and physical range of Sazonava's and Rusakevich's performances. Their performances veered from intense rage, aggression and terror to tenderness, playfulness and comedic satire. This playfulness was contained in a dramaturgy which was structured around the idea of confinement and incarceration. Sazonava and Rusakevich returned repeatedly to the act of banging, clawing and knocking on the walls at intervals throughout the play, and climbing onto a grate which made up part of the site in which the performance took place. In the projection of the original production, which took place in a bar, the performers can be seen hiding themselves below the bar and under chairs. This treatment of space in both versions of the production laid out a boundary around the performance, creating a physical sense of oppression and confinement. The contrast between this evocation of physical confinement and the sheer breadth of emotional and physical movement in the performance generated a counterproductive dissonance. The performers found intimacy and expressive range in the face of their confinement. Incarceration in this production did not render expressions of inner life illegitimate, and this inner life was allowed to expand to enormous proportions for the hour in which the performance took place.

Attending to these hidden temporal practices is not in itself revolutionary – it does not overturn and often does not even directly challenge the temporal order. Rather it invites the audience to deliberately opt out of the chrononormative logic in which time spent living with and in despair is understood as valueless, erasable experience. We might understand this invitation as queering – a queering both of the time of illness/cure and of the power relations which seek to regulate inner life. A re-evaluation of the philosophy and politics of time in relation to reproduction has been an important element of queer theory and critical disability studies in the past two decades, building especially on Lee Edelman's polemical text *No Future* (2004). Edelman's concept of queer, futureless time asks what it means to live without investing in a future structured around heterosexual social reproduction. Heterosexual social reproduction is a version of the future which reproduces heterosexual family units as the building blocks of capitalist progress. It encourages the sacrifice of one generation (often through arduous productive work) for the sake of the next. Like productive and cure-oriented times, it is *end-oriented* and linear. Edelman's anti-reproductive proposition suggests a 'refusal of linear narrative as the ground for establishing meaning and the unfolding of time in normative patterns of progression'.[81]

Edelman's critique of reproductive futurism has an ethical-political line, which has been developed further by disabled and 'crip' theorists. According to reproductive futurism, any appeal which is framed as 'fighting for the kids' becomes 'the affirmation of a value so unquestioned, because so obviously unquestionable, [. . .] of the child whose innocence solicits our defence'.[82] It does so through a universalizing epistemological move which structures childhood as inevitably innocent and of the future. As bearers of social hope in reproductive futurism, the Child of the future is generalized and stands in for conservative norms. As Alison Kafer notes, the Child in this construction is inevitably white and able-bodied, as '"the future", especially figured through the "Child", is used to buttress able-bodied/able-minded heteronormativity'.[83] Kafer points to the ways in which disabled lives trouble the productivist and heteronormative assumptions which underpin reproductive futurism, and can be co-opted into its vision of futurity through the orientation towards cure: 'In our disabled state, we are not part of the dominant narratives of progress, but once rehabilitated we play a starring role: the sign of progress, the proof of development, the triumph of mind over body.'[84] Kafer moves beyond Edelman's simple rejection of futurity, arguing that '"fucking the future", at least in Edelman's terms, takes on a different valence for those who are *not* supported in their desires to project themselves (and their children) into the future in the first place', such as disabled people.[85]

In place of rejecting the future, Kafer proposes an attention to the 'strange temporalities' of crip and disabled experience in order to figure the future in a radically different mode – a process she proposes as a 'cripping' of time. '"To crip" like "to queer"', according to Robert McRuer, 'gets at processes that unsettle, or processes that make strange or get twisted. *Cripping* also exposes the ways in which able-bodiedness and able-mindedness get naturalised and the ways that bodies, minds and impairments that should be the absolute centre of a space or discussion get pushed from that space, issue or discussion'.[86] 'Cripping' involves a deliberate centring of bodies and minds that are distant from the norm and is thus a necessarily activist position. In developing the critique of reproductive futurism into a vision for 'crip futures', Kafer 'find[s] both disability and desire where they don't belong', in a future which is outside of productive and normative time.[87]

Kane's late works could be understood as queering time as insofar as they offer pockets of time in which productive and reproductive futures are on pause. Time filled by counterproductivity becomes another tool through which the plays orientate themselves queerly, into the present. In the Belarus Free Theatre production of *4.48 Psychosis* moments of counterproductivity were generated through dissonant relationship between text and performance. The relationship between text/speech and performance in this production was playful, and veered away from the tendency to force the poetic sections of the text into concrete meaning. Quite the opposite, the performance reached into and queered the play's medical dialogues. A striking example occurred in the scene which lists eleven drug treatments for psychosis and depression and their consequences for the patient-voice. In this scene, Rusakevich brought out a large glass container of brightly coloured fruit, whilst Sazonava danced and sang 'dum dum dum dum' to a parodically dramatic tune. The pair took it in turns to announce the name and dosage of a drug, whilst feeding the fruit to their counterpart. The gestures of feeding throughout the scene ranged from tender, to erotic, to aggressive and back again. The clinical tone of the list of prescriptions and the detachment of the patient-voice's sarcastic commentary was contrasted with the intense physical connection between the bodies on stage.

The scene could be interpreted in a number of ways: lovers playing at being doctors; doctor and patient playing at being lovers; an ambiguous experience of force-feeding; an illicit relationship taking place in a ward or prison. By leaving these options open the performance filled the clinical text with an unstable narrative of desire, preventing the audience from separating 'medical' and 'personal' sections of the play. As in most of the other clinical exchanges and doctor–patient dialogues, Sazonova and Rusakeivich shared both the clinical and patient positions, passing the more powerful speech position between them. Not only was the reductionism of the clinical language in this scene exposed by the gestures which accompanied it, but it was also transformed into the conditions for intimate physical exchange. The performance took a section of the play which sarcastically challenges psychopharmacological reductionism, and used it as a space for the exploration of queer desire, power and despair.

In being transformed into the site of intimate exchange, the scene's temporality is also modified. The scene narrates the failed attempts at treatment which are conducted according to linear time, in which cure and conformity are understood as the end goal. The BFT's interpretation of the scene overlays this failed attempt at productive linearity with a form of erotic togetherness which participates in a temporality which is quite different. The actions of tasting, touching, smearing and feeding are repetitive and looping – geared neither towards cure nor towards a heteronormative understanding of climax. The vase of fruit from which the performers feed each other is enormous, giving the impression of a possibly endless game of fruit-play. The play of queer desire itself becomes a form of resistance to psychopharmacological determinism here, whilst simultaneously offering a different way of being with and (literally) nourishing a suffering other.

The BFT production of *4.48 Psychosis* thus exploited the open and queered approach to time offered in the playtext to explore the richness of interpersonal possibility in the midst of suicidal despair. In place of reproductive futurism, Kafer imagines 'futures that imagine disability differently, futures that support multiple ways of being'.[88] Essential to these futures is the coexistence of desire and despair. The BFT production explores queer tenderness alongside troubling non-narrative expressions of pain which go beyond the erotic-nihilistic. At the end of the production, for example, Rusakevich and Sazonova approach each other once more holding candles up to each other's faces, repeating the play's penultimate line in Russian: 'it is myself I have never met, whose face is pasted on the underside of my mind.' They touch one another's faces and each holds the other's gaze. The projection of the previous production returns showing the 2005 Belarus version of the scene, with a smattering of applause from the audience in the recording. They blow out each other's candles (on projection and in the live performance), and the venue is immediately plunged into complete darkness. We hear the performers retreat from the audience behind the archway at the back of the performance space. Just before the audience can start applause, the final line is screamed by both performers, in voices filled with terror:

'please open the curtains'. Just as the production seemed to be ending on a nihilistic celebration of doomed queer love, the tables were turned. The play's final screams drew the audience attention back to the understanding that confinement, torment and the criminalization of desire continued to be the conditions in which the performance existed.

Desire does resolve despair in this dramatic world. They are folded into one another forming what we might think of as a politics of the chronic. This politics makes a demand upon the audience to sit with a performance of unresolved psychic suffering, which is at the same time a portrayal of a rich and varied inner life. It asks us to resist the idea that pain erases political personhood. The BFT production expressed a parallel between the experience of having one's inner life surveyed, regulated and deemed transparent and illegitimate in the psychiatric setting of *4.48 Psychosis*, and in the context of living under dictatorship in Belarus. In this context theatre becomes a temporal holding space in a radical sense. For the time that the underground production is staged or streamed (often in private homes or unlicensed public locations) an alternative circulation of affects is enabled. Psychic life is allowed to be dense, contradictory, demanding and painful. The Belarus Free Theatre production enveloped its multiple-located audience in a complex, demanding affective field which legitimates an experience of psychic life in which queer desire and political despair are intertwined. Maintaining the playtext's rejection of futurity and dramaturgical emphasis on with despair, the production offered an alternative present in the place of future hope.

## Notes

1 Lisa Baraister, *Enduring Time* (London: Bloomsbury, 2017), 136.
2 A notable exception here is De Vos, *Cruelty and Desire*. As will become clear, I approach desire from a very different position to De Vos in this chapter. De Vos uses Kane as an ahistorical bridge between Antonin Artaud and Samuel Beckett, to argue that both Beckett and Kane continue Artaud's artistic project of destroying literary language. De Vos focuses on the fragmentation of language in the works of both playwrights, arguing that they attempt to reach beyond language in order to access the Lacanian Real.
3 Saunders, *About Kane*, 50.
4 Robert McRuer, *Crip Times: Disability, Globalisation and Resistance* (New York: New York University Press, 2018). Jasbir K. Puar, 'Prognosis Time: Towards a Geopolitics of Affect, Debility and Capacity', *Women & Performance: A Journal of Feminist Theory* 19, no. 2 (2009): 161–72.

5   Baraitser, *Enduring Time*.
6   Rebellato, 'Sarah Kane before *Blasted*, the Monologues', 28–44, 37.
7   Edward Said, 'Thoughts on Late Style', *London Review of Books* 26, no. 15 (2004). Available online: https://www.lrb.co.uk/the-paper/v26/n15/edward-said/thoughts-on-late-style (accessed 6 May 2022).
8   Ibid.
9   Ibid.
10  Sarah Kane, '4.48 Psychosis', in *Complete Plays* (London: Methuen Drama, 2001), 202–45.
11  Said, 'Thoughts'.
12  A position crudely taken by Edward Bond for example. See Saunders, *Love Me*, 191.
13  Ian Burrows, 'Warning My Students about a Lecture on Assault Does Not Make Them Snowflakes', *Guardian*, 31 October 2017. Available online: https://www.theguardian.com/commentisfree/2017/oct/31/shakespeare-trigger-warning-students-snowflakes-cambridge-university-sexual-abuse-victims (accessed 6 May 2022).
14  Anna Harpin, *Madness, Art, and Society: Beyond Illness* (London: Routledge, 2018), 11.
15  Peggy Phelan, *Unmarked: The Politics of Performance* (London: Routledge, 1993), 4.
16  Green, *The Tragic Effect*, 18. See Chapter 4 for a discussion of Green's ideas about welcome/solicitation in the theatrical space.
17  Dictionary of Psychology (American Psychological Association). Available online: https://dictionary.apa.org/suicidality (accessed 3 May 2022).
18  Jon Venn, *Madness in Contemporary British Theatre: Resistances and Representations* (London: Palgrave Macmillan, 2021), 117.
19  Jon Venn, 'It Didn't Happen Like This: Suicide, Voice and Witnessing in Dead Centre's Lippy', *Journal of Interdisciplinary Voice Studies* 4, no. 1 (2019): 21–36, 24.
20  Venn, *Madness*, 120.
21  Edwin S. Shneidman, *The Suicidal Mind* (Oxford: Oxford University Press, 1998), 4, emphasis original.
22  Ibid.
23  Diedrich, 'Last in a Long Line of Literary Kleptomaniacs', 374–98, 394. Shneidman coins the term *psychache* to describe the psychic pain of the suicidal patient.
24  Shneidman, *Suicidal*, 27–8.
25  Ibid., 28.
26  Ibid., 64.
27  Ibid., 98.
28  Shneidman, *Suicidal*, 71; Kane, '4.48 Psychosis', 230.
29  Shneidman, *Suicidal*, 121; Kane, '4.48 Psychosis', 233–5.
30  Shneidman, *Suicidal*, 120.

31 Kane, '4.48 Psychosis', 214.
32 Shneidman, *Suicidal*, 115 and 121; Kane, '4.48 Psychosis', 214 and 215.
33 Sarah Kane, 'Crave', in *Sarah Kane: Complete Plays* (London: Methuen Drama, 2001), 180.
34 Ibid., 179.
35 This was heightened, for example, in the Chichester Festival performance in 2021, in which C's face was projected, covered in scars and bruises, on the back screen.
36 Kane, 'Crave', 193.
37 Ibid., 198.
38 Sara Ahmed, *Queer Phenomenology: Orientations, Objects, Others* (Durham, NC: Duke University Press, 2006), 27.
39 Ibid., 55.
40 Alison Kafer, *Feminist, Queer, Crip* (Bloomington, IN: Indiana University Press, 2013), 27.
41 Anna Harpin, *Madness, Art, and Society: Beyond Illness* (Abingdon, VA: Routledge 2018), 194.
42 H-Dirksen L. Bauman and Joseph J. Murray, 'Deaf Studies in the 21st Century: "Deaf-gain" and the Future of Human Diversity', in *The Oxford Handbook of Deaf Studies, Language, and Education, Vol. 2*, ed. Marc Marschark and Patricia Elizabeth Spencer (Oxford: Oxford University Press, 2010), 222.
43 Sarah Kane, '4.48 Psychosis', in *Sarah Kane: Complete Plays* (London: Methuen Drama, 2001), 237.
44 Saunders, *Love Me*, 132.
45 Barbara Johnson, 'The Frame of Reference', *Yale French Studies* 55, no. 56 (1977): 457–505, 481.
46 Rebellato, *Brief Encounter with Sarah Kane*.
47 Ibid.
48 Kane, 'Crave', 155.
49 Ibid., 182.
50 Craigie, correspondence.
51 Kane, 'Crave', 171.
52 Ibid., 173.
53 Ibid., 158.
54 Ibid., 184.
55 Kane, '4.48 Psychosis', 208.
56 Ibid., 208–9.
57 Ibid., 210.
58 Barbara Johnson, 'Apostrophe, Animation and Abortion', *Diacritics* 16, no. 1 (1986): 28–37, 29–31.
59 Kane, '4.48 Psychosis', 215.
60 Ibid.
61 Johnson, 'Apostrophe', 31.

62  Johnson, 'The Frame of Reference', 458.
63  Kane, '4.48 Psychosis', 214.
64  Ibid., 244.
65  Ibid., 432.
66  Alicia Tycer and Jon Venn both suggest that the play facilitates the kind of witnessing that Shoshannah Felman and Dori Laub advocate as a response to trauma.
67  Bollas, *The Shadow of the Object*, 5.
68  Ibid., 4.
69  Stephenson and Langridge, *Rage and Reason*, 131. My emphasis.
70  Venn, *Madness*; and Tycer, 'Victim. Perpetrator. Bystander', 23–36.
71  Winnicott, *Playing and Reality*, 3.
72  Belarus Free Theatre, '*Tomorrow I Was Always a Lion* Program', November 2016, 4.
73  Shcherban, '4.48 Psychosis Post Show Talk', Belarus Free Theatre: House of Correction, Farringdon, London, 2 November 2015.
74  Baraitser, *Enduring Time*, 47.
75  Each of these modes of being in time is a chapter of Baraitser's book.
76  Ibid., 48.
77  Ibid.
78  See Chapter 4 for a longer discussion of the relationship between mental health, behavioural therapy and work.
79  Baraitser, *Enduring Time*, 49.
80  Ibid.
81  Ibid., 80.
82  Lee Edelman, *No Future: Queer Theory and the Death Drive* (Durham, NC: Duke University Press, 2004), 2.
83  Kafer, *Feminist*, 29.
84  Ibid., 28.
85  Ibid., 31.
86  McRuer, *Crip Times*, 23.
87  Kafer, *Feminist*, 46.
88  Ibid., 45.

# Afterword

## Sarah Kane and psychic life today

To research and write about Sarah Kane today is to write across a time span of about three decades – decades of perhaps unprecedentedly fast change. It is to go from reading faxes and typewritten letters in boxes at the Royal Court's archive, to joining a live stream of a performance of *4.48 Psychosis* which is being transmitted all over the world. It is also to see how productions of Kane's works are remade and form new significations in the contexts of globalization, heightened neoliberalism, third-wave feminism, new populisms and a host of other contexts. The apparent ease with which Kane's works can be brought to bear on these contemporary contexts is remarked on with every new production and seems to signify a kind of proximity between her theatrical vision and the ills of contemporary life.

This project has opened up the historical distance between Kane's writing and contemporary performances, to better understand the intense sense of involvement which many productions of Kane's works produce. Kane's works take on the spatial disruptions and discursive flux of 1990s mental health care, and they return to it an understanding of psychic life and 'mental illness' as spatially enacted and socially communicable. This spatiality is itself a politicization of mental health discourses in the context of the upheavals of deinstitutionalization. It points to the moulding of psychic life by environmental conditions as well as social encounters and suggests that both are dictated by dynamics of power and disempowerment.

Introducing this historical perspective to Kane's theatre, both illuminates her representations of mental experience and reveals her works to be important cultural critiques of the 1990s mental health care moment. To date, many important studies of the cultural history of mental health care have tended to either end with the closure of asylums or present a direct transition from asylum care to diagnostic psychiatry, without considering the evolving spatial and social dynamics that this transition entailed. Reading Kane's works alongside a cross-section of material including mental health legislation and media coverage uncovers the importance of the 1990s as a transitional decade in the history of UK mental health care. Here too, the proximity of this moment often leads it to be situated somewhere in-between history and contemporaneity. The spatial and epistemological decentralization of care following the closure of asylums, how it was experienced and represented, are areas which warrant further exploration and research in and beyond the medical humanities.

Investigating the historical conditions in which and through which Kane staged experiences of psychic life illuminates her contemporary relevance. Her works journey to the present through many iterations and a rich performance history, to present a vision of psychic life outside of the rigid constraints of the neoliberal framework which seems to dominate today's culture. Her theatre has influenced other female writers and artists who work against this trend to produce some of the most interesting writing of mind today, such as playwright Alice Birch and novelist Eimear McBride. To stage Kane's works now and in the future is to build on this tradition and reveal how Kane's radical invitation to experience psychic distress 'from within' challenges new structures regulating mental life, suffering and desire.

Throughout this book, theatre emerges as a privileged site for exploring certain experiences of mental distress. This includes theatre's capacity to stage new environments of mental illness in the 1990s, in both Kane's works and the works of her contemporaries such as Sarah Daniels, Anna Reynolds and Joe Penhall. Among these voices, Kane most emphatically placed spatial dislocation and involvement at the centre of her representations of psychic suffering, to suggest a new mode through which to communicate the experience of mental pain. It is this mode that I have named a 'dramaturgy of psychic life'. It is one that exploits the shared nature of the theatrical site in order to generate an overlap between the transitional spaces of audience and artwork, and repeatedly throws out demands to the audience for specific kinds of attention.

In the hands of Sarah Kane and many of the creatives who have produced her works, this dramaturgy of psychic life creates a holding space for confusion and despair. The dynamics of the theatrical site itself allow psychic suffering to be held in sustained irresolution for a fixed period of time, without being resolved through narrative or translated into meta-discourse. The dramaturgy of Kane's works demands the holding and enduring of the pain of an other without recourse to narrative. As such dramaturgy itself becomes a mode of thinking and communicating which includes, but is not reducible to, the linguistic. In this way, dramaturgy functions *like* the play theorized by D. W. Winnicott, Christopher Bollas and André Green: 'it is a form of thought (like the dream)' which can contain and mediate an experience which presents itself as intolerable.[1] The status of dramaturgy as a discursive tool would benefit from future research and theoretical exploration. Such exploration would consider what kinds of knowledge are allowed to develop when interior life is considered spatially, building on the suggestion here that the dramaturgical is a particularly apt mode for communicating the unredemptive.

Beneath the ceiling of a theatre, which both is and simultaneously is not the 'ceiling of a mind', Kane's works find new ways of holding open despair. In this space the relatability of pain itself is reimagined, as is the scope of theatre's capacity to present psychic life.

# Note

1 Green, *Play and Reflection in Donald Winnicott's Writings*, 12.

# Bibliography

## Primary sources

### Performances cited

*4.48 Psychosis*, by Sarah Kane, composed by Philip Venables, dir. Ted Huffman, 28 May 2016, Lyric Hammersmith.
*4.48 Psychosis*, by Sarah Kane, dir. Vladimir Shcherban, 2 November 2015, Belarus Free Theatre: House of Correction, Farringdon, London.
*Blasted*, by Sarah Kane, dir. Richard Wilson, 12 February 2015, Sheffield Theatre: Crucible Theatre, Sheffield.
*Cleansed*, by Sarah Kane, dir. Katie Mitchell, 12 March 2016, National Theatre: Dorfman Theatre, London.

### Sarah Kane plays and interviews

Armitstead, Claire. 'No Pain, No Kane'. *Guardian*, 29 April 1998, 12.
Christopher, James. 'Her First Play Was About Defecation, Cannibalism, and Fellatio. The New One's About Love'. *Observer*, 2 November 1997.
Kane, Sarah. *4.48 Psychosis*. In *Sarah Kane: Complete Plays*, 202–45. London: Methuen Drama, 2001.
Kane, Sarah. *Blasted*. In *Sarah Kane: Complete Plays*, 1–62. London: Methuen Drama, 2001.
Kane, Sarah. *Cleansed*. In *Sarah Kane: Complete Plays*, 105–51. London: Methuen Drama, 2001.
Kane, Sarah. *Crave*. In *Sarah Kane: Complete Plays*, 153–202. London: Methuen Drama, 2001.
Kane, Sarah. 'Crave by Sarah Kane'. 1997, accessible via the Royal Court Theatre Archive. Reproduced by kind permission of Simon Kane.
Kane, Sarah. *Phaedra's Love*. In *Sarah Kane: Complete Plays*, 63–103. London: Methuen Drama, 2001.
Kane, Sarah. 'The Only Thing I Remember Is . . .'. *Guardian*, 13 August 1998, 12.
Rebellato, Dan. *Brief Encounter with Sarah Kane*, online interview recording, 3 November 1998. Available online: http://www.danrebellato.co.uk/sarah-kane-interview/ (accessed 31 January 2017)
Stephenson, Heidi and Natasha Langridge. *Rage and Reason: Women Playwrights on Playwriting*. London: Methuen, 1997.
Talbert, Nils. 'Interview with Sarah Kane'. In *Playspotting: Die Londoner Theatreszene der 90er*, edited by Nils Talbert, 8–65. Reinbeck, IA: Rowohlt Taschenbuch Verla, 1998. English manuscript available via Graham Saunders' private archive.

## Other literary and dramatic works

Daniels, Sarah. *Headrot Holiday*. In *Sarah Daniels: Plays 2*, 189–262. London: Bloomsbury Methuen Drama, 1994.
Daniels, Sarah. *Masterpieces*. In *Sarah Daniels: Plays 1*, 161–230. London: Methuen Drama, 1991.
Daniels, Sarah. *The Madness of Esme and Shaz*. In *Sarah Daniels: Plays 2*, 189–262. London: Bloomsbury Methuen Drama, 1994.
Orwell, George. *1984*. London: Penguin, 1949.
Penhall, Joe. *Blue/Orange*. London: Metheun Drama, 2000.

## Sarah Kane production history and reviews

Ahad, Nick. 'The Lasting Legacy of Sarah Kane's Genius'. *Yorkshire Post*, 13 February 2015. Available online: http://www.yorkshirepost.co.uk/what-s-on/theatre/the-lasting-legacy-of-sarah-kane-s-genius-1-7105126 (accessed 15 February 2019).
Allfree, Clare. 'Sarah Kane's Pageant of Torture Tests the Furthest Boundaries of Love'. *The Telegraph*, 24 February 2016. Available online: http://www.telegraph.co.uk/theatre/what-to-see/sarah-kanes-cleansed-tests-the-furthest-boundaries-of-love/ (accessed 17 February 2017)
Barry, Elizabeth. 'Introduction: Beckett, Language and the Mind'. *Journal of Beckett Studies* 17, no. 1–2 (2008): 1–8.
Bassett, Kate. *Independent on Sunday*, 8 April 2001, in *Theatre Record* 21, no. 7 (2001): 420.
Bassett, Kate. *The Times*, 22 May 1996, in *Theatre Record* 16, no. 11 (1996): 651.
Belarus Free Theatre. '*4.48 Psychosis*, Post-Show Discussion'. The House of Detention, Farringdon, London, 3 November 2015.
Benedict, David. 'Real Live Horror Show'. *Independent*, 9 May 1998.
Billington, Michael. *Guardian*, 20 January 1995, in *Theatre Record* 15, no. 1–2 (1995): 39.
Billington, Michael. *Guardian*, 14 February 2016, available via the British Newspaper Archive.
Billington, Michael. *Guardian*, 4 April 2001, in *Theatre Record* 21, no. 7 (2001): 421.
Billington, Michael. *Guardian*, 29 October 2010, in *Theatre Record* 30, no. 22 (2010): 1240.
Billington, Michael. 'How Do You Judge a 75-Minute Suicide Note?'. *Guardian*, 30 June 2000, 5.
Braun, Terry. 'Another Angle on Smack City'. *Sunday Business: Life Section*, 10 May 1998.

Brown, Georgina. *Mail on Sunday*, 8 April 2001, in *Theatre Record* 21, no. 7 (2001): 422.
Burrows, Ian. 'Warning My Students About a Lecture on Assault Does Not Make Them Snowflakes'. *Guardian*, 31 October 2017. Available online: https://www.theguardian.com/commentisfree/2017/oct/31/shakespeare-trigger-warning-students-snowflakes-cambridge-university-sexual-abuse-victims (accessed 6 May 2022).
Callan, Paul. *Daily Express*, 5 November 2010, in *Theatre Record* 30, no. 22 (2010): 1242.
Cavendish, Dominic. 'Debut: Interview with Kate Ashfield'. *Independent*, 9 September 1998.
Clapp, Susanna. '*Cleansed* Review – The First Cut was the Deepest'. *Observer*, 28 February 2016.
Clapp, Susanna. 'Kane's New Play is a Howl of Horror with the Sensibility of a Damien Hirst'. *Observer*, 10 May 1998, in *Theatre Record* 18, no. 9 (1998): 566.
Clapp, Susanna. *Observer*, 31 October 2010, in *Theatre Record* 30, no. 22 (2010): 1240.
Coveney, Michael, *Observer*, 26 May 1996, in *Theatre Record* 16, no. 11 (1996): 653.
Craigie, Ingrid. Private correspondence with Graham Saunders, reproduced with kind permission from Ms Craigie.
De Jongh, Nicholas. *Evening Standard*, 4 April 2001, in *Theatre Record* 21, no. 7 (2001): 418.
Deller, Ruth. *Broadway World Reviews*, 14 February 2015. Available online: www.broadwayworld.com/uk-regional/article/BWW-Reviews-BLASTED-Crucible-Studio-Sheffield-February-10-2015-20150214 (accessed 15 August 2016).
Denham, Jess. *Independent*, 24 February 2016.
Evans, Martha Noel. 'Portrait of Dora: Freud's Case History As Reviewed by Hélène Cixous'. *SubStance* 11, no. 3 (1982): 64–7, 65.
Foss, Roger. 'Blasted Review'. *The Stage*, 10 February 2015. Available online: https://www.thestage.co.uk/reviews/2015/blasted-2/ (accessed 15 September 2016).
Foss, Roger. *What's On*. 25 January 1995, in *Theatre Record* 15, no. 1–2 (1995): 38.
*Front Row*, BBC Radio 4, 2 February 2016, 7:15pm. Available online: http://www.bbc.co.uk/programmes/b071fyq9 (accessed 20 April 2016).
Gardner, Lyn. 'Blasted Review – Unflinching Revival of Sarah Kane's Prescient Horror Show'. *Guardian*, 11 February 2015. Available online: https://www.theguardian.com/stage/2015/feb/11/blasted-sheffield-crucible-sarah-kane-richard-wilson-review (accessed 15 February 2019).
Gross, Joss. *Sunday Telegraph*, 8 April 2001, in *Theatre Record* 21, no. 7 (2001): 420.
Harrington, Illtyd. 'Cleansed – Royal Court'. *Camden New Journal*, 14 May 1998.

Harris, Velda. 'Blasted Review'. *British Theatre Guide*, 3 February 2015. Available online: http://www.britishtheatreguide.info/reviews/blasted-crucible-studio-11191 (accessed 15 February 2019).

Healy, Verity. 'Blasted - Crucible Theatre Sheffield'. *Theatre Bubble*, 16 February 2015. Available online: http://www.theatrebubble.com/2015/02/blasted-crucible-theatre-sheffield/ (accessed 15 February 2019).

Hemming, Sarah. *Financial Times*, 13 February 2016.

Hitchins, Henry. *Evening Standard*, 29 October 2010, in *Theatre Record* 30, no. 22 (2010): 1240.

Kellaway, Kate. *Observer*, 22 January 1995, in *Theatre Record* 15, no. 1–2 (1995): 40–1.

Logan, Brian. *Time Out*, 11 April 2001, in *Theatre Record* 21, no. 7 (2001): 422.

Mitchell, Katie. 'Katie Mitchell Platform'. public interview with Katie Mitchell, National Theatre, London, 2 March 2016.

Murphy, Siobhan. *Metro (London)*, 3 November 2010, in *Theatre Record* 30, no. 22 (2010): 1241.

Nathan, David. *Jewish Chronicle*, 15 May 1998, in *Theatre Record* 18, no. 9 (1998): 568.

Nightingale, Benedict. *The Times*, 5 April 2001, in *Theatre Record* 21, no. 7 (2001): 421.

Peter, Jon. 'Short Stark Shock'. *Sunday Times*, 10 May 1998.

Shuttleworth, Ian. *Financial Times*, 1 November 2010, in *Theatre Record* 30, no. 22 (2010): 1240.

Smith, Andrew. *Observer*, 8 April 2001, in *Theatre Record* 21, no. 7 (2001): 421.

Spencer, Charles. *Daily Telegraph*, 20 January 1995, in *Theatre Record* 15, no. 1–2 (1995): 39–40.

Spencer, Charles. *Daily Telegraph*, 5 April 2001, in *Theatre Record* 21, no. 7 (2001): 419.

Spencer, Charles. *Daily Telegraph*, 21 May 1996, in *Theatre Record* 16, no. 11 (1996): 652.

Spencer, Charles. *Daily Telegraph*, 1 November 2010, in *Theatre Record* 30, no. 22 (2010): 1240.

Stratton, Kate. *Evening Standard*, 21 May 1996, in *Theatre Record* 16, no. 11 (1996): 653.

Szalwinska, Maxie. *Sunday Times*, 7 November 2010, in *Theatre Record* 30, no. 22 (2010): 1242.

Taylor, Paul. *Independent*, 23 May 1996, in *Theatre Record* 16, no. 11 (1996): 651–2.

Taylor, Paul. *Independent*, 2 November 2010, in *Theatre Record* 30, no. 22 (2010): 1241.

'The Play the Critics Blasted'. *Sheffield Telegraph*, 6 February 2016. Available online: http://www.sheffieldtelegraph.co.uk/what-s-on/theatre/the-play-the-critics-blasted-1-7091051 (accessed 15 February 2019).

Tinker, Jack. *Daily Mail*, 19 January 1995, in *Theatre Record* 15, no. 1–2 (1995): 42.

Trueman, Matt. 'Blasted (Sheffield Crucible) - Anniversary Revival Does Sarah Kane's Play Full Justice'. *What's On Stage*, 11 February 2015. Available online: http://www.whatsonstage.com/sheffield-theatre/reviews/blasted-sheffield-crucible-sarah-kane_37128.html (accessed 15 February 2019).

Trueman, Matt. '*Cleansed* is More Than Just Shock Theatre'. *What's On Stage*, 29 February 2016. Available online: http://www.whatsonstage.com/london-theatre/news/matt-trueman-cleansed-sarah-kane-national_39853.html (accessed 1 January 2017).

Trueman, Matt. 'I'm Drawn to Plays I Don't Know How To Do'. *Independent*, 19 January 2016.

Venables, Philip. '4.48 Psychosis: Opera as Music and Text. A Mini-Site for the Doctoral Submission About the Opera 4.48 Psychosis'. 2016. Shared by kind permission of Philip Venables.

Williams, Holly. *I*, 25 February 2016.

## Mental health legislation, policy documents and reports

Jarman, Kevin. 'Employment Advisers in IAPT – Providing Integrated IAPT and Employment Support'. New Savoy Partnership Conference, 2017. Available online: https://www.newsavoypartnership.org/2017presentations/kevin-jarman.pdf (accessed 18 February 2019).

*NHS and Community Care Act 1990*. London: Department of Health, 1990.

Robinson, Anne. 'System That's A Sick Joke'. *Daily Mirror*, 14 February 1990.

Ross, Tim. 'Tories Discuss Stripping Benefits Claimants Who Refuse Treatment for Depression'. *Telegraph*, 12 July 2014. Available online: https://www.telegraph.co.uk/news/politics/conservative/10964125/Tories-discuss-stripping-benefits-claimants-who-refuse-treatment-for-depression.html (accessed 18 February 2019).

# Secondary sources

## Psychoanalytic theory, theatre, literary and cultural criticism

Ablett, Sarah. 'Approaching Abjection in Sarah Kane's Blasted'. *Performance Research* 19 (2014): 63–71.

Ahmed, Sara, *Queer Phenomenology: Orientations, Objects, Others*. Durham, NC: Duke University Press, 2006.

Anderson, Laurel, et al. 'Responsibility and Well-Being: Resource Integration Under Responsibilization in Expert Services'. *Journal of Public Policy and Marketing* 35, no. 2 (2016): 262–79.

Appignanesi, Lisa. *Mad, Bad and Sad: A History of Women and the Mind Doctors from 1800 to the Present*. London: Hachette UK, 2008.

Aston, Elaine. 'Feeling the Loss of Feminism: Sarah Kane's *Blasted* and an Experiential Genealogy of Contemporary Women's Playwrighting'. *Theatre Journal* 62, no. 4 (2010): 575–91.

Aston, Elaine. *Feminist Views on the English Stage: Women Playwrights 1990–2000*. Cambridge: Cambridge University Press, 2003.

Aston, Elaine. 'Reviewing the Fabric of Blasted'. In *Sarah Kane in Context*, edited by Graham Saunders and Laurens De Vos, 13–27. Manchester: Manchester University Press, 2010.

Baraitser, Lisa. *Enduring Time*. London: Bloomsbury, 2017.

Barham, Peter. *Closing the Asylum*. London: Penguin, 1992.

Barnett, David. 'When Is A Play Not Drama? Two Examples Of Post-Dramatic Theatre'. *New Theatre Quarterly* 24 (2008): 14–23.

Barthes, Roland. *A Lover's Discourse: Fragments*. Translated by Richard Howard. London: Vintage, 2002.

Bauman, H-Dirksen L. and Joseph J. Murray. 'Deaf Studies in the 21st Century: "Deaf-Gain" and the Future of Human Diversity'. In *The Oxford Handbook of Deaf Studies, Language, and Education, Vol. 2*, edited by Marc Marschark and Patricia Elizabeth Spencer. Oxford: Oxford University Press, 2010.

Beck, Judith S. *Cognitive Therapy: Basics and Beyond*. New York: Guildford Press, 1964.

Beresford, Peter and Jasna Russo. *The Routledge International Handbook of Mad Studies*. Abingdon, VA: Routledge, 2021.

Berlant, Lauren. *Cruel Optimism*. Durham, NC: Duke University Press, 2011.

Berrios, B. E. and H. Freeman. *150 Years of British Psychiatry 1841–1991*. London: Royal College of Psychiatry, 1991.

Bersani, Leo. *Is the Rectum a Grave?: And Other Essays*. Chicago, IL: University of Chicago Press, 2010.

Bersani, Leo. *The Culture of Redemption*. Cambridge, MA: Harvard University Press, 1990.

Blackman, Lisa. *Hearing Voices: Embodiment and Experience*. London: Free Association Books, 2001.

Blackman, Lisa. 'The Challenges of New Biopsychosocialities: Hearing Voices, Trauma, Epigenetics and Mediated Perception'. *The Sociological Review Monograph* 64, no. 1 (2016): 256–73.

Bollas, Christopher. *Catch Them Before They Fall: The Psychoanalysis of Breakdown*. London: Routledge, 2013.

Bollas, Christopher. *The Shadow of the Object: Psychoanalysis of the Unthought Known*. London: Free Association Books, 1987.

Bollas, Christopher. 'The Transformational Object'. *International Journal of Psycho-Analysis* 60 (1979): 97–107.

Bollas, Christopher. *When the Sun Bursts: The Enigma of Schizophrenia*. New Haven, CT; London: Yale University Press, 2016.

Borowski, Mateuz. 'Under the Surface of Things: Sarah Kane's *Skin* and the Medium of the Theatre'. In *Sarah Kane in Context*, edited by Graham

Saunders and Laurens De Vos, 184–94. Manchester: Manchester University Press, 2010.
Bourke, Joanna, *Rape: A History from 1860 to the Present*. London: Virago, 2007.
Brown, Wendy, *Undoing the Demos: Neoliberalism's Stealth Revolution*. New York: Zone Books, 2015.
Butler, Judith. *Giving an Account of Oneself*. New York: Fordham University Press, 2005.
Butler, Judith. *The Psychic Life of Power: Theories of Subjection*. Stanford, CA: Stanford University Press, 1997.
Carney, Sean. *The Politics of Contemporary English Tragedy*. Toronto: University of Toronto Press, 2013.
Carney, Sean. 'The Tragedy of History in Sarah Kane's *Blasted*'. *Theatre Survey* 46 (2005): 275–96.
Caruth, Cathy. 'Introduction'. In *Trauma: Explorations in Memory*, edited by Cathy Caruth. Baltimore, MD: John Hopkins University Press, 1995.
Caruth, Cathy. *Unclaimed Experience: Trauma, Narrative and History*. Baltimore, MD: John Hopkins University Press, 1996.
Chen, Mel Y. *Animacies: Biopolitics, Racial Mattering and Queer Affect*. Durham, NC: Duke University Press, 2012.
Chen, Mel Y. 'Lurching For the Cure? On Zombies and the Reproduction of Disability'. *GLQ: A Journal of Lesbian and Gay Studies* 21, no. 1 (2015): 24–31.
Chute, Hilary. '"Victim, Perpetrator, Bystander": Critical Distance in Sarah Kane's Theatre of Cruelty'. In *Sarah Kane in Context*, edited by Graham Saunders and Laurens De Vos, 161–72. Manchester: Manchester University Press, 2010.
Culik, Hugh. 'Neurological Disorder and the Evolution of Beckett's Maternal Images'. *Mosaic* 22 (1989): 1.
Davies, William. *The Happiness Industry: How the Government and Big Business Sold Us Well-Being*. London: Verso, 2016.
Delgado-Garcia, Cristina. 'Subversion, Refusal, and Contingency: The Transgression of Liberal-Humanist Subjectivity in Sarah Kane's *Cleansed*, *Crave*, and *4.48 Psychosis*'. *Modern Drama*, 55 (2012): 230–50.
De Vos, Laurens. *Cruelty and Desire in the Modern Theater: Antonin Artaud, Sarah Kane, and Samuel Beckett*. Madison, NJ: Fairleigh Dickinson University Press, 2011.
*Diagnostic and Statistical Manual of Mental Disorders*, 3rd edn. Washington, DC: American Psychiatric Association, 1980.
Dictionary of Psychology (American Psychological Association). Available online: https://dictionary.apa.org/suicidality (accessed 3 May 2022).
Diedrich, Antje. '"Last in a Long Line of Literary Kleptomaniacs": Intertextuality in Sarah Kane's *4.48 Psychosis*'. *Modern Drama* 56, no. 3 (2013): 374–98.
Drescher, Jack. 'Out of DSM: Depathologizing Homosexuality'. *Behavioural Science* 5 (2015): 565–75.

Duggan, Patrick. *Trauma-Tragedy: Symptoms of Contemporary Performance.* Manchester: Manchester University Press, 2012.
Edelman, Lee. *No Future: Queer Theory and the Death Drive.* Durham, NC: Duke University Press, 2004.
Fassin, Didier, and Richard Rechtman. *The Empire of Trauma.* Princeton, NJ: Princeton University Press, 2009.
Felman, Shoshanna. *The Juridical Unconscious: Trials and Traumas in the Twentieth Century.* Cambridge MA: Harvard University Press, 2002.
Felman, Shoshanna and Dori Laub. *Testimony: Crises of Witnessing in Literature, Psychoanalysis and History.* London: Routledge, 1992.
Fenn, Kristina, and Majella Byrne. 'The Key Principles of Cognitive Behavioural Therapy'. *InnovAiT* 6, no. 9 (2013): 579–85.
Ferenczi, Sándor. *The Clinical Diary of Sándor Ferenczi.* Edited by Judith Dupont, translated by Michael Balint and Nicola Zarday Jackson. Harvard, MA: Harvard University Press, 1988.
Fitzgerald, Des, and Felicity Callard. 'Entangling the Medical Humanities'. In *The Edinburgh Companion to the Medical Humanities*, edited by Anne Whitehead and Angela Woods, 35–49. Edinburgh: Edinburgh University Press, 2016.
Fletcher, Paul, and Chris D. Frith. 'Perceiving is Believing: A Bayesian Approach to Explaining the Positive Symptoms of Schizophrenia'. *Nature Reviews Neuroscience* 10, no. 1 (2009): 48–58.
Fordyce, Ehren. 'The Voice of Kane'. In *Sarah Kane in Context*, edited by Graham Saunders and Laurens De Vos, 103–14. Manchester: Manchester University Press, 2010.
Foucault, Michel. *Madness and Civilisation: A History of Insanity in the Age of Reason.* Translated by Richard Howard. New York: Vintage Books, 1988.
Foucault, Michel. *The Birth of Biopolitics: Lectures at the Collège de France, 1978–79.* Translatted by Graham Burchill. Basingstoke: Palgrave Macmillan, 2008.
Frankel, Jay. 'Exploring Ferenczi's Concept of Identification with the Aggressor: Its Role in Trauma, Everyday Life and the Therapeutic Relationship'. *Psychoanalytic Dialogues* 12, no. 1 (2002): 101–39.
Freud, Sigmund. 'Beyond the Pleasure Principle'. In *The Standard Edition of the Complete Psychological Works of Sigmund Freud, Volume XVIII (1920–1922): Beyond the Pleasure Principle, Group Psychology and Other Works*, translatede by James Strachey, 1–64. London: The Hogarth Press and the Institute of Psychoanalysis, 1955.
Freud, Sigmund. 'On Narcissism'. In *The Standard Edition of the Complete Psychological Works of Sigmund Freud, Volume XIV (1914–1916): On the History of the Psycho-analytic Movement, Papers on Metapsychology and other works*, translated by James Strachey, 67–102. London: Hogarth Press, 1957–66.
Freud, Sigmund. 'Psychoanalytic Notes on an Autobiographical Account of a Case of Paranoia (Dementia Paranoides) (Schreber)'. In *The Standard Edition*

*of the Complete Psychological Works of Sigmund Freud, Volume XII (1911–1913): The Case of Schreber, Papers on Technique and Other Works*, translated by James Strachey, 3–84. London: The Hogarth Press and the Institute of Psycho-analysis, 1958.

Freud, Sigmund. 'Psychopathic Characters on the Stage (1942 (1905 or 1906))'. translated by James Strachey, in *The Standard Edition of the Complete Psychological Works of Sigmund Freud, Volume VII (1901–1905): A Case of Hysteria, Three Essays on Sexuality and Other Works*, edited by James Strachey, 303–10. London: The Hogarth Press and the Institute of Psycho-Analysis, 1958.

Freud, Sigmund. 'The Loss of Reality in Neurosis and Psychosis'. In *The Standard Edition of the Complete Psychological Works of Sigmund Freud, Volume XIX (1923–1925): The Ego and the Id and Other Works*, translated by James Strachey, 181–8. London: Hogarth Press, 1961.

Goffman, Irving. *Asylums: Essays on the Social Situation of Mental Patients and Other Inmates*. London: Penguin, 1991.

Gottlieb, Vera. 'Lukewarm Brittania'. In *Theatre in a Cool Climate*, edited by Colin Chambers and Vera Gottleib, 201–12. Oxford: Amber Lane, 1999.

Green, André. *Play and Reflection in Donald Winnicott's Writings*. London: Karnac, 2005.

Green, André. *The Tragic Effect: The Oedipus Complex in Tragedy*. Translated by Alan Sheridan. Cambridge: Cambridge University Press, 1969.

Greig, David. 'Introduction'. In *Sarah Kane: Complete Plays*, ix–xviii. London: Methuen Drama, 2001.

Groves, T. 'After the Asylums: Can the Community Care?'. *British Medical Journal* 300, no. 6733 (1990): 923–1188.

Harpin, Anna. 'Dislocated: Metaphors of Madness in British Theatre'. In *Performance, Madness and Psychiatry: Isolated Acts*, edited by Julia Foster and Anna Harpin. London: Palgrave Macmillan, 2014.

Harpin, Anna. *Madness Art and Society: Beyond Illness*. Abingdon, VA: Routledge, 2018.

Hayward, Rhodri. *Psychiatry in Modern Britain*. London: Bloomsbury Continuum, 2013.

Heddon, Dee. 'The Politics of the Personal: Autobiography in Performance'. In *Feminist Futures? Theatre, Performance, Theory*, edited by Elaine Aston and Geraldine Harris, 130–48. Basingstoke: Palgrave Macmillan, 2006.

Hohwy, Jakob. *The Predictive Mind*. Oxford: Oxford University Press, 2013.

Iball, Helen. *Sarah Kane's Blasted*. London: Continuum, 2008.

Johnson, Barbara. 'Apostrophe, Animation and Abortion'. *Diacritics* 16, no. 1 (1986): 28–37.

Johnson, Barbara. 'The Frame of Reference'. *Yale French Studies* 55, no. 56 (1977): 457–505.

Kafer, Alison. *Feminist, Queer, Crip*. Bloomington, IN: Indiana University Press, 2013.

Kane, Nina. 'Breath And Light: Blasted, Sheffield Theatres And New Directions In The Staging Of Sarah Kane'. *Litro*, 19 April 2015. Available online: http://www.litro.co.uk/2015/04/breath-and-light-blasted-sheffield-theatres-and-new-directions-in-the-staging-of-sarah-kane/ (accessed 31 January 2017).

Kane, Nina. *Sarah Kane: Queer Desires and Feminist Continuums*. Abingdon, VA: Routledge, upcoming.

King, David. *Moving on from Mental Hospitals to Community Care: A Case Study of Change in Exeter*. London: The Nuffield Provincial Hospitals Trust, 1991.

Klein, Melanie. 'Notes on Some Schizoid Mechanisms'. In *The Selected Melanie Klein*, edited by Juliet Mitchell, 175–200. London: Penguin, 1990.

Kohon, Gregorio. *The British School of Psychoanalysis: The Independent Tradition*. London: Free Association Books, 1986.

Kristeva, Julia. *Powers of Horror: An Essay on Abjection*. Translated by Leon Roudiez. New York: Columbia University Press, 1982.

Lahr, John. 'Walking with Arthur Miller'. *The New Yorker*, 1 March 2012. Available online: https://www.newyorker.com/culture/culture-desk/walking-with-arthur-miller (accessed 2 November 2021).

Leader, Darian. *What is Madness?* London: Penguin, 2011.

Lehmann, Hans Thies. *Postdramatic Theatre*. Translated by Karen Jürs-Munby. London : Routledge, 2006.

Lepage, Louise. 'Rethinking Sarah Kane's Characters: A Human(ist) Form and Politics'. *Modern Drama*, 57 (2014): 252–72.

Leys, Ruth. *Trauma: A Genealogy*. Chicago, IL: University of Chicago Press, 2000.

Linton, Samara and Rianna Walcott. *The Colour of Madness: Explore BAME Mental Health in the UK*. Edinburgh: Stirling Publishing, 2018.

Lublin, Robert I. '"I Love You Now": Time and Desire in the Plays of Sarah Kane'. In *Sarah Kane in Context*, edited by Graham Saunders and Laurens De Vos, 115–25. Manchester: Manchester University Press, 2010.

Luckhurst, Mary. 'Infamy and Dying Young: Sarah Kane 1971–1999'. In *Theatre and Celebrity in Britain*, edited by Mary Luckhurst and Jane Moody, 107–24. London: Palgrave Macmillan, 2005.

Luckhurst, Roger. *The Trauma Question*. Abingdon, VA: Routledge, 2008.

Malabou, Catherine. *The New Wounded: From Neurosis to Brain Damage*. New York: Fordham University Press, 2012.

Marsh, Ian. *Suicide: Foucault, History and Truth*. Cambridge: Cambridge University Press, 2010.

Marshall, Hallie Rebecca. 'Saxon Violence and Social Decay in Sarah Kane's Phaedra's Love and Tony Harrison's Prometheus'. *Helios*, 38 (2011): 165–79.

Masson, Jeffrey Moussaieff. *Assault on Truth: Freud's Suppression of Seduction Theory*. New York: Farrar, Straus and Giroux, 1984.

McRuer Robert. *Crip Times: Disability, Globalisation and Resistance*. New York: New York University Press, 2018.

Mitchell, Juliet. 'Introduction'. *The Selected Melanie Klein*, edited by Juliet Mitchell, 9–32. London: Penguin, 1986.

Mitchell, Katie. *The Director's Craft*. London: Taylor and Francis, 2008.
Morin, Emilie. 'Look Again: Indeterminacy and Contemporary British Drama'. *New Theatre Quarterly*, 105 (2011): 71–85.
Oppenheim, Lois. 'A Twenty-First Century Perspective on a Play by Samuel Beckett'. *Journal of Beckett Studies* 17, no. 1–2 (2009): 187–98.
Oyebode, Femi. *Madness at the Theatre*. London: The Royal Institute of Psychiatry, 2012.
Phelan, Peggy. *Unmarked: The Politics of Performance*. London: Routledge, 1993.
Philo, Greg,. *Mediating Madness: Glasgow Media Group*. London and New York: Longman, 1996.
Puar, Jasbir K. 'Prognosis Time: Towards a Geopolitics of Affect, Debility and Capacity'. *Women & Performance: A Journal of Feminist Theory* 19, no. 2 (2009): 161–72.
Rabey, David Ian. *English Drama Since 1940*. London: Pearson Education Limited, 2003.
Radosavljević, Duška. 'Sarah Kane's Illyria as the Land of Violent Love: A Balkan Reading of Blasted'. *Contemporary Theatre Review* 22, no. 4 (2012): 499–511.
Rebellato, Dan. 'Katie Mitchell, Learning from Europe'. In *Contemporary European Theatre Directors*, edited by Maria M. Delgado, Dan Rebellato, 317–38. Abingdon, VA: Routledge, 2010.
Rebellato, Dan. 'Objectivity and Observation'. In *The Cambridge Companion to Theatre and Science*. edited by Kirsten Shepherd-Barr. Cambridge : Cambridge University Press, 2020.
Rebellato, Dan. 'Sarah Kane before *Blasted*, the Monologues'. In *Sarah Kane in Context*, edited by Graham Saunders and Laurens De Vos, 28–44. Manchester: Manchester University Press, 2010.
Roberts, Mathew. 'Vanishing Acts: Sarah Kane's Texts for Performance and Post-Dramatic Theatre'. *Modern Drama* 58 (2015): 94–110.
Robinson, Michael. 'Chronology'. In *The Cambridge Companion to August Strindberg*, edited by Michael Robinson, xxv. Cambridge: Cambridge University Press, 2009.
Rogers, Anne and David Pilgrim (eds). *A Sociology of Mental Health*. Maidenhead: Open University Press, 2005.
Rosenfeld, Herbert. 'Consideration Regarding the Psycho-Analytic Approach to Acute and Chronic Schizophrenia (1954)'. In *Psychotic States: A Psychoanalytic Approach*, edited by Herbert Rosenfeld, 117–27. London: Karnac Books, 1965.
Rosenfeld, Herbert. 'Note on the Psychopathology of Confusional States in Chronic Schizophrenia' (1950) In *Psychotic States: A Psychoanalytic Approach*, edited by Herbert Rosenfeld. London: Karnac Books, 1965.
Rosenfeld, Herbert. 'Notes on the Psycho-Analysis of the Superego Conflict in an Acute Schizophrenic Patient (1952)'. In *Psychotic States: A Psychoanalytic Approach*, edited by Herbert Rosenfeld, 52–62. London: Karnac Books, 1965.

Said, Edward. *The World, the Text, the Critic*. Cambridge, MA: Harvard University Press, 1983.
Said, Edward. 'Thoughts on Late Style'. *London Review of Books* 26, no. 15 (2004). Available online: https://www.lrb.co.uk/the-paper/v26/n15/edward-said/thoughts-on-late-style (accessed 6 May 2022).
Saunders, Graham. *About Kane: The Playwright and the Work*. London: Faber and Faber, 2009.
Saunders, Graham. '"Just a Word on the Page and There is Drama": Kane's Theatrical Legacy'. *Contemporary Theatre Review* 13 (2003): 97–110.
Saunders, Graham. *Love Me or Kill Me: Sarah Kane and the Theatre of Extremes*. Manchester: Manchester University Press, 2002.
Saunders, Graham. '"Out Vile Jelly": Sarah Kane's Blasted and Shakespeare's King Lear'. *New Theatre Quarterly* 20 (2004): 69–77.
Shneidman, Edwin S. *The Suicidal Mind*. Oxford: Oxford University Press, 1998.
Sidi, Leah. 'After the Madhouses: The Emotional Politics of Psychiatry and Community Care in the UK Tabloid Press 1980–1995'. *Medical Humanities* 2021.
Sierz, Aleks. *In-Yer-Face Theatre: British Drama Today*. London: Faber and Faber, 2000.
Sierz, Aleks. '"Looks Like There's a War On": Sarah Kane's *Blasted*, Political Theatre and the Muslim Other'. In *Sarah Kane in Context*, edited by Graham Saunders and Laurens De Vos, 45–56. Manchester: Manchester University Press, 2010.
Sierz, Aleks. '"We All Need Stories": The Politics of In-Yer-Face Theatre'. In *Cool Brittania? British Political Theatre in the 1990s*, edited by Rebecca D'Monte and Graham Saunders, 23–7. Basingstoke: Palgrave Macmillan, 2008.
Singer, Annabelle. 'Don't Want to Be This: The Elusive Sarah Kane'. *TDR: The Drama Review* 48 (2004): 139–71.
Solga, Kim. '*Blasted's* Hysteria: Rape, Realism, and the Thresholds of the Visible'. *Modern Drama* 50, no. 3 (2007): 346–74.
Sontag, Susan. 'Introduction'. In *Antonin Artaud: Selected Writings*, edited by Susan Sontag. Berkely and Los Angeles, CA: University of California Press, 1973.
Srinivasan, Amia. *The Right to Sex*. London: Bloomsbury, 2021.
Stockernström, Göran. 'Crisis and Change: Strindberg the Unconscious Modernist'. In *The Cambridge Companion to August Strindberg*, edited by Michael Robinson. Cambridge: Cambridge University Press, 2009.
StopSIM: Mental Illness is Not a Crime. Available online: https://stopsim.co.uk/ (accessed 13 May 2022).
Strindberg, August. 'Author's Note'. In *Six Plays of Strindberg*, translated by Elizabeth Sprigge, 192. New York: Doubleday Anchor, 1955.
Tausk, Victor. 'On the Origin of the Influencing Machine in Schizophrenia'. *Journal of Psychotherapy Research and Practise*, translated by Dorian Feigenbaum 1, no. 2 (1992): 184–206.

Taylor, Barbara. *The Last Asylum: A Memoir of Madness in Our Time*. London: Penguin, 2015.
Turner, Cathy and Synne Behrndt, *Dramaturgy and Performance*. Basingstoke: Palgrave Macmillan, 2008.
Tycer, Alicia. '"Victim. Perpetrator. Bystander.": Melancholic Witnessing of Sarah Kane's 4.48 Psychosis'. *Theatre Journal* 60, no. 1 (2008): 23–36.
Urban, Ken. 'An Ethics of Catastrophe: The Theatre of Sarah Kane'. *PAJ: A Journal of Performance and Art* 33, no. 3 (2001): 36–46.
Venn, Jon. 'It Didn't Happen Like This: Suicide, Voice and Witnessing in Dead Centre's Lippy'. *Journal of Interdisciplinary Voice Studies* 4, no. 1 (2019): 21–36, 24.
Venn, Jon. *Madness and Contemporary British Theatre: Resistances and Representations*. London: Palgrave Macmillan, 2021.
Voigts-Virchow, Echart. '"We are Anathema" – Sarah Kane's Plays as Postdramatic Theatre Versus the 'Dreary and Repugnant Tale of Sense'. In *Sarah Kane in Context*, edited by Graham Saunders and Laurens De Vos, 195–208. Manchester: Manchester University Press, 2010.
Waddington, Juliet. 'Post-Humanist Identities in Sarah Kane'. In *Sarah Kane in Context*, edited by Graham Saunders and Laurens De Vos, 139–48. Manchester: Manchester University Press, 2010.
Wallace, Clare. 'Sarah Kane, Experiential Theatre and the Revenant Avant-Garde'. In *Sarah Kane in Context*, edited by Graham Saunders and Laurens De Vos, 88–99. Manchester: Manchester University Press, 2010.
Wang, Esmé Weijun. *The Collected Schizophrenias*. London: Penguin 2019.
Watson, Ariel. 'Cries of Fire: Psychotherapy in Contemporary British and Irish Drama'. *Modern Drama* 51, no. 2 (2008): 188–210.
Winnicott, D. W., *Playing and Reality*. London: Routledge, 2005.
Wixon, Christopher. '"In Better Places": Space, Identity, and Alienation in Sarah Kane's *Blasted*'. *Comparative Drama* 39, no. 1 (2005): 75–91.
Woods, Angela. *The Sublime Object of Psychiatry: Schizophrenia in Clinical and Cultural Theory*. Oxford: Oxford University Press, 2011.
Young, Allan. *The Harmony of Illusions: Inventing Post-Traumatic Stress Disorder*. Princeton, NJ: Princeton University Press, 1997.
Young, Allan. 'Trauma and Harm'. Podcast recording, The Birkbeck Trauma Project, 14 April 2016. Available online: www.bbk.ac.uk/trauma/events/trauma-and-harm (accessed 2 February 2017).

# Index

*4.48 Psychosis*, Belarus Free Theatre, 2011   15, 156, 163, 181–90
*4.48 Psychosis*, Deafinitely Theatre, 2018   15, 163, 173–5
*4.48 Psychosis*, Lyric Hammersmith, 2018   15, 140–2, 154–6

ableism   50–1, 53–5
Ahmed, Sara
  *Queer Phenomenology: Orientations, Objects, Others*   172, 175
American Modernism   27
Appignanesi, Lisa   65, 66
Appolinaire   95
Artaud, Antonin   27–9, 31, 85, 95, 124
Aston, Elaine   14, 20, 54, 81 n.84
asylums. *See* deinstitutionalization

Balkan conflict   61, 66, 71, 80 n.59
Baraister, Lisa
  *Enduring Time*   31–2, 161, 162, 184–6
Bardem, Jessica   73–4
Barham, Peter   37, 39
Barthes, Roland
  *The Lover's Discourse*   113
Basset, Adam. *See 4.48 Psychosis*, Deafinitely Theatre, 2018
Beck, Aaron. *See* Cognitive Behavioural Therapy (CBT)   143
Beck Depression Inventory   143, 166
Beckett, Samuel   29–31, 35, 41, 49, 71, 190 n.2
  interest in neuroscience   29–30
  *Rockaby*   29

Belarus Free Theatre. *See 4.48 Psychosis*, Belarus Free Theatre, 2011
Bersani, Leo
  *The Culture of Redemption*   124, 126, 127
biography   2–4, 85–6
Birch, Alice
  *Anatomy of a Suicide*   150–3
*Blasted*, Crucible Theatre, Sheffield, 2015   14, 72–6
*Blasted*, first production   34, 51–3, 61
Bollas, Christopher   88, 94–5, 136, 196
  *The Shadow of the Object*   94, 136, 181
  *When the Sun Bursts: The Enigma of Schizophrenia*   94–5, 100–2, 114, 130, 133–4, 154
Bond, Edward   49, 124–5
Borowski, Mateuz   87
Bosnia. *See* Balkan conflict
Bourke, Joanna   66
British Sign Language (BSL)   173–4
Brook, Peter
  Living Theatre   28
Büchner, Georg
  *Woyzeck*   14, 85–7, 96
Bulimia
  in *Starved*   21, 34, 35, 85, 166, 170
Butler, Judith
  *The Psychic Life of Power*   32, 42–3

Carney, Sean   72, 125
Caruth, Cathy   57, 70

child abuse   35–7, 40, 57–9, 66–7, 69, 73–5, 78 n.30
chronic time   162, 190
Churchill, Caryl   6, 31, 49
Cixous, Hélène
   *Portrait of Dora*   30–1
Clarke, Hannah. *See 4.48 Psychosis*, Lyric Hammersmith, 2018
Cleansed, National Theatre, 2017   15, 89, 107–13, 115–16
Cognitive Behavioural Therapy (CBT)   143–50
   role in IAPT   149
comedy   9, 53
Community Care
   backlash   6–11
Community Care Act. *See* NHS and Community Care Act
Craigie, Ingrid   35–6, 41, 86, 177
   *Beside Herself*   6
   *Headrot Holiday*   53
   *The Madness of Esme and Shaz*   39
   *Masterpieces*   54

Davies, William   145, 149
Deafinitely Theatre. *See 4.48 Psychosis*, Deafinitely Theatre, 2018
Deaf Studies   173–4
deinstitutionalization   5–6, 34, 38–9, 42, 195
depression   3, 6, 9–11, 21, 31, 71, 86, 91, 122–5, 142–3, 149, 166, 182
desire   8, 15, 27, 41, 49–51, 96, 99, 106, 161–3, 175–81
De Vos, Laurens   29, 190 n.2
Diagnostic and Statistics Manual (DSM)   4, 66, 90–1
Diamond, Elin   30
Diedrich, Antje   3, 168
distillation
   as a dramaturgical technique   30, 105, 170, 180
dramaturgical analysis   23
dramaturgy
   Kane's dramatrugy as incomplete   15, 110–11
   of residing   127–38
dramaturgy of psychic life
   as a concept   19–34
Duffy, Brian. *See 4.48 Psychosis*, Deafinitely Theatre, 2018

Edelman, Lee   187–8
ES3   2–3, 34, 86, 113
experientialism   2, 13, 15, 19–22, 29, 34–42
Expressionism   25–7, 31, 87

Fassin, Didier and Richard Rechtman   58
Featherstone, Vicky   14, 24, 34–6, 41–2, 175
Felman, Shoshanna   81 n.80
Felman, Shoshanna and Dori Laub   56–7
feminist theatre
   criticism   165
   interpreting Kane's work as   46–56
   second wave feminist theatre   30–1, 65, 76
Ferenczi, Sandor   58–9, 67–71
Foucault, Michel   10
   *The Birth of Biopolitics*   148–9
Frankel, Jay   69–70
Freud, Sigmund   161
   *Beyond the Pleasure Principle*   56–7
   *The Case of Schreber*   117 n.23, 118 n.25
   *Dora*   30
   *On Narcissism*   91–4
   *Psychopathic Characters on the Stage*   24–5, 127

on psychosis 91–4
on trauma 56–8, 78 n.30

Garfield, Paula. *See 4.48 Psychosis*, Deafinitely Theatre, 2018
Green, André 33, 135, 165, 196
Greig, David 124–5
Grotowski, Jerzy
  Laboratory Theatre 28

Halberstam, Judith (Jack) 162
Hamlet 24–5
Herbert, Jeremy
  set design for *Cleansed* 100
  set design for *4.48 Psychosis* 135–9
Herman, Judith
  feminist trauma theory 59, 66–9
historical avant-garde 27–30
Homes, Sean. *See Blasted*, Lyric Hammersmith 2010
Huffman, Ted. *See 4.48 Psychosis*, Lyric Hammersmith, 2018

Iball, Helen 20
innoculation
  theatre as 21, 24, 29, 33
irresolution
  dramatrugy of 15, 23, 88, 95, 100–2, 116, 196

Jaspers, Karl 90
Johnson, Barbara 176

Kafer, Alison
  Feminist, Queer, Crip 162, 173, 187–9
Kane, Nina 14
Kane, Sarah
  *4.48 Psychosis* 1–3, 12, 15, 22, 31, 76, 85–7, 93, 111, 113, 115, 123–94

*Blasted* 1, 6, 14, 20, 22–3, 31, 34, 44, 49–86, 88, 96, 98, 108, 111, 112, 114, 127, 134, 161, 164, 166
*Cleansed* 1–3, 12, 14–15, 22, 24, 29–30, 44, 76–7, 85–122, 161, 164, 166, 168
*Crave* 1–3, 7, 8, 12–15, 22, 24, 31, 34–49, 62, 85–7, 96, 111, 115, 126, 127, 150–2, 161–74
interview 19–20, 49, 64, 80 n.61, 86, 93, 112–13, 116 n.1, 137
*Phaedra's Love* 1, 4, 6–12, 22, 24, 49, 84–8, 144, 164, 166–7
*Sick* monologues 21–2, 34–5, 65, 68, 76, 85, 127, 163, 166, 170
*Skin* 86–7
Klein, Melanie 88, 93, 118 n.27

Lacan, Jacques 29, 92–3
Layard Report 149–50
Leader, Darian 145
Lehmann, Hans Thies 27–8, 43–4
Leys, Ruth 59, 61

Macdonald, James 97, 100, 111, 115, 123, 135
McIntyre, Clare 49
Macmillan, Duncan
  *People, Places, Things* 150, 152–3
McRuer, Robert 188
Mad Pride 4, 14
Mad Studies 4
Malabou, Catherine 104–5
Marsh, Ian 3, 125
Maudsley Hospital. *See* ES3
memoir. *See* biography
Mental Health policy 3–7, 34–42, 142–50

Mitchell, Katie   15, 89, 107–15, 151

naturalism   26, 108
neoliberalism   4, 15, 144, 147–56, 195–6
neuroscience
    influence on Beckett. *See* Beckett, Samuel
    theories of psychosis   88, 91, 102–7
NHS and Community Care Act   5–7, 9–10, 12–13, 34, 37–9, 42, 147, 152
Nielson, Anthony
    *The Wonderful World of Dissocia*   6, 106–7
non-coherence. *See* irresolution

Object Relations School   118 n.27
*Oedipus Rex*   25, 127
Orwell, George *1984*   97

Paine's Plough. *See Crave*, first production
Penhall, Joe
    *Blue Orange*   6, 40, 106–7
    *Some Voices*   6
*Phaedra's Love*, first production   12, 24, 86–8
Phelan, Peggy
    *Unmarked*   165
play
    psychoanalytic approaches to   12–13, 32–3, 136–8
postdramatic theatre   28, 43–4, 126
post-traumatic stress disorder (PTSD). *See* trauma
prediction   95–106
Predictive Error Minimization (PEM)   102–5
psyche
    as a critical term   31–2
psychiatry   3–6, 10, 89–92, 125, 145, 172, 195

psychic life
    definition   31–3
psychosis
    in dramaturgy   85–122, 127–38
    experience of   103
    psychiatric approaches to   89–92
    psychoanalytic approaches to   91–5, 100–2, 114, 130, 133–4, 154
psychotic empathy   114, 132–3
Puar, Jasbir   162

Rabey, David Ian   20
Rame, Franca   12
Rand, Gweneth-Ann. *See 4.48 Psychosis*, Lyric Hammersmith, 2018
Ravenhill, Mark
    *Shopping and Fucking*   6, 20, 182
Rebellato, Dan   34, 68, 163, 166
Reynolds, Anna
    *Jordan*   39–40, 196
Rosenfeld, Herbert   94

Said, Edward   52
    *Late Style*   163
Saunders, Graham   2, 12, 96, 124, 125
Schechner, Richard
    The Performance Group   28
schizophrenia   89–95, 103–5, 132–7, 139
sexual violence   2, 8–11, 14, 21, 37, 44, 49–84, 105, 161, 177
Shcherban, Vladimir. *See 4.48 Psychosis*, Belarus Free Theatre, 2011
Shneidman, Edwin
    *The Suicidal Mind*   166, 169–70
Sierz, Aleks   5, 20
Solga, Kim   14, 55, 72
Stafford Clarke, Max

allegations of sexual misconduct
 at Royal Court   75
Strindberg, August   14, 25–7, 31, 36,
 85, 96, 110
  *A Dream Play*   25–6
  *Ghost Sonata*   96
suicidality   151, 153, 161–94
suicide
 Kane's suicide   1–2, 19–20, 71
 representation of in Kane's
  theatre   31, 98, 113,
  123–4, 166–71
surrealism   27–9, 108–9

tabloids   2, 6–7, 10–11, 51–2, 75
Thatcher, Margaret   5
trauma
 feminist trauma theory   14, 66–9
 mimetic trauma theory   56–9, 66–71
 PTSD   56–66
 trauma theory   56–71
Tycer, Alicia   143, 181

vaccine. *See* innoculation
Venables, Philip   15, 140–1, 154–5
Venn, Jon   13, 38, 139, 167, 181

Waddington, Juliet   125
Wallace, Clare   20
Wang, Esmé Weijun
 *The Collected Schizophenias*
  103–4
Watson, Ariel   134, 143
Webb, Danny. *See Blasted*, Lyric
  Hammersmith 2010
Weller, Jeremy
 Mad   20–2, 31, 137
Wertenbaker, Timberlake   49
Wilson, Lynda. *See Blasted*, Lyric
  Hammersmith 2010
Wilson, Richard
 directing *Blasted*, Crucible
  Theatre, Sheffield,
  2015   72–6
Winnicott, D.W.   13, 32–3, 136–7,
 165, 196
Wison, Robert   28
Woods, Angela   90–2, 116
Wurtzel, Elizabeth   6

Young, Allan   58

Zola, Emile   26

www.ingramcontent.com/pod-product-compliance
Lightning Source LLC
Chambersburg PA
CBHW062220300426
44115CB00012BA/2156